The V

Dilly Court is a No.1 *Sunday Times* bestselling author of over fifty novels. She grew up in North-East London and began her career in television, writing scripts for commercials. She is married with two grown-up children, four grandchildren and three beautiful great-grandchildren. Dilly now lives in Dorset on the Jurassic Coast with her husband.

To find out more about Dilly, please visit her website and her Facebook page:

www.dillycourt.com
 /DillyCourtAuthor

Also by Dilly Court

Mermaids Singing
The Dollmaker's Daughters
Tilly True
The Best of Sisters
The Cockney Sparrow
A Mother's Courage
The Constant Heart
A Mother's Promise
The Cockney Angel
A Mother's Wish
The Ragged Heiress
A Mother's Secret
Cinderella Sister
A Mother's Trust
The Lady's Maid
The Best of Daughters
The Workhouse Girl
A Loving Family
The Beggar Maid
A Place Called Home
The Orphan's Dream
Ragged Rose
The Swan Maid
The Christmas Card
The Button Box
The Mistletoe Seller
Nettie's Secret
Rag-and-Bone Christmas
The Reluctant Heiress
A Thimble for Christmas
The Snow Angel
The Winter Belle

AS LILY BAXTER

Poppy's War
We'll Meet Again
Spitfire Girl
The Girls in Blue
The Shopkeeper's Daughter
In Love and War

THE RIVER MAID SERIES

The River Maid
The Summer Maiden
The Christmas Rose

THE VILLAGE SECRETS SERIES

The Christmas Wedding
A Village Scandal
The Country Bride

THE ROCKWOOD CHRONICLES

Fortune's Daughter
Winter Wedding
Runaway Widow
Sunday's Child
Snow Bride
Dolly's Dream
The Lucky Penny
Poppy's Choice

Dilly Court

The Wild Rose

HarperCollins*Publishers*

HarperCollins*Publishers* Ltd
1 London Bridge Street,
London SE1 9GF

www.harpercollins.co.uk

HarperCollins*Publishers*
Macken House, 39/40 Mayor Street Upper
Dublin 1, D01 C9W8, Ireland

First published by HarperCollins*Publishers* Ltd 2026
1

A catalogue record for this book is available from the British Library.

ISBN: 978-0-00-858094-0 (HB)
ISBN: 978-0-00-858095-7 (PB)

This novel is entirely a work of fiction. The names, characters and incidents
portrayed in it are the work of the author's imagination. Any resemblance to
actual persons, living or dead, events or localities is entirely coincidental.

Typeset in Sabon Lt Pro by HarperCollins*Publishers* India

Printed and bound in the UK using 100%
Renewable Electricity at CPI Group (UK) Ltd

MIX
Paper | Supporting
responsible forestry
FSC™ C007454

This book contains FSC™ certified paper and other controlled
sources to ensure responsible forest management.

For more information visit: www.harpercollins.co.uk/green

For Suzanne Muggeridge

Chapter One

Devonshire, 1865

The chill March wind soughed and cried like souls in torment as it swept across the wild expanse of tors and moorland. Dartmoor was not the ideal place to be when the light was fading fast, and fingers of frost were already beginning to form on the gnarled branches of stunted trees.

Rosina Wills clutched her shawl more tightly around her slim body. Its soft woollen folds were not much protection against the wintry weather, but she could see a dim light in the distance, and she could only hope that she had reached Moonshadow Manor at last. It was two days ago that she had left her old home in Islington, and since alighting from the train at Exeter, she had walked. The thin soles of her boots leaked, and she could feel broken blisters on her heels, but those were the least of her worries. She had come from her relatively comfortable home in London to this completely unknown new life, and it had not been from choice.

Perhaps she could have tried harder to get along with her new stepmother, but Rosina's attempts to get on the right side of a woman who was only six years her senior had fallen on stony ground. It had been two years since Rosina's mother had succumbed to consumption and Humphrey Wills had met and married Dora, a charming twenty-eight-year-old widow. But the new Mrs Wills's initial show of eagerness to be pleasant had soon worn off and then she had made it clear that there was only one mistress in the house, and it was she. Rosina had been forced to watch her father change from being the master in his own home to retreating to an almost childish state whereby he did everything his wife asked and gave her all that she desired. Rosina had found herself relegated to a position close to being a housekeeper, and when Dora announced that she was in the family way she had demanded that Rosina's bedroom, being the second largest in the house, be turned into a nursery. Rosina found herself relegated to a small room on the second floor, overlooking the busy street, but had she objected she knew she would have found herself sleeping in one of the attics together with Maggie, the maid of all work.

Rosina's free hand went automatically to the pocket in her linsey-woolsey skirt, to touch the letter from her aunt Jane, Mama's only living relative. It had come at an opportune moment, when Rosina had been about to give way to the anger and resentment she had been harbouring against her stepmother. The note had been short and to the point.

> *Moonshadow Manor*
>
> *Dearest Rosie,*
> *I find myself unwell and unable to cope on my own. Please come and help.*
> *Your fond aunt,*
> *Jane Maddern*

It had taken less than an hour for Rosina to pack a valise with everything she might need for an indefinite stay in Moonshadow Manor. The rest of her belongings were stowed in a trunk beneath the eaves, to be sent on at a later date. Her father had tried to persuade her to stay at first, but Dora's barely concealed expression of triumph was enough to goad Rosina into leaving the house that evening. She had slept in the ladies' waiting room on Paddington Station and had caught the first train bound for Devonshire next morning.

Now, feeling a little more confident, she quickened her pace. Darkness was swallowing up the moor to the accompaniment of sounds unfamiliar to the city-bred Rosina. The eerily human cry of a dog fox calling to his mate and the hoot of an owl, hunting its prey, together with the sound of water gurgling over the gravel in a nearby stream – all combined to make her break into a run as the dark shape of Moonshadow Manor grew closer.

She was out of breath by the time she reached the main entrance, and she clutched her side as a stitch made her gasp with pain. She raised the heavy iron knocker and allowed it to fall on the metal plate with a loud clang that echoed around the entrance hall, seeming to mock her as she stood outside in the cold, where sharp spikes of sleet slapped her cheeks. Automatically she turned the doorknob and to her surprise the door opened with a scream of rusty hinges. Glad to be free from the harsh weather, she stepped inside. A single candle guttered and was almost extinguished in the draught, but to her relief it recovered and shone with a wavering light. She put her valise down and lifted the candlestick to get a better view of her surroundings. A wide, shallow-stepped staircase led to a galleried landing with wainscoted walls in the same dark oak. More surprising was not the way the large entrance hall was furnished, but the lack of anything that might be considered fitting for a house of this quality. Instead of chairs, tables or settles, there were boxes placed haphazardly, as if long forgotten. A pervasive smell of damp and soot from an unswept chimney added to the gloomy atmosphere.

'Aunt Jane.' Rosina found her voice, but it echoed as if mocking her. She tried again. 'Aunt Jane. It's me, Rosie. I'm here at last.'

There was still no answer, and Rosina edged her way between the boxes, heading towards her aunt's morning parlour. She remembered the layout of the old house from past visits with her parents, but in those days Moonshadow Manor had been a much livelier place. There had been servants to tend to their needs, and she remembered vases of flowers filling the air with their delightful scent. She plucked a cobweb from her hair as she negotiated a narrow passageway where the walls were hung with gloomy oil paintings. It was too dark to see them clearly, but they did nothing to improve the ambience.

She managed to reach the parlour without treading on any of the articles that littered the floor, and opened the door. 'Aunt Jane?'

'Is that you, Alice?'

Rosina winced at the mention of her mother's name. 'No, Aunt Jane. It's Rosie. You sent me a letter asking me to come.'

She gazed round the room in horror to see that there was just as much chaos in here as there was in the entrance hall. Boxes and piles of clothes, books and all manner of odds and ends covered every available surface.

Aunt Jane sat huddled up in a wing-back chair beside a feeble fire. Rosina trod carefully, making her way to her aunt's side. She leaned over to drop a kiss on her forehead, which felt cold and clammy. A candle flickered and was about to go out, but Rosina snatched another from a candelabra and lit it from the guttering flame. She placed it in a candlestick and held it so that she could take a better look at her aunt.

The Aunt Jane she remembered seemed to have shrunk into a wizened old woman. Dark shadows beneath her eyes made them appear sunken in their sockets and her skin was deathly pale.

'I don't know you, girl. Where is Alice?'

'Mama passed away over two years ago, Aunt Jane. I'm your niece, Rosina. You sent me a letter, asking me to come and help you.'

'No, dear. It must have been someone else. I just sit here all day, and sometimes all night, too.' Jane waved her away with a feeble movement of her hand.

Rosina stared at her in dismay. 'Where are the servants, Aunt? Is there no one here to do anything for you?'

'I think they left. Or maybe they are in the servants' quarters. I don't see anyone much.'

'But someone must be bringing you food. Have you eaten today?'

'I can't remember, Alice.'

'This won't do,' Rosina said firmly. 'It won't do at all. I'm going to the kitchen to see what I can find. I'll bring you something to eat and drink. I'll be as quick as I can.'

The large kitchen was at the back of the house and reached through what was once the housekeeper's office and the butler's pantry, although Rosina could only vaguely remember those long-past days. She entered the kitchen, expecting the worst, and was pleasantly surprised to find it relatively clean and tidy. In fact, it did not look as though much food preparation had taken place recently, but the fire in the range had been banked up and embers glowed beneath the grey ashes. Rosina went around the room opening cupboard doors until she found the larder, but the only edible food on the marble slab was a heel of cheese, a bowl of eggs and a pitcher of milk. It was obvious that someone was attempting to take care of her aunt, but they did not appear to be here now.

She placed the candlestick on the long pine table and set about riddling the ashes and coaxing the fire back into life. She picked up the kettle and took it to the scullery to fill it from the pump at the stone sink. Memories of childhood came back to her, making her smile for the first time that day. She had spent many hours in the kitchen helping the cook, who spoiled her with slices of fruit cake, jam tarts, and biscuits hot from the oven. Her mouth watered at the thought, and she realised that she had not eaten since she had bought a ham roll and a cup of coffee from a food cart in one of the small towns she'd passed through on her way. She put the kettle on the hob and went in search of a teapot, cups and some tea, which she found in the bottom of a tea caddy with the lock broken. There was just enough to make one pot of tea. Tomorrow she would need to go shopping or they would starve. There must be a grocer in the nearest village, and hopefully the person who came in to tend to Aunt Jane's needs would be able to give her directions. While she waited for the kettle to boil, Rosina scrambled some eggs and laid a tray ready to take the food and hot tea to the morning parlour.

While her aunt ate, Rosina took the opportunity to go upstairs to see if a fire had been lit in Jane's room. A draught whistled through an ill-fitting casement window, and it did not seem as if there had been fire in the grate for some time. Rosina felt the bed sheets and they were damp. The air was thick with dust and the room smelled of sickness. It was not the sort of place that was suitable for a frail old lady. Rosina left quickly and hurried back downstairs to the parlour.

Jane looked up and managed a weary smile. 'Thank you, Alice. You were always a good sister to me.'

Rosina bit back a sharp retort, tempering her words with a smile. 'I am not Alice, Aunt. I am her daughter, but it doesn't matter now. Do you always sleep in this chair? Your room does not seem to have been used for some time.'

'It's easier if I stay here by the fire,' Jane said,

nodding. 'My room is too cold. I think there's a ghost lady who walks at night. I feel her cold breath on my cheek when I am trying to sleep.'

'I think that's probably the draught from the ill-fitting window, Aunt. Tomorrow I will see what can be done, but tonight I'll try to make you more comfortable.'

'Thank you, dear.' Jane handed her the plate of half-eaten egg. 'I cannot manage the rest. Give it to the scullery maid. She looks as if she could do with fattening up.'

'Yes, Aunt.' Rosina took the plate from her and put it back on the tray. It was obvious she had come to Moonshadow Manor not a moment too soon. 'Drink your tea and I'll make you a bed on the sofa.' Rosina looked round the chaotic room and saw what looked like a pile of blankets and a couple of pillows. She decided she would sleep down here herself rather than risk getting a lung infection by sleeping in a damp bed.

Next morning Rosina awakened early. She was cold and stiff after a night in a chair by the fire, which had now burned down to ashes. She rose to her feet and stretched. It was still dark, and she had to pick her way carefully over the detritus on the floor so that she could draw back the heavy velvet curtains. Dawn was just breaking and a cold, grey wintry light streamed into the room, making it look even more untidy and depressing than it had by candlelight the previous evening. Aunt Jane was snoring gently on the sofa and Rosina crept past her and made her way to the kitchen.

As she opened the door, she was aware of warmth and in the glow of the fire she could see a young woman taking a loaf from the oven. The smell of hot bread filled the room as she placed the tray on a wooden board.

'You must be Miss Wills,' she said in a matter-of-fact tone. 'I'm Merrilees Pavey. I come in every day to take care of things for Miss Jane. Did she tell you about me?'

Rosina shook her head. 'No, I'm afraid not. My aunt was a little confused last evening when I arrived.'

'She do get that way often, miss. She's probably forgot my name anyway, poor soul. She weren't always like this.'

'No, she wasn't. I used to visit with my parents when I was much younger, and Aunt Jane was quite different then. She must be very grateful for what you do, Miss Pavey.'

Merry laughed. 'Call me Merry, if you please. I'm Merry by name and Merry by nature, as my ma always says.'

'It's a very pretty name, and it's nice to have someone cheerful around the house. I'm afraid it has been neglected for some time, by the look of things.' Rosina realised what she had said, and she shook her head. 'I don't mean that as a reflection on your efforts, Merry. I can see that matters must have been out of hand for some time.'

'Indeed, they have. There used to be many servants, but gradually they all left, and Miss Maddern likes to keep hold of things, if you get my meaning. I'm not allowed to throw anything away.'

'We'll see about that,' Rosina said firmly. 'But for now we'll concentrate on what is more important. For instance, we need to light fires in the bedrooms and air the bedding. There doesn't seem to be much in the larder. Is there a shop in the village?'

'There's a grocer in the High Street, miss. My uncle Fred Pavey owns it. He'll be happy to supply your needs.'

'Do we need coal? We probably should get candles in, and oil for the lamps.'

'My uncle Bob Pavey delivers coal and kindling, miss. He also supplies lamp oil, if requested.'

Rosina laughed. 'You have a large family, Merry.'

'Larger than you think, miss. Put it this way, the Paveys can get you most things, and if you need anyone to work on the house or the grounds there's my mother's brothers, Tom and Sid Bragg. Both strong men and very trustworthy.'

'How does my aunt pay you, Merry? I'm afraid I don't know how she has managed to run her household in her present condition.'

'That's the trouble. Miss Jane was most capable

until about six months ago, when she was took poorly. Dr Clarke said it was just a chill, but I think it were something more serious.'

'So, you have been working for nothing since then?' Rosina frowned. Things were worse than she could have imagined.

Merry nodded. 'I couldn't allow Miss Jane to suffer on her own. She was good to me and my family when she was her old self.'

'There must be money somewhere,' Rosina said thoughtfully. 'Do you know if my aunt has a solicitor or a man who handles her business matters?'

'I know that there's a gentleman by the name of Jack Dimond, who is a solicitor in Ivybridge, and he handles Miss Jane's finances.' Merry took a knife and cut two slices off the loaf. She crumbled one of them into a bowl and added some hot milk from a saucepan she took from the range. 'Miss Jane likes bread and milk, miss. It's the only thing she eats nowadays. I'll take it to her with a cup of tea. We do need sugar as well as tea and just about everything, miss.'

'I'll make a list, and if you give me directions to your uncle's grocery shop I'll go there and introduce myself,' Rosina said slowly. 'I suppose he is owed money, too?'

'Everyone in the village who's done anything for Miss Maddern of Moonshadow Manor is owed money, miss.' Merry placed everything on a tray.

'I'll just take this to Miss Jane.' She hurried from the kitchen, leaving Rosina with even more problems than she had anticipated.

Later, after settling Aunt Jane in her chair by the fire with a blanket wrapped around her knees and legs, Rosina accompanied Merry to the village, which consisted of outlying farms and cob cottages with thatched roofs, set about one main street. There appeared to be one shop only and that was owned and run by Fred Pavey, who greeted Merry with a genuine smile.

'Good morning, maidy.' Fred's gaze shifted to Rosina, and he frowned. 'And who might this be?'

'She be Miss Jane's niece from London, Uncle.' Merry nudged Rosina so that she had to move closer to the counter. 'She's got a list of provisions needed for Moonshadow Manor.'

Fred Pavey's expression hardened. 'I don't want to cause unnecessary embarrassment, miss. But until the account for Moonshadow Manor is settled I am afraid I cannot fulfil your requirements.'

Rosina had been expecting this, and she managed a smile. 'Of course I understand, Mr Pavey, but I only arrived last evening, and I haven't had time to go through my aunt's accounts. I will, however, be visiting her solicitor in town and then I will be able to settle all outstanding bills. If you could see your way to supplying what is on my list, I will be most grateful.' Rosina took the piece of paper from her reticule and laid it on the counter in front of him.

Fred studied it, frowning. 'This is going to be costly, miss.'

'Yes, I realise that, but Merrilees will vouch for the fact that the larder is empty, and my aunt is a sick woman. I will go into town now and draw the necessary funds.'

'If Merry trusts you then I suppose I can give you the benefit of the doubt, but this is the last time I will allow Miss Maddern to have credit, sick woman or not.'

'Thank you, sir.' Rosina shook his hand. 'I will honour the debt by the end of the day.' She turned to Merry. 'Thank you, too. I will see you tomorrow morning.'

Merry opened the shop door. 'It's about six miles to town, miss.'

'I walked four times that distance yesterday, and I have blisters to prove it,' Rosina said with a wry smile. 'However, I won't let you or your uncle down.' She stepped outside, followed by Merry, who waved frantically at a man driving a farm cart.

'Ho, there, Seth. Stop a minute.' Merry turned to Rosina with a wide grin. 'Seth works at Applegate Farm, miss. He's a friend of mine.'

The ruddy-faced young man, with a shock of red hair and an impressive beard, drew his old shire horse to a halt. 'Morning, Merry.' His gaze wandered to

Rosina. 'You'm the maid from London, Miss Jane's niece?'

'That's right. I am Rosina Wills, and you are Seth . . .?'

'Seth Tully, miss.'

'Where are you off to, Seth?' Merry demanded impatiently. 'Miss Wills needs to get to town. She wants to see Mr Dimond, the solicitor in Fore Street.'

'I'm going that way. Are you coming, too, Merry?'

'No, Seth. I have my job at Daumerle House to go to. I daren't arrive any later or I'll be given the sack.'

Seth leaned down, extending his hand to Rosina. 'Come on then, miss. I've got to get these chickens to market. You can sit beside me, if you've a mind.'

Rosina accepted his help to climb up onto the cart. 'Thank you, Seth.'

'Good luck in town, miss,' Merry called as Seth cracked the whip over the horse's head and it shambled off at a stately plod.

The drive through farmland and wooded valleys was pleasant enough as the sun was shining, although it was bitterly cold, and Rosina was glad that she had borrowed an old boat cloak that she had discovered in one of the many cupboards in the house. It smelled of wet dog and it was none too clean, but as the road climbed higher and they were out of the shelter of the trees there was a noticeable drop in the temperature.

Seth was a man of few words and Rosina gave up attempts at conversation after a few minutes.

'You be staying long with Miss Jane?' Seth asked as he drew the horse to a halt in what appeared to be the main street in Ivybridge.

'I don't know,' Rosina said warily. She alighted from the cart. She looked around but could not see any indication as to the nature of the house where they had stopped. 'Is this where I will find Mr Dimond? There is no brass plate.'

'I should try knocking if I was you, miss. Good day to you.' Seth flicked the reins, and the cart rumbled off, leaving Rosina standing on the narrow pavement, wondering whether she should follow Seth's advice.

'Are you lost?'

Rosina spun round to see a tall, slim man, dressed entirely in black with a shirt and stock so dazzlingly white that they made her avert her eyes. With an opera cloak over his formal jacket, he looked more like a city gentleman than a country solicitor. He doffed his top hat, and his dark eyes twinkled with amusement as he looked her up and down.

'I – I'm not lost,' Rosina said hastily. 'I'm looking for Mr Jack Dimond, but I don't see a nameplate anywhere.'

He laughed and produced a key from his pocket, which he used to open the front door. 'In a small town like this, one is so well known that a nameplate is quite unnecessary. Whom have I the pleasure of addressing?'

Rosina met his smile with a suspicious frown. She had the uncomfortable feeling that he was teasing her, which was annoying when she needed to be taken seriously.

'I am Rosina Wills,' she said evenly. 'I am here on behalf of my aunt, Miss Jane Maddern of Moonshadow Manor. Are you Mr Dimond? If so, I have business to discuss with you.'

He flung the door open. 'I am he. Step inside, Miss Wills. We do not discuss important matters on the street.'

Chapter Two

Rosina sat on the edge of an upright chair in Dimond's office at the rear of the building. It was more like a comfortable study in the home of a wealthy gentleman than a place where serious business was carried out daily. The wainscoted walls were studded with paintings in gilt frames, mostly of country scenes with a few still lifes included. Rosy apples and pears looked tempting, with luscious grapes tumbling from a cut-glass fruit bowl, and wrinkled walnuts spilling onto a polished mahogany table. Another was not so cheerful, and Rosina averted her eyes from the dead game birds artistically draped over a chopping block.

Dimond was busy stoking the fire and Rosina found her attention wandering from the artwork to the ornate marble mantelshelf with a garniture of silver-gilt candlesticks and an ormolu timepiece. It all seemed oddly out of place for a country solicitor.

Dimond straightened up and brushed a strand of dark, wavy hair back from his forehead. He went to stand beside a huge kneehole desk, eyeing her with the annoying glimmer of amusement she had noticed when they met in the street.

'Now then, Miss Wills. What is it you want to ask me?'

'I received a brief note from my aunt asking me for help. I only arrived at Moonshadow Manor late yesterday and I found her in a parlous state.'

Dimond was suddenly serious. He leaned against the desk, giving her his full attention. 'In what way?'

'She seems quite confused and very unwell. There was barely any food in the larder, and I understand from the young woman who goes in once a day to care for my aunt that there is hardly any coal or kindling, let alone candles and oil for the lamps. I was told that you handle her finances.'

'Her late father, Mr Phillip Maddern, appointed me executor of his will, and I do manage her affairs. Are you asking me to make funds available?'

Rosina sighed, wondering why he felt it necessary to make her feel as though she was begging for something to which she was not entitled. 'Yes, Mr Dimond. My aunt apparently owes money to all the local tradesmen and has run out of credit. It doesn't seem to me that you have been very conscientious when it comes to taking care of your client.'

Dimond straightened up and walked slowly round the desk to take a seat in the buttoned leather chair. 'It appears that I have reneged on my promise, for which I apologise.' He leaned over to open a safe and took out a cheque book, writing on it with a pen dipped in a silver inkwell. 'This should cover the debts and provide you with enough money to live on for a month or so, but I should warn you that the money left by the late Mr Maddern is running out.'

Rosina stared at him in dismay. 'But I was told that my grandfather was a man of substance.'

'He was, but he also dabbled in the stock market, which appealed to his love of gambling. A few unwise or unlucky investments were enough to deplete the fortune he had inherited from his father.' Dimond replaced the cheque book in the safe and closed the door with a loud clang. 'I'm sorry, Miss Wills. I can see this has been a shock to you.'

'But you were given the responsibility of acting as executor. Couldn't you have invested the inheritance in something that would assure my aunt of an income, however small?'

'I did what was required of me, Miss Wills.' Dimond handed her the cheque. 'If you take this to the bank in Plymouth they will cash it for you.'

Rosina stared at the amount, frowning. 'But I

have no means of getting to Plymouth, Mr Dimond. I need money today.'

'As it happens, I have business in Plymouth tomorrow,' Dimond said thoughtfully. 'I can advance you money against the cheque and give you the rest when I return.' He leaned over once again and took a cash box out of the safe. He counted out coins and laid them on the desk. 'This should see you through and ensure you have enough provisions to keep you in comfort for a few days.'

Rosina handed him the cheque and picked up the money. She stowed it into her reticule and rose to her feet.

'Thank you. As I seem to be my aunt's only living relative, I will need to speak to you again about her situation. From what I have seen she is not going to be able to handle her own affairs or take care of herself. I need to know her financial position before I can make any arrangements.' Rosina walked to the door and opened it. 'Good day, Mr Dimond.'

Inwardly fuming, she left the house and slammed the front door behind her, which did not prove anything, but it gave vent to some of her anger. She would have expected more help and a little more sympathy for her aunt's condition from the man who was paid to take care of her affairs. He might be good-looking in a classical way, but Jack Dimond was not Rosina's idea of a person who was best suited to look after her aunt. There must be someone else who could handle her affairs with a little more care and understanding. Rosina decided she must look into this urgently.

It was only when she stood on the pavement outside the house that she realised she had no means of getting back to Moonshadow Manor other than on foot. There did not seem to be anyone about, which she thought odd, but then she remembered that Seth had said it was a market day, and she set off in the direction he had taken when they parted. Clutching her reticule as tightly as if it held gold bullion rather than merely copper and silver coins, she took the main road and followed the sounds that led her to the busy marketplace.

It was easy to spot Seth Tully amongst the crowd as his red hair stood out like a beacon. He was dealing with a farmer, who was gesticulating wildly and appeared to be bargaining for the last of Seth's hens. The animated discussion ended with a handshake just as Rosina reached them.

'It's a pleasure doing business with you, Seth, my boy.' The farmer obviously had a good bargain as he slapped Seth on the back and strolled off.

'It looks as if you've had a profitable morning,' Rosina said, smiling.

'Aye, maidy. That's all my hens sold in no time at all. I'm off to the pub for a glass of cider and a pie.'

Rosina hid the reticule beneath her mantle. 'I was hoping you might be going home, Seth.'

'I will be when I've had some sustenance, maidy. I've fair lost my voice shouting to make myself heard above this din. I need a drink to soothe me throat.'

Rosina could tell from his tone and the stubborn set of his jaw beneath the fuzzy red beard that he would not change his mind.

'Perhaps I could come with you. I don't want to be left on my own in a strange town.'

Seth gazed at her with a hint of irritation. 'They don't approve of women in the taproom, miss. It ain't the place for a maid like yourself.'

'Perhaps if I buy you a glass of cider and a pie it might change your mind,' Rosina suggested casually.

'It would be rude to refuse a lady.' Seth proffered his arm. 'Never let it be said I ain't a gentleman.'

They walked briskly to the inn, where Seth was obviously well known. The landlord looked askance at Rosina, but Seth found her a secluded place in the inglenook and left her seated on a wooden settle while he went to get their drinks and a pie for himself. Rosina had declined the offer of food, but she was thirsty, and she assured him that a glass of cider would be most welcome. The taproom was busy with farmers and labourers taking time to refresh themselves after an early start. A city girl born and bred, Rosina was fascinated by the difference in the country way of life from that of people in her part of London. Not that she would have entered a public house in Islington, but the countrymen's smocks and billycock hats were outfits she had never seen in the city. The air was filled with smoke from the log fire and the clay pipes clenched in the teeth of the older men as they leaned on the bar or sat round small oak tables with pints of cider or ale in their hands. The general hubbub made it impossible to listen to any individual conversation and the Devonshire burr made it even more difficult for her to understand what was being said. Rosina waited patiently for Seth to remember her presence as he was leaning on the bar, alternately taking bites from a pie and washing them down with mouthfuls of cider. She was shocked and surprised by his apparent capacity to down a few pints in quick succession. Eventually he strolled over, licking crumbs from his lips as he set two tankards of cider on the table and sat down.

'I'm sorry, maidy. I took longer than I intended but market day is the only time I gets to chat with other farm workers like meself.'

Rosina took a sip of the cider and found it quite agreeable. 'It's all right, Seth. I understand, but I would like to get back to Moonshadow Manor as soon as possible.'

'I'll finish my drink and then we'll leave.' Seth sat back in his chair taking long draughts of the cider and growing redder in the face with every mouthful.

Rosina eyed him warily. She could only hope that his horse knew the way home as Seth was beginning to look a trifle tipsy and, judging by the rate at which he was swallowing the amber liquid, he might soon be incapable. She looked round as the door opened and there was a sudden lull in the conversation. Most of the men tipped their hats as Jack Dimond strode into the bar. He acknowledged them with a casual lift of his hand as he took the landlord aside and they conversed in low voices away from curious onlookers. Rosina sat quietly, hoping that he would not see her, but just as he turned to leave, he spotted her and made his way between the tables to stand beside Seth.

'You're drunk, Tully,' Jack said coldly. 'What do you mean by bringing a lady into a common taproom?'

Seth rose to his feet, his colour deepening. 'I'm taking the maid home, sir.'

'Not in that condition, my friend. And what do you think you were doing, plying her with that strong cider? What would Miss Maddern say?'

'Just a minute, sir,' Rosina said angrily. 'It really is none of your business. Seth was kind enough to offer to drive me back to Moonshadow Manor, and if I wish to drink a little cider that is my business.'

'I'm afraid it is very much my concern as a representative of your aunt.' Dimond grasped her arm. 'I'm taking Miss Wills home, Tully. You'd best sober up before your father sees you in this condition.'

'I'm quite sober, sir,' Seth said, hiccuping.

'Come with me, Miss Wills.' Dimond met Rosina's angry stare with a look that made it impossible to defy him without causing a scene.

Rosina allowed him to lead her from the bar, but once outside she wrenched free from him. 'I don't know who you think you are, sir, but I don't have to do what you say.'

Dimond shrugged nonchalantly. 'It's your choice, Miss Wills. Either you allow me to drive you back to Moonshadow Manor or you wait for that boy to sober up enough to hold the reins. Besides which,' he added, moderating his tone, 'you were right. I have not given Miss Maddern enough attention recently. I think it's high time I visited her.' He opened the door of a smart-looking chaise and tossed a coin to a youth who was holding the horse's reins.

Rosina knew when she was beaten, and she climbed into the spanking new vehicle. It was infinitely more comfortable than the farm wagon, and at least Dimond was sober, if annoying.

'All right,' she said coldly. 'I accept your offer, but only because I feel you should see my aunt for yourself. You will find that I have not exaggerated her condition.'

'I don't doubt your veracity,' Dimond said as he climbed in beside her and took up the reins. 'I have the greatest respect for Miss Maddern and a vested interest in Moonshadow Manor.' He flicked the whip over the horse's head. 'Walk on.'

Dimond did not seem inclined to talk, and Rosina was not in a mood to make conversation. She was still smarting from his high-handed treatment, but she was also relieved to be on her way back to Moonshadow Manor, and Dimond was obviously an expert when it came to handling a spirited horse. She would not have admitted it in his hearing as he was conceited enough already, but she felt infinitely safer sitting beside him than she would have done with an inebriated Seth Tully holding the reins.

When they arrived at the Manor, Dimond leaped down from the chaise and went round to the horse's head. He spent a few moments patting the animal's neck and talking to it in a low voice, which Rosina noted with reluctant approval. At least Dimond had a less confrontational side to his character if he could show compassion for the horse, even if he seemed to have little patience with people. She climbed down unaided and went to open the front door.

'Where are the servants?' Dimond followed her into the hall. 'Surely you didn't leave Miss Maddern on her own?'

Rosina turned on him, stung by the accusatory tone of his voice. 'Mr Dimond, I only arrived here yesterday afternoon. I am not acquainted with my aunt's household, although as far as I can gather, she only has Merrilees Pavey, who comes in early each morning and then leaves to do her work at Daumerle House.'

Dimond pushed an offending box out of the way with the toe of his boot. 'This place is a mess. The air is thick with dust, and all this should have been cleared up ages ago.'

'Maybe you should visit your client more often then,' Rosina said sharply. 'My aunt seems to have been existing this way for some time.'

'Where is she?' Dimond moved to the foot of the stairs. 'Is she in her room?'

'No, I left her in the morning parlour. It was warmer there than upstairs, and anyway, I found that her bed was unaired and the sheets felt damp. I intend to remedy that today.' Rosina stood aside as Dimond walked past her and made his way to the morning parlour. He entered without knocking and it was obvious that he was accustomed to having a free run of the house. Rosina struggled to understand his relationship with her aunt. Dimond was supposed to be her man of business, yet apart from his admitted recent period of neglect he seemed to have an almost proprietorial attitude to everything pertaining to the house. Rosina followed him into the morning parlour.

'Good afternoon, Jane.' Dimond leaned over the chair where Jane sat, wrapped in a blanket. 'This is a sorry state of affairs. I apologise for not having visited you for some time. It was very remiss of me.'

Jane opened her eyes, and a faint smile curved her thin lips. 'You never apologise, Jack Dimond.'

'Well, I am now. I had no idea that you were managing without help in this old mausoleum. The place is a mess, and I'm not surprised that you are feeling unwell.' Dimond straightened up, turning to Rosina. 'The fire is almost out. Will you see to it, please?'

It was on the tip of Rosina's tongue to tell him that she was not a servant, but it was bitterly cold in the room, and she would have seen to the fire immediately even if he had not mentioned it. She shrugged off her mantle and tossed it onto a nearby chair, before going down on her knees in front of the hearth to riddle the ashes. There were a few feeble embers, and she arranged some lumps of coal so that they would catch light easily. Finally, she picked up the bellows and used them vigorously, until small tongues of flame licked the shiny black coals. As the fire took hold, she added more fuel until there was a decent blaze. She rose to her feet and turned to see Dimond holding her aunt's hand.

'That's better,' he said calmly. 'Now, what about food for your aunt? You said you had bought groceries in the village.'

'They are still in Pavey's shop,' Rosina said reluctantly. 'I had to get money to repay Aunt Jane's creditors.'

'I'll collect the order.' Dimond released Jane's hand. 'I must leave now, Jane, but I will be back shortly. A word with you before I go, Miss Wills.'

He walked out of the parlour, leaving Rosina little alternative but to follow him.

'What is it now, Mr Dimond? Are you going to scold me for something else that was not my fault?'

'I was merely going to say that I will engage some full-time help for you in the village. Do you have anything to say about that?'

'I am capable of finding someone suitable, providing I have enough money to pay their wages.' Rosina faced him angrily. He seemed hellbent on putting her in the wrong and making her feel inadequate to the task she had taken on.

'I was thinking of Miss Maddern, not you.' Dimond frowned thoughtfully. 'Merrilees would be ideal as she knows Jane and she is familiar with things as they are at Moonshadow Manor.'

'What do you mean by that?' Rosina demanded suspiciously.

'You will oblige me by not questioning everything I say.' Jack walked to the front door and opened it. 'I'll be back shortly with the food, and I'll send the coal merchant to fill the outside store.'

'I'm not sure you gave me enough money to pay for that,' Rosina protested.

'Don't worry. It will come out of the funds. From tomorrow onwards you will have Merrilees all day. She's very reliable and Jane knows and trusts her.'

'But Merrilees works at Daumerle House – you know that. Surely, they won't release her to come here?' Rosina was not going to allow him to get away without some explanation.

'Sir Hugo Charteris is an old friend. We've known each other for many years. He will agree if I ask him nicely,' Jack said with a wry smile.

He left the house before Rosina had a chance to question him further. She returned to the parlour where her aunt had dozed off in front of the fire, but Jane seemed to sense Rosina's presence, and she opened her eyes.

'You look so like your mother, my dear. I used to envy her lovely dark hair, and I would have given anything for green eyes like hers, instead of grey, like mine. She was always the beauty of the family, and you've inherited her looks.' Jane sighed. 'Is there any chance of a cup of tea, Rosina? I am rather thirsty.'

'Of course, Aunt. I'll go and make some, right away.' Rosina hurried out of the room. Her aunt's description of her late mother had brought tears to her eyes. She knew that she was not nearly as beautiful as Alice had been, but the mere mention of her brought all the pain of losing a loved one back in a rush. Perhaps she was being over-sensitive after her difficult time with Jack Dimond, who was probably the most unsympathetic man she had ever met.

She made her way to the kitchen where, to her relief, the fire in the range was still hot enough to boil the kettle.

Minutes later Rosina returned to the parlour

carrying a tray of tea and a plate of bread and butter, which she set on a table close to her aunt's chair. She filled a cup and handed it to her aunt.

'What do you know of Mr Dimond, Aunt? Is he trustworthy?'

Jane's hands shook as she held the cup and saucer, rattling the teaspoon against the porcelain. 'Why do you ask, Alice?'

'I'm Rosina, Aunt. Alice was my mama, if you recall?'

Jane took a sip of tea. 'Yes, I remember now. Poor Alice, she was such a good sister.'

'Mr Dimond, Aunt – what do you know of him?'

'Jack's father, Roland Dimond, was our family solicitor before he passed away. He was a good man, unlike his notorious grandfather, Jabez Dimond. Rumour has it that he was a smuggler, but in those days most people on the coast had a hand in what was known as free trade.'

'Try to eat something, Aunt.' Rosina picked up the plate of bread and butter and offered it to her. 'I'll make us a proper meal when Mr Dimond returns with the groceries.'

'I'll eat something in a moment.' Jane lay back in her chair and closed her eyes.

Rosina finished her tea and took the tray back to the kitchen. She did not fancy another night sleeping in the chair, and she went upstairs. The first thing she did was to fling open the windows in her room and in her aunt's room. Then curiosity overcame her and she checked the other rooms on the first floor. To her surprise there were more boxes in the bedrooms, together with piles of garments and oddments of silver plate and broken jewellery. Discarded ornaments, books and framed paintings were lying about and obviously forgotten. The top floor, which had once been the servants' sleeping quarters, was similarly stacked with discarded items. Rosina shook her head. It would take a long time to go through everything and sort out what might be of use, but she had no intention of starting right away.

She returned to her aunt's room and set about clearing the ashes from the grate so that a fire could be lit when the coal was delivered. She took the sheets and pillowcases off the bed and did the same in her own room. The air was much fresher now, and the dust had settled, making it possible to close the windows and shut out the cold air. She took the laundry downstairs and went in search of a linen cupboard to find clean bedding. The irony of the situation was not lost on her. The household tasks that her stepmother had thrust upon her had unexpectedly come in useful, and she was undaunted by the prospect of going through what appeared to be a lifetime of hoarded things.

She found the linen cupboard and was satisfied that there was enough bedding to make the rooms ready, providing fires could be lit. She took the laundry outside and, as she had expected, she found the washhouse with a large copper. It was too late to start the process of filling the tub with water from the outside pump and lighting the fire beneath it; that could wait until tomorrow. She was on her way back to the kitchen, still clutching the linen, when she heard the clip-clop of horses' hoofs and the rumble of carriage wheels on the cobblestones as Dimond drove the chaise into the stable yard. Not only had he collected the baskets of groceries, but he had brought Merrilees with him.

Rosina uttered a cry of pleasure. 'I've never been so pleased to see anyone in my whole life, Merry.'

'I thought for a moment you meant me, Miss Wills,' Dimond said with a wry smile. 'But as you see, I have brought you someone who will be of much more assistance than I could be, given the circumstances.'

Merry leaped down to the ground and took the bundle of washing from Rosina. 'You shouldn't be doing this sort of thing, miss. I'll put this in the scullery. If I leave it in the washhouse the rats will have chewed it into shreds by morning.'

Dimond alighted more slowly. 'I'll put the baskets in the kitchen. You should have a delivery of coal soon. Bob Pavey promised to treat the matter as urgent.'

'I'm very grateful for your help,' Rosina said earnestly as she followed him into the house. 'But I have a question.'

Dimond placed the groceries on the kitchen table. 'What is it?'

'Do you know what's in all the boxes that I keep finding? They are everywhere, even in the attics.'

Dimond's winged eyebrows snapped together in a frown. 'They are here for a reason and it's nothing to do with you. Leave them where they are, and I will have them removed as soon as possible.'

'They belong to you?' Rosina stared at him in surprise.

'They belong to my law practice,' Dimond said abruptly.

'Might I know what's in them? I mean, they could contain almost anything, even contraband.'

'Don't be ridiculous. I'm a respected solicitor. Would I risk my reputation on anything that wasn't above board?'

Rosina met his angry gaze with a steady look. 'I don't know, Mr Dimond. I suppose it might have something to do with the value of whatever is concealed in those boxes.'

'You've been reading too many penny dreadfuls, Miss Wills.'

Rosina bit back a sharp retort. She merely shrugged and turned away. 'My aunt is asleep in the morning parlour, if you wish to see her before you leave, sir.'

'I won't wake her,' Dimond said calmly. 'I'll leave now, but I will be back tomorrow or the next day. Remember what I said, Miss Wills. Do not on any account pry into matters that do not concern you.' He walked out of the kitchen, leaving Rosina staring after him.

She turned to Merry, who had just deposited the laundry in the scullery.

'What do you know about Mr Dimond, Merry? Tell me what people say about him.'

'There are all kind of tales about the family, especially Jabez Dimond, and none of them fit for your ears, miss.'

'It sounds fascinating.'

'The Dimond family used to own Moonshadow Manor. Jabez made a fortune in trade – some say it was free trade, although that's never been proved – but he liked to gamble, and he lost this house to Miss Jane's father, Phillip Maddern, in a card game.'

'How interesting. Tell me more,' Rosina said eagerly.

'Jabez sent his only son, Nathaniel, to study law and he set him up in business. Some say it was a way to make up for his own shortcomings, others think it was to cover up his dealings with the smuggling gangs.'

'Do you think there are items of contraband in the boxes? I thought that free trading had been virtually stamped out when the import taxes were lowered. I heard my pa say so.' Rosina eyed Merry curiously. Once again, she felt she had stepped into another world, far from home and everything she had known.

'I don't know, miss. And that's the truth,' Merry said firmly. 'There's always talk going round in the village, most of it far from true. What I do know is that Miss Maddern doesn't throw anything away, which is the reason for all the articles scattered about the house. She's been like that ever since I first came here as a little maid.'

Rosina squared her shoulders. 'Then it's time things changed. Tomorrow I am going to begin sorting out some of the things that can be put aside for the poor and needy. Maybe I can sell some things, too. That would help the funds. My aunt is not a wealthy woman, according to Mr Dimond, anyway.'

'Some would say she was very fortunate, miss. There are families in the village who have little enough to eat, let alone clothing for the little ones.'

'Then we can help people who are really down on their luck. I'm sure my aunt would approve if she understood. Now to be practical – we'd best make a start. If you light a fire in the bedrooms, I will make up the beds.'

Merry frowned. 'I should be doing all that, miss.'

'Don't worry, there is plenty of work for you. Can you cook, Merry?'

'Not very well, miss.'

'We'll manage tonight, but tomorrow I will see if I can find someone to take over in the kitchen. You make very good bread, though.'

'Yes, miss. Ma taught me how to bake, and I can manage quite well in the kitchen. It's the fancy food I can't do.'

Rosina laughed. 'I don't think we'll be doing much entertaining. Just good plain food will do very well. Now let's start on the bedrooms.'

Rosina was pleased to find that she and Merry worked well together. The bedrooms were prepared speedily, and fires blazed up the chimneys, warming and airing the rooms. They worked together to make a meal of vegetable soup, which Rosina insisted that Merry should share before she set off for home. Jane had not moved from her chair in the morning parlour, but she awakened enough to swallow mouthfuls of soup and a little bread and butter. With Merry's help Rosina managed to get her aunt upstairs to her bedchamber, where they undressed her and put her into a flannel nightgown before tucking her up in bed.

'Thank you, Alice,' Jane said sleepily as Rosina leaned over to brush her thin cheek with a kiss.

'Good night, Aunt. I'll see you in the morning.' Rosina picked up the chamber candlestick and followed Merry out of the room.

'Why does she call you, Alice?' Merry asked as they negotiated the stairs.

'She thinks I am my mother,' Rosina explained with a sigh. 'If it makes her happy, I don't mind. My mother was a lovely person, so kind and loving. I really miss her.'

'I'm sorry for your loss, miss. I'd like to stay longer and help, but my ma will worry if I don't get home soon,' Merry said apologetically. 'I'd best be on me way.'

'Of course. Thank you for all you've done, Merry. I couldn't have managed without you.'

'Get on with you, miss. I'm sure you could handle anything, given the chance. I'll say good night and be off.'

Rosina patted her on the shoulder as they reached the foot of the stairs. 'Good night, Merry. I'll see you tomorrow.'

Merry hurried out through the kitchen and scullery, closing the doors behind her. Suddenly the house was eerily quiet, except for the occasional hiss from sap seeping out of logs on the fire. Rosina took the supper plates to the scullery and pumped water vigorously into the stone sink. She added hot water from the kettle and washed the dishes. Outside it was pitch dark and she could feel the cold seeping up through the flagstone floor. Having completed her task, she made a pot of tea and took it to the morning parlour, where it was warm and cosy, but the sounds of the old house as it settled down for the night were disconcerting. Odd creaks had her turning her head, but of course there was nothing to be seen. She tried to settle down, sipping her tea, but the tale that

Merry had told her of the Dimond family and their rumoured connection to the former smuggling gangs was intriguing. However, she could not imagine Jack Dimond, the respected solicitor, being involved in anything of the kind.

Eventually, as the flames died down to glowing embers, she decided that bed was the answer. She placed a guard across the fire, extinguished the candles on the mantelshelf and made her way upstairs to her room. She undressed by the fire and made herself ready for bed, but outside the wild March wind was racketing round the old house, rattling the windows and doors. She had experienced nothing like this living in London, and although common sense told her that it was merely the last of the winter weather, she struggled with the concept.

There was only one of the boxes in her room, and she had managed to ignore it, even though Jack had warned her against prying into matters that did not concern her. She sat for a moment on the edge of her bed, but she knew she would not sleep until she discovered the secret of Moonshadow Manor. If she was going to live in this house, she needed to know the truth.

Chapter Three

Rosina stood up, staring at the large wooden box, which was tied up with strong cord. She walked over to it and started to pick at the knots. It was not as easy as she had thought it would be, but eventually she managed to untie them, and with trembling fingers she lifted the lid. Quite what she had expected to find was not something to which she had given much thought, but a gasp of disappointment escaped her lips. Jack Dimond had not lied. There appeared to be nothing but handwritten notes and legal documents, but the formal jargon and the spidery writing made them difficult to understand. She folded the top one neatly and put it back in the box. Perhaps tomorrow she would take another look and see if she could make sense of why such papers needed to be hidden away, although Dimond himself was probably the only person who could give her a reason. At least if she were to read some of the documents, it would give her at least a hint of what was going on. After all, the papers must be much more important than Dimond had implied. She climbed into bed, but she left the candle burning despite the flickering shadows on the walls and ceiling. She pulled the covers up to her chin and closed her eyes.

Daylight was streaming through a gap in the curtains when Rosina was awakened by a sound of horses' hoofs and wagon wheels on the cobblestones. The sound of raised male voices made her leap out of bed and she wrapped her robe around her. She hurried out onto the landing and leaned over the banister rail. It was a shock to see two men taking boxes out through the open front door. She ran downstairs barefoot, with her hair flying loose around her shoulders.

'Stop. What are you doing? Where are you taking those things?'

The younger of the two men came to a halt, grinning at her over the top of a pile of the smaller boxes. 'Boss's orders, miss.'

'Who gave you such instructions?' Rosina demanded, clutching the wrap closer around her body.

'Not my place to say, miss.' The cheerful young man staggered out of the house, passing his companion in the doorway.

The older man looked up at Rosina and doffed his cap. 'Morning, miss. We're to take all the boxes from the house. Mr Dimond's orders.'

'He didn't mention it to me,' Rosina said anxiously. 'Maybe I should check with him.'

'It's a long ride to town, miss. We'll have packed up and taken the goods to the storehouse before you get there.' He put his hand in his pocket and took out a crumpled piece of paper. 'He said to give you this.'

Rosina negotiated the last few steps and took the paper from his hand. She read it hastily. 'All right. It seems genuine so you'd better carry on.' She hurried back to her room and dressed quickly. She had barely finished tying back her hair when someone knocked on the door and the cheerful young man burst into the room.

'Excuse me, miss. I was told to check all rooms. Is there a box of papers in here?'

Rosina had hoped they might forget this one, but there seemed little point in denying it.

'Over there, by the clothes press.'

'Thankee, miss.' He crossed the floor and hefted the box onto his shoulder. His booted feet clattered on the bare boards as he left the room and headed towards the stairs.

Faint cries from Jane's room made Rosina forget everything other than her aunt's needs. She hurried to her aid and found her cowering in her bed.

'There was a man,' she said, weakly. 'He took things from my room. I'm supposed to keep those boxes safe.'

'It's all right, Aunt.' Rosina clasped her aunt's hand. 'There's nothing to worry about. It was Mr Dimond who asked for the papers to be taken to a more secure storage place. He sent a note to say so.'

'Roland always was a law unto himself,' Jane said, smiling. 'You should have married Roland, Alice. He always had a soft spot for you.'

'I'm Rosina, Aunt Jane. I'm Alice's daughter.'

'Alice could have had any man in the county, but she chose Humphrey.' Jane closed her eyes. 'I think I could manage some breakfast. Please tell Cook to lightly boil an egg for me, Alice.'

'Yes, Aunt.' Rosina gave up trying to establish her identity. She went to draw back the curtains and found the sun shining despite the bitter cold. She riddled the embers in the fire and added more coal before going downstairs.

The men were taking the last of the boxes to the wagon although there were still clothes, books and other discarded items littering the floor. However, seeing to them would be a task for later. Rosina made for the kitchen, where she found Merry already at work. The familiar aroma of baking bread filled the kitchen, and the kettle bubbled on the hob. Merry looked up and grinned.

'Good morning, miss. Are you ready for breakfast?'

'Good morning, Merrilees. Yes, please. I'm starving, but my aunt is awake and asking for a lightly boiled egg. I ought to see to her first.'

'You need food more than Miss Jane. I'll see to her next. There's tea in the pot, freshly brewed. I'll scramble some eggs for you, and I dare say a slice or two of bacon wouldn't go amiss.'

'Thank you, that would be wonderful.' Rosina pulled up a chair and sat down at the table. She poured tea into a cup and added a splash of milk. 'You've even brought fresh milk.'

'I called in at Applegate Farm on the way here. Seth looks out for me, and his ma lets me have the best and biggest eggs. She's got a soft spot for me.'

'That doesn't surprise me.' Rosina sipped the tea. 'Do you know the men who came to take the boxes away?'

'No, miss. They come from Ivybridge, but they did tell me they do jobs for Mr Dimond. I must say, I'm glad to see the back of those boxes. We never did find out what's in them.'

'Mr Dimond said they were full of old documents. Nothing very interesting,' Rosina said casually, although she found it hard to believe that explanation.

'Seems a bit odd, if you ask me.' Merry cracked eggs into a bowl and whisked them vigorously. She added bacon to a pan on the range and scrambled the eggs in another, and when they were ready, she plated them and set them in front of Rosina at the table.

'Thank you, Merry. This looks and smells wonderful.' Rosina attacked the food with enthusiasm while Merry placed two eggs in a pan of boiling water.

'I love cooking, miss.' Merry sliced bread and buttered it liberally. 'We can manage without a cook if you'll allow me to take over in the kitchen.'

'I'm happy with that. We will need someone to help with the cleaning. I can't manage the whole house on my own.' Rosina placed her knife and fork back on the empty plate.

Merry raised her eyebrows in disdain. 'You are above stairs, miss. You don't do housework. We need a scullery maid and a cleaning woman, every day. Even then it will take a while to get the house back to what it was.'

'What was it like? I can't recall very much as I was quite young when I last visited.'

'I remember coming here as a little maid when Ma worked in the kitchen. There was parties and all sorts of goings-on. I used to hide on the stairs and watch people arriving all dressed up in their finest.'

'That must have been in my grandfather's day,' Rosina said slowly. 'The family obviously had money in those days.'

'I shouldn't repeat tittle-tattle, but old Mr Maddern was a bit of a gambler. It was Mr Dimond's grandfather, Mr Nathaniel Dimond, who tried to get the deeds to the property restored to the family.

There was a court case about it.' Merry arranged thin slices of bread and butter on a plate. She turned back to the range and scooped the eggs out of the boiling water 'These should be done enough for Miss Jane. She do love them soft-boiled.'

'That would account for all those boxes filled with documents, but it seems ridiculous to continue the fight after so many years.'

'Best ask Mr Dimond about it, miss.'

'I will, when I see him next.' Rosina frowned thoughtfully. 'My aunt must have had a hard life, trying to keep this place going on her own.'

'I can remember when Miss Maddern kept a herd of Red Devons. I used to come here with Ma and help to make butter in the dairy, but it all stopped suddenly. I don't know why but I was very young.'

'What happened to the animals?' Rosina glanced out of the window as if expecting to see a Ruby Red Devon cow grazing on the tussocky grass.

'They was all sold off. Miss Maddern needed the money, so Ma said. She hasn't been able to do much for a few years now.'

'Mr Dimond advanced me some money so I can settle most of the outstanding bills, but what I don't understand is, if the Dimonds and the Madderns are so much at odds, why did Aunt Jane entrust Jack Dimond with her financial affairs?'

'I don't know for sure, miss. But I believe it was Mr Phillip Maddern, Miss Jane's pa, who entrusted his affairs to Mr Dimond's father when he agreed to drop the court case, and Mr Jack took over when his pa died.'

'And now Jack wants all the old documents,' Rosina said thoughtfully. 'I wonder if he is going to start it all up again. He doesn't seem like the sort of person I would entrust with my financial affairs.'

'The Dimond family aren't like most folks,' Merry said, shaking her head. 'Mr Jack's father, Roland Dimond, married a gypsy woman called Naomie.'

'Were they happy together?' Rosina needed there to be an uplifting ending to what sounded like the makings of a doomed relationship.

'Naomie was a wild 'un, so they say. She ran away several times, but Mr Roland always found her and brought her home. That is, until Master Jack was sent to boarding school and his ma ran off for the last time. She was never heard of again and Mr Roland devoted himself to building up the law firm. He died a couple of years ago.'

'Then, in the circumstances, I suppose Jack Dimond has done well for himself, despite his difficult start in life.'

Merry nodded wisely. 'You have to start somewhere. That's what Ma always says.'

Rosina pushed her plate away and rose to her feet. 'You're right, and it's time I took charge of matters here. I will give my aunt her breakfast, and then you can help me to sort through all the piles of things scattered round the house.'

'I've been dying to get my hands on all that rubbish, miss. I can't abide a mess.' Merry filled a cup with tea and added a dash of milk. 'But you make a start on that, and I'll take Miss Jane her breakfast. She's used to me helping her so don't you worry.'

'You're right. We will keep to her usual routine. I don't want to upset her.'

Rosina left the kitchen and made her way to her grandfather's study, where she assumed that her aunt would keep all her correspondence. It was bitterly cold in the small room and, as she had feared, the place was in a terrible state of confusion. Bills, receipts and scraps of paper were piled up on the desk and scattered around the floor. It looked as if Jane had made a vain attempt at sorting matters but had given up and simply shut the door on the chaotic scene.

Rosina set about the task in the light of a single oil lamp, while outside rain hurled itself at the windows and the wind whistled down the chimney. She was too busy to feel cold, and she worked methodically, sorting the papers into separate piles with the most urgent bills on top. By the end of the morning, it had become obvious that the amount of money Jack Dimond had given her was not going to cover all the debts. In fact, by the time everything was settled there would be nothing left to live on, and that was worrying. One thing had become obvious and that was a need to visit Dimond's office again. Rosina was determined to find out exactly how much or how little money there was in the bank. She knew she could not contain her curiosity when it came to the documents that Dimond had decided he needed so urgently, and she was eager to get answers.

She cleared the desk and had a pile of out-of-date papers and notes ready to put on the fire, with the most urgent bills in a tray on the desk, which she would see to as soon as funds permitted. At least she could see the floor now and she knew how much money she would need to care for Jane and pay for necessities.

She left the study and took the excess papers to the morning parlour. Merry had tidied the room. It was warm and welcoming with a fire burning in the grate and Rosina spent the next few minutes adding the wastepaper to the flames. Watching it consumed by the fire, she felt she had accomplished something. It was a start, and she intended to go on until she had restored order to Moonshadow Manor and sorted her aunt's finances. Despite her reservations about Jack Dimond, she was beginning to feel a little sorry for the boy abandoned by his mother at a tender age. She would, however, need to ensure that past family feuds were set aside so that they could deal with today's problems like sensible adults, and she must see him as soon as possible. It would be difficult without any transport of her own, but it would not do to keep asking Seth Tully to drive her when she needed to go to town.

Rosina found Merry in the kitchen, peeling vegetables at the kitchen table.

'Merry, how did my aunt get into Ivybridge when she needed to do business there? Before she became ill, of course.'

'There's a gig in the stables, miss. Although poor old Toby passed away two years ago.'

'Was Toby a horse or was he a coachman?'

Merry's brown eyes brimmed with laughter, and she giggled. 'Toby was a horse. He was old when he just went to sleep in the field and didn't wake up again. Miss Jane cried all day when Toby died.'

'That is sad. I must go to the stables and take a look at the vehicle. It might be falling apart, for all I know.'

'I think it's still in one piece,' Merry said, reaching for another carrot. 'Do you know how to harness a horse and put it between the shafts?'

Rosina shook her head. 'I grew up in London, Merry. There are omnibuses that will take you anywhere, and cabs passing the house by day and most of the night. I am a townsperson, and I have a lot to learn if I am going to survive in the country.'

'I told you about my uncles, miss. They will be more than happy to help out in the stables or in the grounds. Maybe you could get a few sheep and start up the farm again, or we could get a market stall and sell all those things that Miss Jane's been hoarding for years.'

Rosina had been about to leave the kitchen, but she came to a halt by the door. 'I think you have something there. A market stall sounds like a very good idea.'

'Seth might be able to help you, miss. He deals with the market manager all the time. We could stock up on provisions if we managed to sell things.'

'It sounds like a good idea, Merry. I'll look into it, but first I'm going to inspect the gig and see if it's roadworthy.'

Stopping only to wrap her shawl around her head and shoulders, Rosina left the house through the scullery and made her way across the back yard to the stable block. It was bitterly cold, but the sleet had given way to a misty drizzle, which blotted out the moors, giving the area a mystical if slightly eerie atmosphere. However, Rosina was more interested in exploring the stables than in flights of fancy. The old doors creaked as she opened them, and she noted that one of the hinges was broken, having rusted through. That would be the first job for Tom or Sid, Merry's uncles, and there were obvious leaks in the roof, judging by the damp patches on the packed earth floor. Cobwebs hung from the rafters, and the air was thick with dust. The empty stalls had been cleared of any detritus, so at least there would be little to do here other than general cleaning and fixing the roof and broken door hinge.

She found the gig shrouded in sacking, and although Rosina was no expert, she could see that it needed some work before it could be taken out on the public roads. However, she was determined to be optimistic and to get advice from people who knew what they were talking about.

She was about to leave when she heard footsteps, and she turned to see a man standing in the doorway. His sudden appearance made her jump, but it was clear from his mode of dress that he was a gentleman of some means.

He swept off his top hat, revealing a head of thick wavy hair the colour of ripe corn. His eyes were an unusual shade of blue-green, and he had a charming smile.

'I hope I didn't startle you, Miss Wills. Merry told me that I might find you here.'

Rosina took a deep breath. She was not going to admit that she had been a little scared, not even for one moment. 'You have the advantage over me, sir. You know my name; might I know yours?'

'I'm your neighbour, Hugo Charteris. I live at Daumerle House. I believe Jack Dimond mentioned me to you.'

'Of course, Sir Hugo. Yes, he did, and Merry told me that you had kindly released her so that she could help me in the house.' Rosina held out her hand. 'How do you do, sir?'

He took off his riding glove and raised her hand to his lips. 'How do you do, Miss Wills?'

'Shall we go outside?' Rosina said hastily. 'It is very stuffy in here.'

He followed her out into cold, damp air. 'Merry said you were considering the use of Miss Maddern's old gig. Even at a distance I can see that it needs some attention.'

'Yes, it does seem rather dilapidated, not that I know anything about vehicles. I'm afraid I am a townsperson born and bred. I know nothing about country living. It's all very new to me.'

'Jack told me that you had recently come from London, and that is the main reason for my call today. Firstly, this is a neighbourly visit to welcome you to Ugstock, but also, I wish to offer my help if needed.'

Rosina laughed. 'Thank you, sir. I won't say no to the latter. I would be very grateful for some advice about getting the gig roadworthy, and I will need a horse, but I wouldn't know where to start.'

'It depends upon how much you wish to spend, but I can lend you a good reliable carriage horse until you are suited. I'll get one of my men to have a look at the gig, if that's agreeable to you.'

'That's very kind, but Merry said one of her uncles would be pleased to help,' Rosina said warily.

She was a little suspicious of someone who was so amenable, especially on their first meeting.

'Tom and Sid work for me,' Charteris said, smiling. 'At least they are supposed to carry out repairs and do general labouring, but between you and me they are a lazy pair. My estate manager has to keep an eye on them, or they will renege on their duties.'

'I don't think Merry realises that they are not good workers, Sir Hugo.'

'We're neighbours, Miss Wills. I hope we will be able to drop formalities, and you feel able to call me Hugo. I hate standing on ceremony.'

'Thank you, Hugo. My name is Rosina.'

'You will bring a breath of fresh air to Moonshadow Manor, Rosina. The old house has been silent and brooding for too long. It's almost as if the moor has been trying to reclaim its own.'

'I don't understand. Why would you say that?' Rosina asked nervously.

He shrugged. 'Take no notice of any wild stories you might hear. The people of Ugstock are very superstitious and I believe they used to spread stories about mysterious happenings on the moors as a way of maintaining the village's isolation.'

'Now I'm more intrigued than ever, Hugo. Why would they think like that?'

'Ugstock is a good few miles from the coast, but in a way that made it more attractive to those who dealt in contraband. It was quite far for the excisemen to extend their search for smuggled brandy, tea or silk, and the moor is inhospitable, especially in winter.'

Rosina stared at him in amazement. 'Surely that all happened many years ago.'

'Talk to some of the more elderly people in the village and they will speak about it as if it were yesterday.'

'Was Moonshadow Manor involved in all that skulduggery?'

'The old house seems to have been at the bottom of many things, including the old feud between the Madderns and the Dimonds. Maybe Jack could tell you more about the goings-on at Moonshadow.'

'All that seems to have been settled now,' Rosina said carefully. She had no proof that Jack Dimond intended to pursue ownership of Moonshadow; it was all surmise on her part.

'With your permission I will call later in the week,' Hugo continued, smiling. 'I haven't paid my respects to Miss Maddern for some time, which is very remiss of me.'

'Of course. I'm sure she would appreciate that, but why wait? Won't you come into the house? I can offer you tea or a glass of sherry wine. At least I think I saw a decanter on the sideboard in the dining room. Perhaps Aunt Jane enjoys a little tipple occasionally.'

'I would love to, but today I have a meeting with my estate manager and then I'm going into Ivybridge to see Jack. Have you a message for him?'

Rosina shook her head. She had plenty of questions

she would like to ask Jack Dimond but it would be better to do so in person.

'No, but thank you for offering. When I get the gig mended, I will drive myself into Ivybridge and then I will call on him.'

Charteris eyed her with some amusement. 'Have you ever handled the reins, Rosina?'

'No, but I can learn.'

'Of course you can, and I will be more than happy to give you some lessons, should you need them. Now, I really must go, but I am very glad that we have met. I'm sure we will be good neighbours.' He put on his top hat and walked towards his chestnut gelding, untethered it and mounted with ease. He tipped his hat. 'Goodbye, Rosina. I will see you again soon.' He rode off at a smart trot.

Rosina stood very still, gazing back at the house with smoke curling up into a wintry blue sky. Beyond it the moor was now lazing in the pale sunlight, looking quite welcoming and far from the misty, sinister place that it appeared earlier. She wondered if the stories about smugglers and the hint at other criminal activities were true and she felt an apprehensive tingle run down her spine as she walked slowly across the yard to the back door. Whatever secrets Moonshadow Manor held it was keeping them hidden beneath its tiled roof and granite walls. A blast of cold air rushed past her as she opened the door and stepped inside.

Chapter Four

Rosina returned to the house and found Merry in the kitchen.

'I've given Miss Jane her breakfast,' Merry said cheerfully as she placed the tray of used crockery on the table. 'And I've made her comfortable in the morning parlour. She's quite chirpy this morning, but she's always more cheerful when the sun shines.'

Rosina smiled. 'I can understand that. It's lovely to see the sun but it's quite chilly outside.'

'Did you find the gig in the stables? I would think it's in a bit of a state.' Merry eyed her expectantly. 'What did Sir Hugo say? I thought you wouldn't mind if I told him where to find you,' she added hastily.

'He was very helpful. He's going to send one of your uncles to take a look at the gig and make any necessary repairs, and then Sir Hugo is going to lend me a horse until I can get one of my own.'

'Well, then, there's a happy outcome. Sir Hugo is a real gentleman. I can't speak highly enough of him.'

'He seems very nice,' Rosina said guardedly. She did not want to seem too effusive in her praise for her neighbour. She doubted that Merry was a gossip, but she was not going to take a chance.

'He isn't married,' Merry continued eagerly. 'Well, he would have been if tragedy hadn't put an end to his hopes, poor man.'

'What sort of tragedy, Merry?' Rosina could not allow this to pass without asking for more information.

'Miss Belinda was so beautiful, but delicate. She came from a wealthy family down Teignbridge way, and she looked like a fairy princess. Everyone knew that it was a love match.' Merry paused, dashing tears from her eyes. 'But a few weeks before the wedding she took sick and died. It was a terrible upset and the whole village mourned her passing.'

'That is sad,' Rosina said earnestly. 'Poor Sir Hugo.'

Merry sniffed and dabbed her eyes with her apron. 'It was eight years ago but he's never shown any interest in another woman. I think his heart is buried in the grave with his one love.'

'Thank you for telling me,' Rosina said gently. 'I

might have said something to Sir Hugo that upset him, and I wouldn't want that.'

'Of course not, miss.'

'I'll go and check on my aunt.' Rosina left the room, putting an end to the conversation.

Jane was as usual dozing by the fire. She opened her eyes briefly when Rosina rearranged the blanket around her knees.

'Alice, you're here again. How nice.' Jane smiled and went back to sleep, leaving Rosina frustrated. She had hoped perhaps her aunt could throw some light on the family business, but it seemed more and more unlikely. She banked up the fire and put the fireguard in place while she tidied the room. She put things in separate piles, one for clothes and blankets, one for books and another for oddments like an old clock, porcelain ornaments and pieces of bric-a-brac. She found a gold watch that seemed to work when she wound it up, and several books, all in good condition. The idea of having a stall in the market seemed to be quite possible, and this was only the first room she had attempted to sort out.

Encouraged by her finds, some of which were only fit to be thrown on the rubbish heap, while others might be worth something to someone, Rosina went from one downstairs room to another. She found some empty boxes in the attic and filled these with her trophies.

She had to stop for a while when Merry's uncles

arrived. Rosina had to accompany them to the stables where they discussed what needed to be done to make the gig roadworthy. Tom and Sid Bragg were light-hearted and seemed to find everything funny. They made Rosina laugh so much that she had tears running down her cheeks and she had to tear herself away from their company, or she might have spent the entire day watching them work and listening to their amusing banter.

After a light luncheon of soup, made by Merry, and some bread and cheese, Rosina started on the upstairs rooms. Soon she needed more boxes, and she had not even begun on the top floor where the servants would have slept. With Merry's help she took the boxes to what had been the butler's pantry in bygone days and set them out neatly labelled. Merry was as excited as a small child as she examined some of the articles, and she was thrilled when Rosina said she could keep a rather ugly trinket probably won at a fair, that was of little value but had an obvious appeal to Merry.

At the end of the day, after she had given Jane her supper and had her tucked up in bed, Rosina was exhausted but triumphant. She felt she was making progress. Tom Bragg had come to the kitchen with a promise to have the gig ready for use next day. Sid followed him into the house, and he affirmed Sir Hugo's promise of a reliable horse to pull the gig.

After they had gone Rosina sat for a while in the

now tidy drawing room, having lit a fire earlier in the day. The furniture might be old-fashioned and slightly worn but it was comfortable, and with the curtains drawn against a rainy night, Rosina was beginning to feel that this old house might one day feel like home. She sipped a cup of cocoa and planned her trip to Ivybridge where she intended to ask Dimond if the ownership of the house was still being contested. She needed to know mainly because, he being her aunt's solicitor, it would almost certainly be a conflict of interests. He alone would have the answers she needed, or so she hoped.

After a while, she went to her room feeling tired but satisfied that she had made progress that day. The nighttime noises of the old house as the ancient timbers settled for the night were no longer as frightening as they had been the previous day. Despite the tales of smugglers and feuding families, Moonshadow Manor seemed to embrace Rosina as she undressed and slipped on her nightgown. She went to the window and drew back the curtains, peering out into the darkness. The rain had ceased but the moon was obscured by thick clouds. She was just going to turn away when a flash of light made her look again. There was nothing and she sighed with relief, thinking it must have been her imagination, but suddenly there it was again. This time the light bobbed up and down as if carried in some invisible hand. Rosina took a step away from the window, her heart beating at twice its normal rate. Then the light disappeared and there was nothing but darkness. She climbed into bed and pulled the covers up to her chin.

Next day, after settling Jane in her chair by the fire, Rosina devoted herself to a thorough exploration of the top floor and attic rooms. Once again, she found enough discarded items to fill several boxes, and with Merry's help she took them down to the butler's pantry where they were added to the existing piles.

They had barely finished when Sid arrived to announce that there would be a delay in repairing the gig as they had to take off one of the wheels and get it to the wheelwright in the next village. Rosina was disappointed, but there was still plenty to do in the house, and she would just have to be patient. The weather had improved a little and there was a hint of spring in the air as she set off for a walk, heading for the open moorland. She had casually mentioned the mysterious light to Merry, who nodded wisely and said it was often seen. Some attributed it to a will-o'-the-wisp; others said it was the spirit of smugglers who had been caught and executed for their crimes. Rosina decided that perhaps the former was more likely, and this left her with a sudden desire to explore her surroundings.

She started off enthusiastically, walking at a brisk

pace along a well-trodden path. The cold air was exhilarating, and the moor seemed to stretch into infinity. The pale sunshine bathed the tussocky grasses with a silvery sheen, and in the distance Rosina could see granite outcrops. It was all so different from the streets of Islington, and the air was so fresh it was intoxicating. She lost track of time and although she knew she ought to turn back, it was as if the moor was drawing her in, urging her to walk further and further into its depths. Then, quite suddenly the sun disappeared behind the clouds and a white mist came rolling across the moor, enveloping her in a cold fog. She lost all sense of direction, and she seemed to have stepped off the path. Then, just as she was beginning to panic, she heard the muffled sound of a horse's hoofs and the rumble of carriage wheels. At first, she thought it was her imagination playing tricks on her, but it seemed to be getting nearer. She opened her mouth and uttered a loud cry for help.

Then, as if by magic, she heard a voice calling her name.

'I'm here,' Rosina shouted. 'I can't see you.'

'Stay where you are. Don't move. I'll find you.'

The reassuringly calm tone of the man's voice made her take a deep breath. She struggled to deal with the panic that threatened to overcome good sense, but it was almost impossible. She wrapped her arms around herself, shivering convulsively as the cold, damp mist seemed to eat at her bones. Then, just as suddenly as it had come, the mist seemed to evaporate. Not only that, but a horse-drawn chaise was not a stone's throw away. The man, swathed in a caped greatcoat and wide-brimmed hat, drew the horse to a halt and leaped to the ground.

'Don't move, Rosina. One step in the wrong direction and you'll find yourself sinking into the marsh.' He strode towards her and without a by your leave he lifted her off her feet and carried her to the chaise. 'You're safe now,' Charteris added as he set her down on the seat and climbed up beside her. 'What on earth were you thinking off, going walking on the moor?'

'It was a lovely d-day when I s-set off,' Rosina said through chattering teeth.

Charteris took off his coat and wrapped it around her shoulders. 'That's one thing you need to learn about the moor. The weather can change from one minute to the next, particularly at this time of the year.'

'How did you know where to find me?' Rosina shot him a sideways glance, but he was concentrating on guiding the horse onto the track.

'Merrilees told me you had gone for a walk. Just remember that even those born and bred here are cautious when it comes to taking on the moor.' He flicked the reins. 'Walk on.'

'That's something I am not likely to forget now,' Rosina said, pulling the heavy folds of his coat close around her. The scent of leather and sandalwood exuded from the thick woollen material, which was oddly comforting. It reminded her of her father, in happier days, before he had met and married the young widow. He had been a good parent and no matter how much he was occupied by business matters he had always found time to take Rosina for a carriage ride to one of the many places of interest in London. It had been a weekly treat to go to the Zoological Gardens or visit the National Gallery or the British Museum. Sometimes he would take her for tea at Gunter's or take a picnic to Victoria Park and listen to the band, or take a boat out on the lake. Pa had loved sandalwood soap, and the scent of it reminded her of him before he became besotted with Dora.

'Were you headed anywhere in particular?'

Charteris's voice broke into Rosina's thoughts, and she turned her head to give him a wary glance.

'No, not really. Although last night I looked out of my bedroom window and I saw a light moving about, almost as if someone was carrying a lantern.'

'I'm sure there was a rational explanation,' Charteris said casually. 'What did you hope to find?'

'I don't know. I suppose I just wanted to see what was out there. I don't believe in ghosts.'

'Neither do I, and anyway, it would have been a very substantial phantom who could carry a lantern.'

'A lantern? What do you mean?'

Charteris laughed. 'I found one discarded outside the stables. It certainly wasn't there when I visited you yesterday.'

'That means someone was skulking round after dark,' Rosina said nervously. 'I don't like the sound of that. Who would come all the way out here at night? What were they looking for?'

'Sometimes you get gypsies in the area. Maybe someone was seeking shelter for the night. I had a quick look in the stables and there didn't seem to be any damage and no evidence of anyone sleeping there.'

'Even so, that makes me a little nervous. There is only Aunt Jane and me in the house at night. Merry goes home after supper.'

'I doubt if whoever it was will return, Rosina. They obviously didn't find anything of interest, but make sure that all doors are locked at night and close the windows.'

'Yes, I will. I most certainly will do that.'

Charteris drew the horse to a halt outside the stable, but instead of alighting he handed her the reins. 'To take your mind off such things, how about a lesson in driving the chaise? It's why I came here in the first place.'

Rosina was about to refuse, but she could tell by his expression that he was not going to let her get away so easily. She clutched the reins nervously.

'Tell me what to do.'

Charteris proved to be a good teacher. Under his guidance Rosina turned the horse in the direction of the main road and soon they were tooling along the lane that led into the village. At first, she was biting her lip and concentrating hard on what she was doing, but as she gained confidence, she found she could virtually leave the horse to do the thinking. It was only when she needed to change direction or to bring the vehicle to a halt that she had to take over. As they circled the village green with its large duck pond and a leafless weeping willow, she was aware that they were attracting some attention. People were staring and men tipped their caps to Charteris while the older women acknowledged him by bobbing a curtsey.

'You really are the lord of the manor, aren't you?' Rosina eyed him curiously. 'Where is Daumerle House? Is it far away?'

'We're coming to a crossroads. Keep going straight ahead and I'll show you my home – if you have time, that is.'

'I'd like that very much,' Rosina said eagerly. 'How do you think I'm doing? Will I be able to drive myself to Ivybridge when the gig is mended?'

'I don't see why not, although you will have to learn how to harness the horse and put him between the shafts.' Charteris frowned. 'You could do with a man on the premises, Rosina. Both for security and to help in the stables.'

'I will need to be more independent,' Rosina said firmly. 'I can't keep relying on my neighbours for assistance.'

'I am always there to help if you need me.'

'I didn't mean you, Hugo. I am extremely grateful for everything you've done for me, but I was thinking of Seth Tully. I had to ask him to take me to Ivybridge and I want to speak to him about getting a market stall.'

'A market stall?' Charteris stared at her in astonishment. 'Why would you wish to do something like that?'

Rosina smiled at his shocked expression. 'It's not exactly what I want to do but more a necessity. I need money and I've been sorting out the odd collection of items that my aunt has been hoarding for years. It seems the logical way to go about solving both problems.'

'You are indeed a resourceful woman, Rosina. I'm not sure whether to encourage you to set yourself up in business, but I admire your determination to put matters straight.' Charteris leaned over to add a touch to the reins. 'We're here. The gatekeeper will come out the moment he sees us, and he'll let us through. Just trust the horse; he knows he's come home.'

As Charteris had said, the gatekeeper hurried out of his cottage to unlock the tall, iron gates and Rosina encouraged the horse to walk on. The animal did seem to know he was close to home and he broke into a trot. Daumerle House came into view at the end of an avenue of stately beech trees. Rosina had been concentrating so hard on driving that she had barely noticed the sun emerging from a bank of clouds. Its rays reflected off the white stucco and the columned portico of the classic frontage.

'It's a fine house,' she said earnestly as she drew the horse to a halt outside the front entrance.

'We think so.' Charteris alighted and looped the reins over the horse's head before handing them to a stable boy, who had appeared from somewhere at the rear of the building.

The front door opened, and a footman emerged to assist Rosina as she stepped down from the chaise. He stood aside as Charteris proffered his arm and led Rosina into the entrance hall.

Rosina shot him a sideways glance. 'Do you live here with your family? It's a splendid house, but isn't it rather large for one person?'

'It's been in my family for a couple of hundred years. The front is a façade built on by my great-grandfather in the last century, but the main part of the house is much older. However, to answer your question, my parents are both deceased. There is just me and my sister, Ariadne.'

At that moment, before Rosina had a chance to respond, a door on the far side of the hall opened and a young woman came hurrying towards them.

Her fair hair, almost the exact colour of Hugo's, and her lively blue eyes would have marked her out as being his sister, even before she introduced herself.

'You brought her here, Hugo. I thought you had forgotten.' Ariadne rushed up to Rosina and embraced her as if they were old friends. 'How do you do? I'm Ariadne Charteris and you must be Rosina Wills.'

'How do you do?' Rosina said faintly. 'I'm afraid you have the advantage over me, Miss Charteris. I didn't know of your existence until a few moments ago.'

'Ariadne, please. I'm sure we are going to be great friends. It's all very well living in a grand country house, but it does limit one's social life somewhat.' She grasped Rosina's hand. 'Come into the drawing room and I'll send for some refreshment. You look as though you need some sustenance.' Ariadne turned on her brother. 'What have you been doing to her, Hugo? The poor girl looks exhausted.'

'No, really,' Rosina protested. 'It was my fault entirely. I went for a walk on the moors, and I lost my way. If your brother hadn't come looking for me, I hate to think what might have happened.'

Ariadne laughed. 'I don't see Hugo as a knight errant, but perhaps you bring out the best in him, Rosina.'

'Don't overwhelm her, Ariadne,' Charteris said firmly. 'I brought Rosina here simply to show her where we live, and then I intend to take her back to Moonshadow Manor. I think she's had enough excitement for one day.'

'That is so typical of you, Hugo,' Ariadne said scornfully. 'You imagine that you know what's best for everyone, but you're wrong. I think a little chat and a cup of coffee will do wonders for Rosina. Then you may take her home.'

'I am all right, Hugo.' Rosina managed a bright smile even though she had the beginnings of a headache. 'Some coffee would be most welcome, and then perhaps you would be kind enough to take me home. I think I've had enough driving practice today.'

'You made her take the reins, Hugo?' Ariadne shook her head. 'And the poor girl had been lost on the moors. What were you thinking of?'

Charteris followed them into the spacious drawing room and went to stand in front of the fire. 'It seems that whatever I do today is wrong in your eyes, Ariadne. Perhaps I should leave you two alone for a while and you can continue denigrating me without interruption.'

'Don't be so sensitive, Hugo. I am only teasing you.' Ariadne flounced over to the sofa and sat down amidst a swirl of silk skirts. She patted the empty space beside her. 'Come and sit with me, Rosina. And you, Hugo, dear. Please ring for Ethel.'

Hugo shrugged, but he rang the bell before leaving the room.

Ariadne waited until the door closed on him before turning to Rosina with an eager smile. 'Tell me all about yourself, Rosina. What brings you to this part of the world? I was told that you come from London.'

Rosina could see that she was not going to get away without a full explanation and she sat down. 'My aunt Jane owns Moonshadow Manor. She sent me a letter inviting me to stay with her and the circumstances at home made it impossible to refuse.'

A knock on the door preceded the appearance of the housemaid. 'You rang, Miss Ariadne?'

'Yes, Ethel. Please bring a tray of coffee and cake.'

Ethel bobbed a curtsey and hurried from the room.

'Well now,' Ariadne said, smiling. 'You can't leave the story like that, Rosina. What happened to make you flee to the country? If it's not too painful to relate, of course.'

'My mother died two years ago. Pa and I were very close but then he met Dora, a young widow, and he married her.'

Ariadne rolled her eyes. 'Don't tell me she turned out to be the classic wicked stepmother?'

'Not wicked, but rather spiteful, and she certainly doesn't like me. Anyway, now she has a baby, and I am *de trop*.'

'That's very sad. I'm sorry, Rosina, but on the other hand it's brought you to Moonshadow Manor and we are close neighbours. I look forward to enjoying your company and I'm sure that Hugo does, too.'

'You're very kind,' Rosina murmured, embarrassed by Ariadne's effusive manner. 'I mean to say you are welcome to visit us, too. Although Moonshadow is nothing like Daumerle House.'

'I have been there a couple of times, and it is comparatively small and rather quaint, but very atmospheric. I can imagine it in days gone by as a haunt for the smugglers on the run from the excisemen.'

Rosina stared at her in surprise. 'I feel that, too. But I thought it was my imagination.'

'There are tales of smugglers and wreckers on the coast, although we are several miles inland. Grandpapa used to tell Hugo and me stories about such goings-on that made us shiver with excitement and, to be honest, gave me nightmares.' Ariadne paused as the door opened and Ethel entered carrying a tray of coffee and cake, which she set down on a table close to the sofa. 'Thank you, Ethel. That will be all for now.'

'Yes, Miss Ariadne.' Ethel shot a curious look in Rosina's direction as she left the room.

'Your presence here has been noted,' Ariadne said, laughing. 'It will be all round the village by noon. That's just how it is here.' She poured the coffee and handed a cup to Rosina. 'Do help yourself to cake.'

Rosina took a sip of the coffee. 'Thank you, I will. It looks so good.'

'Have you got a good cook at Moonshadow Manor? Our cook is a real treasure and she's been here ever since I can remember.'

'I've only got one servant. Merrilees Pavey is very willing, and she can handle basic cooking, but I doubt if she's ever made a cake.'

'Just one servant?' Ariadne stared at her in horror. 'How do you manage?'

Rosina could not resist the cake, and she put a slice on a plate. 'We get by, but the worst thing has been clearing up the shocking jumble of things that my aunt has never bothered to throw away. I'm going to get a stall in Ivybridge market and sell some of the better things.'

Ariadne's eyes widened. 'No! A market stall? Surely not.'

'I need the money, and what better way to sell items for which I have no use? Someone might find them worth buying.'

'But a lady should never dabble in commerce, Rosina. Especially in public view.'

'I don't think I classify as a lady, Ariadne. My father is a cloth merchant, and I have no illustrious ancestors.'

'Even so, you are not a common girl. You should not mix with market traders, although it does sound rather a lark.'

'You could help me, if you so wished.' Rosina forked cake into her mouth. 'This is as delicious as it looks.'

'I suppose I could borrow some old clothes set aside for the poor and needy and cover my hair with a mobcap. It would be fun to see if anyone would recognise me, just so long as Hugo doesn't find out. He wouldn't approve of such behaviour.'

'Do you always do what your brother says?' Rosina said warily. 'I don't want to cause a rift in your family.'

'You're right,' Ariadne said, laughing. 'I am too much under my brother's thumb, although he would refute that. I'm with you, Rosina. Tomorrow I will ride over to Moonshadow Manor, and we can make plans together. Never mind what Hugo thinks.'

Chapter Five

'Thank you for bringing me home, Hugo,' Rosina said when they reached the front entrance at Moonshadow Manor. 'And thank you for inviting me into your wonderful abode and introducing me to Ariadne. I hope we will be good friends.'

'My sister is inclined to flights of fancy and sometimes she acts without thinking. I hope you won't encourage her. She can be very reckless at times.'

Rosina eyed him thoughtfully. 'It must be quite difficult being her brother and yet having to act as if you were the parent.'

'I love my sister, but yes, sometimes I lose patience with her. Perhaps having a friend like you will make her act more like a young lady.'

'I'm not sure I'm the best person for that,' Rosina said hastily.

'I think you have good sense, which is more than I can say for Ariadne.' Hugo took a step back. 'I'll send one of the Braggs over with the horse I'm lending you, and I don't want to interfere, Rosina, but I suggest you allow me to send one of my stable boys. You will need someone to care for the animal and to harness the horse when you wish to go for a drive.'

'I don't know, Hugo,' Rosina said doubtfully. 'It seems I am too much in your debt already. There is no reason for you to feel responsible for what happens here. I don't want to seem ungrateful, but it's almost overwhelming.'

'I'm sorry. I don't mean to make you feel that way. I suppose I am so used to taking care of my sister that when I see someone like you in need I have to help.' Hugo smiled ruefully and tipped his hat. 'I should go now, but Ariadne has asked me to bring her here tomorrow morning. I'll see you then.'

'Yes, I look forward to seeing her, and I would be very grateful to have someone to care for the horse. I've never had to do anything like that in my life, and I can see that I will need transport, living out here in the wilds.'

'Then I am exonerated.' Hugo walked back towards his waiting horse and carriage, leaving Rosina staring after him with mixed emotions. She entered the house and was met by Merrilees, whose agitated expression was enough to make Rosina forget about the Charteris family.

'What's happened, Merry? Is it my aunt?'

'She's been taken poorly, miss. I sent Seth to fetch the doctor because I didn't know where you were.'

'I'm sorry, I should have told you that Sir Hugo was showing me how to handle a horse, and he took me to Daumerle House to meet his sister.' Rosina peeled off her gloves and shook off her mantle. 'Has the doctor been?'

'Not yet, miss. I'm glad you're back. You can speak to him, and he will tell you what to do. I get flustered when I'm faced with Dr Clarke. He makes me nervous.'

'Is my aunt in bed or is she still in the morning parlour?'

'I managed to get her upstairs to her room, miss, but she was proper poorly and she didn't know me.'

'I'll go and see her. When Dr Clarke arrives, please sent him upstairs.' Rosina did not wait for an answer. Merry was clearly upset by the whole episode and Rosina struggled with guilt as she hitched up her skirts and took the stairs two at a time. She entered her aunt's room to find it in semi-darkness with the curtains drawn. It was impossible to see properly, so she drew them back and went to stand by the bed.

'How are you feeling, Aunt?'

She was answered with a faint moan. Rosina laid her hand on her aunt's forehead.

'You might have a touch of fever, Aunt. But don't

worry, the doctor should be here soon. I'm sure he will give you something to make you feel better.' She knew she was chattering, but the sound of her voice seemed to calm her aunt, and Rosina perched on the edge of the bed, taking Jane's thin hand in hers. 'We'll have you up and about before you know it.' She tried to sound positive, but her aunt's breathing was ragged and her skin ashen.

Rosina lost all track of time as she sat clutching her aunt's hand. She found herself gazing at a portrait in oils that hung on the wall opposite her aunt's bed. At first Rosina thought it was a painting of her mother, but then she realised that the gown the young woman was wearing was of a much earlier date than her mother would ever have worn. The background was obviously Moonshadow Manor, and it must have been midsummer, judging by the rose bushes in full bloom, tall hollyhocks and clusters of white daisies. Rosina remembered that Mama had loved roses and had often bought them from street sellers, much to the annoyance of Papa, who said it was an extravagance. The lovely young woman in the painting was a great beauty and there was an almost impish twinkle in her eyes as she gazed from the canvas.

The arrival of Dr Clarke made Rosina rise to her feet and she stood back from the bed.

'Thank you for coming, Doctor.' Rosina clasped her hands tightly. 'I wasn't here when my aunt was taken ill. Merry found her and put her back to bed.'

Dr Clarke, a distinguished-looking man in his early sixties, gave her a genuine smile.

'Don't worry, I am here now.' He opened his leather bag and took out a stethoscope. He held it up for her to get a closer look. 'I am probably the first physician in this area to have this new binaural method of listening to a patient's heart,' he said proudly. 'I attend lectures in London on a regular basis, hence the cost of my professional visits. However, Jane is an old friend and there is no charge, Miss Wills.'

Rosina watched as he examined Jane. 'She will be all right, won't she, Doctor?'

'I'm sorry, Miss Wills. I'm afraid your aunt's heart is very weak, and there is congestion in her lungs, which is probably the winter fever. I'm afraid the prognosis is not very hopeful.'

'Are you saying that she is going to die, Doctor?' Rosina asked anxiously, hoping that Dr Clarke would correct her, but he merely nodded.

'Miss Maddern is not a young woman, and her health has been failing for some considerable time.' He took his watch from his waistcoat pocket and glanced at it, frowning. 'I'm sorry but I have another patient to visit now.' He swung his watch back into its resting place with the ease of long practice. 'I will call again in the morning, but if you are worried, please send for me at any time of the day or night.'

'Thank you, Doctor. Is there anything I can do for her?'

He picked up his medical bag. 'Give her sips of water, or tea if she prefers it. Some thin gruel or anything she might fancy. I suppose you will return to London eventually, Miss Wills?'

'I hadn't thought that far, Doctor. I don't know what I'll do if my aunt passes away. I came here to look after her.'

A shadow of sympathy crossed Dr Clarke's lined features, and he shook his head. 'I don't know the circumstances that brought you here in the first place, but the young women in the Maddern family never seem to have much luck. I suppose you have met Jack Dimond.'

'I have, yes. He is my aunt's solicitor.'

'I don't wish to speak out of turn, but you should know there is bad blood between the Dimonds and the Madderns, going back several generations.'

'I'm beginning to find that out, Doctor. But it won't affect me.'

'Be careful, that's all I can say. You are young and beautiful and very vulnerable on your own in Moonshadow Manor.'

'I'm sure I can take care of myself, Doctor. And I'll look after Aunt Jane to the best of my ability.'

Dr Clarke glanced at the portrait on the wall. 'Do you know who that woman is, Miss Wills?'

'She is very beautiful,' Rosina said carefully. 'What are you trying to tell me, Dr Clarke?'

He looked away, clearing his throat noisily. 'It's

not the sort of thing I ought to tell a young lady, Miss Wills. But with Jane so poorly I feel you ought to know.'

'I'm not a child. I've already found out quite shocking things about my family here.'

'If you're certain . . .?' Dr Clarke eyed her warily.

'I understand perfectly, but please tell me. I have no one else to ask.'

Dr Clarke pointed to the portrait that had attracted Rosina's attention earlier.

'That striking young woman is Roxanne Maddern. Her story is one of tragedy.'

'I've never heard her name mentioned. Can you tell me anything more about her?'

'Roxanne was orphaned at the age of ten and sent to live here with the Dimond family, who had owned Moonshadow Manor for many generations.' Dr Clarke hesitated, eyeing Rosina warily.

'There is obviously more to the story than that,' Rosina said curiously. 'What happened to Roxanne?'

'She was barely fifteen when she caught the eye of Phillip Maddern, but apparently Jabez Dimond had also fallen in love with her. He was well known in the area for dealing with the smuggling gangs on the coast. It's said that he used this house for storing contraband before selling it on.'

'I heard something of the sort,' Rosina said thoughtfully. 'So, what happened, did Jabez and Phillip fight a duel over her?'

'It didn't quite come to that. She went away but she returned almost a year later. In the meantime, Jabez had married someone else, leaving the way clear for Phillip Maddern. In comparison to Jabez he was a well-respected member of the community. Phillip had also won Moonshadow Manor in a card game and he and Roxanne married in secret, but a short time later she left once again, presumably after a heated row. That was the last time anyone saw her.'

'But Phillip must have loved her to have her portrait painted.'

'There's no disputing that fact. But Roxanne had gone and was believed to have perished on the moor. It can happen to unwary travellers. Phillip remarried and his daughter is lying there, in that bed.'

'So, in a way it had a happy ending for my grandfather?'

'Not entirely, I'm afraid. His wife, Ellen, died in childbirth a year later and Jane was raised by a series of nursemaids and nannies. You might as well know the whole truth, Rosina. If I don't tell you, someone else will. Jane was sixteen when she fell in love with a married man and gave birth to his child, your mother, Alice. But she would never divulge the father's name.'

Rosina stared at him in disbelief. 'That must mean that she is my grandmother. But I thought she was Mama's sister. Why didn't anyone tell me?'

'Poor Jane has had to live with the shame ever

since. Ugstock is a small village, and I know for a fact that it hasn't been easy for her. There are some pious souls locally who shun a woman taken in sin.'

Rosina struggled to comprehend the enormity of the lies she had been told. 'My mother allowed me to think that Jane was her older sister. I thought that Phillip Maddern was my grandfather.'

'Phillip was, in theory, your great-grandfather, and he not only married the girl that Jabez loved, but he took Moonshadow from him. All this has contributed to the feud between the two families. I'm sorry to be the bearer of such news, but you did ask me to tell you.'

'Do you know who my grandfather was?'

'There were vague rumours in the village, but I can't give you a name because I don't know. Jane would never reveal the truth. She was quite a beauty in her day, but she never married.'

Rosina sighed, staring at the pale face of her grandmother. There were still traces of the beauty of her youth.

'You said that the Maddern women didn't have much luck, but it seems to me that it's more than that. You could almost say they were cursed by their beauty.'

'Which they have passed on to you,' Dr Clarke said with a wry smile. 'Let's hope you do not fall into the same trap as your predecessors, Miss Wills.'

Rosina tossed her head. 'I won't do that, Doctor. Moonshadow Manor has seen enough scandal and troubles in the past, and they are not over yet.'

'Why do you say that?' Dr Clarke said sharply.

'I think Jack Dimond is trying to prove that his family still owns this house.'

'That's as may be, but I suggest you tread carefully when dealing with the Dimond family. They are difficult people. I'll say no more, but you should heed what I advise.'

'Thank you, Dr Clarke. I'm grateful for your honesty. I doubt if anyone else would have told me the truth about my family.'

'You would have heard snippets of the story, so it's best that I told you what I know. Anyway, Miss Wills, I'll call again tomorrow, but if your grandmother's condition deteriorates further, please send for me.'

Dr Clarke turned and left the room.

Rosina could hear his footsteps growing fainter as he descended the stairs, followed by a thud of the front door closing behind him. She returned to Jane's bedside, staring down at her grandmother with a sympathetic smile.

'You poor thing. I can't imagine what you've been through in your life, but I wonder if Mama had any idea that you might be her mother and not her sister.' Rosina straightened the coverlet. 'I promise you that I won't allow Jack Dimond to take back

Moonshadow Manor. It seems to have been the only thing you really care for, Grandmother.'

Jane stirred and her eyelids fluttered. For a moment Rosina thought that her grandmother was going to speak, but then she sighed and went back to sleep.

'Miss Rosina.' Merry entered the room without knocking. 'How is Miss Jane?'

The sound of Merry's voice brought Rosina back to the present and she turned her head.

'She's sleeping now, but Dr Clarke didn't sound very hopeful.'

'The poor lady. She wasn't always the easiest person to work for, but she was good to me in her own way. The odd thing is that this illness came upon her so suddenly.'

'She was obviously unwell when I arrived here, Merry.'

'And yet earlier that morning she had been outside feeding the hens and collecting their eggs. It don't make much sense to me, but then I'm not a doctor. I dare say he knows best.'

'She sent for me, Merry. Perhaps she knew that her health was failing. I believe she has had quite a hard life,' Rosina said carefully. How much of Jane's history was common knowledge was something she was sure she would find out whether she wanted to or not.

'We all have our ups and downs, miss. Anyway,

I know it's late for luncheon but it's my guess you haven't eaten, so I've left a bowl of soup on the kitchen table for you. I'll sit with Miss Maddern, if that would help.'

'Thank you, but she's sound asleep. Come downstairs with me. I have some questions I need to ask you.'

'Of course, miss.' Marry hurried from the room with Rosina following her.

Downstairs in the kitchen Rosina took a seat at the table. 'Dr Clarke told me some things about my family that I didn't know.' She spooned the vegetable soup into her mouth. 'This is so good. Thank you, Merry.'

'There's always stories going round the village about one person or another,' Merry said slowly. 'Ma says it's wrong to pass on gossip.'

'I expect she's right, but I just want to know what is said about the Maddern family. Is there anything you can tell me?'

Merry pulled up a chair. 'Do you mind if I sit down for a while, miss? I've been on my feet since dawn.'

'Of course not.' Rosina tried to sound casual. 'Is there anything you can tell me about Moonshadow Manor and the family?'

'Only what I told you before about Mr Dimond wanting to take the land back. It's common knowledge. Miss Maddern has been standing up to him, although the poor lady is obviously quite worn out by it all.'

'My aunt never married.' It was a question as much as a statement, but Rosina was desperate to find out what was being said about Jane Maddern. Not that she would be ashamed to acknowledge Jane as her grandmother, but she did not want to rake up an old scandal, especially at this time.

'No, miss. Ma knows more about the Madderns than I do. Maybe you should ask her.'

'I will, but has my aunt lived here all her life?'

'I can't say, miss. I believe she grew up here, and her ma died when she was born. I do know that much.'

'This soup is really good. Just what I needed.' Rosina spooned the last dregs into her mouth. 'Thank you, Merry.'

'I could ask Ma to call in and see you, if that would help,' Merry said eagerly. 'She knows everything that has gone on in Ugstock since she was a girl. She could answer your questions.'

Rosina stood up. 'It's not important. Don't bother her, Merry. If I happen to see your mother in the village, I'll ask her myself. Now I'd better check on my aunt.' Rosina could see that Merry was speaking the truth and to try to elicit any further information from her would only make her suspicious. It seemed that the Maddern family had been involved in too many past scandals. She made her way back to her grandmother's room and pulled up a chair to sit at her bedside. There did not seem to be any change in Jane's condition and there was very little that Rosina could do other than keep her company.

Outside the sky was darkening and the wind getting up. The day was ending with the threat of a storm, and there was a definite chill in the room. Rosina got up only to add more coal to the fire and then draw the curtains. She did not want to look out onto the moor in the darkness in case she saw another unexplained light moving erratically.

She resumed her seat at Jane's bedside, gazing up at Roxanne's portrait. From what Dr Clarke had told her it did seem that the women in the Maddern family were cursed by their good looks and undeniable charm. But what bothered Rosina the most was the gap in her knowledge. Jane had obviously been in love with the father of her child, but now there was no one who could identify him. Was he still alive? Did he live in Ugstock or in Ivybridge? Rosina closed her eyes, trying to picture the man whom Jane Maddern had been protecting for so many years.

Rosina awakened with a start as someone tapped her on the shoulder. She blinked and found herself looking at Merry's round face illuminated to a rosy glow in the firelight.

'It's getting late, miss. I have to go home, but I've left your supper in the oven.'

'Thank you.' Rosina glanced at Jane and was

relieved to see that she had not moved, and her breathing was soft but audible. Rosina stood up and lit a candle with a spill from a jar on the mantelshelf. 'And thank you for all that you've done today, Merry. I don't think I could have managed without you.'

'It's what I'm here for, miss. I'll be back early tomorrow morning, so don't worry about the fire or anything. I'll see to it when I arrive.'

Rosina followed her from the room. 'I'll lock the door after you. I'm a bit nervous here at night.'

'I could sleep in if that helps, miss. Ma wouldn't mind. She says she has too many of us in our cottage anyway.'

'Would you really? I'd like that very much. We'll get a room ready for you tomorrow.' Rosina could have hugged her but that would not be proper, so she merely patted Merry on the arm.

As Rosina said goodbye to Merry and locked the door behind her, she felt suddenly very alone in the big house with the sick woman lying in her bed upstairs. It would be good to have someone else living in the house.

She went back to the kitchen and took her supper from the oven. The pie looked and smelled appetising, and she helped herself to a large slice, but thinking of her ailing grandmother lying alone in her room made it impossible for her to enjoy the food. Rosina set it aside and made her way upstairs.

She was almost afraid to go into her grandmother's room for fear of what she might find, but she forced herself to open the door.

The sight that met her eyes made her drop the candlestick.

'Aunt Jane, I mean Grandmama.' Rosina rushed to the bedside where her grandmother was sitting upright, staring at the portrait of Roxanne. For a moment Rosina thought she must be in the last throes, but when Jane turned her head, she appeared to be very much alive.

'I'm sorry, Rosina,' Jane said slowly. 'I didn't hear you coming.'

'You – you're not – I mean . . .' Rosina was at a loss for words. She sank down on the chair she had only recently vacated. 'You look and sound so different. What's going on?'

'I'll tell you everything, but first would you be kind enough to bring me a pot of tea and a slice of that pie I can smell? I am starving.'

Rosina stared at her incredulously. 'It must be a miracle. You were close to death when the doctor was here. He didn't hold out much hope for your recovery.'

'I know, dear. I am truly sorry, but I couldn't carry on with the deception. I heard everything you said to Albert, and I need to tell you the truth. You are worth that, Rosina.'

'I'm utterly confused,' Rosina said wearily. 'One

moment you are sickly and on the point of death and now you are asking for something to eat and drink. Why have you gone through this cruel charade? I think I have a right to know.'

'I won't argue about that.' Jane swung her legs over the side of the bed. 'But I need sustenance. Have I got to make it for myself, or are you going to help me?'

Rosina faced her and for a moment they locked wills, but then Rosina relented, and she laughed.

'I believe you are the most difficult woman I have ever met. Mama always told me I had a mulish streak and now I know where I got it from.' Rosina reached for her grandmother's wrap, which was draped over a chair, and handed it to her. 'You'd best put that on, and your slippers if you are coming downstairs with me. I don't see why I should carry a tray all the way upstairs if you are capable of coming down to the kitchen.'

'You are more like me than you know, Rosina Wills. Go ahead and put the kettle on, I'll follow you downstairs.'

In the kitchen Rosina put the kettle on the hob and set about making a pot of tea. The initial shock of finding her grandmother very much alive and seeming quite well was wearing off, leaving her more angry than anxious. She cut a slice of the pie and put it on a plate, passing it to Jane, who had seated herself at the kitchen table.

'There now. Eat up and I'll make the tea, but I want a full explanation of this, Aunt Jane or Grandmama, whichever person you are now. What was the purpose of all this? Did you bring me here to make a mockery of me? And why should I not expose you for a fraud and a liar?'

Chapter Six

'I will tell you everything when I have eaten. Last night I had to go out to the barn to fetch the meal I had hidden there while you were out, but tonight I want to enjoy my food in peace.'

Rosina stared at Jane and her eyes narrowed. 'So, it was *you* wandering about last night. I saw the light and I thought we had intruders. I was really worried.'

'This pie is delicious. Just give me a few moments to enjoy it, Rosina.'

There was little that Rosina could do other than to sit, sipping tea, while her erstwhile dying grandmother ate what was left of the pie, washed down by numerous cups of the rapidly cooling brew.

'Well?' Rosina said eventually. 'I think I'm due an explanation.'

'That was so good. Yes, it was me you saw last night. I had to creep downstairs after you were in bed, or I would not have had anything decent to eat.' Jane smiled apologetically. 'I am so sorry you were scared, Rosina.'

'That's not good enough. Are you telling me that all this has been an act? You pretended not to know me when I arrived, and you convinced me that your mind was wandering. I thought you were dying.'

'I am sorry you were distressed, but I thought I put up a good performance.' Jane pushed her empty plate away, shaking her head with a heartfelt sigh. 'I am truly sorry, my dear. I know what I did was wrong. You have been very patient, and all this has been a shock to you, but it wasn't meant to be so. When I sent for you, I had every intention of telling you the truth, but even to my mind it sounded far-fetched. I suppose I took the easy way out, with Albert Clarke's help.'

'What did you imagine would happen?' Rosina demanded. 'Were you going to pretend to be dead? How was that going to benefit you or anyone?'

'Albert told you a little of my story, and we hoped that would help you to get over the shock of my demise.'

'I can't believe that the doctor would take part in such a deception.'

'I've known Albert all my life. He was my childhood friend, and he alone stood by me when everyone in the village shunned me.'

'You mean when you found you were expecting a child out of wedlock?'

Jane smiled ruefully. 'That does make it sound like a crime, but I was very young, just sixteen when I found out that I was in the family way. When your mother was born my father wanted me to give her to a respectable childless couple, but I was having none of it. I loved my child, and I loved her papa.'

'Why didn't you marry him?' Rosina asked angrily. 'And why did you never reveal his name?'

'He was already married when we fell in love.' Jane shook her head. 'I know that sounds even worse, but he had been coerced into a marriage of convenience when he was young, and I was not going to shame him in front of the whole village.'

'And yet you suffered all these years, according to Dr Clarke. What sort of man allows the woman he loves to bear his child and bring her up alone, open to cruel gossip and censure?'

'I know it sounds so easy when you put it that way, but years ago it was an even more difficult situation than it would be today. I was referred to as "the Maddern woman", and hardly anyone in the village spoke to me, but I had some money that my papa left to me, although most of that is gone now.' Jane toyed with the teaspoon she had used to put sugar in her tea. 'I brought Alice up to be a good girl, and she married your father, who is a respectable man, although I gather from the letter you wrote to me that he has had his head turned by a flighty woman. That is why I sent for you.'

'I still don't understand,' Rosina said, frowning. 'You asked me to come here, but you were preparing to die, or at least to feign death. Why would you do that? And how does it help me?'

'I have a chance for happiness. The man I love, your grandfather, is now a free man. He wishes to marry me and make an honest woman of me after all these years of being a pariah.' Jane laughed, but there was no merriment in her tone. 'We will spend whatever time we have left together, somewhere abroad, away from Ugstock and the moor.'

'So why did you want me to come to Moonshadow Manor, especially if you are planning to escape from your life here?'

'I expect you've already learned of the ongoing battle for ownership of this house and its land. Jack Dimond is trying to prove that my papa cheated at cards and that the deeds of Moonshadow Manor were never transferred legally.'

'Is that why there were boxes and boxes of papers left lying around the house?'

'Yes, that's right. Jack's father started legal proceedings thirty years ago or more, and they have gone on ever since. However, you are the named beneficiary in my will. When I die, Moonshadow Manor becomes yours, Rosina. You are young and strong, as I once was. You will fight Jack, and you will win. There will be Madderns still living at Moonshadow and I will be free at last.'

'You want to continue with this macabre pretence?' Rosina said slowly. 'Surely you could just run away with the gentleman concerned and live happily together?'

'He has a family, Rosina. They are all prominent members of the community, and it would not just be his reputation that was ruined if the truth were known. My name was sullied long ago, but the least we can do is to protect his innocent children and grandchildren. Can you understand that?'

Rosina nodded slowly. 'I suppose so, but it might help if I knew his identity. After all, I am his blood, too.'

'I will tell you when it is time.'

'Are you seriously intending to carry this out to the extreme? Do you intend to have a funeral and everything that goes with it?'

Jane's grey eyes sparkled mischievously. 'How many people can watch so-called mourners pretending to grieve while the vicar trots out the usual platitudes, extolling the virtues of the deceased?'

'Grandmother! I believe you are enjoying this.' Rosina stood up and began clearing the table.

'For more than forty years I've been the fallen woman, a person considered to be of low morals and shunned by the majority. I think I've earned the last laugh.' Jane put her head on one side, eyeing

Rosina curiously. 'I appreciate that I'm asking you to be complicit in a deception, but it will harm no one and it will protect others. Are you with me? You must follow your conscience.'

'I need time to think about it. I mean, what do I call you? Are you my grandmother or my aunt? I'm at a loss as to know how I should behave.'

'You came here to stay with your aunt Jane, so let everyone think that is still the case. I intend to linger for a while, if only so that I can see how you deal with young Jack. From what I can see you are more than equal to the challenge.' Jane sat back in her chair. 'What do you say, Rosina? Are you prepared to go along with my plan?'

Rosina hesitated. She was tempted to refuse, but she felt deep sympathy for her grandmother, whose life must have been difficult and lonely. It seemed so unfair that the man who had put her in such a position had led an outwardly blameless existence, bringing up his family and maintaining the fiction that he was a pillar of the community, while both Jane and her illegitimate daughter suffered the consequences. She took a deep breath.

'I am on your side, Aunt. Just tell me what you want me to do.'

'Thank you, Rosina. I know that can't have been easy for you, but you will be setting me free at last. I intend to enjoy whatever time I have left on this earth with the man I love, and it would be a bonus if

I could see Moonshadow Manor safe in the hands of the surviving Maddern woman. Despite everything, I believe you will come to love this house and even the moor, given time.'

'I don't know about that, Aunt. I almost got lost on the moor this morning. If it hadn't been for Hugo Charteris I might have ended up in a bog when the mist came down.'

'Charteris?' Jane was suddenly serious. 'He's a good man, Rosina. You would do well to cultivate him as a friend, and maybe something more. He is very wealthy and well respected.'

Rosina laughed. 'You are supposed to be on your deathbed, Aunt. I think it's a little late to start matchmaking.'

'All the more reason for me to prolong my stay in this world. I would like to see you settled and happy, my dear.' Jane frowned. 'Just beware of Jack. He's a handsome devil and can put on the charm when it suits him. He will stop at nothing in order to get his hands on Moonshadow Manor.'

'Trust me, Aunt. I am unlikely to fall for a handsome face or for sweet words. I will carry out your wishes, and that's a promise.'

It was late next morning when one of the stable boys from Daumerle House arrived with the horse that Charteris had promised. Rosina had been going through the piles of garments lying around, separating the good-quality items, which she intended to sell, from the worn articles that would go to the poor or to the rag merchant, when she caught sight of a youth riding a solid-looking horse and she hurried outside to greet him.

'Sir Hugo sent me, miss. Shall I put Pixie in the stable?'

'Pixie! That's his name, but what do I call you?'

'I'm Joshua, miss.'

'Well then, Joshua, I am very glad to have your help. Merrilees has cleaned out the groom's quarters and she has lit a fire so you can make yourself at home. She'll tell you what time to come round to the kitchen for meals.'

'Yes, miss. Thank you.' Joshua put his hand in his pocket and took out a slightly crumpled letter, which he handed to Rosina. 'I almost forgot this. Miss Ariadne told me to give it to you, miss.'

'Thank you.' Rosina tucked the letter into her pocket. 'After luncheon I would like to have a go at driving Pixie, if you will have him harnessed and ready, but I'd like you to come along, too. Sir Hugo did allow me to drive him to Daumerle House, but I am still a novice at handling the reins.'

Joshua grinned. 'We'll soon sort that out, miss. Pixie is as gentle as a lamb. You won't have any trouble with him.' He flicked the reins and rode off towards the stable block at the rear of the house.

Rosina was encouraged by the young fellow's

obvious enthusiasm for his job, but she was not so sure about handling the animal on her own. She was no expert when it came to horseflesh, but Pixie did not look very old, and he trotted off at a brisk rate, making her slightly apprehensive about handling the reins.

She had recovered a little from the shocking story that Jane had related, and she had managed to convince Merry that all was well, and nothing had changed since the previous day. Merry was very sympathetic and offered to go for the doctor when she saw that Jane was back in bed and unwilling or unable to rise. It had taken all Rosina's tact and patience to reassure the girl and to convince her that Dr Clarke would be calling later that day.

Now, Rosina was about to go back into the house when she remembered the letter and she took it from her pocket and broke the seal. The handwriting was neat and well-formed.

Dear Rosina,

I am unable to visit you today as I had forgotten a prior appointment with my dressmaker. However, please accept my apologies and I hope you will be able to join us for luncheon tomorrow at Daumerle. Hugo will come for you at midday. If this is not convenient, please send Joshua with a note and we will make alternative arrangements.

I very much look forward to getting to know you better.
Yours sincerely,
Ariadne Charteris

Rosina replaced the note in her pocket. With everything that had happened in the last twenty-four hours she had completely forgotten Ariadne's promise to call upon her, and it was something of a relief to discover that it was not to be. She was about to go inside to write a note of acceptance, when the sound of approaching hoofbeats stopped her once again. She waited in the doorway until the horseman dismounted and came striding towards her. She would have recognised that walk even if he had not swept off his top hat with a flourish.

'Mr Dimond, this is an unexpected pleasure.' Rosina was not sure she meant it, but there was no point in antagonising him before he had explained the reason for his visit.

Jack bowed in acknowledgement of her greeting. 'Good morning, Miss Wills. The pleasure is all mine. I was in the vicinity so I thought I would call on the off chance that we might have a brief conversation.'

'Then you'd better come inside. I'm afraid we are still at sixes and sevens, but I am in the process of sorting out the items that my aunt no longer needs.'

Jack glanced at the piles of clothing as he followed Rosina to the morning parlour, but he refrained from making a comment.

'How is Miss Maddern today? I trust her health is improving.'

'She has chosen to remain in bed. Dr Clarke is going to visit her when he has a moment.'

'Her condition is worsening?'

'I haven't been here long enough to judge that,' Rosina said cautiously. 'Do take a seat. May I offer you tea or coffee? Perhaps something stronger?'

'I dare say there might be a keg or two of French brandy hidden in the cellar and forgotten.' Jack sat down by the fire, holding out his hands to the flames. 'It's a bit chilly today,' he added conversationally. 'Perhaps a glass of sherry wine is called for, if you will join me.'

'You didn't come here to discuss the weather, sir. Might I ask why you wish to see me?'

'Miss Maddern is an old family friend. I am naturally concerned as to her welfare.'

Rosina was not in the mood for prevarication. 'And yet you are doing your best to prove that this property really belongs to your family. She told me so last evening.'

'Did she now? When I last saw her, she could hardly speak a word.'

'Her condition varies,' Rosina said vaguely. 'But it explains why you wanted all those boxes of papers.

Do you really think you can prove anything after all these years?'

'If there has been no transfer of the deeds then legally the property still belongs to my family. I suppose you are here because your mother was a Maddern and therefore you think you have a claim on the estate.'

'Nothing of the sort.' Rosina faced him angrily. 'I came because my aunt invited me to stay with her. I knew nothing about all this. You assume too much, sir.'

'Come now, Miss Wills, or may I call you Rosina? We will be working together to sort out this conundrum, and there is no need for us to fall out.'

'I agree. I don't know you and you don't know me, but I assume we both have my aunt's best interests at heart. Or perhaps you are more concerned about the value of the property?'

'No, not at all. Miss Maddern is ailing, and I will naturally work to support her best interests, and of course those of Moonshadow Manor. Whether or not I can prove that it is still in our possession takes second place. When you understand that perhaps we can discuss matters more rationally.'

Rosina went to the side table and picked up the cut-glass decanter. She was not usually someone given to drinking in the morning but today she made an exception, and she filled two glasses. She gave one to Jack before taking a seat on an upright chair, facing him. She decided that he was a difficult man to judge. At face value he was charming, well-mannered and he seemed to care about Jane, but Rosina had a feeling that this was a façade. There was more to Jack Dimond than he was prepared to let her see, for the time being at least. She sipped the wine.

'So, this is purely a social call,' she said casually. 'Or maybe you have found something in those boxes of papers that your men took from this house?' Rosina experienced the warming effect of the wine, and she put the glass down. She knew that she needed to keep a clear head when dealing with Jack.

'My head clerk is going through the documents, which will take time. This is purely a goodwill visit in order to assure you both of my ongoing support and good faith.' Jack drained his drink in one swallow. 'I must get you a better sherry. This one is only fit for use in the kitchen. Speaking of that, how are you managing without servants to help in the house?'

'I have Merrilees Pavey now. Sir Hugo allowed her to come and work here, which was good of him.'

'You have me to thank for that. I put it to Hugo that your need was greater than his. After all, there are dozens of servants at Daumerle House. Hugo can spare at least one of them,' Jack said dismissively.

'I thought he was your friend.' Rosina eyed him curiously. 'You spoke warmly of him when we first met.'

'We are old acquaintances, but I've always known that deep down Hugo does not approve of me. The family tensions go back years, to my great-grandfather, in fact. Jabez Dimond seems to have upset everyone round here in one way or another. When people tell me I am like him, I know it is not meant as a compliment.'

Rosina laughed. 'Perhaps that is a sign to mend your ways, Jack.'

'My name trips lightly off your tongue, Rosina. I like the sound of it.' Jack rose to his feet. 'Might I see Miss Maddern before I leave? Just to wish her well, of course. Nothing that would upset the dear lady.'

'I'll go to her room and ask her if she would like to see you. She might not wish you to find her in bed. She is rather old-fashioned.' Rosina was on her feet before he could answer, and she left the room without waiting for his response. She took the stairs two at the time and burst into her aunt's bedroom, stopping only to catch her breath.

'What is the matter?' Jane demanded, setting her book aside and peering at Rosina over the top of her steel-rimmed spectacles.

'Jack Dimond is downstairs. He wants to come up to your room and see you. I don't know if he suspects anything.'

'There is no reason why he would be suspicious but bring him to see me. I've had plenty of practice at being too poorly even to speak.' Jane took off her spectacles and handed them to Rosina. 'Put them in the dressing table drawer together with the book.' She threw herself back against the pillows, pulled the coverlet up to her chin and closed her eyes.

Rosina did as she asked before going downstairs to fetch Jack. She found him staring out of the morning-room window, gazing at the mist-shrouded moor.

'My aunt will see you now, Jack, but please don't exhaust her. She is quite poorly today.'

'Of course. I just want to assure her that all is well, although I need to tell her that there are almost no funds left in her account. She needs to start selling items or there will be no income.'

'I will take care of that,' Rosina said firmly. 'My aunt does not need to worry. I had already decided to have a stall in the market.'

'That will keep you going for a while, but I'm afraid Miss Maddern will have to face the truth sooner or later. The only answer would be to sell Moonshadow Manor.'

'To you, I suppose,' Rosina said coldly. 'Is that why you came today? If you can't find the evidence to prove that your family still own this house and the land surrounding it, you will force Miss Maddern to sell it to you, no doubt at a stupidly low price.'

Jack went to open the door. 'You really don't have a good opinion of me, do you, Rosina?'

'I think you are ruthless when it comes to getting

what you want. I'll lead the way, although I have a feeling you know this old house better than I do.' She walked on without waiting for an answer. Now she had at least some idea of Jack's intentions she would be better placed to work out a way to stop him getting his hands on Moonshadow Manor, if only for Jane's sake. She stopped outside the bedroom door.

'Wait here for a minute, please. I'll make sure she is ready to receive you.'

'Of course.' Jack leaned casually against the wall. 'There's no hurry.'

Rosina entered the room, closing the door behind her. 'He's outside,' she said in a low voice. 'Are you sure you want to see him?'

'Yes, indeed,' Jane said, smiling. 'I'm beginning to enjoy the play-acting, especially now I have someone complicit in the deception.'

Rosina opened the door. 'Come in, please,' she said to Jack. 'But don't tire her too much.'

Jack strolled into the room and went to stand at the foot of the bed. 'How are you today, Miss Maddern?'

'Who is he, Rosina?' Jane said feebly. 'I've forgotten already.'

'It's Mr Dimond, Aunt. He's your solicitor and he's come to call on you.'

Jane raised herself on her elbow. 'Is there anything wrong? Do I owe you money, sir?'

'There's nothing for you to worry about, Miss Maddern,' Jack said hastily.

'Who is he again, Rosina?' Jane asked in a low voice. 'I don't remember him.'

'I'm sorry, Jack,' Rosina said apologetically. 'She did wish to see you.'

'I can see that you are unwell today, Miss Maddern.' Jack moved towards the door. 'I'll call again when you are feeling better.' He hurried from the room. 'I'll see myself out, Rosina.'

She nodded and waited until she heard his footsteps on the stairs before helping Jane to sit up.

'Nicely done, Aunt,' Rosina said, suppressing a giggle. 'You should have gone on the stage with that talent for acting.'

Jane smiled. 'Yes, I've always fancied myself as Ophelia or Lady Macbeth, but you never know, my chance might yet come.'

'I think Mr Dimond is angling for you to put Moonshadow Manor up for sale so he can buy it, and that means he hasn't yet found any proof of his claim to the property. What do you want me to say to him?' Rosina plumped up the pillows behind her aunt before retrieving the spectacles and her book.

'Don't agree to anything,' Jane said firmly. 'Keep him on tenterhooks and that way we still have the upper hand. I've known Jack since he was a boy, and his father and grandfather. They had one obsession only, and that was to regain the title deeds for Moonshadow Manor.'

Rosina hesitated in the doorway as she was about

to leave the room. 'Wouldn't it have been easier to let them have it, or rather, to sell it back to them? The Madderns can only have owned the property for sixty or seventy years. I mean, if he offered a fair price, you could take the money and live comfortably for the rest of your life.'

'You are a Maddern, Rosina. This house is for you and your family. Jack Dimond does not deserve to live here.'

Rosina could see that Jane was getting upset. 'I'm sorry, Aunt. I know the old place means everything to you. I'll do whatever you want for now, but I need to know how long you expect to keep up this fiction.'

'I'm just waiting for your grandfather to tell me when the arrangements for our disappearance have been made.'

Rosina stared at her, frowning. 'Why must it be like this, Aunt? If he is a free man – why wait?'

'I told you, he has a family, my dear. All these years he has been protecting them, and he will not simply stop now. It must be done carefully so that no one gets hurt.' Jane replaced her spectacles and opened her book. 'In the meantime, I will simply enjoy your company. Perhaps I will come down to dinner this evening.'

'Won't you trust me enough to share his name with me, Aunt?' Rosina asked, curbing her impatience with difficulty. 'I promise not to divulge it to anyone.'

'It's not that I don't trust you, Rosina, but it's best

for everyone if you remain ignorant of what is to come. That's all I have to say on the matter.'

Rosina could see that this was all she was likely to be told, but that would not prevent her attempting to solve at least that mystery. She stepped out onto the landing and closed the door softly, taking a deep breath. Moonshadow Manor was steeped in conflict and scandal, but the old house held on firmly to its past and it grasped the people involved in its clutches, leaving them unable or unwilling to escape. She wondered what secrets were hidden beneath the cosy thatched roof and the thick cob walls. This was not just a home: there was something else that Jane Maddern had spent the best part of her life protecting, and that several generations of Dimonds had wanted so desperately they were prepared to lie and cheat to get their hands on the property.

Rosina went slowly downstairs with more questions on her lips than answers.

Chapter Seven

Next day it was not Hugo but one of the coachmen from Daumerle House who came to fetch Rosina. She was disappointed as she had spent hours thinking up questions to ask Hugo when they were on their own. She doubted if Ariadne would know anything other than gossip about Moonshadow Manor, and she could only hope to have an opportunity to speak to Hugo privately at some point.

It was a fine day with a definite hint of spring in the air. Great clumps of daffodils spread patches of sunshine at the edge of the neatly ploughed fields as the carriage passed by, and pale yellow primroses lined the hedgerows. Rosina was in an optimistic mood by the time they reached Daumerle House, and she was greeted in the entrance hall by Ariadne, who led the way to the drawing room.

'Hugo sends his apologies, but he had to go into Ivybridge on business. It was unexpected but it was something he had to do, or so he said. I never bother with things like that; they don't concern me.'

'You are very fortunate to have a brother who takes care of you,' Rosina said earnestly. 'I was an only child, although I now have a half-brother.'

'You told me that your papa remarried. That must be very hard to bear, especially if he has a new family.' Ariadne motioned Rosina to take a seat and she settled gracefully on the sofa. 'Is that why you came to Devonshire?'

'It is the real reason, I suppose. I don't get on very well with my stepmother. She is only a few years my senior, which does make it a little difficult, and I think she regarded me as a threat.' Rosina had not meant to blurt out the truth, but Ariadne was a sympathetic listener, and perhaps such matters were better out in the open. Rosina had had enough secrets to keep with regard to her grandmother and Moonshadow Manor without adding to her burden.

'You must put all that behind you, Rosina. I hope you will be happy living at Moonshadow. I, for one, am delighted to have a neighbour of my own age.'

'You have your brother. He seems very fond of you.'

'Oh, well, you know what families are like, Rosina. I do love Hugo, of course, but half of the time I could cheerfully strangle him, had I the strength, of course. Anyway, he has so much to do with running the estate and his business interests that he has little time for me, which was why I was so surprised that he has shown you so much attention. He was very disappointed to miss our luncheon today.'

Ariadne's mischievous expression made Rosina respond with a smile.

'Are you matchmaking, by any chance? You must have heard about the scandal attached to my name.'

'You have obviously discovered that it is almost impossible to keep anything secret in this area. I believe Miss Maddern is in poor health now, but she was a beauty in her day, so they say. I've heard all the tales concerning Miss Maddern, but she has done nothing to upset me or my family. I think people should not be made to bear the burden of their youthful mistakes for the rest of their lives.'

'I agree, of course. I barely know her, which is a shame, but I am determined to take care of her now.'

Their conversation was interrupted by the appearance of a parlour maid to announce that luncheon was served, and Ariadne rose to her feet.

'I'm certainly ready to eat. I hope you are, too.'

'Yes, indeed. The country air seems to have given me an appetite.'

Rosina stood up and followed Ariadne from the room. She had been meaning to question Ariadne about Jack Dimond, but the opportunity was lost, and it proved difficult to introduce him into the conversation over luncheon. The elegant dining room was filled with the scent of hothouse roses and lilies, and the opulence of her surroundings quite took Rosina's breath away. She had thought her home in London was comfortable and well furnished, but Daumerle House made everything she had been used to seem tawdry and commonplace. To Ariadne, all the trappings of wealth and position were obviously second nature, and to comment on their surroundings would make Rosina seem gauche and naïve. She managed to keep her thoughts to herself and settled down to enjoy the delicious meal.

After luncheon they returned to the drawing room, where a maid brought them coffee.

'I was hoping that Hugo might have come home in time to sit with us for a while,' Ariadne said as she handed a cup to Rosina. 'He will be sorry to have missed you. I believe he was meeting Jack Dimond on a business matter.'

Rosina's hand shook and she spilled coffee into the saucer. This was the opportunity she had been hoping for. 'What exactly do you know about Mr Dimond?'

Ariadne's cheeks flushed prettily. 'I've known him all my life. He's absolutely charming when he wishes to be, and at other times he can be quite a devil.'

'A devil?' Rosina eyed her curiously. 'In what way?'

'Oh, well, he's a terrible tease. He's not what I would call a lady's man, even though he is very handsome, and I believe he's quite clever. However, there are stories that go round about him, probably all untrue, of course. Just gossip.'

Rosina sipped her coffee, holding the saucer strategically so that the liquid did not stain her pristine white blouse. 'What sort of gossip?'

'I should not pass it on, of course, but it's more about the Dimond family than Jack himself. I believe that his great-grandfather, Jabez, was a total villain, but Jack's grandfather started the law firm, and you might say the family came full circle. From criminal to lawyer.'

'And where does that leave Jack?' Rosina asked casually. 'Is he on the good side of the family or the bad side?'

'Who knows?' Ariadne giggled. 'I really don't care. Jack is fun to be with, when he is in a good mood, but there is something about him that I can't put my finger on. He never lets anyone know his real self.'

Rosina eyed her curiously. 'I get the impression that you are quite fond of him, despite his flaws.'

'To be honest I do find him rather fascinating, but I know nothing could ever come from it. Apart from the fact that Hugo would never approve of a relationship between Jack and me, I couldn't live in a small house with only a couple of servants.' Ariadne sighed. 'I know that makes me sound shallow, but it's how I've been raised.'

'If you were in love with Jack Dimond, I don't think

you would worry about money and position. He is undeniably a handsome man, but there is something dangerous about him,' Rosina said thoughtfully.

'Perhaps that is what makes him so attractive to women.' Ariadne put her cup and saucer back on the tray and leaned forward, adding in a conspiratorial tone, 'Did you know that his mama was a gypsy? Perhaps that explains why he is so unlike any other man I've met.'

'Yes, I have heard that. I believe she ran away when Jack was sent to boarding school.'

'It was before my time, so of course I never met her.' Ariadne sighed, shaking her head. 'But everyone said that Naomie was wild and exciting, and I dare say very good-looking, too.'

'Poor Jack. He must have grown up wondering why his mother deserted him, but that doesn't explain the reason why he is so desperate to own Moonshadow Manor,' Rosina said slowly.

Ariadne laughed. 'Perhaps he thinks that his great-grandfather Jabez left treasure buried in the cellar.'

'If that is so I think I will be the one who ought to search for it. As I told you before, my aunt has very little money, and I'm serious about taking a stall in the market where I will sell my aunt's discarded and unwanted items.'

'And I want to help you, as I said when we first met. It will be fun, but I don't want Hugo to find out. We mustn't tell him because he would forbid me, and he would try to stop you from going through with what he will consider a wild scheme.'

Rosina tossed her head. 'He's a fine man but this has nothing to do with him, and I really have very little choice. You must do what you wish.'

'I could think of nothing else after we parted last time. I raided the linen cupboard where the servants' uniforms are stored, and I selected aprons and mobcaps for both of us. When shall we do it?'

'The sooner the better. I will speak to Seth Tully tomorrow. He is sure to know how to hire a stall on market day. When I know the details, I'll send Merry to you with a note.'

'A conspiracy!' Ariadne's eyes shone. 'How exciting, but there's no need to wait until tomorrow. If I send for a carriage, you could call on Applegate Farm on the way home.'

Rosina was surprised by Ariadne's obvious enthusiasm, but she could not allow an opportunity like this to slip, and so she nodded.

'That sounds like a very good idea. I've already sorted out some of the items that are saleable, and others are simply rubbish, although they must have meant something to Aunt Jane. I will have to be very careful about how I dispose of them.'

Ariadne jumped to her feet and tugged at the bell pull. 'I'm sure you will do what is right. I can't wait to dress up like a servant and help you on your stall. It will be unlike anything I have ever experienced.'

Rosina laughed. 'If it's successful, maybe we ought to start a business by opening a shop in town.'

She had meant it as a joke, but Ariadne's eyes widened, and she clasped her hands together.

'Do you think that's possible? I would love to see Hugo's face if I announced that I was going into trade.'

'I wasn't serious,' Rosina said hastily. 'I think it very unlikely that will happen.'

Ariadne looked up as the door opened and a maid entered.

'Have a carriage sent round to the front entrance, please, Mary. Miss Wills is ready to return home.'

Not only did Seth find Rosina a stall that was temporarily vacant for the next day, but he volunteered to pack her goods onto his cart and take them into town. Rosina sent Merry to Daumerle House with a note for Ariadne confirming that they were about to go into business, and Merry returned with a small parcel containing a cap and apron. There was only one thing left to do, and Rosina saw the opportunity when she took Jane's supper tray into the drawing room, which she placed on a table close to Jane's chair.

'You look very pleased with yourself, miss,' Jane said, smiling. 'Did you enjoy your luncheon with Ariadne Charteris?'

Rosina pulled a stool closer and sat down. 'Yes, thank you. I was very impressed with Daumerle

House on my first visit, and even more so after today. It's beautiful, but very grand. I felt a little out of place there.'

'Nonsense,' Jane said brusquely. 'You are as good as anyone, and better than most, Rosina.'

Jane dipped her spoon into the soup. 'Vegetable soup again! I really will die of boredom if I have to eat this every day.'

'It's a matter of money, Aunt. That's what I was going to talk about next.'

Jane eyed her over the rim of the spoon. 'You don't have to tell me that there is very little left in the bank. I know that.'

'I've thought of a way to earn money, but I would like your permission, first.'

'What scheme have you thought up? If it's selling Moonshadow Manor to Jack Dimond, the answer is a definite no.'

'Not that, Aunt. You may have noticed that I've been tidying up since I came here.'

'Yes, I did, of course. It was getting a little out of hand.'

'Exactly, and I think there is value in many of the items. I want to sell them from a stall in the market. It would bring in money to buy food. You could have meat or fish for supper.'

'You want to become a market trader?' Jane dropped her spoon into the soup bowl. 'Bother! Now I've made a mess.'

'Don't worry, I'll fetch a cloth.' Rosina was about to rise but Jane motioned her to remain seated.

'I'll mop it up with some bread. But you must tell me why you think going into trade is a good idea. We are the Madderns of Moonshadow Manor and we have a name to keep up.'

Rosina eyed her warily. 'I thought that was tarnished long ago, Aunt. I'm sorry to be blunt, but unless your gentleman wishes to contribute to the housekeeping, I have no choice.'

'I can't ask him for money. I've managed all these years without taking anything from him financially, apart from when your mama was a small child. He did help me then, but afterwards I managed by keeping cows and a few sheep, as well as chickens. I planted vegetables and I sold the produce we didn't need.'

'So you were in business,' Rosina said triumphantly. 'Can you give me one good reason why I should not sell off things you no longer have a use for?'

'Hobnobbing with the common people in the marketplace might damage your chances in the marriage market, Rosina. I have very little left to give you other than this old house and the land surrounding it, but I don't want you to have a life like mine. You deserve to marry well and bring up your children without the scandal that I inflicted on your poor mama.'

'She never spoke of it, Aunt. My mother only had

good things to say about you, and I believe she loved Moonshadow almost as much as you do.'

'That's true, my dear. She was very happy here in spite of the cruel gossip we both had to endure.'

'Did she know the man who was her father?' Rosina asked warily.

'She knew him, but she was not aware of their relationship. He and I agreed to that before she was born. He had a family of his own and a position to keep up. We are both free now. It is just a matter of time.'

Rosina laid her hand on her grandmother's arm. 'If you would only tell me his name, I could speak to him and ask for his help.'

'No, I don't want that. I've never begged him for anything. However, you must do what you must, Rosina. You are Moonshadow's future now. I trust you to care for it as I have and one day it will be yours.' Jane nibbled the bread. 'Sell anything you like, but bring home some sausages or a joint of beef, or even a steak. It's so long since I ate meat I can hardly remember what it tastes like.'

'Thank you, Aunt.' Rosina rose to her feet. 'Who knows, I might have found a real career for myself.'

'I think you will save Moonshadow Manor, and you will set me free to live my last years with the man I have loved for a lifetime.'

When Rosina went to her room that night she peered out of the window, but the moor was shrouded in fog and the stable yard was in darkness. She went

124

to bed and dreamed of Roxanne emerging from the mist, but instead of the beauty as shown in the portrait, Roxanne was a pixie, intent on mischief. The wicked imp seized Rosina by the shoulder and shook her violently.

'Wake up, miss.'

Rosina struggled into consciousness and found herself looking into Merry's anxious face.

'What time is it?'

'Time you was up and dressed, miss. Seth will be here any minute now. If you're not ready you might miss your chance of getting a stall in the market.'

Rosina threw back the coverlet and leaped out of bed. 'I'll be five minutes. If he arrives before I get downstairs, tell him I won't be long.'

The market was busy, even though it was still early morning when Rosina and Ariadne alighted from Seth's cart. He leaped down and hefted the boxes of the goods that Rosina had chosen to sell, and he carried them to a nearby stall, which was a little too close to the animal enclosures for Ariadne's liking. The smell of the farmyard made her wrinkle her pretty nose, but Rosina ignored her complaints and set to arranging the items in a way she hoped would attract customers. Seth's stall was close by, and he set out trays of eggs, slabs of butter wrapped in cabbage leaves and freshly baked bread from the farm kitchen. He placed a milk churn at the side of his stall together with pint and half-pint measures. However, Rosina was too busy to pay much attention to anything other than the contents of her stall. Her stomach was churning with nerves although she tried hard not to worry. If the worst came to the worst, she would have to take the goods back to Moonshadow Manor and think of another way to earn some money. As it was, the smell of the still-warm bread on Seth's stall was tantalising, especially since she had not had time for breakfast.

Ariadne seemed more interested in her unusual attire than actually doing anything helpful. She pirouetted around the stall, holding out her apron as if in a dancing competition, and tossing her head so that her golden curls escaped naughtily from her white mobcap. Rosina was amused to see the reaction of the farm workers, who watched open-mouthed, but she could see that Ariadne might attract the attention of the male shoppers, which was likely to be her only contribution to the work in hand.

'Isn't this fun, Rosina?' Ariadne asked, giggling. 'I wish Hugo could see me now. He would have a fit.'

'In that case we must hope he doesn't come into town this morning.' Rosina shook her head. 'I just want to sell some of these things.'

'It's still early and I'm starving.' Ariadne glanced around at the other stalls. 'I'm going to get something to eat. What about you, Rosina?'

'I am a bit hungry.' The words had barely left

Rosina's lips when Ariadne danced off, weaving her way between the other stalls and stopping occasionally to sample some of the wares on sale. Despite her cap and apron, she seemed to be attracting a great deal of attention and Rosina could only hope that word did not reach Hugo about his sister's antics. However, Ariadne returned a little later with a wicker basket filled with saffron buns, several types of cheese and two large red apples. She was sipping cider from a pint tankard and giggling, which worried Rosina.

'You shouldn't drink cider, especially on an empty stomach, Ariadne. You're a bit tipsy already.' Rosina went to take the tankard from her, but Ariadne moved away.

'It's very refreshing. I wonder we don't serve this at home. Do have a taste, Rosina.'

Rosina could see that people were watching and laughing at Ariadne's antics and she decided to humour her. 'All right, just a sip.'

'You see, you can be fun after all.' Ariadne handed her the tankard.

'Thank you. Now eat something, please. Those buns look very tasty.' Rosina took a step away from Ariadne and tipped the contents of the tankard into a drainage gully. 'Oh, dear. How clumsy of me, I've spilled some.'

'I'll fetch some more,' Ariadne said eagerly. 'They have a big barrel of it on that stall over there.' She waved her hand in the general direction of where she had brought the cider. 'I think I need to sit down, Rosina. I feel a little dizzy.'

Before Rosina had a chance to assist her, Seth appeared at Ariadne's side and he lifted her bodily, setting her down on an empty milk churn.

'You shouldn't allow her to drink cider, miss,' he said firmly. 'She's a bit squiffy.'

'I had nothing to do with it,' Rosina protested.

'She needs to go home,' Seth said, scowling. 'I can't take her because I've got to look after the stall.'

Rosina knew that he was right. Ariadne was smiling happily with her eyes closed and her head resting on Seth's shoulder.

'I should have brought my chaise,' Rosina said regretfully.

'I can't look after her, miss.' Seth tried to edge away and Ariadne lolled against Rosina's stall, snoring gently, with one hand still clutching at Seth's jacket, making it difficult for him to leave.

Rosina looked round in desperation, hoping to see someone who might help, but to her dismay it was Jack who rode up to them and, judging by his expression, he was much amused.

'Well, what have we here?' he said, laughing. 'Unless I'm very much mistaken that is Miss Ariadne Charteris and she is more than a little the worse for wear.' He turned to Rosina. 'And you are holding the evidence in your hand. If you are trying to run this stall you shouldn't allow your staff to drink strong cider.'

'If anyone else accuses me of getting her drunk I will throw this at them.' Rosina slammed the tankard down on the edge of the stall.

'So, the angelic Miss Wills has a temper.' Jack shook his head. 'Tut tut, Miss Wills. Not in front of the servants.'

'It isn't funny.' Rosina took a deep breath. 'Instead of mocking me, perhaps you would do the gentlemanly thing and take Miss Charteris away from the public view. I hate to think what her brother will say when he hears of this.'

Jack dismounted. 'I'll take her, Tully. Get back to your stall, you've got customers waiting, or else they're enjoying the spectacle. Either way you need to sort them out.'

'Thank you, sir.' Seth freed himself from Ariadne's grip and hurried back to his stall.

Jack helped Ariadne to her feet, and she flung her arm around his neck, giggling.

'I knew you had a fancy for me, Jack.'

He lifted her onto the saddle. 'Be a good girl and stop wriggling.'

Ariadne leaned over, seeming to be in imminent danger of falling off the horse. 'No, I don't want to go home. I want to stay here with my friend Rosina and you, Jack.'

Jack steadied her with his hands on her shoulders. 'Hold on, Ariadne. I'm supposed to be meeting your brother in a few minutes. Let's hope he's late.

I'm going to get into the saddle, and I'll take you to my office. Hugo can have you then.'

'Please hurry.' Rosina glanced round anxiously. They were attracting much unwanted attention, but she caught her breath when she saw Hugo riding towards them. It was too much to hope that he had not seen his sister.

Hugo drew his horse to a halt. 'Take your hands off her, Jack.'

'You're just in time to save me the bother of taking her across town, Hugo. This had nothing to do with me.'

'I can see that,' Hugo said bitterly. 'This is all your doing, Rosina. I should not have trusted a Maddern to befriend my sister. What do you mean by bringing her to this place and allowing her to drink. Have you no shame?'

Chapter Eight

'Leave Rosina alone, Charteris,' Jack said angrily. 'Don't blame her for your sister's misdeeds.'

'I didn't ask for your opinion.' Hugo dragged Ariadne from the saddle and gave her a shake. 'You are a silly girl. You've embarrassed yourself and our family. What were you thinking of, coming here, and dressed like that?'

'Please don't scold her,' Rosina said in a low voice. She was aware that everyone around them was listening to the conversation, and while some people were sympathetic, others were openly laughing. 'I asked Ariadne to help me, but someone gave her cider to drink, which was unfortunate.'

'Unfortunate?' Hugo's voice rose an octave. 'You will have nothing to do with my family again, Miss Wills. I'm taking my sister home. Do not try to contact her.'

'Oh, Hugo. Don't be mean,' Ariadne said, sobbing. 'I chose to come today. It's not Rosina's fault.'

'You're making matters worse, Charteris,' Jack said in a low voice. 'Ariadne can ride your horse, and you can borrow my mount. I'll walk back to my office, and you can send the animal back with one of your grooms. Get your sister home before the whole town turns out to enjoy the spectacle.'

For a moment Rosina thought that Hugo was going to refuse, but Ariadne was working herself up into such a state that he merely nodded.

'All right. Thank you. I will take you up on your offer.' Hugo practically threw Ariadne onto his saddle before mounting Jack's horse. 'You'll have him back in an hour or two, Jack.'

He slapped his horse on the rump and the animal took off with Ariadne clinging to it for dear life.

'Thank you,' Rosina said earnestly. 'I don't know how this happened. We were just supposed to be selling the items on the stall.'

'Hugo can be hot-headed at times, but he's very protective of his little sister,' Jack said seriously. 'I might be the same had I any siblings.'

'Well, I appreciate your intervention.' Rosina sighed. 'I haven't sold a single thing.'

Jack laughed. 'You must put more effort into it. You need to attract custom, not send it away with dramatic scenes.'

'That wasn't intentional,' Rosina said with a

reluctant smile. 'If it hadn't been for someone selling cider to Ariadne we might have managed.'

'Don't give up yet. I think I might be able to help.'

Jack strolled off and mingled with the other stall holders.

Rosina perched on the milk churn, wondering what to do next. It was not yet mid-morning and Seth was doing well on his stall. The curious onlookers had dispersed, leaving Rosina feeling as if she had just witnessed a theatrical drama in which she was one of the supporting characters.

It was a matter of minutes before she saw Jack walking purposefully towards her with a woman clutching his hand. Rosina stood up, wondering how a person with suspiciously red hair and a gown that was quite shockingly low cut, especially for daytime, could possibly help on the stall.

'Miss Wills, might I introduce my friend, Lizzie Kettle. She will show you how it's done, won't you, my darling?'

Lizzie gave him a gap-toothed grin. 'As a favour to you, Jack, my love.'

'Er, thank you,' Rosina said uncertainly. 'That is very kind.'

'Kindness got nothing to do with it, maid. Jack has promised me half a crown and a kiss for helping out. Stand back, maid, and I'll show you the ropes.' Lizzie puffed out her chest.

'Roll up, roll up and see what we got to offer. All

good-quality stuff from the mysterious Moonshadow Manor, that old house on the moor with more secrets than will ever be brought to light. Come on, don't be shy. You might find some treasure.' She held her arms open wide as if about to embrace all comers.

Rosina moved closer to Jack as people began to form a crowd around the stall.

Lizzie held up a lace shawl, waving it in front of a woman's nose. 'This would suit you, my lover.'

The prospective purchaser was obviously tempted and, after encouragement from Lizzie, money changed hands and the shawl was sold. After that there was a steady flow of customers. Lizzie seemed to have a natural gift for setting the price just right for the person wanting the article, which Rosina, joining in, tried to emulate. Jack stood back, arms folded, obviously enjoying the spectacle of Lizzie and Rosina attempting to outdo each other in sales.

By midday the last of the items had been sold and Lizzie was triumphant. Jack had left them at some point, although Rosina had not noticed when he walked away, but he appeared again as the church clock struck the hour.

'Come to pay me, have you, me 'ansome?' Lizzie demanded as she sashayed up to him, lips parted.

Jack swept her into his arms and planted a kiss on her full lips. He released her and slipped some coins into her hand.

'You've earned that, Lizzie, my love. Don't spend it all in the pub.'

Lizzie grinned. 'It's a pity we've sold out on the stall. I could have charged you double for my services, Jack.'

'Thank you, Lizzie. I couldn't have done this without your help,' Rosina said hastily.

Lizzie did not seem eager to leave the comfort of Jack's arms and she rubbed her cheek against his chin.

'I'd do anything for this man. Well, almost anything.' Somewhat reluctantly, Lizzie peeled herself off him and walked away, swinging her hips.

Rosina felt the blood rush to her cheeks from witnessing such brazen behaviour, although she could not help wondering what it would be like to enjoy a lingering kiss in Jack's warm embrace. Perhaps this was what Ariadne and Jane had meant when they said he was dangerous. Common sense told her to keep him at arm's length, but the mere thought of a close encounter made her senses tingle. She realised that Jack was looking at her with that all-too-familiar twinkle in his dark eyes.

'You've done well, Rosina. What are you going to do now?'

'I should go home, but Seth is still busy on his stall. It's a long walk to Ugstock.'

'I'd take you in my chaise but, being a poor solicitor, I only have the one horse. I'm afraid I cannot offer you my services until Hugo sends Judge home with one of his grooms.'

'Judge!' Rosina said, laughing. 'You call your horse Judge?'

'He's a wise old animal. I'd trust his opinion more than most people.'

'I suppose it's a fitting name for a lawyer's horse, but that doesn't solve my problem.' Rosina frowned. 'Next time I come to market I will ride.'

'You intend to repeat this exercise next week?' Jack eyed her curiously.

'I haven't had a chance to count my takings, but I seem to have done well. I only brought a small portion of the items my aunt has collected over the years.'

Jack held out his hand. 'You've a substantial sum there. I suggest you come with me to my office, and I will drive you home when Hugo returns Judge.'

Rosina glanced round nervously. Most of the people in the market looked respectable and were intent on their purchases, but there were a few men hanging around who looked as though they might cause trouble.

'All right. I'll come with you. Anyway, I wanted to ask you some questions about Moonshadow.'

'My office is the place for that, not here.' Jack took her hand and tucked it in the crook of his arm. He waved to attract Seth's attention. 'Don't worry about Miss Wills. I'll see her safely home.'

'Yes, Guvnor.' Seth tipped his cap and went back to serving a customer.

'I can speak for myself,' Rosina said stiffly.

'I don't doubt it, but my voice carries above the din in the marketplace better than yours. Don't you agree?'

'I can see why you chose to study the law.' Rosina shook her head. 'You have an answer for everything.'

He laughed. 'Not quite, although I wish it were so. Let's walk quickly. I think it's going to rain.'

There was little opportunity for conversation as they hurried through the crowded streets, and they arrived at Jack's office just as the first drop of rain started to fall from a leaden sky. Jack ushered Rosina into a parlour at the back of the house where a fire burned brightly in the grate.

'Make yourself comfortable, Rosina. I'll ring for Mrs Tarr, my housekeeper. I'm sure you could do with some sustenance while we wait.'

Rosina nodded but he had already tugged at the bell pull, and almost immediately the door opened, and a small grey-haired woman entered as if she had been standing outside waiting for her cue.

'You rang, sir?'

'Yes, Mrs Tarr. I'd like you to meet my client, Miss Rosina Wills. She's living presently at Moonshadow Manor with her aunt, Miss Maddern.'

Mrs Tarr gave Rosina a speculative look as she bobbed a curtsey. 'Good afternoon, Miss Wills.'

'How do you do?' Rosina extended her hand. It was obvious that Mrs Tarr was more than simply a housekeeper. She had the comfortable look of someone who had been a valued member of the household for many years.

Mrs Tarr shook hands gravely. 'Luncheon is nearly ready. There is enough for both of you.'

'Thank you, Mrs Tarr. That will be most acceptable.' Jack's smile was warm and genuine, which surprised Rosina. She waited until Mrs Tarr had left the room.

'Mrs Tarr has been with you for some time, Jack?'

'She has indeed. In fact, she was my nanny until I was sent away to boarding school. She was widowed young and has lived with my family ever since.' Jack went to the sideboard and picked up a decanter. 'I think a sherry would be welcome after standing out in the cold for so long.'

'I thought it was only my aunt who drank sherry before luncheon,' Rosina said, smiling.

Jack filled two glasses and handed one to her. 'Your aunt is a very remarkable lady. I have great respect for her. Please take a seat. Mrs Tarr will let us know when luncheon is served.'

Rosina sat in a chair near the fire. She only now realised that standing in the windy marketplace had chilled her to the bone, but the sherry was warming.

'You surprise me, Jack. When you spoke to me the other day you were threatening to take Moonshadow from my aunt, and now you are telling me that you respect her. Which is it?'

'Moonshadow should still belong to the Dimond family, I have no doubt about that, but Miss Maddern has borne the slights and disrespect of many with dignity and fortitude. Anyone who knows her must acknowledge the fact.'

'I believe some people regard her as a fallen woman,' Rosina said warily. 'You don't agree?'

Jack placed his empty glass on the mantelshelf. 'It's always seemed to me that society regards men and women differently, and in my opinion unfairly. Miss Maddern made a mistake, by conventional standards, but she raised her child on her own and presumably unaided. She has never named the father, who has apparently escaped censure and lived his life free from the stigma that she has suffered.'

Rosina stared at him in amazement. 'I agree entirely but I am astonished that you see it that way.'

'I see things from the point of view of fairness, but I know that is not always the case.'

'And you think your family was treated unfairly by the Madderns when my grandfather won Moonshadow Manor in a game of cards. Do you think he cheated?'

'I wouldn't go that far, but I doubt if the transaction was strictly legal.'

'But you have no proof? There can't have been anything in all those boxes of documents that confirmed your suspicions.'

'You have a good legal brain, Rosina. Maybe you should have studied law.'

'Which we know would be impossible,' Rosina said, smiling. 'I really don't know what to say to you about Moonshadow Manor. I know my aunt loves it dearly and wants to keep it in the family above all things. However, she thinks that Roxanne was the main reason my grandfather wanted to own Moonshadow.'

'The mysterious Roxanne, who apparently disappeared in the mist on the moors, and was never seen again.'

'You've heard the story?'

Jack laughed. 'I've been told many stories about Roxanne, and probably none of them true.' He looked round as the door opened, and Mrs Tarr walked into the room.

'Luncheon is served, sir.'

Jack held his hand out to Rosina. 'I hope you're hungry because Mrs Tarr is an excellent cook.'

Mrs Tarr rolled her eyes and sniffed. 'Flattery won't wash with me, sir.'

'Flattery? It's the honest truth, Mrs Tarr. You know me.'

'Indeed, I do, sir. Come this way, Miss Wills.' Mrs Tarr marched out of the parlour with Jack and Rosina following her to the dining room, which overlooked a small back garden.

Rosina took her seat at the table and was quick

to note the glass vase filled with wood anemones set on a lace mat in the centre. She could tell from the highly polished silver on the sideboard and the warm glow of the mahogany furniture, that Mrs Tarr was very proud of the house that had been her home for so many years. The scent of lavender and beeswax mingled with the aroma of the hot bread rolls that Mrs Tarr placed on the table.

'Everything looks so warm and homely,' Rosina said earnestly.

'You sound surprised.' Jack took a seat opposite her. 'Did you think I would live off gruel in the light of a single candle?'

'Not exactly, but I think how fortunate you are to have someone like Mrs Tarr to take care of you.'

'That is true. I don't know what I would do without her, but I have to say it's very pleasant to have someone to share my table with me.'

Rosina unfolded the white linen table napkin and laid it across her lap. 'I imagine there are plenty of ladies who would be delighted to have a meal with you, judging by Miss Kettle's actions today.'

Dimond laughed and passed her the basket of rolls. 'Lizzie is an old friend, but that is as far as it goes.'

'Your private life is nothing to do with me.' Rosina took a roll and broke it in half. 'What concerns me is your ambition to take Moonshadow Manor from my aunt. Can you really do that?'

'Rest easy, Rosina. I have no intention of throwing Miss Maddern out on the street, but I am going to establish who is the legal owner in one way or another.'

'Then that puts us on opposing sides.' Rosina met his steady gaze with a frown. 'I should not be here.'

At that moment Mrs Tarr returned with a tureen of beef stew, which she placed on the table in front of Jack.

'Can I get you anything else, sir?'

'No, thank you, Mrs Tarr. This looks and smells delicious, as always.' Jack picked up a silver ladle and filled a soup bowl, which he passed to Rosina.

'There's treacle tart for dessert, sir.' Mrs Tarr left the dining room, closing the door behind her.

'She looks after you like a mother,' Rosina said, smiling. She tasted the stew and nodded emphatically. 'You were right, this is delicious. It's worth sharing the table with the enemy just to enjoy Mrs Tarr's cooking.'

'I thought you were going to say supping with the devil,' Jack said with a wry smile.

'That's what Ariadne called you, Jack. Have you been toying with that poor girl's affections?'

'No such thing.' Jack's expression seemed to be one of genuine horror. 'I've known Hugo since we were at school together. I would never take advantage of my situation when it comes to someone like Ariadne. She's like a sister to me.'

Rosina pulled a face. 'In your eyes, maybe.'

'Are you always this forthright, Rosina?'

'I suppose I am, but I didn't grow up in polite circles like you and the Charteris family. My papa is a cloth merchant, and I was raised in Islington. I mixed with ordinary people, not those born into wealth and position.'

'My family were not in the higher echelons of society, nor were they particularly well off.'

'But you went to the same school as Hugo Charteris.' Rosina eyed him curiously. 'That would be expensive, I think.'

Jack laughed. 'My school fees were paid for out of a legacy left by my great-grandfather Jabez Dimond, no doubt his ill-gotten gains from a life of crime.'

'Is that why you are obsessed with regaining possession of Moonshadow Manor? Is there treasure buried in the cellar, as someone has suggested to me?'

'That's an interesting idea, but it had not occurred to me. I want what's mine. Moonshadow Manor was in my family for five generations before Jabez lost it in a game of cards. Can you understand that, Rosina?'

She put her spoon down. 'Yes, I can. I am a practical person, Jack, but I have to think of my aunt. You say you don't want to evict her from the only home she's ever known, but how do I know you will keep your word?' Rosina rose to her feet. 'I am sorry, but it does put us on opposite sides. I think I should leave now.'

Jack reached out to catch her by the hand. 'You can't go until you have tasted Mrs Tarr's treacle tart. For one thing, she would be very upset, and for another, you would be missing out on one of life's great pleasures.' He squeezed her fingers and smiled. 'Please sit down and finish your meal.'

Rosina knew when she was beaten, although it was only a temporary truce. She sat down again.

'All right, just to please Mrs Tarr. I don't know why she is so devoted to you, but she is a wonderful cook.'

'That is one thing we both agree on. You and I might have different aims when it comes to Moonshadow Manor, but I think we are of the same opinion when it comes to fighting for what you believe in. We are not enemies, Rosina. If anything, we are both on the side of what is right.'

'But your idea of what is right is opposite to mine, in this case at least.' Rosina picked up her soup spoon. 'May we change the subject, because I doubt if we'll ever agree?'

'Maybe not, but I will always be honest with you, Rosina. That's the best I can offer.'

'I can't ask any more from you than that.'

The rest of the meal passed without any further disagreements and Jack kept Rosina amused with stories of his early struggles to gain the qualifications he needed to practise the law. His days at university had been eventful and Rosina was amazed that he had not been sent down, judging by some of his antics. She suspected that he had committed even worse misdeeds, but the ones he recounted made her laugh and forget their differences, at least temporarily.

Judge was duly returned by one of Hugo's grooms, and Jack drove Rosina back to Moonshadow Manor as he had promised. They parted amicably at the front entrance.

'If you intend to take a stall in next week's market, just let me know,' Jack said as he picked up the reins. 'I'll make sure that Mrs Tarr puts treacle tart on the menu.'

'That would be lovely.' Rosina smiled as she opened the door. 'Thank you for luncheon and thank you for bringing me home.' She entered the house without waiting for his response and closed the door firmly. Ariadne's warning was never far from her mind. It would be so easy to forget that she and Jack wanted completely different things.

The soft silence of Moonshadow Manor wrapped itself around her as she made her way to the morning parlour. Jane was seated by the fire, her head bent over as if she were studying the piece of paper she clasped in her hand.

'Aunt Jane, I have good news for you.' Rosina held her reticule up, giving it a shake so that the coins jingled.

Jane shook her head, and her free hand searched the folds of her skirt for a handkerchief. 'Not now, Rosina.'

Rosina dropped her reticule onto a side table and crossed the floor, shrugging off her mantle as she went.

'What's wrong, Aunt? Are you crying?'

'No, dear. Well, yes, I suppose I am.' Jane found the errant hanky and blew her nose.

'Can you tell me what has upset you?' Rosina pulled up a stool and sat down. 'It must be bad news indeed.'

'He is dying.' Jane's voice broke on a sob. 'It is too late for us. All these years wasted and now we can only be reunited in heaven.'

Rosina reached out to lay her hand on Jane's knee. 'Don't cry. It might not be as bad as it sounds. Who is the letter from, Aunt? Maybe they have exaggerated.'

'His valet is the only person who knows the truth about us.' Jane mopped her eyes. 'Yarwood has been his trusted servant for over forty years.'

Rosina moved a little closer. This was the first time that Jane had mentioned a name connected to the man she had loved for the best part of her life.

'Where does your gentleman live, Aunt? Is it far from here?'

Jane shook her head. 'I cannot say, Rosina. I have guarded our secret for so long that I cannot tell a soul, not even you.'

'But you told me that the man you love is now free. Surely there is no need for secrecy?'

'He has family. I told you before that they know nothing of this.'

'You must have seen each other every now and then, or your romance would have been forgotten long ago, so he can't live too far away.'

Jane's grey eyes lit with sudden emotion. 'Oh, yes, we met often. He would come here late on a Friday night, after the servants had gone to bed. He used to leave before anyone was up, and we had breakfast together. Then he would ride away and leave me bereft, but it was better than parting altogether.'

'And you were prepared to fake your own death so that you could join him abroad somewhere, and all this to save his family's embarrassment.'

'You don't understand, Rosina. They are a well-known and well-respected family. A scandal would ruin many lives.'

'It seems that the man you love was prepared to ruin your life, Aunt. You are the one who paid dearly for your love affair. He seems to have got off very lightly.'

'No, Rosina. No, you don't understand. He has had a brilliant career in politics, as well as running his country estate. He has taken care of his dependants, as well as me and your mother. She never went without.'

'Did Mama know him, Aunt?'

'She met him rarely and then only as a family friend.'

'So, she lived her life not knowing her own father. I would say that was cruel.'

'You can't begin to understand, Rosina. You never met him, and you didn't know either of us when we were young and in love. Now it's too late. He is going to die, and I cannot be with him.'

Rosina leaned away, gazing at her aunt in disbelief. 'Why can't you? What is to stop you from visiting him, even as an old friend?'

'I am an invalid. I can't walk very far, and I have no money. Moonshadow has taken every penny I ever had.'

'I don't believe you are as ill as you pretend.' Rosina stood up and took hold of Jane's hands. 'Stand up. You managed to get here from your room, which is quite a long walk. You are weak because you sit by the fire all day and you don't eat proper meals. I believe that you've played the part of an invalid for so long that you've forgotten how to live like a normal person.'

'That is unkind. I was very poorly when you arrived here, Rosina.'

'You were acting, Aunt. You had convinced yourself that you were dying, aided by Dr Clarke. Does he know the identity of your lover?'

'Yes, of course.'

'Then he might be able to help us now. Perhaps all

your gentleman needs is a visit from you and a good doctor.'

'Don't tease me, Rosina. How can I travel in my condition?'

'You were prepared to go abroad with your gentleman, having made everyone believe you had died, and then I would be responsible for the upkeep of Moonshadow. Tell me I am wrong.'

Jane shook her head. 'No, dear. It is true and I am sorry for the deception, but it was the only way I could think of to ensure that no hint of scandal was attached to Bertram's name.'

'Bertram!' Rosina stared at her in amazement. 'You have actually spoken his name. Who is this man whom you have spent the best part of your life protecting?'

'I have sworn to keep his identity secret, but now I may never see him again.' Jane's eyes filled with tears, and she turned her head away.

'That is easily remedied. I will take you to him. I am sure you could manage a few miles in a comfortable carriage, if you put your mind to it. Tell me where this person lives and leave the rest to me.'

Chapter Nine

Rosina glanced at the clock on the mantelshelf. 'There is still time to travel if I get Joshua to put Pixie in harness. How far is it to Bertram's estate, Aunt?'

'You would really take me there?'

'Of course I will. If it's as urgent as you say, then there is no time to lose, but I need to know if we can reach it before dark.'

'It takes about an hour on horseback,' Jane said reluctantly. 'I can't just turn up at his door, Rosina.'

'Why not, Aunt? It seems he has felt free to arrive here whenever he feels so inclined. I think I might have a few words to say to Bertram. What is his full name? You might as well tell me now.'

'I can't remember the last time I spoke his full name out loud.' Jane blew her nose in the already soggy handkerchief. 'But I suppose you will find out anyway. Your grandfather's name is Sir Bertram Charteris of Glazewood Hall, in the village of Glazewood. He is a well-respected member of parliament.'

'My grandfather!' Rosina struggled with the knowledge. The only grandfather she had ever known was a crusty old gentleman who lived in an Essex village and kept pigeons in a specially designed loft at the bottom of his garden. Papa had taken her to see him several times a year, until he met Dora, who professed a dislike for birds in general and pigeons in particular. The visits had stopped after that, with no explanation, although Rosina knew exactly whom to blame.

'Yes, your grandfather,' Jane said firmly. 'And before you ask, he is Hugo and Ariadne's uncle. So perhaps you can understand a little why we have kept our relationship secret.'

Rosina nodded. She was too stunned by the knowledge to put her thoughts into words.

'That means I am related to Hugo and Ariadne,' she said dazedly.

'Their father is Bertram's brother, Harold. So, yes, you are related to them, and Bertram has a family of his own to consider.' Jane raised her hand to her forehead, closing her eyes. 'It gives me a headache just thinking about it.'

'All the more reason for going to see him now. I'll ask Merry to pack a bag for you and one for myself,' Rosina said hastily. 'You need to change into something suitable for travelling, Aunt. In the meantime, I'll tell Joshua to get the chaise ready. We'll leave as soon as possible so that we get there before dark.'

'What will you tell the servants, Rosina?' Jane stood up, clutching the arms of the chair for support.

'I'll say we are going to visit a sick relative and will be gone for a day or maybe two. That's all they need to know.' Rosina slipped her arm around Jane's small waist. 'Come, I'll help you upstairs and then I'll send Merry to you.'

Even while she made arrangements for the journey, Rosina's mind grappled with the knowledge that she was related to the Charteris family. If what Jane had told her was true – and she had no reason to doubt it – then Hugo and Ariadne were her . . . she had to pause and work it out . . . her first cousins once removed. She was not an expert in that sort of thing, but it was hard to believe and even harder to realise that she had lived all her life with a lie – until now, and she was driven by a sense of emergency. Joshua volunteered to drive them, but even though Rosina was tempted to take him up on his offer she knew that Jane's closely guarded secret could then be in danger of becoming public property. Just one slip of the tongue on Joshua's part and the news would be round the village in a flash. She was nervous about handling a carriage horse, but she was also determined to put an end to the mystery and to meet the man who had held Jane in thrall for a lifetime.

It was just three o'clock when they set off. Jane was wrapped in a thick cloak with a blanket around her knees, and Rosina had changed into a woollen travelling gown with a warm cape and a velvet bonnet. Merry was overtly curious but had accepted Rosina's explanation of their sudden venture as a visit to a sick relative. However, as Rosina drove off, she caught sight of Merry and Joshua with their heads together. She comforted herself with the fact that they had nothing to go on other than supposition, and it was important to keep it that way.

The sun was shining as she guided Pixie onto the main road and Rosina felt a sudden surge of excitement. This really was an adventure and one that might change the course of her life and that of her grandmother.

Jane said very little during the drive, and eventually she fell asleep, leaving Rosina to concentrate on the road ahead. She had asked Joshua how to get to the village of Glazewood, and it had seemed simple enough, but the narrow lanes all looked alike and when she came to an unmarked crossroad, she had to hazard a guess as to which was the right way. She tried hard to remember Joshua's instructions, and she took a chance on the lane to the right. However, as the light began to fade, she realised that the main road had given way to what was little more than a track and they were on the moor itself. Rocky tors loomed out of the landscape, and the wind grew stronger. The track was too narrow to turn the chaise round and go back the way they had come, and after her first experience of walking on the moor, Rosina was afraid of getting the horse or the wheels of the chaise stuck in a treacherous bog.

The land ahead disappeared suddenly into a white mist, which grew darker and colder as Pixie plodded reluctantly through the swirling miasma. Rosina glanced anxiously over her shoulder but fortunately Jane was sound asleep, and for once she had a healthy colour to her cheeks. Rosina turned her head, peering into what was reminiscent of the London winter fogs, but this was a natural phenomenon and at least it was not choking and sulphurous. There was little she could do but allow Pixie to have his head and put her trust in the sturdy Welsh cob. The cold was seeping into Rosina's bones, and she had to curb a feeling of panic. They could go on until Pixie was too exhausted to take another step, although there seemed to be no other option. To stop here in the middle of nowhere might prove fatal for them all. A cold wind dispersed the fog but darkness was enveloping the moor, which only added to the terrors of being lost. Then, quite suddenly, Rosina saw what looked like tiny lights floating above the ground ahead of them.

Then the track widened out and divided. The lights moved to the right and, as if guided by them, Pixie took that path without any instruction from Rosina. She was so desperate by this time that she made no attempt to tighten the reins. The lights moved on, and even when Pixie quickened his pace the little darting luminosities kept ahead of them. Rosina gazed at them, hypnotised by their presence.

Jane sat up suddenly, pointing a shaking finger at the tiny lights. 'Roxanne,' she whispered, 'is it you? Have you come to show us to safety?'

'Of course not, Grandmama,' Rosina said firmly. 'They are just glow-worms. Roxanne was a flesh-and-blood woman. I don't believe the myths about her.'

'She is there, leading us to safety. Follow her, Rosina, or we will perish out here on the moor.' Jane huddled back beneath the blanket, leaving Rosina to encourage Pixie to walk on.

The dried mud deadened the sound created by Pixie's hoofs and the dull rumble of the chaise on the rough track as they followed the tiny darting lights. Then, suddenly, the glow-worms vanished, and the travellers were faced by a high brick wall, covered in ivy, which loomed above them. They were in almost total darkness but, in the distance, Rosina could make out the spire of a church and the flickering candlelight in cottage windows.

'That must be Glazewood,' she murmured with a

sigh of relief. She leaned over to pat Jane's arm. 'Is this the right place? Are we here?'

Jane peered over the folds of the blanket. 'Thank goodness. I thought we were going to die on the moor. I told you it was Roxanne who led us to safety. Drive on, Rosina. The gates to Glazewood Hall are a little further along.'

Rosina flicked the reins and Pixie obliged by breaking into a trot, or perhaps he sensed that there was a nice warm stable awaiting him. When they reached the impressive wrought-iron gates, Rosina reached out and tugged at the bell pull. Within seconds the door to the gatekeeper's lodge opened and a man hurried out.

'Who's there?'

'It's Miss Jane Maddern and Miss Rosina Wills. Let us in, Bates,' Jane said loudly.

'Yes, ma'am. I'm sorry, I couldn't see you in the dark.' Bates unlocked the gates and opened them wide.

'Thank you,' Rosina called as she drove past him. She turned her head to give Jane a curious look. 'You are obviously well known here.'

'I've only visited rarely when Bertram's family were either in London or staying with relations elsewhere. At first, I used the name Mrs Fox, but after a while I reverted to my real name. The servants are very discreet.'

Rosina laughed. 'Grandmama, you are quite

shocking. I could never have imagined all this when I lived in London. I thought life in the country would be very dull and boring.'

'I'm glad you find it amusing,' Jane said tartly. 'Rein the horse in at the front door. A servant will take the chaise to the coach house.'

Glazewood Hall came into view, lit by flambeaux. Silhouetted against the night sky, it was an impressive sight. Rosina could hardly believe that this grand house belonged to her grandfather. She felt as if she had stepped into the pages of a storybook, or else she was dreaming and would wake up in her bed at Moonshadow, or even back in London. However, as she reined Pixie in and drew the chaise to a halt, the front door opened, and as she alighted from the driver's seat a footman hurried out to take the reins. Rosina turned to help Jane, but she had thrown back the blanket and was about to alight by herself. Rosina took her by the arm and helped her to the ground.

Jane braced her shoulders and marched unaided to the door. 'Good evening, Spencer. We came to see how Sir Bertram is faring.'

'Good evening, Miss Maddern.' Spencer ushered her into the entrance hall. 'If you and the young lady would like to wait here, I will announce your arrival.' With a flick of his fingers, he summoned a maidservant who had been standing to attention a little further away from them, and she hurried up to

Jane and Rosina, taking their outer garments over her arm. She bobbed a curtsey and moved away so swiftly she seemed to disappear into the darkness of a passage.

Rosina could not help but be impressed by the faultless service and Spencer's imperturbable demeanour. He had not displayed any sign of surprise at their unexpected arrival so late in the day and he left them now, walking away in a slow stately fashion. Although, perhaps even more astounding was the change in Jane, who had suddenly taken on a completely different persona. She might well have been a dowager duchess, by the way she conducted herself.

'You are obviously well known here, Grandmama, even if you say you rarely visit this house,' Rosina said in a low voice as Spencer entered a room on the far side of the hall.

'I have had a lifetime of practice, my dear. If anything, it is you who have given me the courage to come here and speak my piece. I have probably been too accepting of the situation over the years, but no longer.'

'What if Sir Bertram's family are here, Grandmama? What will you say to them?'

Jane smiled confidently. 'They always spend several months in London at this time of the year, but it's Bertram I have come to see. That letter intimated that he was very poorly, which is terrifying. Also, I want you to meet your grandfather. He could only ever be a kind friend to your mother, but he should know and be known to you. I just pray we are not too late.'

'After so many years of secrecy I imagine this must be difficult for you.'

'I thought it would be, but now I've confessed the truth I am finding it easier and easier. I want Bertram to have that feeling of release as well. Maybe his sudden illness is a godsend after all.'

Moments later, Spencer returned. 'If you would follow me, please . . .' He led them across the entrance hall, with its elegant curving staircase and galleried landing, coming to a halt outside a room on the far side. He knocked, waited for an answer, opened the door and ushered them inside.

Jane entered first, coming to a halt as a young woman, with dark hair and a fresh, peach-like complexion, rose from a chair by the fire and came to greet them with open arms. She enveloped Jane in a fond hug.

'Aunt Jane, what a lovely surprise.'

Jane returned the embrace. 'It's been a long time, Grace. Too long, in fact.' Jane held her at arm's length. 'But where are my manners? May I introduce you to my granddaughter, Rosina Wills, who is on a visit from London.' She turned to fix Rosina with a set smile. 'My dear, I would like to introduce you to Grace Charteris, Sir Bertram's second daughter.'

Grace held out her hand and her green eyes sparkled with interest. Rosina had the eerie feeling that she was looking in a mirror. If she had harboured any doubts as to her relationship with Sir Bertram and his family, they were banished immediately.

'How do you do, Miss Wills?'

Rosina shook Grace's hand with a feeling of disbelief. The whole journey from Moonshadow to Glazewood Hall had felt like a dream – or perhaps a nightmare – and now she was shaking hands with a woman of a similar age who must in fact be her mother's half-sister, and therefore her aunt. Rosina was, for once, speechless.

'Is your father any better, Grace?' Jane asked, breaking the sudden silence.

Grace stared at her in obvious surprise. 'He's fine, Aunt Jane. Why do you ask?'

'I had a letter from Yarwood, telling me that Sir Bertram was very ill.' Jane clutched the back of the nearest chair. 'Are you telling me that it is untrue?'

'Papa went to his room to change for dinner, Aunt Jane,' Grace said, giggling. 'Poor Yarwood has had to be discharged. His mind wandered sometimes, and he said and did odd things.'

'That is too bad.' Jane uttered a sigh of relief then, clutching her hand to her breast. 'But I am so pleased the report is false. I thought my old friend was dying.'

'I can't think why Yarwood did such a thing. I dare

say he will end up in Bedlam. He might have been confusing Papa with Mama's sudden demise.' Grace rolled her eyes expressively. 'But you've come all this way, so you and Rosina will join us for dinner. I'll ring for Spencer and tell him to pass the message to the kitchen.' Grace walked over to the mantelshelf and tugged at the bell pull. 'And it's too late for you to return home, so I hope you will stay the night. I'll have rooms made ready for you.'

'Thank you, Grace. That's very kind.' Jane sank down on the nearest of two sofas upholstered in pale blue damask, the colours of which were repeated in the rest of the elegant furnishings. 'We did not intend to impose ourselves on you, but I for one will be only too happy to accept. What about you, Rosina?'

'Yes, of course,' Rosina said with a start. 'Thank you, Grace.' She struggled to think of something more to say, but she held her tongue, not wanting to make remarks that would make her appear gauche and naïve.

'Might I ask how you came to be out so late, Aunt?' Grace went to sit beside Jane. 'I mean, it's delightful to see you and Rosina, but you are a long way from home after dark, are you not?'

'It's my fault,' Rosina said hastily. 'I insisted on driving us although I have only recently learned how to handle the reins. I mistook the instructions I had been given and took the wrong road.'

'But enough about us,' Jane smiled. 'I thought you

161

and your sisters would be in London for the season, Grace.'

Spencer appeared in the doorway. 'You rang, Miss Grace?'

'Yes, Spencer. Miss Maddern and Miss Wills will be staying tonight. Please tell Mrs Lawson to have two rooms made ready for them and we will be two more for dinner.'

'Yes, Miss Grace.' Spencer acknowledged her instructions with a small bow and left, closing the door behind him.

Grace resumed her seat by the fire. 'As I was about to say, Aunt Eugenie has taken Clarissa and Cecily to London, and Cecy is to undergo the season, even though we are officially in mourning.'

'I am very sorry for your loss, Grace,' Jane said hastily. 'Your mother was a good woman.'

'She was, of course, and she was adamant that she did not wish us to go into mourning. She wanted us to carry on as if she were still with us.' Grace sighed and wiped back a tear with her hanky.

'You must miss her, though,' Rosina said softly. 'Did you not wish to accompany your aunt and sisters to London?'

'Not I.' Grace shook her head vehemently. 'Thankfully I have been through that ordeal, and I couldn't face the prospect of going through it for the third time. Clarissa enjoys that sort of thing, and she adores London. I myself am a country girl at heart.'

Grace looked up as the door opened again, this time to admit a smartly dressed gentleman, wearing a dinner jacket and pinstriped trousers, with a starched cravat at the neck of a frilled shirt. His dark hair was streaked with silver, and his face – although Rosina guessed he must be well into his sixties – was remarkably unlined. She could see that he must have been extremely handsome when a young man, and his smile on seeing Jane would have melted the hardest heart. However, if he was surprised to see her here now, he managed to hide his feelings. He crossed the floor to take her hands in his.

'Jane, this is an unexpected pleasure. You don't often grace Glazewood with your presence.'

Jane's smile matched his, but she quickly looked away. 'We took the wrong road, Bertram, and were lost on the moor for a while. It was quite terrifying.'

He raised her hands to his lips before releasing them. 'Then I'm very glad you managed to reach here without mishap.' He turned to Rosina, smiling. 'We haven't been introduced, but I am Grace's proud father.'

Grace shook her finger at him. 'Don't tease her, Pa. Rosina will think we are dreadful hosts. This is my papa, Rosina.' She stood up and placed her arm around Rosina's shoulders. 'May I introduce Miss Rosina Wills, Pa? She is Aunt Jane's niece. We have only just met but I am looking forward to getting to know her.'

Bertram and Jane exchanged fleeting glances that were not lost on Rosina, but Bertram recovered quickly and stepped forward to shake Rosina's hand.

'How do you do, Rosina? I may call you that, may I not? I feel I have known you for a very long time.'

'How do you do, sir?' Rosina glanced up at him shyly. His grasp on her hand was warm and firm, and there was nothing but kindness and sincerity in his grey eyes. She understood now why her grandmother had kept his secret for so long. There was something compelling about him that encouraged trust and even devotion.

Grace sank down on the sofa, patting the space beside her. 'Come and talk to me, Rosina. Let the elderly folk chat among themselves.' She laughed and turned to Jane. 'I don't mean you, Aunt Jane.'

'I should hope not,' Jane said, smiling. 'But I am more than happy to let you girls talk together. I haven't forgotten what it's like to be young.'

Bertram moved to Jane's side. 'You will never be old, my dear. You haven't changed since you were a girl of sixteen when we first met. You were beautiful then and you are even lovelier now.'

'I hope you didn't say things like that in Mama's presence, Pa.' Grace was suddenly serious, but her father merely smiled and shrugged.

'Your mama was a wonderful woman, Grace. We might not have stopped the clocks or wear mourning black, but we miss her each in our own way.' He turned to Jane. 'You understand, I'm sure.'

She nodded. 'Yes, Bertram. I've always understood.'

Grace shrugged and turned her attention to Rosina. 'Tell me about yourself. Are you staying long at Moonshadow? Don't you find it rather dull after London?'

'I'm not sure how long I will be living at Moonshadow,' Rosina said evasively. 'As to London, yes, I miss some things there, but I think I could get used to living in the country.'

'That is the correct answer.' Grace patted Rosina on the shoulder. 'I can see that you and I will be good friends. I should ride over to Moonshadow and call on you, although that would necessitate a visit to Daumerle House to see my cousins.'

Rosina eyed her curiously. 'You don't get on with them?'

'You know what families are, Rosina. I love Ariadne – she's a sweet girl – but I find Hugo very pompous and overbearing.' Grace jumped to her feet as the door opened, and a maidservant hurried in, carrying a tray of tea and cakes. 'Put it down there, please, Nell. I'll pour, so that will be all.'

Nell placed the tray on a low table, bobbed a curtsey and left the room, having cast a sideways glance at Rosina. Grace set about filling the teacups and passing them round.

'I'm getting better at this,' she said as she handed

a cup and saucer to Rosina. 'I used to spill the tea into the saucers every time. Mama made me practise until I had mastered the art.'

'You must miss her terribly,' Rosina said earnestly. 'I lost my mama a couple of years ago, but the pain never quite goes away.'

Grace sat down again, glancing at her father and Jane, who were seated side by side, deep in conversation.

'Old people always have a lot to talk about. But they've had years and years of living to mull over. I expect I will be the same when I reach a grand old age.' Grace sipped her tea. 'Tell me about your home in London, Rosina. Whereabouts do you live?'

'Nowhere like this,' Rosina said bluntly. 'We have quite a modest house in Islington, not far from Papa's business.'

'I expect he misses you.' Grace placed her cup and saucer back on the tray. 'How long will he allow you to stay?'

'Papa remarried a year ago.' Rosina smothered a sigh. 'Dora has a baby, and they need my bedroom for the nursery.' She had not meant to blurt out the truth, but there was something sympathetic about Grace that invited confidences.

'You poor thing.' Grace picked up the plate of iced fancies. 'Have a cake. I always find eating something sweet makes me feel much happier. Clarissa says I'll grow corpulent, but I really don't care.'

Rosina took a small cake and bit into it, which helped to stem the unshed tears that threatened to spill from her eyes. She had not cried after leaving home and she was determined not to allow her emotions to overcome her now. The sweetness of the delicacy and the delicious flavour seemed to help. Grace was also indulging with obvious enjoyment and as she swallowed the last crumbs they began to giggle.

'I don't know why I'm laughing.' Rosina dabbed her lips with a starched linen table napkin.

'Me neither.' Grace shook her head. 'Cook does make the most delicious cakes. I hope she has outdone herself at dinner.' She glanced over her shoulder. 'Papa and Aunt Jane aren't eating. Heaven knows what they find to talk about.' Grace stood up, brushing crumbs from her skirt. 'Come with me, Rosina. I'll show you to your room. I know which one Mrs Lawson will have chosen. She is very predictable.'

Rosina could see that her grandmother was too deep in conversation with Sir Bertram to notice and she followed Grace from the room. The vast entrance hall was illuminated by dozens of wax candles, the cost of which would be daunting to any ordinary person. Rosina could not help but be impressed as she followed Grace up the sweeping staircase to the first floor. By the time she reached the bedroom that had been allotted to her she was afraid she might need a map to guide her back to the ground floor. Flickering candles in wall sconces lit their way and as Grace opened the door to the guest room Rosina could see the welcoming glow of a fire.

'It's a pretty little room,' Grace said casually. 'Your valise is on the footstool, but I can send a maid to unpack for you.'

'Thank you, but I can manage.' Rosina took in her surroundings, trying to appear casual when in reality this seemed like a room fit for a princess. The delicate floral wallpaper, no doubt hand-painted, and the carefully selected furnishings, curtains and the coverlet on the bed were all in shades of pink and white with the odd touch of pale green. The four-poster bed looked comfortable enough to make her want to sleep for a week, but Rosina knew her stay here would be short. She might be related to the Charteris family by blood, but that did not mean they would have to accept her. She must not allow herself to imagine that this way of life would ever be hers.

'All right then,' Grace said cheerfully. 'I'll leave you to unpack and settle in. You might care to change for dinner. Papa is a stickler for doing things properly. I thought I had better warn you. It's how they did everything in his day. My sisters and I are much more modern.' Grace whisked out of the room, leaving Rosina to her own devices.

She sank down on a chair by the fire, wondering if they had done the right thing by coming here. Sir

Bertram – she could not think of him as Grandfather – was a splendid gentleman, and Grace was delightful, but how would they feel when they discovered her true identity? She was of their blood and yet her upbringing was so different from theirs. Rosina was beginning to doubt if she could ever fit in. She could only imagine the conversation that Grandmama and Sir Bertram were having at this very moment, and it was not encouraging.

Chapter Ten

Rosina unpacked the few things she had brought with her from Moonshadow and shook out the creases in her best silk gown. She put it on, examining her appearance in the cheval mirror. In the soft candlelight the shade of green in the swirling skirts and tightly fitted bodice brought out the colour of her eyes, and she brushed her long hair until it hung in soft curls around her shoulders.

'You still look like a poor relation,' Rosina told her reflection sternly. Unfortunately, there was no getting away from the fact that the Charteris family were wealthy beyond her wildest dreams. Grace might be open and friendly, but there was little chance of them forming a close friendship, especially if she discovered the complexity of their connection. A wry smile curved Rosina's lips and she wondered how Grace would react if she discovered that they were aunt and niece. A knock on the door made her turn with a start.

'Come in.'

The door opened and Grace breezed into the room. She came to a halt, gazing at Rosina with a delighted smile.

'What a lovely gown. So simple and yet so elegant. You must have bought it in London. I can always tell.'

'I had a good dressmaker,' Rosina said modestly. 'She could copy anything from a fashion plate.'

Grace held out her arms and did a twirl. 'My gown looks over-fussy and rather vulgar in comparison. You must allow me to share your modiste. She is obviously a treasure.'

'I don't know about that.' Rosina had a vision of Hannah Peabody in her one-room lodging above a butcher's shop in Islington. Hannah working by the light of a single candle in winter, straining her eyes as she stitched fine seams by hand.

'I insist,' Grace said firmly. 'You must come with us when we go to London next time and introduce me to this person. She is obviously very skilful. Anyway, enough of that. Let's go downstairs to dinner. We have a surprise guest.'

'I should put my hair up first.' Rosina eyed Grace's elaborate coiffure with a touch of envy.

'Nonsense,' Grace said firmly. 'You have glorious

hair. You just need a couple of combs strategically placed by me. Come to my room and you can choose the ones you like best.'

Rosina had little option but to go along with Grace's request, and anyway, she was quite eager to see her room. She was not disappointed. Grace's bedchamber was luxuriously furnished and decorated in pastel shades, with a chaise longue placed in front of tall windows, overlooking the grounds at the rear of the house. It was a room that any lady would have been proud to call her own, and yet there were memories of childhood cunningly placed, including a large French fashion doll on the bed, propped up with silk cushions so that it looked as if reclining leisurely.

Grace went straight to the dressing table and opened several drawers, uttering a cry of triumph when she came across a box filled with hair combs of varying designs, which she held up for Rosina to see.

'Come and sit down, Rosina. My maid does my hair for me, but I have practised on Cecy, so I know what I'm doing. Let me make you even more beautiful.'

There was nothing for it but to put herself in Grace's hands. Rosina perched on the dressing-table stool and watched in the mirror as her thick raven hair was brushed and then pinned into place with pearl-encrusted combs.

Grace stood back with a triumphant smile. 'There! What did I tell you? That has made all the difference. You look stunning.' She pulled Rosina to her feet. 'Come with me. Everyone will be in the drawing room now, so we need to hurry.'

Rosina followed Grace as she hurried from the room and made her way downstairs, leading the way to the drawing room. She flung the door open and made a dramatic entrance. Rosina followed her but came to a sudden halt, catching her breath at the sight of the tall, smartly dressed man, standing with his back to the fireplace.

'Jack!' Rosina stared at him in astonishment. Of all people, he was the last person she had expected to find in Sir Bertram's drawing room. Moreover, he seemed very much at home, and it occurred to Rosina that this was not simply a casual visit.

'Good evening, Miss Wills,' Jack said with a wry smile. 'I confess I was as surprised to find that you and Miss Maddern were here as you are to see me.'

Sir Bertram looked from one to the other. 'You two are acquainted?'

'More than acquainted, sir,' Jack said smoothly. 'Last time I saw Miss Wills was after her foray into the business of running a market stall. We ate luncheon together earlier today, did we not, Miss Wills?'

Rosina's nerves were stretched to a point where any moment she felt she might rush outside and howl

173

at the moon, although, of course, she had never done anything like that, and probably never would. It was just that this was the sort of situation she could not have imagined. She shot a glance at Jane, who was sitting beside Sir Bertram on the sofa, looking surprisingly serene considering the circumstances. Rosina took a deep breath, forcing herself to sound calm.

'We did indeed, Mr Dimond. Your housekeeper is an excellent cook, and I was grateful for your hospitality. However, I admit that I am surprised to see you here.' She met his amused gaze with a lift of her chin. It was annoying that Jack always seemed to find something humorous about their meetings.

'Jack is an old friend of the family, and my lawyer,' Sir Bertram said calmly.

'Isn't it rather late for a professional visit?' Grace asked casually, but Jack merely smiled.

'I was in the area, Miss Charteris.'

Sir Bertram frowned. 'It's really none of your concern, Grace,' he said severely. 'I asked Mr Dimond to call next time he was in the neighbourhood. We do have some business matters to discuss after dinner, so I have invited him to join us.' He turned to Jane, his expression softening. 'You don't mind, do you, my dear?'

'Of course not. We are the uninvited guests, Bertram.' Jane laid her hand on Bertram's as it rested on his knee. 'Rosina and I lost our way in the mist,

Mr Dimond. We ended up here, which was fortunate for us.'

'Nasty things, the mists that come from seemingly nowhere on the moor,' Jack said, nodding. 'Although I have to say I have never been caught out in such a way, but then I was born and bred here. My mother, as everyone knows, was of Romany stock, so perhaps I have inherited her gift for being at one with nature.'

'No, really?' Grace was suddenly alert. 'You never mentioned that before, sir.'

He shrugged. 'Some people think it not quite the thing, but I am proud of my ancestry. We can't all be born into the gentry.'

The talk of heritage and birthright was making Rosina feel uncomfortable. She shot a sideways glance at her grandmother, but Jane, it seemed, was used to ignoring barbs and insinuations. Once again, Rosina experienced a feeling of pity mixed with admiration for the woman who had stoically borne the stigma of giving birth to an illegitimate child for so many years.

At that moment, with excellent timing, Spencer entered the drawing room to announce that dinner was served.

Rosina found herself seated next to Jack at the vast mahogany dining table. Jane was in the place of honour at Bertram's right hand and Grace was on his left.

'It seems a strange coincidence that you turned up

here at the same time as my aunt and I did,' Rosina said in a low voice.

'Are you suggesting that I followed you?' Jack shot her a quizzical glance. 'That sounds very far-fetched to me, Miss Wills.'

'I thought we had gone past the formal stage,' Rosina said crossly. 'What game are you playing, Jack Dimond?'

He laughed. 'Why is it that when someone uses one's full name, you know they are not amused?'

'Unlike you, it seems. You find everything funny, and that way you don't have to answer my questions.'

'You really are upset with me, Rosina. I promise you that I had no notion that you and Miss Maddern were here. I quite genuinely have business to discuss with my client.'

'What are you two talking about?' Grace demanded. 'Won't you share it with the rest of us, or must I die of curiosity?'

Rosina struggled to think of an answer that would satisfy Grace, but Jack smiled urbanely.

'Miss Wills does not approve of me, Grace. She is of the opinion that I arrived here merely to annoy her.'

'Really, Rosina?' Grace eyed her curiously. 'I think there is something going on between you two that you are trying to keep from us.'

'Grace!' Sir Bertram gave her a warning glance.

'Enough of that, if you please. You are embarrassing our guests.'

'Not at all, sir,' Jack said casually. 'Miss Wills and I have a challenging relationship, although we are the best of friends, are we not, Rosina?'

'I wouldn't put it as strongly as that.' Rosina shook her head. 'But I do find Mr Dimond rather enigmatic.'

Grace laughed. 'I dare say that's the first time anyone has called you an enigma, Mr Dimond. And I thought that lawyers were always so dull and prosaic. You must be the exception.'

'If your definition of a lawyer is such, then I am happy to be the exception,' Jack said, smiling. 'As to being an enigma, I can assure you that I am nothing of the sort. I am what I appear to be, and that is a moderately successful country solicitor with the best interests of my clients at heart.'

'There you are now, Grace.' Sir Bertram signalled to the footman to serve the main course as the soup dishes were cleared away. 'I hope you are satisfied with that. Now let's enjoy the rest of our meal.'

'Yes, Papa.' Grace subsided into silence.

Rosina was relieved, but she sensed that Grace suspected something was not quite right, and no doubt she would question her again as to her exact relationship with Jack. Even as she ate and listened to Jane and Sir Bertram chatting about inconsequential things, with Jack adding his own comments, Rosina felt that something had changed subtly. She could not help wondering why Sir Bertram had chosen Jack Dimond to be his lawyer, when he must have known that Jane had problems with him and his claim on Moonshadow Manor. Rosina decided to challenge Jack about it after dinner, and she sat back to enjoy the delicious food.

However, as soon as the meal ended Grace suggested that the ladies should retire to the drawing room and Sir Bertram gave her an approving smile as he rose to his feet.

'Mr Dimond and I have things to discuss over brandy and cigars, but we will join you soon.'

Grace led the way with Jane and Rosina following her, and they made themselves comfortable in the drawing room where an under-footman brought them coffee.

Grace picked up her cup and sipped. 'Now we are alone, so to speak, Rosina, tell me what is going on between you and Mr Dimond. I sense a mystery or an intrigue, at least.'

'Rosina is just standing up for me, Grace,' Jane said hastily. 'Jack has been my solicitor for many years, but his family used to own Moonshadow, and he has done his utmost to find proof that the transfer of the property to the Madderns was illegal.'

'And yet you still make use of his services.' Grace looked from Jane to Rosina. 'Isn't that rather odd? I mean, if he is trying to take your home away, Aunt

Jane, it does seem to be rather strange. Not that I know much about the law.'

'Well, my dear,' Jane said, smiling, 'ours is an unusual situation.'

Grace blushed and looked away. 'I'm sorry. I didn't mean to pry into your affairs, Aunt Jane. Everyone knows that you were let down by someone you trusted, and you have bravely suffered the consequences. I would never allow anyone to say differently.'

'Of course not. I know that, Grace. I have grown used to being a pariah in Ugstock and the surrounding area. A youthful mistake made me an outcast, as you know.'

'I think you've borne it heroically,' Rosina said hastily. 'I don't think I could have survived public censure as you have. You are a fine woman, Aunt Jane. I admire you for your fortitude.'

'As do I,' Grace added earnestly. 'Papa brought me and my sisters up to respect others and not to judge. It's something that I try my hardest to live up to.'

'Your papa seems like a very kind man.' Rosina picked up a delicate coffee cup and took a sip. 'This is excellent coffee. We always have tea at home, but I do like coffee.'

'Tell me about your home in London, Rosina.' Grace settled herself comfortably in her chair. 'We have a townhouse in Cavendish Square. Do your family live far from there?'

'Quite a way,' Rosina said vaguely. 'Are you acquainted with Islington?'

'No, I'm afraid not. To be honest, I prefer the country to London life, and I avoid going there as much as possible.' Grace sipped the last of her coffee and placed the cup and saucer on the tray. 'Is it a nice part of London? Are there any parks and gardens?'

'It's a very busy part of town,' Rosina said evasively. 'My pa is a cloth merchant. He is in trade.'

Grace laughed. 'Is that meant to shock me? I hear people talking about being in trade as something unmentionable, but I can never understand why. As to you having a market stall, I think that is so exciting. Tell me about that.'

'We needed the money.' Rosina shot an apologetic glance in Jane's direction. 'I'm sorry, Aunt, I have to be honest. I mean, I did quite enjoy my morning in the market, although I didn't do most of the selling.'

'Really?' Jane sat forward in her seat. 'You didn't tell me that, Rosina. I would never have agreed to let you undertake such a task had I known you were unhappy about doing so.'

'No, Aunt. It's quite all right. I thought I knew what I was doing, but it took a woman called Lizzie Kettle to show me how it's done.'

'Lizzie Kettle?' Grace giggled. 'What a strange name. Is she a friend of yours?'

'No, not at all. Jack Dimond summoned her up as

if from nowhere and she knew exactly how to attract customers. I merely assisted her.'

'Your adventures make my life here seem very dull in comparison,' Grace said, smiling. 'Are you going to do it again? If you are, I would love to come and help you. I think I might have a talent for calling out like a barker at a fairground.'

'What do you know about fairgrounds?' Jane shook her head. 'Grace, my dear, does your papa know that you've frequented such places?'

'Of course not, Aunt.' Grace dimpled mischievously. 'I don't tell Papa everything, but I know I can rely on you to keep my secret.'

'You may, indeed.' Jane stood up, shaking out her crumpled skirts. 'It's been a rather tiring day. If you don't mind, I'll retire to bed now.'

'Can you find the way, Aunt?' Grace asked anxiously. 'Or shall I ring for a servant to show you to your room?'

'I think I can manage, my dear.' Jane turned to Rosina with a weary smile. 'Good night, Rosina. We should leave soon after breakfast tomorrow. At least it will be easier finding the way in daylight.'

Rosina jumped to her feet and gave Jane a hug. 'Good night, Aunt. Sleep well.'

'I think there's every chance of that. It's been a long and eventful day. I'm sure I will fall asleep as soon as my head hits the pillow.' Jane walked slowly from the room, closing the door behind her.

'She is a lovely person,' Grace said earnestly. 'I am very fond of Aunt Jane. I just feel so sorry for the way she has been treated by society. People are very cruel and judgemental.'

Rosina was about to answer when a noise at one of the windows made them both turn with a start. 'My goodness, that sounds like hail, but it can't be.'

Grace rushed over to the window and peered out into the darkness. She turned slowly.

'Rosina, can I trust you?'

'Yes, of course. Why do you ask?'

'Can you keep a secret?' Grace asked eagerly. 'Are you ready for an adventure?'

'I think so. Who is outside, Grace?'

'Come with me. You must not breathe a word of this to anyone, not even Aunt Jane. Do you understand?' Grace clasped her hands to her bosom. 'This is life and death to me.'

'Surely not so?' Rosina felt the skin prickle at the back of her neck.

'Come with me. Don't make a sound.' Grace hurried to Rosina's side and grabbed her by the hand. She led her from the room and virtually dragged her to a room at the end of a long passageway. The garden room was lit by moonlight streaming through the French windows. Grace opened the door and stepped outside, falling into the arms of a man who enveloped her in a passionate embrace.

Startled, although not shocked, Rosina remained in

the shadows. Grace had obviously wanted to involve her in what appeared to be an illicit relationship, but it put Rosina in an awkward position. She shifted uneasily from one foot to the other. If Grace wished to have an affair with someone of whom her father did not approve, that was her business. It was unfair to involve someone else. It crossed Rosina's mind that this appeared to be history repeating itself. Aunt Jane and Sir Bertram has been romantically involved for a lifetime, and now it seemed that Grace was embarking on another such illicit affair.

Grace slid her hands up the young man's chest and pushed him just far enough away so that she could catch her breath. She turned her head to give Rosina a smile drunk with love.

'You see why you must not tell anyone, Rosina.'

'I should go to my room,' Rosina said awkwardly. 'I won't say a word, Grace. This is your business, not mine.'

'I wanted you to meet Luke, the love of my life.' Grace looked up at him with an adoring smile. 'We can trust Rosina. She is going to help us, aren't you, Rosina?'

Rosina shook her head. 'I don't see how. Please don't involve me in this, Grace.'

'But, dearest, you are already involved,' Grace said sweetly. 'You have a choice. You either go now and tell my father that I am in my lover's arms – a man who is wonderful and upstanding and who adores me – or you can keep our secret and maybe help us in the future.'

'How d'you do, miss?' Luke said slowly. 'I do love her, miss. I mean Grace no harm.'

'I'm sure you don't.' Rosina could not see his features clearly, but he sounded sincere and almost desperate. She experienced a pang of sympathy for the star-crossed lovers, but tomorrow she would be returning to Moonshadow Manor, and there was little she could do to help them.

'I really should go to bed,' Rosina said firmly. 'You can trust me. I won't say a word about this, Grace.'

'Not even to Aunt Jane?' Grace rested her head against Luke's broad shoulder. 'She is a dear, but I know what she would say, and that would be based on her own sad experiences.'

'I expect you're right.' Rosina backed towards the doorway. 'Good night.' She made her escape before Grace had a chance to say anything further, but once back in the dark corridor she had to find her way to the entrance hall and the main staircase. Straining her eyes, she could see a flicker of candlelight to her left and she hurried towards it, pausing outside a door that had been left ajar. She could hear male voices in conversation, and she stopped, not intending to eavesdrop, but she heard her grandmother's name mentioned and was overcome by curiosity.

'How long have you known?' Sir Bertram's deep voice echoed off the walls in the passageway.

'Quite a long time, sir. I've known Jane since I was a boy, and she was my father's first client when he set up his practice in Ivybridge.' Jack Dimond's unmistakable tones came in answer to the question.

Rosina knew she should walk on, but she found herself unable to move, and she leaned against the wall, scarcely daring to breathe.

'Who else knows, Jack? I thought we had managed to keep our affair secret.'

'I can't answer that for certain, sir. I am the only one, as far as I am aware, but in a small village like Ugstock you can never be absolutely sure.'

'It would ruin me if the truth came out,' Sir Bertram said angrily. 'I know I can rely on your discretion because I pay you handsomely for your service, but I can't afford to have it known publicly that I fathered Jane Maddern's child.'

Rosina stifled a gasp of dismay. Even though she could not see Sir Bertram's expression she could hear the coldness in his voice, and there was a slight pause before Jack spoke again.

'You don't intend to make amends to Miss Maddern for the suffering she endured at the hands of others?' Jack's tone was icy.

'I looked after her financially when the child was small, Jack. I will do so again, on the understanding that our relationship has to cease immediately. I am a grieving widower, and I have a position to uphold in society. Besides which, I am hoping to be re-elected in the next general election. I don't want anything to tarnish my reputation.'

It was all that Rosina could do to prevent herself from crying out in anger, but she covered her mouth with her hand, controlling her breathing with difficulty.

'I have done my bit, Sir Bertram,' Jack said sharply. 'I imagine our business is just about concluded now.'

'Perhaps, but I was thinking you might be interested in working for me, should I succeed in the election. I will need someone trustworthy at my side.'

'I'm a country solicitor, sir. I have no interest in politics. With regret, I am not your man.'

Rosina flattened herself against the wall as the door was wrenched wide open and Jack strode out. He came to a halt when he saw her, placed his finger over his lips and took her by the arm.

'Don't speak,' he said in a low voice as he marched her towards the light at the end of the corridor. 'We need to have a conversation.'

Chapter Eleven

'What are you doing?' Rosina demanded angrily as Jack came to a halt at the foot of the stairs. 'Have you been spying on my aunt all this time?'

He released her with an apologetic grin. 'Don't you mean your grandmother? Yes, I suppose it was spying of a sort. Sir Bertram paid me to keep an eye on Miss Maddern and the whole village, if it comes to that. Before his wife died, he was content to let matters lie, but now he is ready to start a new episode in his life.'

'You knew this all along, but you pretended to be my friend? What sort of man are you, Jack?'

'I thought I was protecting Miss Maddern. Despite the feud between our families, I have the greatest respect for Jane. She is a brave and loyal woman, who did not deserve to be ostracised by society, but

I've always thought that Sir Bertram, although he had done her wrong, did have her best interests at heart.'

'I'm ashamed to have him as my grandfather,' Rosina said bitterly. 'He has tricked my grandmother into believing that they would have a happy life together when he was a free man. Everything he promised her was all lies, according to what I just heard.'

Jack shook his head. 'He might have meant it at the start, Rosina. Men sometimes make promises they can't keep when they are in love. Sir Bertram and Miss Maddern have been in a relationship for forty years or more. Things are bound to have changed.'

'Not for her, Jack. My grandmother was prepared to fake her own death in order to be with him. She had it all arranged with Dr Clarke.'

'If the village gossips are to be believed, Miss Maddern could have married, even allowing for the scandal, but she chose to remain single.'

'She loved and still loves that man,' Rosina said in disgust. 'If I hadn't overheard your conversation I would have continued to encourage her in her fantasy.'

'What were you doing lurking outside Sir Bertram's study?' Jack's generous mouth curved into a smile. 'I suppose you got lost in the dark.'

'Something of the sort, and it's none of your business.' Rosina mounted the stairs. 'I'm going to bed. I don't know what I'll say to Grandmama in the morning, but I will need to give it a great deal of thought.'

'It would be best not to interfere, Rosina,' Jack said seriously. 'Those two have been lovers for nearly half a century. They need to end it by mutual consent. If you try to come between them, you might come off worst.'

'I'll take my chances. Good night, Jack.'

Rosina continued up the stairs, heading towards her bedroom. Tomorrow they would leave Glazewood Hall, and she had no desire to return, even though she had found family she had not known existed. Grace was lovely and fun to be with, but now it seemed that she was involved with a man she dared not introduce to her father. Illicit affairs seemed to run in the family. Rosina could feel Jack staring after her from the bottom of the stairs, but she did not look back.

Next morning, after a night when she tossed and turned and had little sleep, Rosina was up early. She washed, dressed and put up her hair before going downstairs to the dining room, where she found Jack already at breakfast.

'You look tired, Rosina,' he said casually. 'Do try the devilled kidneys – they are delicious.'

Rosina took a seat opposite him. 'No, thank you. I'll just have tea and toast.'

'You don't know what you're missing. I must get the recipe from Cook and pass it on to Mrs Tarr.'

Rosina took a slice of toast from the rack and reached for the butter. 'I wouldn't do that, if I were you, Jack.'

He looked up from his plate, frowning. 'Why not?'

'It's hardly tactful. You obviously don't know much about women if you think you can get on the good side of your housekeeper by praising another woman's cooking. I think Mrs Tarr would be mortally offended.'

'I don't think I'll ever understand women,' Jack said, shrugging.

'Obviously not.' Rosina buttered the toast and added a spoonful of marmalade to the side of her plate. 'I will finish this and then I'd better go upstairs and see if Grandmama is awake. She wanted to leave early.'

'Are you still intent on telling her what you heard last night?' Jack met her gaze with no hint of humour in his dark eyes. 'Think hard before you break her heart.'

'It is not I who will do so, Jack. I think it's a foregone conclusion that Sir Bertram will do that. I just want to prepare her for the shock of what is to come.'

'He's not a man to be trifled with,' Jack said, frowning. 'He is intent on standing for re-election. I don't think anything or anyone will stop him.'

Rosina pushed her plate away, her appetite gone. She rose to her feet. 'Just thinking about the way he's treated her makes me feel sick, to say nothing about what my poor mother must have endured as a child and as a young woman. Grandmama did not bear the stigma of having a child out of wedlock alone. My mother had to live with it all her life.'

'I'm not denying the hardships they endured.' Jack stood up, holding out his hand. 'I am not your enemy, Rosie.' He smiled ruefully. 'I'm sorry, your name is too long. I think of you as Rosie.'

Rosina stared at him in amazement. 'We are having a serious conversation about a situation that might destroy my grandmother, and all you can say is that you don't like my name? What sort of person does that?'

'Someone like me, I'm afraid. I'm done with making apologies, Rosie. All I can say is that I have Miss Maddern's best interests at heart. I think she is better off without him, if you want my honest opinion.'

'I'm not sure that I do. You say you have her best interests at heart and yet you want to prove that Moonshadow Manor belongs to the Dimond family. I call that hypocritical.'

'It would be, if true.'

'If that is so then why did you want all those boxes of documents? If it wasn't the ownership of Moonshadow Manor that you wanted to find, what was it?'

'It was a record of birth.'

'Surely there are baptismal records in the local church that would tell you all you need to know,' Rosina said slowly. She could see that whatever he was seeking was important to him and that made it all the more mysterious.

Jack shook his head. 'This birth would have been kept secret.'

'Was it recent, or some time ago? Why is it so important to you, Jack?'

'I can't prove anything yet, but it could have a bearing on everything I've been brought up to believe. I don't want to say any more yet.'

Rosina was just trying to make sense of this when the door opened and Jane walked into the room, followed by Sir Bertram. They were both smiling and Jane looked so happy that Rosina knew she had not the heart to spoil that moment.

'You both look very serious,' Jane said, looking from one to the other. 'Is everything all right, Rosina?'

'Yes, Aunt.' Rosina forced herself to smile. 'I was just coming to wake you up if we are to start out early.'

Sir Bertram strolled over to the sideboard and helped himself to bacon and devilled kidneys from a silver breakfast dish. 'You must have something to eat before you go, Jane. I insist.' He walked over to the table and sat down at the head. 'You seem to have left your food, Rosina. I hope you are not coming down with a chill after your experience on the moor.'

'No, sir. I feel well enough. I am not very hungry.'

'Well, sit down again anyway. I like to eat with everyone in harmony. You, too, Jane, my dear.'

Jane went to the sideboard and took a small portion of buttered eggs before joining Sir Bertram at the table. 'I'm not very hungry either, but I will eat, if only to keep you happy, Bertram.'

Rosina exchanged wary glances with Jack as she resumed her seat. She could not force herself to eat, and she sipped her coffee in silence, glancing now and then at her grandmother and Sir Bertram as they chatted in low intimate voices. It struck Rosina to the heart to see her grandmother so happy and loving with a man who was going to take away everything she had lived for. It was as much as Rosina could do to sit quietly during the rest of the meal, and she could see that Jack was also feeling uncomfortable.

'You're unusually quiet, Jack,' Sir Bertram said, wiping his lips on his table napkin. 'Didn't you sleep too well?'

'I had an excellent night's sleep, sir.' Jack sent a warning glance to Rosina, who was finding it harder and harder to keep from blurting out what she had overheard the previous evening. 'I was just planning my day, and I realise that I should also leave early. I have a business appointment later this morning.'

'Quite so.' Sir Bertram buttered a slice of toast. 'I,

too, have important business, which necessitates a trip to London.'

Jane eyed him in surprise. 'I thought you had retired from such matters, Bertram.'

'Not at all, my dear. I am seeking re-election. I was going to keep it to myself until my seat was assured, but you are like family to me. I cannot keep secrets from you, Jane.'

'What secret is this, though, Bertram? You told me that you were thinking of buying a property abroad and taking life easier now.' Jane's voice shook with emotion.

'I can still do that, Jane,' Sir Bertram said uneasily. 'Nothing has changed as far as you are concerned.'

Jane rose to her feet, staring at him in horror. 'Are you going back on your word, Bertram? After all these years of waiting and suffering the consequences of our relationship, are you telling me that it was all for nothing?'

'Hush, my dear. Not in front of your niece and my man of law. We will talk about this when I return from London.'

Jane drew herself up to her full height. 'Rosina is my granddaughter, Bertram. She is also your granddaughter. I think it's time you acknowledged her, although it's too late for our dear dead daughter, Alice.'

'Papa!' Grace erupted into the room, her face pale with shock. 'Is this true?'

Sir Bertram's pleasant smile faded and was replaced by a look that made Rosina shiver.

'This has nothing to do with you, Grace. Kindly go to your room. I'll speak to you later.'

Grace stood her ground. 'No, Papa. I won't be sent away like a child. I'm a grown woman and I deserve to be told the truth.'

'Please, Bertram,' Jane said, holding out her hands. 'Don't create a scene. We need to speak in private.'

Rosina jumped to her feet. 'Come with me, Grace. I'll tell you all you need to know.'

'No!' Sir Bertram's voice rose to an angry roar. 'You will do no such thing, Rosina. This is my house, and you are a guest. You will not interfere in family matters.'

Rosina could see that her grandmother was close to tears, but she was not going to back down. 'I'm sorry, sir. I was under the impression that I am part of your family. You, unfortunately, are my grandfather and that makes poor Grace my aunt. I agree it is a ridiculous situation, but I am not afraid of you, and I will do as I think fit.' She grabbed Grace by the arm. 'Come with me. I think Sir Bertram needs to speak to my grandmother alone.' She propelled Grace from the dining room, avoiding meeting Jack's eyes as she walked past him.

Outside the dining room Grace collapsed onto a spindly gilt chair. 'Is all this true, Rosina?'

'I'm sorry to say it is.' Rosina leaned against the wall. 'I've only recently learned the truth and it was just as much of a shock to me.'

'But my parents were devoted to each other,' Grace said shakily. 'I don't understand how Papa could have had another family without any of us knowing.'

'I know how you feel, Grace. It's not easy to understand. All I know is that my grandmother has loved Sir Bertram for a lifetime. She was prepared to go to any lengths to be with him when he was a free man.'

Grace shot her a venomous glance. 'You mean when my mother died. They were waiting for her to pass away.'

'I don't think that's the case, even if it seems so. I can only speak for my grandmother, but I know her feelings are genuine. You saw how upset she was just now.'

'My suffering is equal to hers. But it's the hypocrisy of the affair that infuriates me. I have been forced to see Luke in secret for nearly a year, because my papa would not allow me to marry beneath me. Now I find that Papa has been behaving abominably for a lifetime.' Grace stood up, taking a deep breath. 'At least the knowledge sets me free. Papa would not dare to forbid me to see Luke, or I will tell my sisters, and I'll make sure that his parliamentary career is in ruins.'

'You wouldn't go so far, not to your own father,' Rosina said in dismay.

'You don't believe me?' Grace tossed her head. 'Wait and see – that's all I have to say.' She flounced off, leaving Rosina standing in the hallway.

She was wondering what to do next when the dining-room door opened and Jane rushed out, holding her handkerchief to her face.

'Grandmama.' Rosina caught her in a gentle hug. 'Don't cry. I'm sure there is an explanation to all this.'

Jane pulled away from her. 'I heard what Bertram said. I'm shocked, and yet I think I've known for some time that he has changed his mind. We're going home, Rosina. Please find a servant and have our carriage brought round to the front entrance. I'm going to my room to pack my valise.' Jane walked away before Rosina had a chance to respond.

Once again, the dining-room door opened and this time it was Jack who stepped into the hallway.

'Are you all right, Rosie? That was quite a scene to witness so early in the morning.'

'I suppose you find it funny, as you seem to view everything that way,' Rosina said crossly.

'Not at all. As a matter of fact, I am deeply sorry for Miss Maddern. She does not deserve to be cast aside so casually.'

'At last, we agree on something.' As Rosina made to walk away, Jack caught her by the hand.

'Stop a minute and hear me out.'

She paused, staring straight ahead. 'I can't think of anything you could say to make this better.'

'For a start I had no idea that Sir Bertram would treat Miss Maddern this way. I knew he was considering the purchase of a villa somewhere abroad where the weather would be considerably more clement. I also knew that he was intent on pursuing his political career. However, I could not have known about the promises he made to Miss Maddern. If he has broken those it is inexcusable.'

'I couldn't agree more. I'm taking my grandmother home now. I, for one, will not be returning to Glazewood Hall, and I doubt if Grandmama will wish to come here again.'

'It is a sorry state of affairs, Rosie,' Jack said with a sigh. 'I am truly ashamed to have had any part of it.'

Rosina gave him a searching look. 'I suppose I must believe you, but you seem to have an ulterior motive for everything you do, Jack. Now I need to find a servant and have the chaise brought to the front entrance.'

'I'll do that, Rosie. It's the least I can do to help. I'm leaving now as well, but I'll call in on you and your grandmother in a day or two to make sure you are both all right.'

'Thank you, but that won't be necessary. I think Grandmama and I are better off on our own.' Rosina walked off with as much dignity as she could muster. She felt angry, sad and bruised, as if she had been tossed from a horse, but it was more for her grandmother's sake than her own. She could only imagine how Grandmama must be feeling after a lifetime of devotion to a man who had destroyed her reputation and left her to struggle on her own to raise his child. Rosina clenched her fists so hard as she ascended the stairs that when she looked down at her palms there were small semicircular bleeding cuts.

Rosina and Jane left Glazewood Hall half an hour later and set off for home. The sun was shining from a cloudless sky, and the moor was in a more forgiving mood than it had been the previous day. Rosina took the reins with much more confidence this time and they reached Moonshadow Manor without further incident. Jane had said little during the drive, but as Rosina drew Pixie to a halt in the stable yard Jane sat very still.

'I don't think I can continue with my old life, Rosina,' she said, sighing. 'This house holds so many memories.'

Rosina handed the reins to Joshua, who had come running from the coach house.

'Will you be needing the chaise again today, miss?' Joshua asked warily.

'I don't think so, thank you.' Rosina alighted nimbly and went to assist Jane, who was staring straight ahead as if in a trance.

Merry hurried up to them, eyeing Jane curiously. 'Is the mistress unwell?'

Rosina shook her head. 'She's a little tired, I think. Come on, Aunt Jane, allow us to help you to the ground. Joshua needs to take care of Pixie.'

Unprotesting, Jane allowed them to assist her.

'I'll take Miss Jane to her room, Merry. Would you be kind enough to make a pot of tea? I think perhaps a tot of brandy in my aunt's cup might be beneficial.'

'Yes, miss. Right away.' Merry picked up her skirts and raced back into the house, leaving Rosina to help Jane across the cobbled yard.

'He doesn't care what happens to me,' Jane said in a low voice. 'All these years I've wasted, waiting and hoping, and it's all been for nothing. I wish I had died when I pretended to be ill.'

'You're upset, quite naturally. I would be in similar circumstances, and you're exhausted. I'm taking you to your room and I'll send for Dr Clarke. Maybe he can give you something to make things a little easier.'

'I don't want to rely on laudanum to keep me from fretting,' Jane said angrily. 'I need to suffer for being such a fool.'

They had reached the scullery door and Rosina pushed it open with her booted foot.

'You are not a fool. The only stupidly ignorant person in this sorry tale is Sir Bertram. I hope he suffers when he realises that he has lost you for ever.' Rosina looped Jane's arm around her shoulders and guided her through the maze of passages to the front hall, and up the stairs to Jane's bedroom.

Merry had thought to light a fire, which was welcome as it was still chilly outside, despite the spring sunshine. Jane allowed Rosina to help her into a clean nightgown, and she sat in bed to sip the tea that Merry brought to her.

Rosina plumped up the pillows. 'Lie back and get some rest, Aunt Jane. Ring the bell if you need anything and one of us will come straight away.'

'Thank you, dear.' Jane lay back and closed her eyes.

'I'll come and check on you in an hour or so, anyway,' Rosina said softly. She followed Merry from the room and closed the door.

'I don't think I've ever seen the mistress in such a state.' Merry stopped at the head of the stairs and turned to Rosina, frowning. 'What happened to upset her so?'

'It was a private matter, Merry. I can't give you any details, but I think we ought to send for Dr Clarke. Would you ask Joshua to take a message to him?'

'Yes, miss. Of course.' Merry went on ahead, leaving Rosina to go downstairs more slowly. She was at a loss as to how best to treat her grandmother in the circumstances, but Dr Clarke was an old friend, and he had been Jane's confidant over the years. He might be able to offer some sound advice.

* * *

Dr Clarke entered the morning parlour where Rosina had been waiting patiently while he examined her grandmother.

'Well, Doctor, what do you think? I'm at a loss as to how to deal with this.'

Dr Clarke placed his leather medical bag on a chair and went to stand by the fire.

'It's a delicate situation, Rosina. I can deal with broken bones, but broken hearts are another matter, and much more difficult to heal.'

'You were prepared to go along with her preposterous plan to feign death. You must have some idea as to how I could help her through this. Please take a seat, Dr Clarke. May I send for some tea, or something stronger, perhaps?'

He drew up a chair and sat down, shaking his head. 'I don't want anything, thank you, Rosina. As to your grandmother's condition, I think you will simply have to be patient with her. I will give you a bottle of laudanum, but use it sparingly, or she will grow dependent on it. You aren't thinking of returning to London in the near future, are you?'

'No, certainly not, Doctor. I wouldn't dream of leaving Grandmama at such a time. For one thing, she has little money, and I will need to have another go at selling in the market.'

Dr Clarke smiled. 'I heard about that, Rosina. It was a brave move on your part, but I gather you had some help from Lizzie Kettle. She is an old patient of mine.'

'I couldn't have managed without her, but I think I've learned from an expert, and I will have better success this time.'

'Sir Bertram should offer Jane some financial compensation. After all, the man has taken advantage of her good nature all these years. It grieves me to see her cast aside because he has political aspirations.'

Rosina eyed him curiously. It dawned on her that perhaps Dr Clarke had always been a little in love with Jane Maddern, even if he had not acknowledged his feelings. She was about to reply but he was already back on his feet.

'I have another patient I need to see, so I must take my leave of you, Rosina, but I promise to return tomorrow. In the meantime, try to persuade your grandmother to eat something when she wakes up. Also, please keep the laudanum bottle in your care. I have had patients who were far too generous in their use of the drug, with disastrous results.'

'Don't worry, Dr Clarke. I will keep it safe and make sure she has it only when absolutely necessary.' Rosina stood up, holding out her hand. 'Thank you for coming so promptly.'

'Good day, my dear. I am so glad you are here with Jane. She needs you even more now.' Dr Clarke left the room, snatching up his medical bag as he went.

Rosina sat down again, staring into the fire, as she mulled over the events of the past twenty-four hours.

But, ever practical, she got to her feet and went in search of suitable items for her next stall in Ivybridge market. As she investigated the low-ceilinged attics, she found a thick coating of dust on everything. However, there were many articles that would be saleable, if cleaned, and with this in mind she went downstairs to the kitchen to find Merry.

'What did the doctor say, miss?' Merry asked eagerly.

'He's given me laudanum to use sparingly, but he said that we must be patient. My aunt needs rest, and she must not be bothered with anything trivial.'

Merry stopped cutting up carrots to give Rosina a straight look. 'It's that Sir Bertram, isn't it, miss? He was always here on one pretence or another. It's been said in the village that he was Miss Alice's father, although I don't pass on gossip.'

Rosina stifled a gasp of dismay. 'Who says such things, Merry?'

'Nearly everyone, miss. It's common knowledge in Ugstock, but we keep it to ourselves. It don't get spread to the other villages. It's our business and we look after our own.'

'I'm glad to hear it,' Rosina said carefully. 'Spreading rumours can cause such a lot of unnecessary heartache.'

'Precisely so, miss.'

'I know I can trust you not to tell anyone in the village about my aunt's condition, Merry.'

'My lips are sealed, and so are Joshua's. We're Moonshadow people now, like Roxanne was all those years ago.'

Rosina stared at her in surprise. 'Why does Roxanne's name keep cropping up? What did she do that turned her into a legend?'

'They say she was a witch,' Merry said eagerly. 'She was very beautiful, and she had Jabez Dimond mad with desire for her, but she disappeared for nearly a year, and when she came back to Ugstock it was Phillip Maddern who wed her. Some say she only married him because he had won Moonshadow from Jabez.'

'So Phillip Maddern gained both Moonshadow Manor and the woman Jabez loved? Is that right?'

'That's how the story goes. Jabez Dimond lost Roxanne, and he forfeited Moonshadow Manor into the bargain.' Merry sighed. 'I've always felt a bit sorry for Mr Jabez. They say he was a smuggler and wanted by the revenue men, but I dare say most of the people in the village and further down along the coast were involved in one way or another.'

'What happened to Jabez, Merry? He obviously married and had children. Did he have a happy life?'

Merry shook her head. 'He married Lily Philbrick, an heiress, but they only had one child, Nathaniel. He was born with a club foot and everyone in the village said that Roxanne was jealous and had put a curse on Lily.'

'Why would Roxanne do that? She obviously wanted Phillip Maddern and not Jabez.'

'Roxanne might not have wanted to marry Jabez, but that didn't stop her being jealous of Lily. Then Jabez died when Nathaniel was a baby.'

Rosina laughed. 'It all sounds like a story from a penny dreadful. Poor Nathaniel, with the club foot, but that was unlikely to have been caused by a curse.'

'You can laugh, miss. But I'd be careful if I was you. They say that Roxanne's ghost still wanders the moor. She don't like being mocked.'

Rosina could see that Merry was serious. 'Yes, of course. I'll be sure to remember that. We don't really have such tales in London, so you'll have to forgive me if I find it a little hard to believe.'

'Believe what you will, miss. But Roxanne is out there, somewhere, along with the pixies and the souls who perished on the moor. It's my belief that she has put a curse on Miss Jane and that is why she is in such a state now. Something has disturbed Roxanne. Who knows what will happen next?'

Chapter Twelve

Next morning, after a quiet night, Rosina was busy packing the last of the saleable items she had found in the attics when Merry rushed into the parlour.

'Sir Bertram's carriage has pulled into the stable yard, miss. I didn't stop to see who's in it.'

Rosina dropped the ornament she had been about to pack and hurried after Merry as she made her way back to the kitchen. She opened the scullery door just as Sir Bertram alighted from the carriage followed by Grace.

'I'll put the kettle on,' Merry said, backing into the kitchen.

Rosina stepped outside, eyeing Sir Bertram warily.

'This is a surprise, sir. I wasn't expecting to see either of you again.'

Grace pushed past her father. 'I persuaded Papa to

come, Rosina. I think he has something he wants to say to Aunt Jane.'

'I can speak for myself, Grace,' Sir Bertram said stiffly. 'Your visit to my home did not end well, Rosina, and for that I apologise.'

'It is not I to whom you should be addressing your apologies, Sir Bertram.' Rosina drew herself up to her full height. 'My grandmother is too unwell to see you at present, so I'm afraid you have had a wasted journey.'

'Please don't send us away so quickly.' Grace took Rosina's hands in a firm clasp. 'I understand how you must be feeling, but surely it should be Aunt Jane who decides whether or not to hear my father out?'

'You had better come inside. I will tell my grandmother that you have come to see her. The decision is hers.' Rosina turned on her heel and headed into the house. She led the way to the morning parlour and opened the door. 'Please wait in here.'

Grace followed her father into the room, but she came to a halt at the sight of the boxes overflowing with a seemingly random selection of articles.

'Are you thinking of moving house?' Grace picked up a book, examined its cover, but replaced it quickly. 'I don't read much, myself.'

'What is the meaning of this?' Sir Bertram demanded angrily. 'I recognise some of those items.'

'If you must know, I am taking them to Ivybridge

on market day. My grandmother is rather short of funds, so I am renting a stall and hoping to sell all these things for a reasonable price. I did quite well last time.'

'Jane is in need of money?' Sir Bertram's shocked expression seemed genuine.

'How do you think she has managed all these years, Sir Bertram?' Rosina demanded angrily. 'I believe you helped her financially after my mother was born, but my grandmother has managed to support herself until fairly recently, so I gather.'

Sir Bertram sat down abruptly. 'Jane had only to ask. I have never begrudged her anything.'

'She has her pride, sir.' Rosina left the room, fighting down the desire to tell Sir Bertram exactly what she thought of him. But this was not the right time to start a bitter argument, and she hurried upstairs to her grandmother's room.

Jane was sitting up in bed with a cup of tea that Merry had just brought her.

'I thought Miss Jane might need it,' Merry explained as she brushed past Rosina on her way out of the room. 'Shall I make tea for the other two?'

'Not yet,' Rosina said tersely. 'I'm not sure how long they will be staying.'

'What is that about, Rosina?' Jane asked anxiously. 'Have we visitors?'

'Yes, Grandmama. Sir Bertram has just arrived, and he wants to speak to you. Grace is also here, although I'm not quite sure why she has come with her father. You don't have to speak to him if you don't wish to. I can send him away.'

Jane handed the cup and saucer to Rosina before flinging back the coverlet and sliding her legs cautiously over the side of the bed.

'I will see him. I didn't think I would ever be able to speak to him again after his betrayal, but I will hear him out.'

'You won't weaken, will you?' Rosina placed the teacup on a side table. 'I mean, he seems determined to pursue his career in politics, and it didn't sound as if it involved you. I'm sorry to be so blunt, but I don't want to see you hurt again.'

'What happened yesterday came as a terrible shock, Rosina. But over the past forty years I have developed a hard shell, and it has protected me from the worst of the innuendoes and gossip that have circulated around my name. I have done my grieving for what might have been, and it is Bertram who will be the ultimate loser.'

Rosina gave her a hug. 'I'm so proud of you, Grandmama. Let me help you to dress and we'll face him together.'

'No, my dear.' Jane shook her head. 'This is my problem, and I will deal with it. By all means help me to make myself presentable, and then I will speak to Bertram on my own.'

Rosina did not argue. She could see that her

grandmother was determined to deal with Sir Bertram, and there was no gainsaying her.

An hour later Grace and Rosina were in the drawing room, still waiting for the conversation between Jane and Sir Bertram to come to an end.

Grace paced the floor, stopping to finger the contents of one of the boxes that Rosina had packed with goods for sale.

'Do you really intend to set up a market stall again? You'll be happy being a common trader, Rosina?'

'It's not so bad, and I made enough money to keep us in necessities for a while,' Rosina said calmly. 'But that will run out before long.'

'I imagine it would be quite exciting. Perhaps I ought to help you, considering the part my family has played in your life already.' Grace picked up a pair of pot dogs and pulled a face. 'I can't imagine anyone wanting these hideous things.'

'You would be surprised.' Rosina took them from her and replaced them in the box. 'As to helping me on the stall, your cousin Ariadne tried to assist me last time, but she gave up quite soon. It is not for everyone.'

Grace tossed her head. 'I am made of stronger stuff than poor Ariadne. She is scared of her own shadow.'

'You are welcome to assist me if you wish,' Rosina said doubtfully. 'But you need to be in Ivybridge very early on Thursday morning.'

'Luke will drive me there. It's a good excuse for us to spend time alone.'

'Are you determined to continue your relationship with Luke, even though your papa will oppose it?'

'All the more so. Papa likes to rule everyone's life, but I have my own ideas. I watched my mother fade away because of the way in which he treated her. Now I understand the reason and it was because of your grandmother.'

'If you disapprove so much, what are you doing here today, Grace?' Rosina was growing tired of Grace's habit of turning the conversation back to herself at the slightest opportunity.

'Don't look so disapproving, Rosina. I came today to make sure that Papa was honest with Aunt Jane. Even though their relationship must have cost my mother much heartache, I do have some sympathy for my father in his predicament.' Grace turned away and went to open the door. 'I thought I heard voices. We're in here, Papa.'

Rosina hurried into the hallway but was relieved to see her grandmother apparently calm as she walked beside Sir Bertram.

'Come and sit down, Grandmama,' Rosina said firmly. She took Jane by the hand and led her to a chair by the fire.

'Well, Papa? Have you done as you promised?' Grace demanded, frowning.

'I don't have to answer to you, Grace. Whatever

your opinion of me I am still your father.' Sir Bertram eyed the decanters on a side table. 'Is there any brandy? I could do with a tot.'

Rosina glanced over her shoulder. 'There might be enough for one glass. We can't afford such luxuries, Sir Bertram.'

'If that's a hint for financial assistance, I have already settled an annuity on your grandmother, Rosina, which she will receive quarterly.'

Rosina turned back to Jane. 'You've been paid off?'

'I wouldn't put it quite like that,' Jane said hastily. 'Bertram and I have had a meaningful talk. We've decided that it's time to go our own separate ways, no matter how painful that might be, for me at least.'

'So, the villa on the Continent was a mere fantasy, was it?' Rosina fixed Sir Bertram with a penetrating stare.

He poured what was left in the decanter into a glass and took a sip. 'You might say that with some justification. In my present position I cannot afford to have any scandal attached to my name.'

'I suppose that must include me,' Rosina said coldly. 'The child of your illegitimate daughter would not fit with the image you wish to create amongst your voters.'

'Rosina, that's enough.' Jane raised a hand and then let it drop to her lap. 'Bertram and I have decided that it would be best for everyone if we were to keep things as they are. The scandal surrounding your mother's birth has been forgotten and your background is perfectly respectable.'

'That's all very well,' Rosina said slowly. 'But there are other family members to consider. What, for instance, am I to tell Hugo and Ariadne? They are Grace and her sisters' cousins, so they are related to me, too. Do I tell them or do I pretend ignorance?'

'Rosina has a point, Papa.' Grace emptied the last of the sherry into a glass and took a large mouthful. 'They are bound to find out. You know Hugo; I don't think he will take it lightly.'

Sir Bertram drained his glass and placed it back on the table. 'I don't see why they need to know. It isn't as if Rosina is going to be presented at Court. I'm sure we can trust her to keep our relationship a secret.' He shot a sideways glance in Rosina's direction. 'You have done well enough for yourself, my dear. After all, you will inherit Moonshadow Manor one day, which is more than most young women in your position could expect.'

Rosina kept her temper with difficulty. She faced Sir Bertram with a defiant lift of her chin. 'I knew nothing of you until I came to live with my grandmother, and I want nothing from you. I will keep your secret, but only for my grandmother's sake.'

'Well said.' Grace clapped her hands. 'You see, Papa. You cannot rule everyone as you have done with us at home. Anyway, I think it's time for us to leave now. I will see you at market on Thursday, Rosina.

I am happy for our kinship to be made public, even though I refuse to allow you to call me aunt.'

Rosina laughed. 'Don't worry, Grace. Nothing could be further from my mind. I will see you on market day but be early or it will all be over.'

'Goodbye, Bertram.' Jane tried to stand but sank back into the chair. 'I realise now what a gullible fool I've been. I just wish you had been more honest with me when you decided to go your own way. That is something I will find very hard to forgive.'

'I will always remember the happy times we have shared, my dear. But you knew my situation and I thought you had accepted it.' Sir Bertram cleared his throat nervously. 'I will miss you, Jane.'

'Really?' Jane raised an eyebrow. 'I'm afraid I don't believe you. I've wasted a lifetime listening to your promises, which you obviously never intended to keep. It's best if we don't meet again. Now kindly leave my house. You are no longer welcome here.'

Sir Bertram hesitated for a moment, but then he picked up his top hat and strode out of the drawing room.

Grace followed him to the door, but hesitated, turning to Rosina. 'I see no reason why we cannot be friends. We are blood relations, after all.'

'If you wish,' Rosina said warily.

'I do, and I always get my own way. Until market day, Rosina.' Grace left the room, closing the door firmly behind her.

Rosina stifled a sigh of relief. Surely the worst must be over now. Grandmama had borne the meeting with her ex-lover with fortitude, although only she knew what it had cost her to control her feelings to such an extent.

'Are you all right, Grandmama?' Rosina asked anxiously. 'I'm so sorry it has ended badly for you.'

Jane sighed. 'I think it was over a long time ago, but I would not admit it to myself. Bertram is an ambitious man, and he will no doubt do well in politics. He can be quite ruthless when he feels he needs to be.'

'As I have just witnessed. I just hope you are not too upset. You won't go into a decline again, will you? I really thought you were dying when I first came to Moonshadow.'

'No, my love. I will depart this world when my Maker decides it's time, but until then I intend to live my life with the aid of Bertram's annuity, which is quite substantial. More than I imagined he might give me. I assume it is to salve his conscience and to make sure I remain silent.'

'When can we access some of this money, Grandmama? Do I need to have a stall in the marketplace this week?

'Bertram told me that Jack Dimond is handling it, as previously. Have we enough to live on for now?'

'We are all right for a while, but don't worry, I quite enjoyed having the market stall. I'll get a message to Seth Tully. He's been very helpful, and I'll make an appointment to see Jack Dimond. We need to know exactly where we stand.'

After a quick meal at midday Rosina left her grandmother enjoying a nap. Joshua, at Rosina's request, had the chaise ready and she drove herself to Applegate Farm, where she had a word with Seth about a market stall. He was more than happy to oblige, and he confided in Rosina that he had hopes of getting together personally with Merry, who had proved evasive in the past. Rosina could not help thinking that Merry was exactly the sort of woman whom Seth's mother might be delighted to welcome as a daughter-in-law, although Merry seemed to have other ideas. However, Rosina decided, it was none of her business and she kept her opinions to herself.

Once again it was a lovely spring afternoon. It would not be dark for several hours, and on the spur-of-the-moment, Rosina set off to drive to Ivybridge. She needed to speak to Jack about the annuity and find out when they might expect the first payment. She had half expected him to call, if only to enquire how her grandmother was faring after their visit to Glazewood Hall, but there had been no sign of him. She flicked the reins and with renewed confidence set off in the direction of town.

Pixie trotted on, needing very little guidance as he obviously remembered the way, and Rosina was able to enjoy the view of cows grazing on the fresh green grass, the trees with their tightly furled buds ready to burst into leaf, and the bustling new life in the hedgerows. Catkins waved in the breeze and overhead a skylark warbled its melodious song. Despite the upheaval at Moonshadow and her grandmother's heartache, Rosina had a feeling that all would be well. As a born-and-bred city girl, Rosina had not found adjusting to life in the countryside easy, but she was warming to a rural existence. She might even begin to enjoy living on the edge of the mysterious moor with its legends, ghosts and fairy stories.

When Rosina drew Pixie to a halt outside Jack's house, she was lucky enough to spot a boy idling on the street corner and he was eager to earn tuppence for taking care of Pixie.

Mrs Tarr opened the door, and her serious expression was replaced with a smile of welcome.

'Miss Wills, this is a pleasant surprise.'

'Good afternoon, Mrs Tarr,' Rosina said, smiling. 'I haven't booked an appointment with Mr Dimond, but I wonder if he would see me?'

'You're fortunate that he's just arrived home, miss. Come inside and I'll let him know that you're here.' Mrs Tarr ushered Rosina into the parlour. 'I'll be two shakes of a lamb's tail, as my late mama used to say.'

Rosina went to look out of the window, checking on the boy, but she need not have worried. He was stroking Pixie's nose, and they seemed to have struck up a rapport, which was a relief. She turned at the sound of the door opening and was expecting to see Mrs Tarr, but Jack strolled into the room.

'Rosie! This is a nice surprise.'

'I'm sorry to turn up without an appointment,' Rosina said cautiously. His smile seemed genuine enough, but she never knew when Jack was being serious. His somewhat capricious attitude to life was quite different from that of most people she had known.

'Nonsense, you are welcome at any time. Although, I am often out on business, so it is a matter of taking a chance on my being at home. However, here I am and here you are. I really am pleased to see you, especially after the unfortunate incident at Glazewood Hall. How is your grandmother?'

'She is better than I would have expected. Sir Bertram and Grace called at Moonshadow this morning. He came to apologise, although I'm not sure of his motive. Perhaps he hoped he might continue his relationship with my grandmother.'

'That seems unlikely in the circumstances. I hope Jane threw him out.' Jack's slanting eyebrows drew together in an ominous frown. 'I think he behaved abominably to the woman he professed to love.'

'I thought you were on his side, Jack?' Rosina

gazed at him in surprise. 'You seemed very much at home with Sir Bertram and his family.'

'I'm paid to be polite to clients,' Jack said curtly. 'Sir Bertram is a man driven by ambition. He tramples on everyone who gets in his way. I'm sorry to be so blunt, Rosie. I know he's your grandfather, but you must have seen through him.'

Rosina nodded. 'I had come to that conclusion on my own. I like Grace, but I don't see us becoming close friends. Our stations in life are so different.'

'I agree entirely. Grace Charteris is charming but spoiled. She will use you when she has a mind to and then she will drop you when she is bored. My advice, if needed, would be to keep her at arm's length.' Jack was about to tug at the bell pull when the door opened, and Mrs Tarr entered carrying a tray of tea and cakes.

'I know you didn't ask for this, sir, but I thought Miss Wills looked a little peaky, and it's a long drive back to Moonshadow Manor.'

'Thank you, Mrs Tarr.' Jack took the tray from her and placed it on a side table close to Rosina. 'That's very thoughtful.'

Mrs Tarr gave him a smile that Rosina decided she kept especially for him. 'Ring the bell if you need anything else, sir,' she said, before leaving the room.

'You have a treasure there, Jack,' Rosina said, smiling. 'She is your devoted servant.'

'I rely on Mrs Tarr entirely. She is more like a

mother to me than a mere housekeeper.' Jack picked up the teapot and filled two cups. 'I'll leave you to add the milk. I either pour too much or too little.' He handed a cup to Rosina.

'Thank you, Jack.' Rosina added a dash of milk. 'I expect you're wondering why I came here today.'

'I was hoping it was my undeniable charm and intelligent company you were seeking.'

'Well, that, too. Actually, it was something that Sir Bertram said this morning. I don't know if he was trying to make things right with my grandmother, or whether he simply wanted to look good, but he said he had arranged an annuity for her, which would be paid quarterly by you.'

'That is true. He spoke to me about it yesterday. I think he was suffering from an attack of conscience because it will enable you both to live quite comfortably, although not in any lavish style. You'll receive the first payment at the beginning of next month.' Jack added milk to his tea and sipped it, gazing at Rosina as if assessing her reaction to the news.

'I will consider it as dues earned by my grandmother,' Rosina said firmly. 'I intend to support myself, as far as possible.'

'I assume you intend to repeat your attempt to make money in the market.'

There was no hint of mockery in Jack's eyes or in the tone of his voice, which surprised Rosina.

'I won't make a fortune, but I can earn my keep,' she said defensively. 'My grandmother knows what I'm doing and she approves.'

'Shall I alert Lizzie Kettle? I'm sure she would be only too pleased to assist you.'

'Not this time, Jack. I intend to do it all by myself.'

'There is certainly a lifetime of odds and ends at Moonshadow Manor. I never knew why Jane didn't simply throw them out or give them away.' Jack selected a small cake and bit into it. 'Do try one of these. They're quite delicious.' He proffered the plate to Rosina, and she took one, if only to please him. However, when she tasted it, she had to agree.

'Mrs Tarr could set up a bakery, and she would sell out every day.'

Jack laughed. 'Please don't tell her that. She might think it would be better than slaving away for a bachelor like me.'

'I won't say a word.' Rosina brushed cake crumbs from her lips. She replaced her cup and saucer on the tray. 'I'd better be going, Jack. It's a long drive home and I don't want to get caught out in the darkness again. It was quite frightening when Grandmama and I were surrounded by mist on the moor. It came down so suddenly.'

'The moor needs to be treated with caution at all times. I was planning on driving over to Moonshadow Manor in the morning. I need to speak to Jane in person about the annuity.'

Rosina stood up. 'Are you still hoping to find documents to prove you own Moonshadow? You only told me half the tale.'

'If you will grace my table by having luncheon with me after the market closes on Thursday, I will tell you everything. I believe I can trust you to keep a secret.'

'I can't wait,' Rosina said, smiling. 'Until Thursday then.'

Jack rose to his feet, leaving his teacup and saucer on the mantelshelf. He opened the door and ushered Rosina into the hallway. 'If you are nervous driving back to Ugstock on your own I could have my horse saddled and ride with you.'

Rosina stared at him in amazement. 'No, but thank you for the offer. Sometimes you are quite human, Jack.'

He laughed. 'I suppose I must take that as a compliment, Rosie.' Jack opened the front door and stepped out, calling to the boy who was keeping watch on Pixie and the chaise.

The drive home was unexceptional, and it was still daylight when Pixie trotted into the stable yard. Rosina handed the reins to Joshua, who as always was quick to run out to greet her.

'You have visitors, miss,' he said, jerking his head in the direction of the house. 'Sir Hugo Charteris and Miss Ariadne arrived not half an hour ago.'

Rosina was feeling quite exhausted after the events

of that morning and the drive to and from Ivybridge. No doubt she would become accustomed to handling the reins, but it was still a novel experience and took all her concentration. She had hoped for a quiet cup of tea and a rest, but it was not to be.

'Thank you, Joshua.' She crossed the yard and entered the house through the scullery.

Merry was in the kitchen kneading bread dough as if it were her worst enemy. She brushed a strand of hair back from her forehead.

'I hope they don't want to eat with us, miss. There's barely enough for Miss Jane, you, me and Joshua, let alone Miss Ariadne and Sir Hugo.'

'I'm sure they won't be expecting to be fed,' Rosina said hastily. 'They turned up unexpectedly, so they are not likely to stay long.'

'You never know with people.' Merry gave the dough a last smack before placing it in a bowl and covering it with a damp cloth. 'I need to get some groceries from Uncle Fred tomorrow, miss. Can we afford to pay for them?'

'I'll make sure I do well at market, Merry. You may tell Mr Pavey that our account will be settled on Friday.' Rosina left the kitchen, taking off her gloves, bonnet and mantle, which she draped over a hall chair before entering the drawing room. She had no idea why Sir Hugo and Ariadne had called, but she crossed her fingers nervously, hoping that there was not going to be another inquisition.

Sir Hugo was standing with his back to the fire while Ariadne perched on the window seat and Jane was seated in her usual chair.

'There you are, Rosina, dear,' Jane said with obvious relief. 'I was beginning to get worried.'

'I had business in Ivybridge, Aunt.' Rosina acknowledged Hugo with a nod. 'I might have missed you had I been any later.'

'Don't play the innocent, Rosina,' Hugo said coldly. 'Grace called on us this morning. She told us the shocking truth, which you and Miss Maddern kept from us.'

Ariadne slid off the window seat and rushed over to clutch Rosina's hand.

'It was such a surprise to find out that we are related. I, for one, am delighted. I'm afraid Hugo was not so pleased with the news.'

'I don't see what it has to do with Hugo,' Rosina said stiffly. 'I had no knowledge of the affair when I came down from London. My late mother never thought to burden me with the knowledge that she was Sir Bertram's illegitimate daughter, and Aunt Jane, or should I say, Grandmama, has kept the secret all her adult life.'

'I am so sorry.' Ariadne raised Rosina's hand to her cheek and her eyes filled with tears. 'How awful for you.'

'Don't be so sentimental, Ariadne,' Hugo snapped. 'Control yourself or we'll go home right away.'

'Why are you so nasty to your sister?' Rosina demanded angrily. 'She is being sympathetic, which is more than anyone could say for you, sir. I didn't choose to be your cousin, or second cousin or whatever relation I am to you. I dare say it doesn't count as it was on the wrong side of the blanket, as we common people might say.'

Jane held up her hand. 'Stop this at once. Hugo, you are being insufferable as usual. I am the person whom you should be castigating, although I cannot see that my relationship with your uncle Bertram is any business of yours.'

'The family name is besmirched, Miss Maddern.' Hugo's handsome features reddened, and a vein throbbed in his neck. 'Or rather it will be if this gets out. I think I have a right to be angry.'

'Then direct your ire at me,' Jane said simply. 'I loved your uncle, and I gave my whole life to protecting him from scandal. We have, however, come to a mutual agreement that the affair has come to an end. If you choose to make it public that will be up to you. As far as I am concerned it is over and done with.'

Ariadne released Rosina's hand and went to kneel in front of Jane. 'Miss Maddern, you have my sympathy and my admiration for your selfless bravery. I wish I had as much courage as you.'

'Get up, Ariadne. You're making a spectacle of yourself, as usual.' Sir Hugo raised her to her feet. 'We will leave now, and I doubt very much if we will return to Moonshadow Manor. It was always said to be cursed and now I believe that to be true.'

Ariadne sent a beseeching look to Rosina as her brother propelled her from the room.

'I hope to see you again, Rosina.' Ariadne's voice faded away as Hugo slammed the door.

Rosina shook her head. 'To think I thought he was the perfect gentleman. It just shows how wrong you can be.'

'He was always a pompous child,' Jane said, sighing. 'He takes after his father, Harold, who was Bertram's younger brother. They did not get on well together.'

'It seems to me that the whole family spends their time fighting each other,' Rosina said sadly. 'I'm not sure I want to be related to any of them. Grace is nice enough, but she is rather spoiled, and Ariadne needs to stand up for herself.'

'I agree, which is why I have kept to myself all these years. I still love Bertram, but it was the old Bertram I fell in love with. The person he is now is almost unknown to me, but I wish him well in his political career.'

'I don't know how you can be so forgiving, Grandmama.'

Jane laughed. 'No, dear. I am rather surprised myself. I suppose I have had to be so independent and self-reliant that I have built a protective shell around my heart. Thank goodness I have you, Rosina.'

'And Dr Clarke,' Rosina said mischievously. 'He is your devoted slave, Grandmama.'

'Really?' Jane shrugged. 'Yes, I suppose he is. Dear Albert, what would I have done without him. Anyway, dear, why did you go to Ivybridge? Was it to see Jack Dimond?'

'Yes, it was. He is coming here tomorrow morning to give you all the information about the annuity. He told me that it is quite generous.'

'I suppose Bertram is pensioning me off, like an old retainer.' Jane pulled a face. 'Then I will enjoy the freedom it gives me, Rosina. You and I will live comfortably off it.'

'You will have the benefit of the money, Grandmama,' Rosina said firmly. 'I intend to earn my living. I'm not qualified to do anything, but I rather enjoyed selling goods in the market. I wouldn't mind having a nice little shop in town, although I'm not sure what I would stock.'

'You intend to go into trade?' Jane smiled. 'That would upset Hugo even more. I think you should do it, Rosina. The Charteris family is in need of shaking up, and you are the right person to do just that.'

Chapter Thirteen

Market day dawned cloudy but mild and Rosina experienced a sense of excitement as she waited for Seth to bring his farm cart to the stable yard. It was still very early and Merry had only just lit the fire in the range, which meant that there would be no time for breakfast. Rosina buttered a slice of bread and ate it while she loaded her items for sale onto the straw-lined bed of the cart. Seth was a willing helper, but Rosina suspected that his main interest was Merry, who continued to treat him with casual disdain. However, this only seemed to serve to make him even more determined to win her favour. They set off in good time with Seth driving his vehicle and Rosina riding Pixie.

Seth had managed to acquire the same pitch as before and Rosina found it much easier to set up this time. Not only had she cleared the attics, but she had gone through the various cupboards in the kitchen and the utility rooms, where she had found several pieces of porcelain that were in good condition, although they appeared to be very old. There was a mantel clock and a couple of rather dull etchings. Rosina did not hold out much hope for a sale for the latter, but they added a contrast to the more mundane articles.

She had just finished setting up the stall when she saw Grace alighting from a chaise driven by Luke. It had been dark when Rosina had seen him briefly for the first time, but she recognised the shock of fair hair visible beneath his cap, and the athletic build as he handled the reins. He was a good-looking young man, and it was easy to see why Grace would be attracted to him. Rosina braced herself for another encounter with her aunt. However, Grace seemed to have forgotten the strained atmosphere of their last meeting, and she made her way through the gathering crowd with arms outstretched.

'Rosina, that looks wonderful. You are so clever.' Grace enveloped Rosina in a friendly hug. 'I simply had to come and help you.'

'I'm not sure there is much for you to do,' Rosina said doubtfully. 'But it was good of you to think of me.'

'We are family, after all.' Grace selected a straw bonnet from the stall. 'This is quaint. I suppose Miss

THE WILD ROSE

Maddern must have worn it when she was tending her cattle on the moor.'

'I really couldn't say. I only saw her on rare occasions when I was growing up.'

'And yet you are so close now.' Grace put her head on one side. 'Would inheriting Moonshadow Manor have anything to do with that?'

'Of course not. How can you say such a thing?' Rosina met Grace's knowing smile with a frown. 'I came because I was invited by Grandmama.'

Grace shrugged. 'Perhaps it would be best to refer to her as "Aunt Jane" in public. You know how people gossip.'

'Exactly why did you come here today, Grace?' Rosina demanded crossly. 'Was it to lecture me, or to spy on me so that you could tell your father that I am disgracing the family by going into trade?'

Grace took a step backwards. 'No, of course not. How could you think such a thing of me? I came to help you, but I can see that you neither need nor want me.'

'I'm sorry. I didn't mean to upset you, but you must admit that things are not easy between our families. My grandmother says she accepts the situation, but I still think your father behaved abominably towards her.'

'I agree with you. I think Papa behaved abominably to both my mother and Miss Maddern, and that is my honest opinion.' Grace turned to Luke and

231

waved. 'Isn't he handsome, Rosina? You must agree that he is a fine figure of a man.'

Rosina nodded, torn between irritation and amusement. 'Yes, Luke is a good-looking fellow. But perhaps you need to be a bit careful, Grace. I mean, your father is never going to allow you to be with Luke in any permanent relationship.'

'Papa will come round eventually, especially when he sees how much I love Luke, and how he adores me,' Grace said confidently. 'I am not afraid to stand up for myself, Rosina.'

'I doubt if your father would wish one of his daughters to associate with a servant. It seems to me that he puts his political career above everything.'

'Things change,' Grace said airily. 'I know what you're saying, Rosina, but I won't think about that now. As a matter of fact, if you really don't need my help I will spend some time with Luke. He has permission from the head groom to stay with me as long as necessary, so that means a whole day as far as I am concerned.'

Grace turned away as a woman asked the price on a woollen muffler. She handed over the coins, grinning widely, which made Rosina think she had not charged enough for the item. However, that was threepence in her pocket and the first sale of the day. She turned to speak to Grace again, but she was already on her way back to the chaise. Luke jumped to the ground and lifted her off her feet. He kissed her on the lips before swinging her into the vehicle and climbing up beside her. Grace waved to Rosina as they drove off.

'Abandoned you, has she, love?'

Rosina turned with a start and found Lizzie Kettle standing behind her. 'I'm sorry? I don't know what you mean, ma'am.'

'It's Miss Kettle, my duck. I was talking about that la-di-da flibbertigibbet. She thinks she's above us peasants.' Lizzie snorted and wiped her nose on her sleeve. 'She ain't your friend, dearie.'

'Is there anything I can help you with, Miss Kettle?' Rosina asked cautiously. 'Are you interested in purchasing something?'

'Lor' love you, girl. I come to offer me services, not spend me hard-earned money. Do you want me help or not?' Lizzie stood, arms akimbo, waiting for an answer.

'Could you shout out as you did last week?' Rosina looked round at the market-goers, most of whom were only giving her stall a cursory glance.

Lizzie slapped her on the back. 'Leave it to me, ducks. I got a voice what carries. Got me training in Spitalfields Market up London way, when I was a nipper.'

'I thought you must be a Londoner,' Rosina said, smiling. 'I used to live in Islington. Please do your best, Lizzie.'

Rosina stepped aside as Lizzie puffed out her

chest and took a deep breath. The sound that emanated from her vocal cords was loud and clear and certainly had the desired effect. People began milling round the stall, encouraged by Lizzie, who clearly had a way with people. Either that, or taking in her impressive size and raucous voice, they were scared of what she might do or say if they did not cooperate.

The morning passed quickly and most of the clothing had been snapped up, leaving a pile of books, the mantel clock and the etchings. Rosina was considering selling them off at ridiculously low prices when a well-dressed gentleman stopped by the stall. He picked up the clock and examined it closely, repeating the process with the two etchings.

'How much are you asking, miss?' He replaced the items. 'I'll offer sixpence for the lot.'

'Take it, miss,' Lizzie said in a low voice. 'A tanner is better than nothing. We've sold out then.'

Rosina knew instinctively that the three items were worth more than sixpence, but the gentleman looked as if he knew a bargain when he saw one. She was about to accept when Jack strolled over to join them. Rosina had noted his arrival in the marketplace earlier, but she had been too busy to acknowledge his presence.

'Good morning, Wingate,' Jack said pleasantly. 'You always did have an eye for a bargain. I see nothing has changed.'

Wingate eyed him warily. 'Don't interfere, Jack. This has nothing to do with you.' He fixed Rosina with a hard stare. 'Sixpence, miss. Not a penny more.'

'Come now, old chap,' Jack said, smiling. 'The young lady is just trying to make a living. If you want the items, I suggest you make a realistic offer.'

'I'm asking a shilling for the clock.' Rosina met Wingate's gaze with a steady look. 'And the etchings were done by a famous artist. I think half a crown each is reasonable.'

'Bah! Daylight robbery.' Wingate's fleshy features reddened angrily.

'Come on, old fellow,' Jack said amicably. 'You know they are worth more than that.'

'I don't know what your connection is with regard to this young woman, but I would be grateful if you would mind your own business, Jack.' Wingate took a deep breath. 'I'll give you a crown for all three and not a penny more.'

Rosina held out her hand. 'Five shillings it is, sir.'

'I'll wrap them for you, mister.' Lizzie grabbed a sheet of newspaper, but Wingate shook his head.

'No, thank you. I don't want printing ink over everything. I'll take them as they are.' He took a silver crown from his inside pocket and placed it in Rosina's outstretched hand. 'Good day to you, Jack.' Wingate snatched up his purchases and strode off towards a waiting carriage.

'How do you know that man?' Rosina demanded, glaring at Jack. 'Why did you intervene?'

'I know him through business. He's a dealer in antiques, which apparently are becoming quite a profitable line of business. He spotted the value of those items, and he would have cheated you had I not realised what he was doing.'

'You're so clever, Jack,' Lizzie said, fluttering her eyelashes. 'I love a man with brains, particularly if he's handsome as well.'

Jack laughed. 'You're a flatterer, Lizzie.'

'I know, and it works most of the time. But you're not an easy mark, Jack Dimond. I'll be on me way, then.' Lizzie held her hand out to Rosina. 'We done well enough this morning, miss. I'm sure you're grateful.'

Rosina placed some coins in Lizzie's hand. 'I am, indeed. Thank you, Lizzie. I couldn't have managed without you.'

'Don't spend it all in the pub,' Jack said as Lizzie's fingers closed over the money.

'I'll have you know I'm a lady, Jack.' Lizzie tossed her head. 'Ladies don't frequent such places, unless a gent decides to treat them to a nip or two.'

'I'll bear that in mind, thank you, Lizzie.' Jack waited until she sashayed away. 'I believe we have a luncheon arrangement today, Rosie.'

She nodded. 'I think we do, Jack.'

He proffered his arm. 'Allow me to escort you to your mount.'

'I think I can find Pixie without assistance.'

'And you are carrying a purse filled with your takings.' Jack glanced over his shoulder. 'There are persons loitering in this marketplace who would gladly relieve you of your hard-earned cash.'

A shiver ran down Rosina's spine as she followed his glance. It was true, there were ill-clad individuals, both male and female, who were standing around as if waiting for the chance to pick a pocket or steal a purse. She tucked her hand in the crook of Jack's arm.

'Thank you, Jack. I'm looking forward to Mrs Tarr's cooking. Merry is coming along nicely but she's unlikely to come up to Mrs Tarr's standards.'

'Tell Mrs Tarr that and you'll have a friend for life, and probably as much cake as you can ever eat.'

There was little chance of continuing the conversation as the market square was crowded and it took time to make their way to the spot where the horses were tethered. Jack helped Rosina onto Pixie's saddle before mounting his horse.

'Keep close to me, Rosie. Market day attracts all sorts and not all of them are trustworthy. Ride on.'

Luncheon was as good, if not better, than Rosina had anticipated. Mrs Tarr had outdone herself with a steak and kidney pudding, buttered cabbage and roast potatoes. The dessert of pears stewed in red wine with cinnamon and sugar was also delicious. Rosina was a little disappointed that treacle tart was not on the menu, but she refrained from saying anything. Conversation had been general during the meal, but afterwards, when Rosina and Jack adjourned to the front parlour for coffee, it was obvious that Jack had something on his mind.

'What is it that you are not telling me, Jack?' Rosina eyed him curiously. 'I know there's something.'

'How are you off financially, Rosie?' Jack took a seat opposite her. 'I mean, do you get any allowance from your father?'

'No, not a penny. He needs all his money to support his new family. I am perfectly willing to work, Jack.'

'You must have sold just about everything that Jane collected over the years.'

'Yes, it's all been sorted and, surprisingly, people have bought the items. I need to find something else to do. Grandmama's money won't keep us both.'

'It could, with care, but perhaps you need more independence, just in case she decides to do something unpredictable.' Jack drained his cup and placed it back on its saucer. 'After the life she has led I wouldn't be surprised if Jane Maddern suddenly decided to kick over the traces.'

'Grandmama?' Rosina stared at him in disbelief. 'What makes you say that?'

'Jane has been a prisoner of love for over forty years. She gave up everything to raise her child on her own and to my knowledge has never asked anything of anyone. Now she is free. What might you do in similar circumstances?'

Rosina laughed. 'Maybe run away and join a circus? I don't know, Jack. I hadn't thought about it like that.'

'I'm just saying that perhaps you need to consider carefully how you are going to manage if it did happen.'

'I don't imagine for a moment that Grandmama will do anything out of the ordinary, but I want to stand on my own two feet. That man, Wingate, the antique dealer, has given me an idea.'

'Go on,' Jack said warily. 'Tell me more.'

'I may be wrong, but I think I have an eye for quality, and there is money to be made selling good-quality items, like the clock and the etchings.'

'How would you go about that?' Jack leaned forward, eyeing her with renewed interest.

'I would go to house sales and buy things, which I would sell on.'

'You would keep the market stall? That would be an expense.'

Rosina frowned thoughtfully. 'You're right. Perhaps I would have a sale of my own at Moonshadow. There's the old barn where Grandmama kept the cattle in winter.'

'Ugstock is on the edge of Dartmoor, Rosie. How would you persuade people with enough money to buy your antiquities to travel all the way to Moonshadow?'

Rosina stood up and walked over to the window. 'I would advertise in the local newspaper, or perhaps in the *Illustrated London News* or some such magazine.'

'That would cost money, Rosie.' Jack shook his head.

Rosina shot him a sideways glance. 'You don't think I could do it, do you, Jack?'

'To be honest, I think it's an ambitious project, but I suppose you could start in a small way, to see if the market is there.'

'That is what I'm trying to tell you,' Rosina said impatiently. 'I would make use of what little money I have and spend it on items that I think might be saleable. If I use the barn I won't have any overhead expenses.'

'You're forgetting that Miss Maddern owns the property, Rosie. What do you think she would say to the idea?'

'I think she would be very enthusiastic. Grandmama kept Moonshadow going on her own for forty years. She managed and so can I.'

Jack rose to his feet. 'I admire your spirit.'

'You think I should give it a try?'

'I imagine you will do it whatever I have to say,' Jack said, laughing. 'I can see a likeness to your grandfather in you.' He held up his hand as Rosina opened her mouth to protest. 'Sir Bertram is a self-made man. He earned his fortune and his title by hard work.'

'I really know nothing about him, Jack.' Rosina stared at him in surprise. 'Are you saying that Sir Bertram made his money in trade?'

'He owns a granite quarry. A very profitable one, too.'

'That makes the way he has paid my grandmother off even more despicable,' Rosina said angrily. 'If he is so wealthy then the amount he has settled on Grandmama is paltry.'

'I agree, but he could simply have walked away. I'm not defending the man, but Miss Maddern has no legal hold over him.'

'Grandmama is better off without him. I'm ashamed to be related to such a person. That makes me all the more intent on earning my own living, Jack. I won't be beholden to someone like Sir Bertram, regardless of the fact that we are related by blood.'

'In that case, perhaps I can help you. There is a bankrupt sale at Grandtor House on Saturday. If you would like to go, I will bring the chaise to Moonshadow and pick you up after breakfast. We need to get there early so that you can look round and decide if you want to bid on anything. What do you say?'

'Thank you, Jack.' Rosina stared at him in

disbelief. 'That's a very generous offer. I won't have much to spend but it will be a start, and I might find some bargains.'

'I don't know why you look so surprised. I'm not an ogre, Rosie. I want you to succeed but I didn't want to give you false hopes.'

'I know what I'm doing. If I fail it's my fault, but I must try.'

'I understand that, and I'm prepared to lend you money to purchase your first stock, on a business level. You may repay me when you begin to make a profit.'

'You mean we'll be business partners?'

Jack laughed. 'If you want to put it that way, yes. Business partners.'

'I'll give it some thought, but I should leave now,' Rosina said firmly. 'I hadn't noticed the time but it's getting late.'

'I will ride with you.'

'I'm perfectly capable of finding my own way to Moonshadow, Jack. Thank you for the offer but I don't need an escort.'

'You have a pouch filled with money. Any number of villains might have spotted you leaving your stall. They might even have seen you last week and they know where you live. Humour me, Rosie. Let me see you safely home.'

'If you put it like that it would be mean-spirited of me to refuse. Thank you, Jack. I will accept your offer, but if I am to go into business, I think I will need a more permanent protector.'

Jack raised an eyebrow. 'Do you mean to get married?'

It was Rosina's turn to laugh. 'No, I intend to get myself a guard dog.'

When Rosina arrived back at Moonshadow she was surprised to see Dr Clarke's chaise in the stable yard with Joshua tending to the doctor's aged horse.

Rosina entered through the scullery and found Merry making tea in the kitchen.

'I see the doctor's vehicle is outside. Has Miss Jane been taken ill?' Rosina asked anxiously.

'No, miss. Dr Clarke came earlier, and they've been chatting away like a couple of magpies. I've been in and out of the room until I'm sick of hearing that blooming bell tinkling over my head.'

'I'll take the tea in to give you a rest,' Rosina said, giggling. 'It's not like Aunt Jane to be so demanding.'

'I think it's him, miss. Not that I have a bad word to say about the doctor, but gentlemen do seem to want a lot of looking after. First, he was thirsty after the long drive, then he was hungry, and then she wanted her afternoon tea and cake. Then, just as I was cleaning up, they want more tea. They must have talked their heads off in there. That's all I can say.'

Rosina took off her bonnet and mantle, which she hung on a peg behind the door. The tea tray was ready, and she picked it up and carried it to the drawing room. Sure enough, Dr Clarke and Jane were seated together on the sofa deep in conversation. They both looked up with a start when Rosina placed the tray on a low table.

'I didn't hear you come in.' Jane moved a little away from her companion. 'Thank you, dear, but you should have sent Merry in with the tea.'

'Good afternoon, Dr Clarke. I was a bit worried when I saw your chaise in the yard. I thought maybe it was a professional visit, and Merry is busy, Grandmama, so I offered to help.'

'It is a purely social call, Rosina,' Dr Clarke said hastily. 'I am keeping an eye on my patient after the shocking events concerning Sir Bertram. That man should be shot, in my opinion. He has made a fortune out of the labour of the men working for him in the quarry – at great cost to their own health and wellbeing, I might add – and he has treated your grandmother disgracefully.'

'Yes, I agree. I see that Merry has put out three cups so why don't you join us?'

'Thank you, I will.' Rosina filled each cup, added a dash of milk and passed them round. 'I am rather thirsty after the ride from Ivybridge. I sold out on the stall today, Grandmama, although I did have a little help from Lizzie Kettle.'

'Well done, but I don't like you having to work with common people. I don't know Miss Kettle personally, although I do remember her mother and she was a wild one. You are better than that.' Jane sipped her tea.

Rosina noticed that her grandmother's small fingers sought for the comfort of Dr Clarke's much larger hand as they sat side by side. Not for the first time Rosina wondered if there was something deeper than mere friendship going on between her grandmother and the doctor.

'Lizzie is an excellent salesperson, Grandmama. And she has a voice that would make any town crier proud. She can attract customers to the stall so much better than I ever could.'

'Her father was a drunkard,' Dr Clarke said mildly. 'Lizzie's mother had to cope with ten children and a useless husband. It's a wonder that any of the surviving children managed to make a decent living.'

'I dare say you helped the family.' Jane patted his free hand. 'I know you only too well, Albert. You would never charge the family for your services, or any other patients who had fallen on hard times, if it comes to that.'

Dr Clarke laughed. 'You make me sound like a saint, Jane. I am far from that.'

'Thank goodness,' Jane said, smiling. 'A saint would be very poor company, in my opinion, anyway. We have had some amusing times together, you and I.'

'And many more to come, I hope,' Rosina added earnestly. 'I think you have both suffered over the years.'

'I was devastated when Bertram told me that it was over between us,' Jane said slowly. 'I slept very little last night. I lay in my bed staring at Roxanne's portrait – such a beauty; no wonder Jabez Dimond and my father both loved her – and then the strangest thing happened.'

'She stepped out of the frame and spoke to you.' Dr Clarke smiled and raised Jane's hand to his lips. 'Poor Jane, you were obviously in a state.'

'That painting scares me at the best of times.' Rosina shivered. 'Maybe we should move it to another room, Grandmama.'

'Roxanne told me that life is short, and I should seek happiness for myself.' Jane shook her head. 'I don't know if Roxanne died as my father said, or whether she merely walked out onto the moor and never returned.'

'From what I heard, half the male population of Ugstock and Ivybridge were in love with Roxanne,' Dr Clarke said, frowning. 'Your papa had the good sense to pick a sensible woman the second time.'

'I don't remember Mama,' Jane said sadly. 'She died when I was born. I think Roxanne put a curse on her. I've heard it said that she was a witch.'

'I'm sure that's not true.' Rosina shook her head. 'That is the stuff of fairy stories. I think Roxanne was just a very beautiful woman who knew how to make men fall in love with her, and all these myths have been created around her.'

'But we saw her on the moor, just before we ended up at Glazewood Hall, Rosina,' Jane said urgently. 'I think she was trying to warn me about Bertram, just as she came and spoke to me last night.'

'What did she say to you, my dear?' Dr Clarke asked gently.

Jane turned her head to look him in the eye, her expression bleak. 'She said if I was not careful, I would lose the one person who has stood by me all these years. She meant you, Albert.'

He kissed her on the cheek. 'I will never leave you, Jane. Never!'

Rosina turned with a start as somewhere in the house a door slammed, and she felt a cold breeze brush her cheek. It must be her imagination, but she was certain that there was a movement in the shadowy corner of the room.

'I had better go and help Merry to prepare supper.' Rosina stood up, her heart beating so fast she could scarcely breathe. 'You will be staying to dine with us, won't you, Doctor?'

'I have a surgery this evening, Rosina. But thank you anyway.' Dr Clarke rose to his feet. 'I will come again tomorrow, Jane.'

'Albert, perhaps Roxanne was right. I think we need to get away from Moonshadow,' Jane said urgently. 'Maybe you and I ought to run away together.'

Rosina hesitated in the doorway. She could see genuine fear in her grandmother's eyes, and she shivered. Perhaps there was a malignant spirit haunting the old house.

Chapter Fourteen

Despite Rosina's questions next day, Jane denied having suggested that she and Albert should run away together. She even laughed at the idea, putting it down to flights of fancy that were associated with the mists on the moor and the general ambience of Moonshadow Manor. As to her conversation with Roxanne, Jane brushed it off as having been in a dream, and Rosina had to be satisfied with that explanation. However, Jane's refusal to acknowledge her fears only added to Rosina's suspicion that all was not well. She could understand her grandmother's state of agitation after being treated so badly by Sir Bertram, but her sudden changes in mood were disturbing.

It was not until Saturday morning, when Jack was driving her to the house sale, that Rosina felt able to talk about the strange conversation that had taken place the other evening.

Jack listened intently. 'Your grandmother has been through a distressing experience, Rosie. I wouldn't take too much notice of things she says or does for a while. She's not a young woman and she's had her life turned upside down by a man who has taken her loyalty for granted all these years.'

'Do you think she really sees Roxanne, or is that her disturbed imagination?'

'Roxanne has been dead for many years, but she has become something of a myth locally.'

'You say she died, but other people think she wandered onto the moor and changed into some sort of spirit that still haunts the place.'

'That's nonsense, of course. But the people round here are superstitious, and it's easier to explain things supernaturally than to believe the plain honest truth.'

'I suppose so.' Rosina was not entirely convinced. Until the other evening she had thought her grandmother to be one of the most sensible and down-to-earth women she had ever met, but now she was beginning to wonder if the shock of Sir Bertram's duplicity had left Jane Maddern incapable of rational thought.

'I think we need a plan for this morning,' Jack said conversationally.

Rosina turned her head to stare at his profile as he handled the reins. 'A plan?'

He smiled. 'Yes, you need to decide what sort of items you might bid for and how much money you intend to spend. Or perhaps I should say how much you intend to invest.'

'I have four pounds and ten shillings,' Rosina said proudly. 'And I settled Fred Pavey's bill yesterday.'

'You won't be buying a grand piano then,' Jack said, smiling.

'You think this is all a joke, don't you, Jack? You are taking me to the sale to demonstrate the impossibility of my ambitions.'

'No, not at all. However, you need to be realistic. I can help you financially, but you need to purchase articles that will sell quickly as well as make a profit.'

'I'm not stupid,' Rosina said crossly. 'I understand commerce to an extent. My pa is in trade, and he has made a good living from buying and selling cloth.'

'But he doesn't help you in any way.'

It was a statement rather than a question and too true to be comfortable.

'My father has another family to bring up now. I am an adult and capable of fending for myself.'

They lapsed into silence for a while. Rosina sat back to enjoy the fresh air and the sunshine that was showing the moor off to its best advantage. The frightening mists that had enveloped Rosina and her grandmother were a distant memory, and spring was touching the land with gentle fingers, caressing and beautifying the moor, while banishing the last remnants of winter. The mere thought of evil spirits and mischievous pixies seemed ridiculous on a day like this.

Almost before Rosina realised it, they had reached their destination. Jack slowed the horse to a walk.

'Here we are,' he announced as he drew his horse to a halt outside the gates of an imposing mansion. 'Grandtor House, and we seem to be the first to arrive.' He glanced over his shoulder. 'Unless I'm mistaken, that is Hugo Charteris's carriage coming towards us. I recognised the matched greys and Hugo himself is holding the reins, with his coachman at his side. Your family like to show off, Rosina. I'm afraid we look like the poor cousins.'

'I am the poor cousin,' Rosina said bleakly. 'Hugo was not pleased to discover that I am related to them, although I don't think Ariadne minds too much.'

'Hugo is a terrible snob. Don't take any notice of him.'

'Why would he want to attend a bankrupt sale?' Rosina tried not to look at the carriage that pulled up behind them as they waited for the gatekeeper to come out of his cottage.

'Hugo enjoys participating in the humiliation of others. I believe he used to be friends with Sir Thomas Fairbanks – that is, until they fell out. Perhaps I'm being too hard on Hugo. Maybe he has come to purchase something in an attempt to help out his former friend's family.'

'From the little I know of Sir Hugo I think your first assumption was correct. However, I wish he had not come. I don't want him looking down on me because I need to earn my own living.'

'Shame on him if he does. I know I tease you, Rosie, but I am proud of the way you are dealing with the difficulties you are facing.'

The gatekeeper rushed out of his cottage and unlocked the gates before Rosina had a chance to answer.

'Drive round to your left, sir,' the man said, tipping his cap. 'There'll be stable boys to take care of the horses.'

'Thank you.' Jack flicked the reins, and his horse ambled off at a steady pace. However, moments later they were overtaken by Hugo's carriage, being driven at a reckless pace.

'What on earth does he think he's doing?' Rosina said shakily. 'He could have scared your horse, Jack.'

'He's trying to prove that I am an inferior. Take no notice.'

'Why does he care what you think?'

'We went to the same school and we were in the same year at Oxford, but different colleges. Hugo always has to prove himself to be the best in whatever situation.' Jack tossed the reins to a waiting stable boy before alighting from the vehicle. He helped Rosina to the ground.

'Let's go into the house. I'm not waiting for Hugo.'

Rosina giggled as Hugo stormed past them, heading for the entrance at the rear of the building where a footman had just opened the double doors.

'It seems as though you were right. Hugo has to be the first in everything.'

Jack proffered his arm. 'We have more important things to think about than going into competition with Hugo Charteris. What shall we look at first?'

'Everything,' Rosina said breathlessly. 'I feel so nervous. I have butterflies in my tummy.'

'I'm not sure if that's good or bad, but we'll start slowly, shall we? Take a good look round and when we've seen everything you will be able to decide what you want.'

They entered the building and walked slowly, taking in all the items listed in the sale catalogue. Rosina was impressed by the scale and grandeur of the house, but she could feel the sadness of the family who were losing everything they owned and valued. She caught sight of two small girls peering over the banisters on the top floor, which she assumed must be where the nursery was situated. Their pale faces were pressed against the ornately carved balusters as they watched their home being invaded by strangers.

Rosina stopped at a table where children's playthings were displayed, and her heart sank. She turned to Jack with tears in her eyes.

'How awful. They are selling off the children's toys.'

'I'm sure they have plenty more,' Jack said

dismissively. 'Concentrate on what you are doing, Rosie.'

'I can't. Not while those poor little girls are gazing down at us.' Rosina picked up a doll with a beautiful porcelain head and a mass of golden curls. Even at this distance she heard a small sob and on looking up she saw the older of the two girls cover her face with a handkerchief. Rosina glanced at the ticket price. 'I'll have this one,' she said firmly.

'A doll? You are going to sell children's toys?' Jack stared at her in disbelief.

'No. I'm not going to do anything of the sort.' Rosina glanced up again and saw the younger child pointing to another doll. Rosina picked it up and the child nodded eagerly.

'Rosie, no, you can't do this,' Jack said hastily. 'They are asking far too much for the dolls anyway.'

'You can't put a price on love,' Rosina said in a low voice. She clutched the dolls in her arms. 'Would you want to break the hearts of two small children, Jack?'

She left him and walked away to find the person who seemed to be in charge of the sale. Payment for the dolls left her funds seriously depleted, but Rosina was oblivious to anything but seeing the little girls smile. She climbed the stairs and was quite breathless by the time she reached the nursery suite. The two small girls were curled up on the floor outside the open door. They scrambled to their feet as Rosina approached.

DILLY COURT

'Don't be scared,' Rosina said, smiling. 'I saw you looking at the toys. Are these yours?'

The elder of the two, a pretty dark-haired child, eyed her warily. 'We weren't supposed to watch. Miss Bowering will cane us for being disobedient.'

'Cane you?' Rosina stared at her in disbelief. 'What's your name?'

'I'm Flora and I'm five, and this is my sister, Lottie. She's only three and a half.'

'How do you do, Flora and Lottie?' Rosina said seriously. 'My name is Rosina, and I think these belong to you.' She held the dolls up for them to examine. 'Now, let me guess which one belongs to each of you.' Rosina frowned thoughtfully. 'I think that this one is yours, Flora, and so this one must belong to you, Lottie.'

Flora snatched the doll from Rosina and cuddled her, rubbing her cheeks against the doll's silky hair. Lottie took hers shyly, staring at Rosina with pansy-soft brown eyes.

'Thank you, Rosina,' Flora said firmly. She nudged her sister. 'What do you say, Lottie?'

'Thank you.' Lottie wrapped her arms around the doll, but her eyes widened in alarm as a tall, well-dressed man emerged from a room on the floor below. He stood on the landing, looking up and his expression darkened when he saw Rosina. He took the stairs two at a time.

'Excuse me, miss. This part of the house is not

256

open to the public. The items for sale are all on the ground floor.' He stared at the dolls and his brows drew together in a frown. 'Give me those, Flora. You know they no longer belong to you.'

Rosina stepped between them. 'I don't know who you are, sir, but I purchased those dolls, and I have given them back to their rightful owners. What sort of father sells his children's precious things?'

'He's not our papa,' Flora said sulkily. 'He's Uncle Monty. Our papa went to heaven.'

'He rode there on his horse,' Lottie added, nodding wisely.

'They shot his horse,' Flora said scornfully. 'You are such a baby, Lottie.'

Rosina could see that Lottie was upset and she instinctively placed her arm around the little girl's shoulders. 'Don't cry, dear. I'm sure that the horse did go to heaven with your papa.'

'Don't encourage her in such nonsense. The girls will have to grow up quickly now that they have lost both parents.'

Rosina glared at the children's uncle. He was younger than she had first thought, perhaps in his mid- to late twenties, but his angry expression marred his otherwise handsome face.

'If you are their guardian, sir, I pity the poor mites,' Rosina said angrily. She turned her head in time to see Jack as he reached the top of the stairs.

'What is this?' Jack glanced from one to the other.

'Are you entertaining guests in the nursery suite, Monty?'

'You know each other?' Rosina said incredulously. 'Why didn't you tell me, Jack?'

'You two are together?' Monty frowned. 'Your companion is creating a scene involving my nieces, Jack.'

'I am not,' Rosina protested hotly. 'You are the one who has taken the poor little orphans' toys from them and put them up for sale. I paid good money for those dolls, and I've given them back to the girls. Don't you dare take them away.'

Jack laid his hand on Rosina's shoulder. 'I expect there's a reasonable explanation, Rosie. Perhaps I should make the necessary introductions. Rosie, may I introduce Montague Fairbanks. Monty, this lady is my good friend Rosina Wills, from Moonshadow Manor, Ugstock.'

Monty's expression changed subtly. 'From Moonshadow? That explains a lot. How do you do, Miss Wills?'

Rosina was too angry to be polite. 'What do you mean by that, sir? What has Moonshadow got to do with anything?'

'Nothing, I assure you.' Monty opened the nursery door. 'Miss Bowering, are you there? Why are my nieces out here on their own?' He stepped into the room and emerged almost immediately. 'Where is your nanny?'

Flora eyed him warily. 'She's gone, Uncle.'

'What do you mean by that? Where has she gone? I told her specifically to keep you two in the nursery.' Monty leaned over the balustrade. 'The place is filling up. I'll have to go down and make sure that everything is going as it should be. The smaller items are all available to purchase but the auction for the furniture and fittings takes place this afternoon. Have you come to gloat or to purchase, Jack?'

'Neither. In fact, I didn't realise that your brother had died. My condolences, Monty.'

'Thank you. I'm afraid Tommy was deep in debt before the hunting accident. I am here merely to ensure that all goes smoothly. I didn't put you down as someone interested in antique furniture.'

'I came with Rosina. She is going into business as a dealer in second-hand articles, and she hoped to buy stock.' Jack took a hanky from his pocket and bent down to wipe Lottie's runny nose. 'Who is supposed to be looking after these little ones?'

'The wretched Bowering woman. I had no real faith in her, but it seems that she's walked out on them.'

'Have you no one to take care of them?' Rosina demanded incredulously. 'Surely you have a wife or a female relation who would look after them? There must be someone in the family.'

Monty shot her a withering look. 'If I had such a person, do you not think I would have arranged for them to be here today? The girls have been looked after by servants since the accident.'

'Rosie, don't even consider such a possibility,' Jack said, frowning. 'I know you have a generous heart, but you came here for a purpose, and sad as the children's plight is, it is not our business.'

'How can you say that?' Rosina stamped her foot. 'You and their uncle are a disgrace. These are two defenceless little children, and you are talking about them as if they were chattels. I'm surprised you haven't put a price ticket on them and left them in the entrance hall.'

'Now there's an idea,' Monty said with a glimmer of a smile. 'How much do you think they're worth?'

Flora began to howl, and Lottie covered her ears with her hands. Rosina put her arms around them both. 'Shame on you, Mr Fairbanks. I can't believe you said that, even in jest.'

Monty shook his head. 'Unfortunately, the only staff left on duty are the butler and some of the groundsmen. I suppose they must have a wife or two tucked away somewhere. But I have to go downstairs to oversee the sale. It's the only thing I can do for my late brother.'

'I think his children would be more important to him,' Rosina said angrily. 'What about you, Jack? You're just standing there. Could Mrs Tarr help out until Mr Fairbanks can find a replacement for the nanny?'

'It wouldn't be fair to place such a burden on her, Rosie. She isn't a young woman, and my house isn't a suitable place for two little ones.'

'Then there's only one solution. I will take them home with me.' Rosina turned to Monty. 'When you have finished your business and had time to decide the best course for your nieces' welfare, you may come and collect them.' She leaned closer to Flora, who was sobbing quietly. 'Don't cry, dear. I'll look after you and Lottie. Show me where your things are kept, and we'll pack a bag each for you and your sister.'

'Where are we going?' Flora asked anxiously.

'To my house. It's not too far from here and there's a lovely lady called Merry, who will be so delighted to see you. Then there's my grandmother. She loves children, and no doubt she will spoil you. We'll give your uncle time to make more permanent arrangements.'

'It's just temporary,' Monty said hastily. 'I do care about them, of course, but this sale is important, otherwise the bailiffs will come in and take whatever they wish. I am trying to salvage a little of my family's fortune, if only for the sake of the little ones.'

'I understand. Come on, girls. Best foot forward, as my mama used to say.' Rosina ushered the children into the nursery with Jack following them.

'Rosie, have you given this any thought at all? You aren't in a position to take care of two small girls.'

'Why not? Someone must see to their needs. Your

friend Fairbanks is even selling off their toys, so he's hardly a paternal type. I will take care of them until he makes appropriate arrangements. There must be someone in his family who would want to care for the children.'

'Very probably, but you're forgetting why you came here in the first place.'

Rosina faced him angrily. 'Yes, I am. It seems quite paltry now, especially when compared to the lot of these two innocents.' She turned away, giving Flora an encouraging smile. 'Show me where your clothes are kept and let's see if we can find a valise or a bag of some sort. Let's make a game of it, shall we?'

When they arrived back at Moonshadow Manor the children were exhausted by the events of the day and had to be lifted from the chaise.

'Not a word of this in the village, Joshua,' Rosina said firmly as she took the girls by the hand. 'These little ones are staying here temporarily.'

Joshua eyed the children as if they were strange animals who had suddenly invaded his territory. 'Aye, miss. I understand.'

Rosina could see that he was not convinced, but she turned away without giving him any further explanation.

'Thank you, Jack,' she said, smiling. 'Are you coming in?'

He shook his head. 'Thank you, but no, I'll drive

back to Ivybridge. You will have your hands full with two small children to look after. How will you manage?'

'Don't worry about that, Jack. I'm sure I will have plenty of help, and your friend Monty gave me some money to pay for the girls' keep. I haven't counted it yet, but the purse feels heavy.'

'It could be filled with pennies and halfpennies, for all you know, but I hope Monty has been generous. He has always lived by his wits, being the second in succession, and all he has inherited is a pile of debt.'

'Not in front of the children,' Rosina said severely. 'I'll say goodbye and thank you for taking me to Grandtor House.'

'I'm afraid it was a wasted journey from your point of view.'

'Maybe, but I know I've done the right thing. Flora and Lottie will be well cared for until Monty finds someone more suitable to take them on a permanent basis. Goodbye, Jack.'

Rosina led the children across the yard and into the scullery.

'What on earth have you got there?' Merry demanded as Rosina entered the kitchen.

'We have guests,' Rosina said cheerfully. 'Girls, I want you to meet my friend Merry. She has brothers and sisters of her own, so she is used to taking care of small children.'

'I'm five,' Flora said firmly. She held her hand

out to Merry. 'My name is Flora Fairbanks, and my mama and papa have gone to heaven.'

Merry shook hands solemnly. 'How d'you do, Miss Flora? I'm really sorry to hear about your ma and pa.' She turned her attention to Lottie, who was clinging to Rosina's skirt. 'And who is this young lady?'

'She's my sister, Lottie. She's three and a half,' Flora said importantly. 'I look after Lottie. She doesn't like strangers.'

Merry held her hand out to Lottie, smiling. 'It's a pleasure to make your acquaintance, Miss Lottie. Do you like jam tarts? I made some this afternoon.'

Rosina was delighted to see both children responding eagerly to the promise of food and, judging by the way they devoured the jam tarts, they were both very hungry. Merry filled two cups with milk and stood back, watching them eat and drink with a satisfied smile.

'It always works with them at home,' she said happily. 'Give nippers something nice to eat and some milk and they'll be happy.' She lowered her voice. 'But are they staying, miss? Why have you brought them here?'

'It's just temporary.' Rosina took a jam tart from the plate and bit into it. 'I am starving, Merry. I hope you've made something nice for dinner.'

'Yes, miss, I have, of course. But you haven't answered my question.'

'I came across them in the house where all the contents were up for sale. They had been left in the charge of a nanny, who had apparently walked out, and their uncle didn't know what to do with them. Apparently, he's a single man with no close female relatives and he was at a loss.'

'So, you brought them home with you.' Merry pursed her lips. 'We've got plenty of room, but looking after little ones takes a lot of time and trouble. What will Miss Maddern say?'

Rosina swallowed the last mouthful of the jam tart. 'That was so good, Merry. Your pastry is delicious. Anyway, I'm going to speak to my grandmother now.'

Merry put two tarts on a plate and handed it to Rosina. 'Give her these. Miss Maddern loves jam tarts. They'll put her in a good mood.'

Rosina laughed. 'Thank you, Merry, I'll remember that for next time.' She left the girls happily settled at the kitchen table and she took the plate to the drawing room.

At first Rosina thought her grandmother must be in the morning parlour as she was not seated in her usual chair by the fire, but a rustle of paper made Rosina turn her head and she was surprised to see Jane sitting at an escritoire in the far corner of the room. She was clutching a pen and dipping it into an inkwell.

'I've brought you something to eat, Grandmama.'

Rosina crossed the floor to stand at her side. 'What are you writing?'

Jane sprinkled sand on the paper, which not only blotted up the ink, but successfully covered the writing.

'Nothing to concern you, dear. How did it go this morning at the bankrupt sale?'

'Well, actually that's what I wanted to talk to you about.'

Jane gave her a knowing look. 'There's something I am not going to like. I can tell by your expression, Rosina. What is it?'

Chapter Fifteen

To Rosina's surprise her grandmother was quite amenable to taking care of the two Fairbanks children on a temporary basis. She said she had met their parents on several occasions when she had been visiting Glazewood Hall and they had been Sir Bertram's guests, although she had not seen them for a year or two. However, Tommy Fairbanks had always been a gambler, and Jane was not surprised that he had lost his entire fortune. The children's mother had succumbed to lung fever when Lottie was little more than a year old, and the girls had been cared for by a succession of nannies.

'Until some responsible relative is found, I am quite happy to have them here,' Jane said firmly. 'That is, if you and Merry can cope, Rosina.'

'We will, Grandmama.' Rosina leaned over to

drop a kiss on her grandmother's forehead. 'Don't worry about a thing.'

She had spoken confidently, but now Rosina was beginning to think she had taken on too large a task. These were small children who had lost their parents and their home. Everything was strange to them, and they would need constant care and attention. Rosina knew she would have to rely heavily on Merry's experience of caring for her younger siblings. Doubts were creeping into her mind, but Rosina put them aside. There was nothing she could not do if she set her mind to it. She returned to the kitchen and was amused to find Joshua capering around, using the broom as a hobbyhorse, much to the delight of the children. He came to a sudden halt when he spotted Rosina.

'I'm sorry, miss. I was just keeping the little ones entertained while Merry makes up a bed for them.'

'That's quite all right, Joshua,' Rosina said, smiling. 'Don't stop on my account. If you're happy to keep this up I will go and help Merry.' She left the room before he could argue, and made her way upstairs.

Merry looked up when Rosina walked into the room. 'I hope you don't mind, miss. I put them next to you. I thought they would feel safer in here. They might not like sleeping in the attic rooms. Them crows stamp about on the thatch, hunting for spiders and such, but the sound would frighten small children.'

'We definitely don't want that, Merry. I think the children will be nervous enough simply being in a strange house.'

'It's ever so dusty under the bed, miss. It will take two of us to pull it out. Maybe I should call Joshua to come and help.'

'He's doing well entertaining the children. I can help you. There might be things stowed away beneath it. I didn't think to look under the beds when I was scouring the house for items to sell.'

Merry took one end and together they moved the heavy iron bedstead away from the wall.

'There's plenty of dust and cobwebs.' Merry reached for the broom she had brought from the kitchen. 'I'll sweep first.' She worked energetically but came to a sudden halt. 'Look there, miss. The floorboards have been cut into. Do you think there's something valuable hidden beneath?'

Rosina laughed. 'I think there is probably even more dust and fluff. But there's no harm in looking.' She kneeled and felt around the edges of the cut boards. There was some movement, and she was able to lift one with relative ease. She peered into the gaping hole and reached down until her fingers curled around a leather-covered scroll. She lifted it out and blew the dust off. 'This must have been down there for some time.'

'What is it, miss? Maybe it's a map of a buried hoard of smugglers' ill-gotten gains.'

'There's only one way to find out.' Rosina sat on the floor, carefully unrolling the outer cover. The document inside appeared to be a will. Rosina took it to the window to examine the faded writing in more detail.

'Is it important, miss?' Merry asked eagerly.

Rosina nodded slowly. 'I think it is very important to someone, but not necessarily to me.' She folded the fragile parchment. 'Can you finish up in here, please, Merry? I need to show this to my grandmother.'

'Of course, miss. Leave it to me.'

'Excellent,' Rosina said vaguely as she hurried from the room.

Jane was in the drawing room, relaxing in her chair by the fire. She opened her eyes with a start when Rosina entered.

'What is it, dear? You look flustered.'

Rosina handed her the document. 'I found this under the floorboards in the room that Merry and I were preparing for the children.'

'I can't find my spectacles. Will you read it out loud?'

Rosina pulled up a chair and sat down, carefully unfolding the document. 'It appears to be the will of Phillip Maddern.'

'My father?' Jane raised her eyebrows in surprise. 'He left everything to me. That can't be a legal document.'

'Probably not,' Rosina said calmly. 'But it is very strange. It says that it is the last will and testament of Phillip John Maddern. It's all legal language, but it looks as if you are his beneficiary.'

'As I said.' Jane settled herself more comfortably in her chair. 'Go on, what else does it say?'

Rosina cleared her throat. She had to read the next few lines twice in order to believe her eyes. 'It says that on your demise Moonshadow Manor and its grounds are to be left in perpetuity to Nathaniel Dimond or his descendants, "being the only son of my late wife, Roxanne Maddern and Jabez Dimond".' Rosina hesitated, gazing at her grandmother. 'I don't understand. What does it mean?'

Jane paled alarmingly. 'There was gossip at the time, so I was told, although I was too young to understand.'

'Understand what, Grandmama? Was Roxanne married to Jabez or to your papa?'

'Jabez courted Roxanne, but she chose my father and there is a record of their marriage in the parish register,' Jane said slowly. 'So that part is true. Jabez married Lily Philbrick, a local heiress. Nathaniel was born just a few months after they married. It might have raised a few eyebrows at the time, but no one dared to offend Jabez.'

'That boy was Jack's grandfather. Are you saying that in fact Roxanne was his mother, and there was some deception about the birth?'

'I thought it was just idle gossip,' Jane said dazedly. 'Maybe that will is a forgery.'

'I suppose it could be, but why take so much trouble to hide it? And why didn't Roxanne marry Jabez, Grandmama? I was told that he was infatuated with her.'

'As were all men, it seems. Roxanne might have married Jabez had he not lost Moonshadow to my papa at a card game. Don't forget that Jabez was not considered a respectable man in those days. He was associated with smuggling and constantly on the run from the revenue men. Perhaps that is why Roxanne chose my papa.'

'Your father must have loved her very much to marry her when she had borne another man's child,' Rosina said thoughtfully.

'Yes, I believe he was completely infatuated with her, which is why he commissioned the portrait. My poor mother had to live with that painting, and the knowledge that Roxanne was the love of his life. It seems that we Madderns are doomed to fall in love with the wrong people.' Jane lay back in her chair and closed her eyes.

'I think this will is what Jack has been searching for.' Rosina replaced the document in its leather case. 'The question now is whether or not I give this to him.'

'I have got my life back, thanks to you, and Albert. Even if you give Jack Dimond that document he can do nothing about it until I die. I am leaving everything to you, as I said before. If Jack wishes to fight it in court, that is up to him.'

'Don't worry about it now, Grandmama,' Rosina said hastily. 'No one wants you to die, least of all me. But now I understand a little better why Roxanne has such a presence in the house, and in everyone's minds. She must have been a remarkable woman, and she's become something of a legend.'

'I would say she was a wanton.' Jane pulled a face. 'I feel sorry for my mama, who had to live with Roxanne's legacy for the whole of her married life, and shame on Papa for marrying Roxanne when he knew about her affair with Jabez and the child she bore him.'

'It's easy to judge.' Rosina stood up, clutching the will tightly in her hand. 'I wonder what really happened to her. Did she wander off onto the moor and vanish into the mist? Or did she die in childbirth as the story goes?'

'Forget Roxanne,' Jane said crossly. 'I have had enough of her today. Best go and see how those two infants you brought home are doing. Just don't get too fond of them. They should go back to their family.'

'Yes, of course, Grandmama.' Rosina made her way to the door. 'I'll ask Jack to speak to the children's uncle again. He seems to be their only relative, so he should make the necessary arrangements.' She left the room and stood for a moment in the entrance hall, listening to the now familiar sounds of the old house. At the end of the day the timbers creaked like the joints of an elderly person as the building settled back onto its foundations. Rosina closed her eyes and tried to picture the beautiful Roxanne as the lady of the manor, but Roxanne had faded into the mists of memory. The silence was broken by the sound of children's voices emanating from the kitchen and Rosina went to investigate.

The girls were seated at the table, finishing off the jam tarts, but both of them looked sleepy.

'I think it's time for bed,' Rosina said in a low voice. 'Have they been good, Merry?'

'Like angels, miss. I wish my sisters and brothers behaved so well. Although they will probably be different in the morning after a good night's sleep. What did Miss Jane say when you told her about them?'

Rosina smiled. 'She's happy to have them here until alternative arrangements can be made. I expected her to put up all sorts of arguments, but she was quite amenable.'

'Much as I love nippers, they do need their own family, miss.' Merry mopped up some milk that Lottie had spilled on the table. 'I think those dollies look very tired, Flora. Perhaps we ought to put them to bed.'

Flora yawned. 'Are we going to sleep here tonight, miss?'

'Merry has made a bed up for you and Lottie, and the dollies, in the room next to mine.'

'Will you read us a story when we are in bed, miss?'

'Of course I will. And you must call me Rosina. Can you do that, Flora?'

'Yes, Rosina.' Flora licked the jam off her fingers. 'Will you give us lessons, like Miss Bowering?'

Rosina and Merry exchanged anxious glances.

'Maybe, but we'll have to see. You finish up your food and I'll go and look for a storybook. I'm sure I saw one the other day when I was tidying up.' Rosina was beginning to realise that she had given no thought as to how she was going to take care of two very small and helpless children. She could see that Merry was thinking the same thing. The next few days were going to be very difficult.

By the end of the following week there had been no contact with Monty Fairbanks and, although the children were sweet and amusing, they took up almost all Rosina's time, and she was still struggling to find a way to support herself financially.

Ariadne arrived one afternoon, no doubt having listened to gossip from the servants' hall, as by now it was all round Ugstock village that Miss Wills had adopted two small girls.

'I hope you don't mind me calling on you this way, Rosina,' Ariadne said as she peeled off her lace gloves and settled herself on the sofa. 'I heard that you went to the Grandtor sale and came home with two children,' she said, giggling. 'That was very brave of you.'

'Someone had to look after them, Ariadne. It was an emergency.' Rosina was getting used to being quizzed about her intentions regarding Flora and Lottie. Everyone, from Seth Tully to Fred Pavey, had been agog with curiosity. She had even had a visit from the vicar, Matthew Horsfall, whose suggestion that the girls should go into an orphanage had not gone down well. Rosina had not exactly ordered Mr Horsfall out of the house, but she had made her feelings plain, and he had left soon afterwards.

Ariadne arranged her skirts and primped her hair. 'Well, you are a better woman than I am. I could not have undertaken such a task. I suppose Monty has visited them often?'

Rosina gave her a cursory glance. So that was why Ariadne had chosen to call in unexpectedly. She was more interested in seeing Monty Fairbanks than she was in the fate of his small nieces.

'No, as a matter of fact I haven't seen Mr Fairbanks since the day of the sale. I am beginning to think he has abandoned the girls.'

Ariadne's eyes widened. 'Oh, no! Horrors! But I'm certain that Monty wouldn't do something so mean. He is an honourable man, and he is a most excellent dancer. He partnered me at many balls last season. I'm sure he would have proposed had it not been for Cousin Grace, who was quite shameless in her pursuit of him.'

Rosina eyed her curiously. She had never heard Ariadne speak so passionately about anyone or anything and it made her suspect that Monty Fairbanks had worked his charm on both Grace and Ariadne.

'Do you know where Monty lives?' Rosina had a sudden desire to learn more about the mysterious Monty Fairbanks. And, of course, there were the children to consider. Their welfare must come first.

'Why yes, of course. Monty, Hugo and Jack were all at the same school. Hugo doesn't see much of Monty these days, but I believe Monty spends most of his time in London. How I envy him the parties and the balls, to say nothing of the theatre and concerts.' Ariadne turned to Rosina with a sad smile. 'Don't you find life in the country terribly dull, especially when you were born and raised in London?'

Rosina shook her head. 'As a matter of fact, I find living here is far more eventful than ever my life was in London. But then I didn't move in the same circles as you, Ariadne.'

'I suppose not. You poor thing.'

'Getting back to the girls' uncle,' Rosina said hastily. 'Do you know his address in London? I really think someone should speak to him seriously. It feels as if he has abandoned his responsibilities.'

'I believe Monty resides with his aunt Maud in Welbeck Street.'

'He has an aunt?' Rosina stared at her, frowning. 'Then he lied to Jack and me on the day of the sale. He said he had no living relations who might take care of the girls.'

'That sounds like Monty,' Ariadne said, giggling. 'Lady Tring is very much alive and very respectable. Monty, however, is an awful liar, but he's so charming he gets away with it. Anyway, where are the children now?' Ariadne glanced around the room as if expecting to see the small girls sitting quietly on the sofa.

'Merry has taken them into the village to play with her younger brothers and sisters. She won't be back for a while. But seriously, I think someone should speak to Monty as soon as possible. I would be happy to go up to London to see him.'

'I could come with you,' Ariadne said eagerly. 'We could stay in the town house. Hugo couldn't raise any objections if we two went together. After all, I do know Monty better than you, Rosina.'

'I think that is an eminently sensible idea,' Rosina said thoughtfully. 'What day do you suggest?'

Ariadne smiled delightedly. 'Excellent. Now, let me see. Tomorrow is Wednesday and I have an appointment with my milliner. On Thursday Hugo is taking me to visit Aunt Tryphena, not that either of us are particularly fond of the old lady, but she is very wealthy and has no children of her own.'

'How about Friday, then?' Rosina was beginning to lose patience.

'Friday is perfect.' Ariadne put on her lace gloves. 'We would need to get to the railway station early in the morning. Smith will come and collect you in the barouche so pack enough for at least one night's stay in town.'

'Perhaps we ought to take the children with us,' Rosina said thoughtfully. 'I'm sure that Monty's aunt would not have the heart to turn them away.'

Ariadne pulled a face. 'Oh, no. I am not travelling with small children who have sticky fingers and burst into tears at the slightest provocation. They will be better off here with your servant. She seems to be a capable woman.'

'Perhaps that would be more sensible,' Rosina said slowly. 'I'll see you out, Ariadne.'

'Yes, I need to get home to sort out what I will wear in London. Monty has an eye for style and elegance. I want to look my best.' Ariadne sailed past Rosina and almost ran from the house. The footman leaped down from the carriage to open the door and put down the steps, and he handed her into the vehicle.

Rosina was left standing on the front step wondering how she had come to be involved in Ariadne's plans. It must be that Monty had hidden charms, for it was not his wealth or status that seemed to have enchanted Ariadne.

The coachman drove off in a cloud of dust, but

just as it was settling a horseman brought his mount to a halt in front of the house and Jack dismounted, handing the reins to Joshua, who had come running from the stable yard.

'That was the Charteris carriage. Was Hugo gracing you with his presence, Rosie?'

'No, it was Ariadne.' Rosina retreated into the entrance hall. 'I haven't seen you since the day of the sale. Have you been avoiding me, Jack?'

He followed her into the house, stopping to take off his hat and gloves, which he left on the side table. 'I'm sorry, Rosie. I've spent most of the time since then in court, defending a client. Has Monty been in contact with you?'

'No, he has not. The girls are still with us and have settled in very well considering the circumstances, but we are not their family and I have not had a word from Monty.'

Jack shook his head. 'I was afraid of that. I am well aware of Monty's reputation, and it doesn't give me much hope.'

'But you allowed me to bring his little nieces to Moonshadow.'

A smile lit Jack's eyes. 'Would anything I said have stopped you?'

'No, I suppose not, especially where small children are concerned, but I am worried about them, Jack. In fact, I'm going to London with Ariadne on Friday. She says she knows Lady Tring, Monty's aunt who lives in Welbeck Street, and that is where he is living at present.'

'Why is Ariadne being so helpful all of a sudden?' Jack said, frowning. 'That doesn't sound like her.'

'I think she is smitten by Monty's charms, although I doubt if Hugo would approve,' Rosina said with a wry smile. 'Or perhaps she's doing it because we are related, and she wishes to avoid a family scandal.'

'That is very unlikely. I've known Ariadne since she was twelve and I don't think she has ever considered the feelings of anyone but herself.' Jack followed Rosina into the drawing room. 'That's not all, is it? There's something on your mind, I can tell.'

Rosina eyed him warily. 'Yes, Jack. I think I might, by accident, have found what you've been searching for.' She walked over to the escritoire where she had left the leather pouch containing Phillip Maddern's will. 'Merry and I were getting a room ready for the children on their first night and we found this hidden beneath the floorboards. It must have been there for decades.'

Jack took it from her and sat down abruptly on the sofa as he unfolded the dusty leather and took out the parchment. He read it slowly, his brow furrowed.

'You didn't have to give me this, Rosie. You could have put it back or even burned it.'

'Why would I do that? It concerns both of us, but you even more than me. You always thought that

Roxanne was more than just a myth, didn't you?' Rosina sat down beside him.

'This could be a forgery, Rosie. I don't know why anyone would want to spread such lies, but it might have been someone with a grudge against the Madderns.'

'But you don't really believe that do you, Jack? This is the document you have been searching for, so why aren't you pleased to have found it at last?'

'It means that Roxanne was my great-grandmother, which is what I suspected all along.'

Rosina gazed at him, frowning. 'Does that knowledge make any difference after all these years? What it does say, if this is genuine, is that one day Moonshadow will come back to your family.'

'Yes, but Phillip Maddern won the property from Jabez. Roxanne was just the link between the two men, and it seems that she had the power to enchant a villain like Jabez. We will never know if he wanted to marry her, but for some reason she chose Phillip Maddern. Maybe it was Moonshadow Manor itself that held such an attraction for her.'

'Phillip must have really loved Roxanne to marry her and leave this house to your family, Jack. Maybe he cheated Jabez out of this old house and he was overcome by feelings of guilt.'

'It all happened a long time ago and this document will never go to probate, and I've changed my mind, Rosie. Moonshadow should come to you. If anyone deserves to benefit from the tangled affairs of our predecessors, it is you.'

'Then perhaps we should put the will back beneath the floorboards, for the time being, anyway. You might change your mind one day, Jack. As we've seen with my grandmother, anything can happen.'

'One minute she was preparing to die, and now she's a changed person,' Jack said, smiling. 'I've always admired Jane Maddern for being a strong woman.'

'Dr Clarke seems to share your opinion of her. He's here almost every day and they've taken to going out for long walks on the moor. That makes me nervous after my experiences with the bogs and the mist, but Grandmama says that Albert knows the moor like the back of his hand.'

'It's a mystical and beautiful place, but not for the unwary.' Jack handed the leather pouch to Rosina. 'Bury it beneath the floorboards. The mystery that has been bothering me for years is now solved and should be left to the annals of history.'

'Perhaps you should have the painting of your great-grandmother, Jack,' Rosina said tentatively. 'It is beautiful and I'm sure that Grandmama would be happy for you to own it now she knows the truth.'

Jack shook his head. 'No, Rosie. Leave Roxanne where she wanted to be. She seems to have loved this house more than anything or anyone, even her own flesh and blood. After all, she gave her child to Jabez when I'm sure she could have persuaded Phillip to raise him as his own.'

'That would have been so strange,' Rosina said slowly. 'You would have been born a Maddern, in that case.'

'Best not to think about it too deeply, Rosie. We have another problem to deal with, which is why I came here today. There are two little girls who desperately need a family to care for them.'

'Yes, of course, and that is why I'm going to London on Friday, with Ariadne, but that's by the bye. I am hoping that Lady Tring will be able to talk sense into Monty, or perhaps she will offer to give Flora and Lottie a home.'

'If you need me to accompany you, I will cancel my appointments for Friday.'

'Thank you, Jack, but I think that Ariadne and I can manage on our own.'

By the time Friday dawned Rosina was not quite so sure of herself. She was beginning to wish that she had accepted Jack's offer to accompany them to London, but there was no turning back. She was up early, washed, dressed and ready to travel with a few things packed in a small valise. She waited eagerly for Smith to arrive with the carriage to take her and Ariadne to the railway station. Merry was to look after the children, but Rosina had been careful to keep the reason for her absence a secret from the small girls. It would be too distressing for them if nothing came of the visit to Welbeck Street and if neither Monty nor Lady Tring could be persuaded take responsibility for the little orphans.

The barouche arrived on time and Rosina climbed in to sit beside Ariadne, who talked excitedly all the way to the station. Rosina was beginning to wonder how she was going to cope with her incessant chatter if Ariadne kept it up for the whole of the journey, but she made a huge effort to be patient, answering in monosyllables until in the end Ariadne ran out of small talk. Rosina had been steadfastly looking out of the window, but when she turned her head to look at Ariadne, she had fallen asleep, curled up like a child with her head resting on the luxuriously upholstered squabs. The rest of the journey passed in blissful silence, and they arrived at the station in good time for the London train.

They were waiting on the platform, when Rosina heard her name being called and the sound of running footsteps. She turned her head and was surprised to see Grace Charteris racing towards them. Her bonnet had come off and was hanging by its ribbons and she was holding up her skirts revealing high button boots beneath lace-trimmed petticoats.

'Wait for me,' Grace cried as the train roared into the station. 'I'm coming with you.'

Chapter Sixteen

There was no time to argue or to demand an explanation. Grace hurled herself into the carriage as the guard blew his whistle and the engine let off steam before starting to move. Grace fell onto the seat next to Rosina.

'What are you doing here?' Rosina demanded, mystified.

'Grace doesn't want me to see Monty – that's why she's come without even a maid to chaperone her,' Ariadne said bitterly. 'Ask her for yourself, Rosina.'

'You've always been jealous of me, Ariadne.' Grace settled herself decorously onto the seat, adjusting her bonnet with a gloved hand. 'And you've made it plain that you're after Monty. Why else would you be travelling up to London with Rosina?'

'Speak for yourself, Grace. I am going because there are two small girls who have been orphaned and abandoned.'

'That is why I am coming, too.' Grace faced Ariadne with a stubborn set to her jaw. 'I will speak to Monty. He always listens to me. He thinks you are just a silly young woman, desperate to find a husband. You were always trying to flirt with him at functions last season.'

Rosina held up her hands. 'Stop it, both of you. Why are you bickering like two schoolchildren? Why on earth would either of you want to get closer to Monty Fairbanks, anyway? As far as I can gather, he is a gambler and a womaniser.'

'That is just gossip,' Grace said crossly. 'People are jealous of his charm and good looks. Ariadne made a fool of herself over him.'

'I am not desperate to find a husband.' Ariadne slumped down in a corner seat and turned her head to stare out of the window. 'I could have anyone I wanted. I'm an heiress and I'm pretty.'

Rosina looked from one to the other. 'The only time I met Monty Fairbanks was at the bankrupt sale of his family home. His brother had gambled away every penny they had. Why would either of you think he is a good match?'

'Monty is due to inherit his uncle's title and fortune when the old gentleman passes away,' Grace said casually. 'Monty will be the most eligible man in the country, and she knows it.' She pointed her finger at Ariadne.

'Everyone knows it,' Ariadne said sulkily. 'You flirted with him outrageously, Grace Charteris, so don't deny it. You are twenty-four and almost on the shelf. I am only twenty-two, and Monty told me that my hair is the colour of ripe corn, and my eyes are blue like the summer sky.'

'Utter nonsense,' Grace snapped. 'Did he also say that you suffer from delusions, and you are the silliest creature he has ever met?'

'That really is enough from both of you.' Rosina raised her voice. 'I think you are behaving like idiots. I am going to London to see Lady Tring, if Monty is not available. There needs to be a serious discussion regarding the girls' future. This isn't about you, Ariadne, or you, Grace. If you can't see that, I suggest you both alight from the train at the next station.'

'We can't do that,' Grace protested. 'How would we get home?'

'That would not be my problem.' Rosina fixed her with a steady look. 'Anyway, Grace, how did you know that Ariadne and I were going to London today?'

'Cousin Hugo was at the sale,' Grace said, pouting. 'He came to see Papa and I happened to overhear their conversation.'

'You mean you were eavesdropping.' Ariadne tossed her head. 'You always were a sneak, Grace.'

'But Hugo wouldn't have known that I was going to London, let alone that Ariadne was coming with me.' Rosina leaned closer to Grace. 'Tell the truth. What did you hear?'

'They were talking about purchasing Grandtor House at a knockdown price. Hugo said that Monty has about as much business acumen as a goat, and Papa agreed. They laughed a lot.'

'That doesn't explain how you knew what we were planning.' The image of a goat with Monty's handsome head made it difficult for Rosina to keep a straight face, but she was determined to get to the truth. 'You must have found out at the last minute, Grace. You came without your maid and no luggage, even though we will have to stop in London for at least one night.'

'Lady Tring won't want to put up all three of us,' Ariadne said sulkily. 'You've made things very difficult, Grace. As always.'

'I accompanied Papa to Daumerle House this morning, because I was bored at home, and I wanted to find out if they had made a decision about Grandtor House.' Grace hesitated, as if considering how much she was going to tell them. 'It's much larger than Glazewood Hall, and if Papa owned it, I am sure Monty would marry me, if only to get his old home back.'

'That wouldn't work, stupid.' Ariadne rolled her eyes. 'You have two sisters, one older, Grace. You wouldn't inherit Grandtor if your papa died. It would go to Clarissa, who is the eldest.'

Grace sat back on the seat. 'Well, I can't think of everything, and I had to act quickly. I persuaded Luke to drive me to the station and here I am.'

'I thought that Luke was the love of your life?' Rosina frowned, remembering the passionate scene she had witnessed at Glazewood Hall.

'Well, he is, of course,' Grace admitted reluctantly. 'But I can't marry a footman. Papa would never allow it.'

'You are a wanton woman,' Ariadne said angrily. 'I'm ashamed to call you cousin.'

'You are such a baby,' Grace said scornfully. 'Anyway, why would Monty want to have anything to do with a foolish girl like you?'

Rosina stood up, ignoring the swaying of the carriage as the train racketed along the track. 'If I hear another word out of either of you, I am getting out at the next station. I will wait for the next train and travel to London on my own.'

'I think she means it.' Ariadne stared at Rosina in alarm. 'I'm not travelling to London with you, Grace.'

'Nor I with you.' Grace sighed. 'I won't say another word providing you keep your silly mouth shut, Ariadne.'

Rosina fell back onto her seat as the engine slowed down. 'All right. We will all go to London, but only if you two stop squabbling and trying to outdo each other. Do you promise?'

Grace and Ariadne nodded reluctantly, and they sank into a sulky silence, which lasted most of the way to London.

The hackney carriage stopped outside the elegant four-storey town house in Welbeck Street. Grace and Ariadne were still arguing between sulky silences. Rosina was heartily sick of them by now and she wished that she had come alone, but it was too late to do anything other than knock on the door and wait.

The maid who opened the door did not seem to be surprised when Rosina asked to see Mr Fairbanks, which made Rosina wonder if young women often called at the house asking for him.

'Mr Fairbanks is not at home, miss.'

'Might we see Lady Tring?' Rosina tried to appear unbothered, although she was not really surprised to find Monty was absent. From what she could gather, he spent most of his time in gaming clubs, parties or at the races. However, she was not going to return home without having at least tried to help Lottie and Flora.

'I will enquire. Please wait here.' The maid stood aside to let them into the entrance hall before closing the front door. She hurried off, returning minutes later to announce that Lady Tring would see them, and she led the way upstairs to the drawing room.

Lady Tring was an imposing figure. She wore a

white lace cap, and her silver hair was confined in a chignon at the back of her neck. It was impossible to gauge her height as she was seated by the fire, the folds of her purple silk gown arranged neatly. As a final touch of elegance she wore several rows of pearls with matching earrings. Rosina could not but be impressed. She felt almost as if she were in the presence of the Queen herself, and it was all she could do to prevent herself from bobbing a curtsey.

'Well, ladies, what can I do for you?' Lady Tring looked from one to the other, her gaze stopping when it settled on Rosina. 'Speak.'

'Thank you for sparing the time to see us, ma'am,' Rosina said nervously. 'We really wanted to speak to your nephew, but I understand he is not at home.'

'What has Monty done now?' Lady Tring sighed, shaking her head. 'Which one of you has been jilted by him?'

'It's not that,' Rosina said hastily. 'It has nothing to do with us individually.'

'Has he proposed to all three of you?' Lady Tring peered at each of them in turn through a lorgnette. 'Monty has excelled himself this time.'

Grace opened her mouth to speak but Rosina forestalled her.

'We are here concerning his brother's children, ma'am.'

Lady Tring stared at her blankly. 'Thomas's children? I thought they were being cared for locally.'

'They have been living with me and my grandmother since the day of the bankrupt sale, ma'am. I took them in because there did not seem to be anyone else to take care of them.' Rosina shifted from one foot to the other.

'That is true,' Grace added firmly. 'The little girls are being looked after by people who are not related to them.'

'And Monty seems to have forgotten them.' Ariadne seemed intent on having her say, or perhaps she was simply making her presence felt.

'And who are you?' Lady Tring demanded imperiously. 'Please introduce yourselves and for heaven's sake sit down. You're giving me neck ache.'

Rosina sank down on the sofa with Grace on one side and Ariadne on the other.

'I beg your pardon, ma'am. I am Rosina Wills from Moonshadow Manor, Ugstock.'

'I am Grace Charteris, ma'am. You will doubtless have met my father, Sir Bertram Charteris, and this is my cousin, Ariadne Charteris.'

'I can speak for myself,' Ariadne said crossly. 'I believe we met once during last season, Lady Tring. Monty was very attentive.'

'Monty is always attentive where pretty girls are concerned.' Lady Tring looked at each of them in turn as if assessing their worth. 'So, apparently, he has not been taking care of my nieces. Why was I not told of this?'

'I cannot say, ma'am.' Rosina eyed her warily. 'All I know for certain is that Flora and Lottie should be with their own family. That is why we wanted to speak to Monty, as he seems to have forgotten their existence.'

'My family have had their fair share of tragedy,' Lady Tring said sadly. 'In fact, there is only myself, Monty and my daughter, Sophia, still surviving.'

'I thought Monty had a rich uncle who was going to leave him everything?' Ariadne said suspiciously. 'Did he make that up?'

A shadow of a smile curved Lady Tring's thin lips. 'Surprisingly, that is true, but Lord Bracklesham is related to Monty on the maternal side. Monty's father married a second time after the death of Tommy's mother.'

'Is your daughter married?' Rosina asked, grasping at straws in her desperation to find a good home for the little girls.

'Sophia? Heavens, no! She will never see thirty-five again and is sadly very much on the shelf. She even talks about going into a nunnery, but I believe that is only to save face. Life is hard for spinsters.'

Grace shot a meaningful look in Ariadne's direction. 'Sad, but true, ma'am.'

Rosina could see that this conversation was taking the wrong turn. She rose to her feet.

'Might I bring the children to see you, ma'am? They should be with their family, much as we love them already, but I am not in a strong financial position to support them.'

'Of course. Yes, it is my duty to look after the orphans, and Monty must play his part. They are his nieces, and he was close to his half-brother. Bring them to me, Miss Wills.'

Rosina glanced round the room with its heavy mahogany furniture, upholstered in maroon velvet with matching curtains and draped pelmets. The room although opulent was not the most cheerful of places. She could imagine a small child being overwhelmed by it all. However, there seemed no alternative but to do as Lady Tring commanded and bring the unfortunate orphans to Welbeck Street. At least they would be looked after, fed and clothed. Perhaps the severe and seemingly unbending Lady Tring would melt when she saw the two little girls.

'Well, what do you say, Miss Wills? I have an appointment at noon, and I need to change into my afternoon gown.'

Rosina came back to the present with a start, and she realised that Ariadne and Grace were staring at her. 'Yes, ma'am. Of course I will bring the children to meet you.'

'Better still, I will send Monty to Devonshire to fetch the children. It's time he took responsibility for something in his life.' Lady Tring stood up and reached for the bell pull. 'My maid will see you out. Good day, Miss Wills, and the Misses Charteris, too.'

She sailed out of the room, leaving all three mutely staring after her.

Grace was the first to regain the power of speech.

'Well, what do we do now? Do we simply return to the station and wait for a train to take us home? I thought at least she would offer us hospitality for tonight.'

'It is late morning,' Rosina said thoughtfully. 'Ariadne and I came prepared to stay for one night, if necessary. I didn't think she would dismiss us so summarily.'

'Hugo has rooms in Dover Street,' Ariadne added, 'but I don't think there would be room for three of us.'

'I'm not going home yet.' Grace made a move towards the door. 'We can all stay at our town house in Cavendish Square. It's not far from here. You will meet Clarissa and Cecily. They might even know where we could find Monty.'

'What would your papa say?' Rosina asked anxiously. 'Maybe we ought to get the train back to Devonshire.'

'No, don't be a spoilsport, Rosina.' Ariadne clapped her hands. 'Let's do what Grace suggests. It will be fun.'

At that moment the maid opened the door and ushered them into the hallway. It was plain that their stay in Welbeck Street had ended.

Outside on the street Rosina still had doubts. 'I'm not sure about this, Grace. Your papa seemed a very strict man. I doubt if he would approve of us inviting ourselves to stay.'

'He's your grandpapa as well as my pa,' Grace said, laughing. 'You have as much right to use the London house as I do. We don't know the times of the trains going to Devon and it will be late by the time we get home, so probably a far better plan is to spend the night in London and return in the morning.'

'I suppose it can't hurt,' Rosina said doubtfully. 'But what will your aunt say? You said she was staying there to chaperone your sisters.'

'Don't worry about her. Aunt Eugenie will do anything to avoid an argument, and my sisters are too concerned with their own affairs to bother what I do or say.' Grace tucked her hand in the crook of Rosina's arm. 'Stop prevaricating, Rosina. It's only a short walk and I am starving. I hope Cook has something tasty to serve to us. Anyway, I feel scruffy and dirty after the train journey, and I have a change of clothes at the house in Cavendish Square.'

'Or you could go home to Islington, if you have a mind to,' Ariadne said slyly.

'I think Cavendish Square is an excellent idea.' Rosina proffered her free hand to Ariadne. 'At least you two agree on something, and that's the first time today.'

'We might even be able to track Monty down,' Grace said thoughtfully. 'I could send our head footman to the places that I've heard Monty frequents.' Grace shot a triumphant glance in Ariadne's direction. 'You see, keeping my ear to the keyhole does come in useful at times. I hear all sorts of things that people want kept secret. I know that Papa disapproves of Monty because of what I overheard last evening, and I also know that Pa will not hesitate to use what he knows when bargaining for Grandtor House.'

'I don't doubt it,' Rosina said drily. 'He certainly took advantage of my grandmother's good nature over the years.'

'Look at it this way, Rosina. You would not be here but for their affair, so things have a habit of working out in the end.' Grace squeezed Rosina's arm. 'I'm glad you are my niece, even if it is rather ridiculous. I'll even put up with Cousin Ariadne while we're here enjoying ourselves.'

The house in Cavendish Square was far grander than Rosina had imagined, but Grace seemed very much at home. She acknowledged the butler with a cheerful greeting and sailed past him, as if she had just come home from a shopping expedition. He cast a supercilious eye over the small cases that Rosina and Ariadne had brought with them, but he did not question Grace's demand for two extra rooms to be prepared for her guests.

'By the way, Horrocks,' Grace said casually, 'are my sisters at home?'

Horrocks paused with a valise in each hand. 'Miss Clarissa and Miss Cecily are attending a house party in Kent with Miss Templeton. They are not expected to return home for several days, Miss Grace.'

'Thank you, Horrocks. Will you ask Cook to send tea and lots of cake to the drawing room, please? And we'll be three for dinner tonight.'

'Very well, Miss Grace. Might I ask how long you and the young ladies expect to stay?'

'A couple of days or so, Horrocks. I'll let you know when we are sure of our plans,' Grace said airily. 'Follow me, girls.' She headed up the wide staircase with Rosina and Ariadne trailing behind her obediently.

'It's a shame that my sisters are not here,' Grace said casually as she entered the large, airy drawing room on the first floor. The curtains were drawn against the sunlight, and she crossed the floor to pull them back, allowing sunlight to flood into the room. 'Not that I miss them terribly; we always argue, a bit like you and I, Ariadne. But they will be up to date with all the parties and where we might find Monty.'

'You did say you would send your footman to ask around,' Rosina reminded her.

'Yes, you did,' echoed Ariadne, stripping off her gloves and mantle. 'I hope Hugo doesn't take it into his head to come after us. I wouldn't put it past him. He always spoils things for me.'

'I can deal with Cousin Hugo,' Grace said firmly.

'First of all, we need to find Monty and then we can enjoy ourselves. I doubt if Papa even knows that I'm missing.'

Rosina peeled off her gloves. 'I just want to make sure that the children are taken care of. Lady Tring seems like a sensible woman, but rather stern and unbending. I'm not sure she's the right person to look after two small girls. They are sweet little things and deserve a loving home.'

Grace rolled her eyes. 'I'm sure they are being well cared for in Devonshire. I intend to enjoy myself. It's a good thing my sisters are away because I can borrow their clothes without any arguments, since I didn't have a chance to pack a case for myself.'

'I haven't got anything very formal to wear,' Ariadne said nervously. 'I hope you don't intend to go to anywhere too grand, Grace.'

'You are about the same size as Cecy, and Clarissa's gowns should fit Rosina.' Grace tossed her head. 'I'm going to search through the pile of invitations that Aunt Eugenie always keeps in the escritoire. There might be something this evening or tomorrow that is worth attending. We can chaperone each other.'

'I don't think Hugo would approve of that,' Ariadne said warily.

'Hugo won't know, will he? You are such a baby, Ariadne. Where is your free spirit?' Grace curled her lip. 'It's hard to believe that you and I are related.'

Ariadne's eyes filled with tears, and she searched in vain for a handkerchief. Rosina took one from her reticule and passed it to her.

'Don't be mean, Grace. We can't all be heroines from a gothic novel.'

Grace tossed her head. 'You should treat me with more respect, Rosina. After all, I am your aunt.' She giggled and took off her bonnet, tossing it onto a table in the corner of the room. 'This is the first time I've been on my own in London. I am mistress of the house for a day or two, isn't that fun?'

Rosina was not so certain. She eyed Grace warily, wondering what mischief she might be thinking up in her new-found freedom. 'Grace, you mentioned a possible list of invitations your sisters might have received. We came to London to find Monty.'

'Yes, I suppose so.' Grace pointed to a mahogany bureau in the far corner of the room. 'Have a look in the top drawer, Rosina. That's where Aunt Eugenie keeps such things.'

'I don't think it's right for me to go through someone else's private things, Grace. You do it,' Rosina said firmly. 'As you said, this is your house.'

'Oh, all right.' Grace stood up and flounced over to the bureau. She took out a sheaf of papers and returned to her seat, leafing through them until she came to one that seemed to catch her attention.

'There's a ball at Springfield House tonight. This is an invitation for my sisters and Aunt Eugenie. If

Monty is anywhere other than a gambling club that is where he will be.'

'I haven't got a ball gown,' wailed Ariadne.

'We cannot attend a ball without an escort,' Rosina said firmly. 'Be practical, Grace.'

'We just need a gentleman, and I know who to ask. Francis Moulton owes me a favour, so I am calling it in, to speak in vulgar parlance.' Grace jumped to her feet again and hurried over to the bureau. She scribbled a note on a sheet of parchment and, having folded it neatly, she tugged at the bell pull. She had barely returned to her seat when the door opened, and a maid entered bearing a tray of tea and cake.

'Put it there,' Grace said imperiously, pointing to a low table. 'And please give this to James. Tell him to take it straight away to Sir Francis Moulton's house in Brook Street and tell him to wait for an answer. It's very urgent.'

'Yes, Miss Grace.' The maid set the tray down, took the note from Grace and hurried from the room.

'Will he oblige, do you think, Grace?' Ariadne asked nervously. 'Won't he get the wrong impression?'

'Darling Ariadne, I have to say that Francis is almost as stupid as you are. He's been trying to get on my right side for months. He even came down to Devonshire, ostensibly to see Papa, but in reality, he wanted to see me. I know exactly how to handle dear Frank, so don't worry on that score.' Grace sank back in her chair. 'Rosina, you are nearest, will you do the honours and pour the tea? I am quite exhausted already.'

Rosina filled the teacups and passed them round. 'Are you sure this is a good idea, Grace? I mean you could get away with attending a social function in place of your sisters, but neither Ariadne nor myself are known to the people who sent the invitation.'

'Don't worry about that,' Grace said airily. 'These functions are so crowded that almost anyone who owns a ball gown can gain entry and be lost in the crowd. You'll see.'

Chapter Seventeen

The carriage drew up outside the mansion in Cavendish Square and a footman leaped down to open the door and assist the ladies to alight. Grace was first and then Rosina, followed by Ariadne and Sir Francis. He proffered his arm to Grace, who laid her hand on his sleeve, glowering at him.

'Don't think this is anything but a favour you are doing me, Frank.'

Rosina felt quite sorry for the hapless Sir Francis, who had accepted the challenge and seemed delighted to be their escort. However, Grace's harsh words wiped the smile from his clean-shaven face and his lower lip quivered.

'I say, Grace, that was uncalled for,' he said wistfully. 'Can't a chap step up when needed without having it thrown back in his face?'

'I'm sure Grace didn't mean it like that.' Rosina spoke more sharply than she had intended, but she could see that Grace's erstwhile suitor was hurt by her remark.

'Don't pander to him, Rosina,' Grace said crossly. 'He is a big baby, and he had nothing better to do this evening, did you, Frank?'

'Please can we go inside?' Ariadne shivered dramatically. 'It might be spring but it's still cold at night.'

'Of course.' Grace smiled up at Francis. 'You know I didn't mean it, don't you, Frank? Now we have an important mission to accomplish, isn't that right, Rosina?'

'Yes, it is. We have to hope that Monty Fairbanks is here or at least find someone who can tell us where he might be.'

'Understood,' Francis said eagerly. 'Follow me.'

The entrance hall was even more impressive than that of Grandtor House, and the ballroom was ablaze with dozens of expensive wax candles in cut-crystal chandeliers and wall sconces. The heat from their flames, together with the warmth of several hundred guests, made it feel quite tropical after the chill outside. The scent of hot wax mingled with the varieties of expensive French perfumes and pomades, and couples were already waltzing round, the women in a swirl of brightly coloured silks and satins, with the gentlemen a stark contrast in black evening suits.

Rosina had never attended such a grand function, and she was overawed by it all. Her relatively quiet existence in Moonshadow Manor and her former modest London home had not prepared her for such a social spectacle, and she almost forgot the reason for their being here. Grace and Ariadne seemed much more at ease, and they lost no time in finding a table that gave them a good view of the entire ballroom.

'May I have the next dance, Grace?' Francis said shyly.

'No, you may not, Frank. I am going to mingle and do what we came to do in the first place. Ariadne, you must follow my example. Remember why we came here tonight.'

'But what about me?' Francis asked anxiously.

Grace turned on him, frowning. 'You should dance with Rosina. She doesn't know anyone here, so she's of little use in this instance.' Grace sashayed off before Francis had a chance to protest.

'I'll dance with you, Francis,' Ariadne said quickly. 'I don't want to look like a wallflower. Rosina can sit there and keep a look out for Monty.'

Francis proffered his arm. 'It's a pleasure, Ariadne,' he said gallantly. He glanced over his shoulder as he was about to lead Ariadne onto the dance floor. 'I'm sure you won't sit there for long, Miss Rosina. If I might be so bold, you look very charming in that blue gown.'

'Come on, Francis. Stop gossiping.' Ariadne tugged at his arm until he led her into the dance.

Rosina managed a smile, but if she were being honest, she would have admitted that she did not feel comfortable in the gown borrowed from Clarissa's extensive wardrobe. It was rather embarrassingly *décolleté*, although the well-cut bodice fitted snugly, emphasising her tiny waist, and the full skirts billowed out around her like a gossamer cloud. Even so, Rosina felt like a fraud, wearing someone else's gown and matching satin slippers. She tried to convince herself that it was all done in the interests of finding Monty, but that was not much comfort.

She had no alternative but to sit at the table and watch the dancers. She scanned the faces of the guests, but none was familiar and there seemed to be no sign of Monty. Attending the ball had seemed like a good idea as they discussed it over dinner that evening, but it now seemed to be a waste of time. They were no nearer finding Monty than they had been at the start of the day, although Grace had found herself a partner and seemed to have forgotten the reason for their gate-crashing the event. She was obviously enjoying herself, and Ariadne seemed quite happy dancing with Francis. However, Rosina was uncomfortably aware of sympathetic glances she was receiving from some of the other ladies present. In one way it was a relief to simply sit and watch the couples as they negotiated the complicated steps of a mazurka. Rosina's experience of dancing to date had mainly been country dances in much more modest venues. She found herself wishing she was back in Moonshadow Manor with the moor stretching out as far as the eye could see, and her grandmother dozing in her favourite chair by the fire.

'Miss Wills, may I have the pleasure of the next dance?'

Rosina looked up with a start. 'Jack! What are you doing here?'

'I came looking for you.' He glanced over his shoulder. 'Hugo is also here. He's come to take Ariadne home. I knew I should have insisted on accompanying you to London.'

'We are managing perfectly well,' Rosina said stiffly. 'Please sit down, people are staring. How did you know we were here?'

'When you weren't at Hugo's town house, we assumed that Grace had insisted on taking you both to Cavendish Square. Horrocks told us where to find you.' Jack pulled up a chair and sat far too close for comfort. 'I know that Ariadne insisted on accompanying you, but why did you bring Grace?'

'To be honest I didn't have any choice. Grace made up her mind to accompany us to London.'

Jack smiled. 'That sounds like Grace. From what I know of her, she is very headstrong.'

'She is, but she is also very resourceful, and she knows more people in London than Ariadne does, so that is why we came here in search of Monty. Lady Tring was not very helpful.'

'You went to Welbeck Street?'

'Are you acquainted with Lady Tring?'

'No, but I made it my business to learn all I could about Monty because I knew that you would stop at nothing when it came to finding a home for the children. Not that Monty Fairbanks is the ideal foster parent for a rabbit, let alone two little girls.'

'Lady Tring is prepared to take them in, Jack.'

He put his head on one side, eyeing her curiously. 'You don't sound too impressed.'

'I pity the girls being raised by an aunt who is only doing her duty. I hoped that perhaps Monty might decide to do the right thing and take them in, with a nanny, of course.'

'Monty is an irresponsible rogue, Rosie.'

'I gather that he's going to inherit a fortune. If he marries someone suitable, he might give the children a good home and the love they desperately need.'

'I can't help thinking you are placing too much trust in Monty Fairbanks, but he is their uncle, and he should take some responsibility for his late brother's children.'

'So, you agree with me?' Rosina met his amused gaze with a steady look.

'I'm not saying that exactly, but I do admire your tenacity and your concern for two little orphans.' Jack turned his head. 'Here comes Hugo. I should warn you, Rosie, he is not happy about his sister coming to London without a proper chaperone.'

One look at Hugo's thunderous expression was enough to convince Rosina that Jack was right.

'Why is my sister dancing with that idiot Francis Moulton?' Hugo demanded, glowering at the dancers as they swept past.

'He was kind enough to escort us to the ball,' Rosina said cautiously. 'We came in search of Monty Fairbanks.'

'I know all that, and in my opinion, you are wasting your time. Monty is a gambler and a lothario. He is the last person I would entrust with the lives of two small children.' Hugo stood with his arms folded. 'We should go as soon as this dance ends. I'm taking Ariadne to my lodgings in Dover Street.'

'But we are staying at the Charteris house in Cavendish Square,' Rosina protested. 'Ariadne has unpacked her valise.'

'We'll take a cab there and she can collect her belongings.' Hugo beckoned to Ariadne as she danced past him in Frank's arms. 'I can't abide that fellow,' Hugo added through clenched teeth.

Rosina and Jack exchanged worried glances.

'Look, Hugo, I know this is far from ideal,' Jack said reasonably. 'But might I suggest that I stay in your lodgings tonight and you leave your sister with Rosina and Grace? We can call for them in the morning and escort them home.'

'That sounds sensible, Jack.' Rosina gave him a grateful smile.

'All right,' Hugo said grudgingly. 'But I'm taking her home in the morning and I don't want any arguments.' He strode off to stand at the edge of the dance floor.

'I hope he doesn't drag her off physically.' Rosina was about to stand up, but Jack laid a gentle hand on her arm.

'There's nothing you can do, Rosie. Just sit there and let Hugo have his say. You'll only make matters worse if you try to interfere.'

Rosina shook off his restraining hand. 'Hugo is a bully. No wonder Ariadne is such a silly thing.'

Jack laughed. 'Well, it looks as if she's found her knight in shining armour. I believe that young fellow she's dancing with is standing up to Hugo.'

Rosina's hand flew to cover her mouth as she stifled a giggle. It did seem that Francis had found the courage to argue with Hugo while Ariadne looked on open-mouthed. The episode was brief, and Hugo escorted Ariadne off the dance floor and brought her back to the table.

'I'm going to call a cab for you girls,' Hugo said grudgingly. 'Don't allow Grace to gainsay you, Rosina. I expect all three of you to return to Cavendish Square immediately.'

Rosina opened her mouth to argue but a warning look from Jack made her bide her time. She waited until Hugo had stormed off to call a cab.

'Why did you let him do that, Jack? Grace might not want to leave the ball yet.'

'That is up to her, Rosie. I can't tell Grace what to do.'

'But you think you can order me to comply with Hugo's demands?'

'Of course not. But I can't see *you* allowing Ariadne to return to Cavendish Square on her own.'

Rosina was saved from replying by Ariadne who was now back at the table, followed by Francis.

'I was never so humiliated,' Ariadne said tearfully. 'We were just dancing, and Hugo was hateful to Frank.'

Francis cleared his throat, eyeing Jack nervously. 'It was all very proper, sir.'

'Don't worry about me, Moulton,' Jack said casually. 'I have no say in what Ariadne does. But if I were you, I wouldn't aggravate her brother any more this evening.'

'We're going back to Grace's house, Ariadne,' Rosina added hastily. 'Your brother is going to take you home in the morning, so I should say goodbye to Frank, if I were you. Hugo has only gone to call a cab.'

Ariadne turned to Francis, blushing and fluttering her eyelashes. 'I'm sorry, Frank. I did enjoy our dance, but I don't think we'll meet again.'

He took her hand and raised it to his lips. 'I will come to Devonshire to see you, if you will allow it, Ariadne.'

'Really? You would travel all that way just to see me?' Ariadne stared at him in amazement.

'I would travel to the moon and back,' Francis said dreamily.

Jack patted him on the shoulder. 'If I were you, I would beat a hasty retreat, old chap. Hugo is coming back.'

Francis took a step away from Ariadne, but Grace chose that moment to rejoin them.

'What is going on?' she demanded. 'Why the long faces? And why are you here, Jack Dimond? And what has upset Hugo? I can tell by the look on his face that he is not best pleased.'

'I think I'd better explain on the way back to Cavendish Square,' Rosina said hastily as Hugo strode towards them.

Grace turned to face him. 'Are you being a killjoy again, Cousin Hugo? Can't you allow your poor sister one evening of fun without ruining everything?'

'Don't make a scene,' Ariadne pleaded, dashing tears from her cheeks.

Grace opened her mouth to argue but Rosina stood up and placed herself squarely between them.

'Don't say another word, Grace. Ariadne is in enough trouble with her brother without you adding your two penn'orth. We are going back to your house now, but you may stay here with Frank if you wish. I cannot tell you what to do.' Rosina slipped her arm around Ariadne's shoulders. 'Come along.

We'll leave now, but this isn't over.' She turned to Hugo. 'I hope you are proud of yourself for making your sister cry. We are leaving and we don't need you to escort us, Hugo.'

Jack rose to his feet. 'I will see you to the cab. Are you coming, Grace?'

She nodded. 'I suppose so, although I am very reluctant to do anything just because Hugo demands it.' She turned to Francis. 'You know where I live. You might just catch us there tomorrow before we leave. Thank you for escorting us here tonight, anyway.'

Hugo stood aside to allow Grace to pass. 'I pity the poor devil who ends up marrying you, Grace Charteris.'

Grace tossed her head and walked past him. 'I could say the same about you, Hugo.' She marched on ahead and was first to climb into the cab, followed quickly by Ariadne. Rosina hesitated, turning to Jack with a grateful smile.

'Thank you for intervening with Hugo.'

'It was nothing, and don't worry, Rosie. We will find Monty and then arrangements can be made for Flora and Lottie.'

Rosina stared at him in surprise. 'You remember their names. Most people refer to them as "the children" or something similar.'

'They are persons in their own right. I'm not overly sentimental, but even very young girls are entitled to be treated like individuals. I would hate to think that any offspring I might have in the future might end up as merely a problem to be solved.' Jack helped Rosina into the cab and closed the door. 'Good night, ladies. I'll see you tomorrow.'

Grace sank back against the worn leather squabs. 'Jack Dimond improves on acquaintance. If he was a rich man I would marry him, but as he's only a lawyer I think I'll hand him over to you, Rosina.'

'I think I might marry Frank,' Ariadne said dreamily. 'I believe he inherited quite a large fortune from his late papa.'

'You hardly know him.' Grace yawned and closed her eyes. 'You are such a silly goose, Ariadne.'

'I like him and he's coming to Devonshire to see me.' Ariadne's mouth drooped at the corners and her eyes reddened.

'Don't take any notice of Grace,' Rosina said hastily. 'She enjoys teasing you, Ariadne. Sir Francis seems a decent enough person. Maybe it is love at first sight.'

'Did you hear that, Grace?' Ariadne poked Grace in the ribs. 'Rosina says that Frank loves me, so there. Anyway, I don't see suitors queuing at your door.'

Grace uttered a pretend snore. 'Shut up, Ariadne. When I am ready to settle down, I will pick the lucky man who is going to marry me.'

'Aren't you both forgetting something?' Rosina demanded angrily.

'What do you mean?' Grace opened her eyes, suddenly alert.

'The reason we came to London in the first place,' Rosina said patiently. 'We need to find Monty Fairbanks and make him come to a decision as to the fate of Flora and Lottie.'

'I suggest we leave it to Jack and Hugo.' Grace yawned. 'All I want now is a nice warm bed.'

'And a cup of hot chocolate, or even cocoa,' Ariadne added, nodding. 'We will sort it all out tomorrow, Rosina.'

After a good night's sleep, Rosina was up early as usual. She washed, dressed and put up her hair before going downstairs to the dining room. There was no sign of either Grace or Ariadne, but they had both been exhausted after the ball, and it was not surprising that they were not yet awake. Breakfast was already set out in silver serving dishes and Rosina helped herself to bacon and buttered eggs. She took her plate to the table and sat down just as a maid entered bringing a pot of coffee and a rack of toast, which she placed in front of Rosina.

'Thank you.' Rosina settled down to enjoy the meal, and the maid left quietly, closing the door behind her. However, she returned within minutes.

'If you please, miss. There is a gentleman who wishes to speak to you urgently.'

'Did he give you a name?' Rosina put her coffee

cup down on its saucer. 'I wasn't expecting anyone this early.'

But before the maid could answer, the door opened and Jack strode into the room.

'It's all right,' he told the maid. 'Miss Wills knows me.'

'Yes, I do,' Rosina agreed, noting the worried expression on the maid's face. 'You may go, thank you.' She waited until the door closed once again on the servant. 'Why are you here so early, Jack? What could be so urgent?'

'You wanted to see Monty – well, I found him last night. He wasn't in a fit state to talk much, but we should be able to get some sense out of him this morning.'

'What about Hugo and the girls?'

'Hugo is going to take them home. You and I will follow later, if that is what you wish.'

Rosina drank the rest of her coffee before rising to her feet. 'I will do anything if it means we can speak to Monty.'

'Then come with me now. We can collect your things afterwards, only I don't want to give Monty the time to move on elsewhere. I believe there is a race meeting later today and I'm quite sure that will be his destination, hence the haste.'

'I'll just fetch my bonnet and mantle, and I'll leave a note for Grace and Ariadne.' Rosina left the dining room and hurried upstairs to pack her bag and put on her outdoor garments. She left a note with her valise so that Grace or Ariadne would find it when they came looking for her, and, having checked her appearance in the mirror, she went downstairs to join Jack.

The hansom cab pulled up in a narrow alley lined with warehouses, tenements and pubs. The smell of the river mud hit Rosina with force as she alighted holding on to Jack's hand. The sounds from the nearby docks were a cacophony of horns hooting, cranes creaking and groaning and barrels being rolled over cobblestones.

'This is a far cry from Welbeck Street, Jack,' Rosina said anxiously. 'Are you sure we've come to the right place?'

'I know it's not a very salubrious part of the city, but this is where I found him. I imagine he had a heavy night, and he was certainly very drunk when I picked him up off the pub floor.'

'You did that?' Rosina stared at him in surprise. 'You didn't need to go that far, Jack.'

'I think I did. Those children deserve better than Monty Fairbanks, but we need to get some sense out of him, or else the girls will be destined to be raised by their great-aunt.'

Rosina hesitated on the pavement outside what appeared to be a cheap lodging house. She was uncomfortably aware that they were being watched by rough-looking men who were loitering in doorways.

'Let's find him then,' she said hastily.

Jack placed his arm protectively around her shoulders as he crossed the pavement and knocked on the door. It was opened just a crack, and an unkempt woman peered out at them.

'What d'yer want? You ain't no dossers.'

'I brought a man here last night. You gave him a room, for an exorbitant price, considering the locality and the amenities.'

'Speak English, you stuck-up toff.' The woman spat on the ground in front of Jack.

Rosina clutched Jack's arm, but she held her head high. 'Could we see the person in question, please?'

'So, the young lady has manners. More than can be said for you, mate.' The woman held the door open just wide enough to admit them into the stinking hallway. The floorboards were filthy and worn thin in places. Wallpaper hung in shreds off the walls as the old woman mounted the stairs, treading on the carapaces of dead cockroaches while the live ones scuttled for safety. When they reached the landing, she thrust open a door and held out her hand.

'That'll be tuppence for me trouble, mister.'

Jack took some coins from his pocket and dropped them onto her outstretched palm.

'Ta, mister. Let's hope you find him still alive. I've seen drunks like him end up corpses.'

'Thank you, ma'am.' Rosina tried hard to remain polite. 'We will check on him.'

'Yes, thank you for your trouble. We can manage from here.' Jack stood aside, jerking his head in the direction of the staircase. 'That will be all.'

'La-di-dah!' The woman stamped towards the stairs and descended, grumbling with each step.

'Let's hope she was being overdramatic,' Jack said cautiously as he opened the door wider. 'Let me go in first, Rosie. This isn't going to be a pretty sight.' He entered the room and Rosina followed, but she came to a halt, holding her hand to her face as the noxious smell enveloped her.

The air was thick with the smell of stale alcohol and vomit. The bare boards were stained, and Monty lay face down on filthy bedding. He stirred when Jack poked him on the shoulder.

'Wake up, Fairbanks,' Jack said sharply. When there was no response, he turned Monty onto his back. 'Sit up. I know you can hear me.'

Monty opened one bloodshot eye and then closed it again. 'Go away.'

Jack leaned over then dragged him into a sitting position. 'You might want to wait outside, Rosie. I think he's going to throw up again.'

Rosina suppressed a shudder. 'I grew up in North London, Jack. I'm not a delicate young lady like Ariadne or even Grace. Let's get him out of this disgusting place.'

'You heard what the young lady said, Monty.' Jack looped Monty's arm around his shoulders and hefted him to his feet. 'Come on. You'll feel better in the fresh air. You go first, Rosie.'

Jack helped Monty to navigate the stairs and Rosina opened the front door. Outside the air seemed quite fresh and clean after the stench of the interior. Rosina took deep breaths and began to feel better. She would not have admitted it to Jack, but she had been feeling quite faint in the stuffy confines of the dosshouse. Jack marched Monty to the end of the street and held his head under the pump while he worked the handle. Water spurted out and Monty struggled, coughing and choking beneath the relentless flow. When Jack released his grip Monty straightened up, shaking water from his head.

'You nearly drowned me,' he protested, wiping his eyes on the back of his hand.

'If I'd wanted to do that, I would have thrown you in the Thames. It's only a few yards away.' Jack brushed droplets of water from the sleeve of his jacket. 'There's a coffee house in Fleet Street. We'll go there and finish sobering you up so that we can have a sensible conversation. Are you coming with us, Rosie?'

The aroma of roasting coffee beans mingled with the smell of pipe smoke in the warm fuggy atmosphere of the coffee house. Rosina and Jack sipped their drinks while Monty drank thirstily, and when he had finished one cup of the beverage Jack ordered another.

Red-eyed, and with steam coming from his wet jacket and shirt, Monty regarded Jack nervously. 'I'm sober enough, Dimond. What do you want from me?'

'I want nothing. It's your orphaned nieces who need your attention, Fairbanks.'

'Yes, Monty, they are still living with me at Moonshadow Manor,' Rosina added firmly. 'It can't go on like that.'

Monty ran his hand through his damp hair. 'What has it got to do with me? I can't look after small children.'

'That's obvious,' Jack said drily. 'It seems that you can't even take care of yourself. But they are your kith and kin. What is to become of them?'

'Aunt Tring will take care of them. She has a large house and plenty of servants. The girls will be brought up to be ladies.' Monty patted the pockets of his waistcoat. 'My pocket watch has gone. That thieving bitch at the dosshouse must have taken it.' He shot an apologetic look in Rosina's direction. 'I apologise for the language, Miss Wills, but you really shouldn't be here.'

'Are you actually going to abandon those children?' Rosina demanded angrily. 'Your aunt paid lip service to their welfare, but it was clear that she really did not want to be bothered with two small children.'

'They are not my responsibility. I haven't got a home of my own and I certainly can't afford to keep them fed and dressed. Aunt Maud is their nearest relative.'

'But I thought you were about to inherit a title and a fortune from some ancient relation,' Rosina insisted. 'Whoever that is must also be some sort of relation to the girls.'

'Perhaps that's an exaggeration.' Monty rose to his feet. 'I can't help you, and to be honest I don't like children. If it were left to me, I would put them in an orphanage, which is probably where they will end up.' Monty walked out of the coffee shop, allowing the door to swing shut behind him.

Rosina stared at Jack in dismay. 'That is so cruel.'

He laid his hand on hers as it rested on the table. 'What now, Rosie? Do you want to go to Welbeck Street and face Lady Tring with the truth about her precious nephew?'

Rosina shook her head. 'Never, Jack. I couldn't face leaving those poor little mites with someone who clearly did not want to have them but was only doing her duty. They deserve better than that. I want to go home to Moonshadow Manor. I've grown used to the wild moor and the clean air. I know I was born and raised in London, but I feel suffocated here.'

'Then we'll get the next train. I'll see you safely home.'

Chapter Eighteen

It was late afternoon when they arrived at Moonshadow Manor.

'Thank you, Jack,' Rosina said as he helped her to alight in the stable yard. 'You didn't have to drive me from the station, but I am very grateful.'

He handed the reins to Joshua, who had emerged from the coach house. 'Just give him a drink. I'll be leaving again soon, Joshua, so don't bother to unharness him.'

'Yes, master.' Joshua led Judge away, chatting to the horse as if he were an old friend.

'You must come in for some refreshment, Jack,' Rosina said firmly. 'It's been a long day.'

'I'll see you safe inside, and give my respects to your grandmother, but I won't stay long, Rosie. It will be dark in an hour or two.'

'She's always pleased to see you, even if she doesn't say so.' Rosina led the way into the scullery and through to the kitchen where she had expected to find Merry preparing dinner, but she was not there.

'Merry,' Rosina called as she made her way to the entrance hall where she stopped to listen for the sound of voices. 'This is strange, Jack. Where is everyone?'

'They can't be far away,' Jack said reasonably. 'Try the drawing room. I expect your grandmother is snoozing by the fire.'

Rosina felt the hairs on the back of her neck tingle, and she sensed that all was not well. She entered the drawing room and found it empty. The fire had burned to ashes and there was a chill in the air.

'Something is wrong, Jack. I can feel it.'

'It does seem strange,' Jack agreed, frowning.

Rosina was about to retrace her steps when the door opened and Merry rushed into the room, her face flushed and her bonnet hanging by its ribbons. She brushed her tumbled hair back from her forehead.

'Oh, miss. Thank goodness you've come home.'

'What's the matter, Merry? Where is my grandmother? She hasn't been taken ill, has she? And where are the children?'

'I just took them to my mother to look after, miss. I went looking for Dr Clarke, but I couldn't find him. His housekeeper said he has packed up and left.'

'What do you mean, he's left? Has he gone away somewhere or was he simply on a visit to one of his patients? And where is my grandmother, Merry? What is going on?'

'I dunno where she be, miss, and that's the truth. She's been acting strange since you went to London, and when I brought her food at midday she weren't here. I went to her room, thinking that she must be having a nap, and she weren't there either. All her clothes have gone, miss. I think Roxanne has spirited her away.'

'Roxanne must have taken the good doctor as well, if, as you say, he is also missing,' Rosina said slowly. She turned to Jack. 'What do you think, Jack? I'm seriously worried now.'

'It seems obvious that they have gone together,' Jack said, frowning. 'But why now?'

'Grandmother wouldn't go away without telling me. Would she?' Rosina sat down on the small sofa, as her knees gave way beneath her.

'Wasn't she planning something of the sort when you first came here?' Jack walked over to the escritoire. 'Maybe she's left a note. I don't believe she would simply disappear.' He leafed through a sheaf of papers. 'These are just bills and receipts. There's nothing here.'

'Ma said it were Roxanne,' Merry said gloomily. 'It were a full moon last night. That's when Roxanne is about and making mischief.'

'That is just superstitious nonsense. Roxanne died years ago.' Rosina glanced anxiously at Jack.

She wondered how he could bear hearing his great-grandmother's name used in folklore.

'That's right,' Jack said firmly. 'Whatever the truth, Miss Maddern and Dr Clarke are both adults with minds of their own. We can do nothing but wait and hope to hear from them, Rosie.'

Rosina peeled off her gloves and rose to her feet. She took off her bonnet and mantle and laid them on a chair. 'I'm going to search her room to see if she left a note or anything that might tell me where she has gone, and why she left so suddenly.'

'I could stay here tonight, if that would ease your mind,' Jack said worriedly.

'I will be fine.' Rosina managed a smile. 'I have Merry to keep me company and Joshua is in the coach house. Not that I expect anything untoward to happen. Perhaps the children could stay with your mother just for one night, Merry.'

'Yes, miss. Of course. Ma loves little ones. She's always saying it's sad when children grow up too soon, so don't worry about the girls.' Merry shot a questioning look in Jack's direction. 'Will you stay for supper, sir?'

He shook his head. 'No, but thank you, Merry. I should be going on my way. I might stop off at the doctor's house and see if his housekeeper knows anything that might help us.' He turned to Rosina. 'I'll come over in the morning, Rosie.'

'Yes, thank you, Jack. I shan't sleep a wink until I know that Grandmama is all right.'

'I think you can rely on Dr Clarke to take care of her,' Jack said gently. 'Try not to worry.' He turned to Merry with a warm smile. 'Look after her, Merrilees. And send Joshua for me if things change dramatically.'

'Aye, sir. I will.' Merry glanced anxiously at Rosina. 'Shall I make a pot of tea, miss? I'll set about making supper, but you've had a long journey. Maybe you should rest?'

'Goodbye, Rosie. Until tomorrow.' Jack hurried from the room and Merry made to follow him but hesitated in the doorway as she waited for Rosina's answer.

'Goodbye, Jack.' Rosina smiled tiredly. 'A cup of tea would be most welcome. I'm just going upstairs to see if I can find a note or anything to give me a clue as to where they have gone.'

Merry grinned. 'Maybe they've gone off to Gretna Green to get wed.'

'No! That's impossible,' Rosina said hastily. 'But I suppose it could be one answer. I'm going to examine my grandmother's room, Merry. I'll be down directly.'

The portrait of Roxanne gazed at Rosina as she went through everything that was left on her grandmother's dressing table and in the drawers. She pulled back the bedclothes and searched underneath in case a slip of paper had fluttered to the ground, but there was nothing. The clothes press was almost empty, with just a few items of clothing left that were old and outdated. Not that Jane Maddern had been a follower of fashion, but the discarded garments were sensible skirts and blouses that Jane might have worn when working in her kitchen garden or tending her cows on the moor. Rosina was beginning to realise how little she knew of her own grandmother, and now she had gone and might never return.

She glanced up at the painting of the beautiful Roxanne. 'You are just a likeness in oils,' Rosina said out loud. 'I don't believe that you haunt the moor or this house.' Acting on impulse, Rosina went to stand in front of the painting. She placed a hand on either side of the ornate gilt frame and lifted it off its hook. It was heavy, dusty and the back was covered in cobwebs, but as Rosina placed it on the floor there was a shower of gilt paint, and a tightly rolled piece of parchment was dislodged from between the canvas and the frame. Rosina propped the portrait against the wall and picked up the document. It was brittle with age, and she had to unroll it carefully to keep it from disintegrating. She took it to the window seat and sat down to study the neat copperplate writing in the last rays of the sun.

Moonshadow Manor, the sixteenth day of
May in the year of our Lord 1800
To my darling baby boy, Nathaniel,
You may never read this, but should it come
into your hands, my darling boy, I want you
to know that your mother loved you dearly. I
was forced to give you up to your father, Jabez
Dimond, which I will regret for the rest of my
days. However, Jabez will give you the life that
only money can buy, and I am certain you will
do well in the world. Do not believe the stories
that you will be told about me.
Your loving mother,
Roxanne

Rosina folded the note gently. This was something that would never have come to light had she not taken down the painting. It was almost as if Roxanne wanted it to be found and given to Jack, who had spent his whole life living in the shadow of a passionate affair between his great-grandfather and Roxanne, the woman who was adored by Phillip Maddern, the man who bested Jabez at a game of cards. Rosina could only begin to imagine the conflict, drama and scandal that the affair between Jabez and Roxanne must have caused, and it seemed as if it were having repercussions to this day.

Rosina tucked the letter into her skirt pocket. It had remained hidden for more than sixty-five years, another few hours would make no difference, but she still had not found anything from her grandmother. After finding nothing in her own room, Rosina went downstairs to the kitchen.

'Any luck?' Merry stopped stirring a pot on the hob. 'Did you find anything from Miss Jane?'

Rosina shook her head. 'No, nothing.'

'The soup will be ready soon, miss. I started it off this morning so I'm just reheating it. You must be hungry after all that travelling.'

'I suppose I am, but I haven't given much thought to eating all day. Do you think the children will be all right at your mother's cottage, Merry? I don't want to take advantage of her good nature.'

Merry laughed. 'Ma would be calling it a kindness to let her have the girls. She misses tucking little ones up in bed and telling them stories.'

'It's very good of her, and much appreciated.'

'You didn't find their uncle in London?'

'We found him,' Rosina said bitterly. 'He was in a drunken state, and he didn't want anything to do with them. His aunt, Lady Tring, said reluctantly that she would take the girls in, but I hate to think what sort of life they would have with her.'

'Poor little mites. What will you do with them?'

Rosina frowned. 'I don't know and that's the truth, but they must stay here until something more permanent is decided upon. I will go to the village first thing in the morning to thank your mother and

I'll bring the girls home. That soup smell delicious, Merry. I am hungry after all.'

Bright and early next morning, with Pixie in harness, Rosina drove the chaise to the Paveys' cottage on the edge of the village. She thanked Mrs Pavey profusely for having the children overnight, and the small girls raced out to give Rosina a hug. They chattered incessantly all the way back to Moonshadow Manor and were still talking over each other when Joshua laughingly lifted them from the chaise.

'Seems like they had a good time with Merry's family, miss.'

'Indeed, they did.' Rosina looked over her shoulder at the sound of a horse neighing in the stables. 'Is that Judge, Mr Dimond's animal, Joshua?'

'Yes, miss. He arrived soon after you left for the village.'

'Thank you, Joshua. Take care of Pixie for me.' Rosina climbed down to the cobblestones and shooed the children into the house. She could hear them calling for Merry as they ran into the kitchen.

Merry caught them both up in her arms and kissed their chubby cheeks.

'I've missed you both. I hope you was good for my mum.'

Flora nodded vigorously. 'We were really good. Mrs Pavey said so, didn't she, Rosina?'

'I was good, too,' Lottie added hastily.

'I'm sure you were,' Rosina smiled.

'Mr Dimond is in the morning parlour, miss,' Merry said firmly. 'Would you like some coffee?'

'Yes, please. I'll leave the girls with you while I go and talk to Mr Dimond.' Rosina hurried from the kitchen and made her way to the morning room.

Jack was standing by the window, gazing out at the moor. He turned at the sound of her footsteps and smiled.

'Good morning, Rosie. How are you today?'

'I'm well, but did you find out anything last evening when you called at the doctor's house?'

He shook his head. 'His housekeeper said he had gone away for a few days, but he had not told her where or when he might return. She said it was very sudden. Did you find a note or anything from Miss Maddern?'

'No, but I found something else.' Rosina took the parchment from her pocket and handed it to him. 'I took down Roxanne's portrait and this was dislodged from the back of the frame.'

Jack unfolded it carefully and read it, his expression barely changing. He looked up.

'You've read it?'

'Yes, Jack. It had to be something important for it to have been hidden so carefully. It's almost as if Roxanne hoped that one of her descendants would find it and be comforted by her words.'

'It seems that she parted reluctantly with

Nathaniel. I dare say my father knew the truth, but it's one of those secrets that families try to keep from public attention.'

'I pity my great-grandmother having to live with the painting of the woman who had caused such heartache.'

Jack gazed down at the letter with a deep sigh. 'But it's good to know that Roxanne was reluctant to give up her child, and she did it for his own good. I respect her for that.'

'I wonder if there is some sort of curse on Moonshadow Manor,' Rosina said slowly. 'Grandmama devoted the best years of her life to Sir Bertram. Now she has gone missing with Dr Clarke.'

Jack slipped the piece of parchment into his pocket. 'Why would they simply disappear without a word?'

'I don't know, Jack. But Merry thinks they might have eloped to Gretna Green,' Rosina said with a wry smile. 'There seems to be little we can do other than wait for them to contact us, but the most pressing problem is finding a good home for Flora and Lottie.'

'Lady Tring is their nearest relative, Rosie. I'm afraid the law is on her side. She has offered to take care of the children and Monty can't look after himself, let alone his small nieces.'

'What are you saying Jack?' Rosina asked

anxiously, although in her heart she already knew the answer.

'I think we ought to take the children to London, and let Lady Tring do her best for them, Rosie.'

'I suppose you're right, but it breaks my heart to condemn them to life in that mausoleum with a woman who is only having them as a matter of duty.'

'They will have a good education and advantages that are denied to most children,' Jack said earnestly. 'You could visit them, if her ladyship agrees, or maybe they could come to Moonshadow to stay in the summer.'

'They could, if Lady Tring would allow it, but if Grandmama doesn't return, for whatever reason, I don't think I will be able to remain here, Jack.'

'Why not?'

'The main reason being that I can't afford it. I have no income other than the money I earned in the market, and no way of earning enough to maintain this old house and pay Merry and Joshua.'

Jack frowned. 'There's the fund that Sir Bertram set up for Miss Maddern.'

'That's just it. The money belongs to Grandmama, not to me. If she does not return soon, I will have no alternative but to go home and live with my father and stepmother.'

'We must hope that your grandmother remembers her responsibilities, Rosie. I've known Miss Maddern all my life. I can't believe that she would desert you.'

'Neither can I, but I have to plan ahead, Jack. I don't want to return to London. I've grown to love Moonshadow Manor and the moor. I feel part of the village and city life has no attraction for me now, but I must be practical.'

'Don't do anything yet. There is still time for Miss Maddern to contact you or even me as I handle her business affairs. Leave it to me, Rosie. I will arrange for us to take the children to London, but first I will contact Lady Tring and make sure she is willing to have them. By that time, we will most probably have had some communication with your grandmother or the good doctor.'

'All right, Jack. I'll try to be patient, and I'll take care of the girls until we know what their fate will be.'

Jack laughed. 'I'm sure that Lady Tring will mellow when she has two young lives to care for. She might unbend enough to become a doting great-aunt, and in any event, she can afford to hire a nanny and a governess when the girls are older.'

Rosina knew that what Jack said made sense, but it did not help to calm the anxiety she felt for the helpless children.

During the next few days Rosina did her best to concentrate on the girls, and she took them for walks on the moor, where they picked wildflowers and looked for butterflies. Flora and Lottie had fun chasing rabbits, which showed little sign of fear when they approached, and then hopped off as if enjoying the game. Rosina laughed at their antics, and it helped her to forget her worries about her grandmother. There had been no word from her or from Dr Clarke, and his housekeeper was telling anyone who would listen that she thought the good doctor had met some terrible fate. It was all round the village and the stories grew more bizarre as they were told and retold. Jane Maddern seemed to have been written off as a subject of interest. Rosina thought that perhaps so much gossip had been centred on her over the years that the tales had been exhausted.

It was almost a week after they returned from London that Ariadne visited Moonshadow, but the only subject that interested her was Monty Fairbanks. Rosina told her frankly about the state in which they had found him, and the fact that he had probably exaggerated his prospects of inheriting a title and a fortune. Ariadne was obviously disappointed and then she was annoyed to think that her brother had been right.

'Hugo is impossible. I hate men,' Ariadne said passionately. 'I think I will go into a nunnery, Rosie.'

'You don't mean that, surely?' Rosina stifled a giggle. She could not imagine Ariadne in a nun's habit, let alone spending the best part of the day in prayer.

'Well, I do.' Ariadne stamped her foot. She glanced out of the drawing-room window. 'That's Sir Bertram's carriage, unless I'm very much mistaken.'

Rosina stood up to see out of the window. 'You're right. It seems we're very popular today.'

'It's Grace. She's probably come to crow because my hopes are dashed,' Ariadne said tearfully.

Rosina tugged at the bell pull. 'We'll have a nice cup of tea and some of Mrs Pavey's seed cake, and you can chat about the ball. Anyway, I thought you were rather taken with Sir Francis Moulton. He was certainly attracted to you, if I recall correctly.'

'He is all right,' Ariadne said grudgingly. 'But Monty is much more fun.'

At that moment the door burst open, and Grace waltzed into the room, followed closely by Merry.

'Why the glum faces?' Grace demanded, frowning.

'You rang, miss?' Merry asked before anyone had a chance to answer Grace.

'Yes, Merry. Please bring tea and cake. Where are the children? It's very quiet.'

'Ma came to take them for a walk,' Merry said, grinning. 'She's going to miss them something terrible when they goes to London.'

'I'm sure we all will.' Rosina turned to Grace, who was staring at her in surprise. 'Jack and I are taking the children to their great-aunt in London.'

'Tea and cake. Right away.' Merry whisked out of the room, allowing the door to swing shut.

'What about Monty?' Grace demanded. 'I thought you were going to find him and make him responsible for the children.'

'He was drunk,' Rosina said bitterly. 'He lied to us, Grace. He only pretended to be heir to a vast estate and a title.'

'Yes, I know he did.' Grace sat down, smiling smugly. 'Frank told me all about Monty Fairbanks.'

'When did you see Francis?' Ariadne glared at her. 'You said you didn't like him.'

'He called on me just before I left Cavendish Square the morning after the ball.'

'I'm sure he came to see me, not you. Why didn't you let me know he had called?'

'I didn't think you were interested in a mere baronet, Ariadne. I thought you had set your cap at Monty.'

'Are you insinuating that I chase after men? I was never so insulted.' Ariadne stamped her foot.

'I find that hard to believe,' Grace said, curling her lip. 'You are so desperate to catch a husband that it's embarrassing.'

Rosina raised her hands in exasperation. 'Could you please stop bickering? I have problems of my own.'

Grace and Ariadne turned to her, open-mouthed.

'Oh dear. What has happened?' Grace asked eagerly. 'Has Jack proposed, and you turned him down?'

'No such thing.' Rosina felt the blood rush to her cheeks. 'Jack is just a friend. No, I'm talking about my grandmother. She and Dr Clarke have vanished.'

'Vanished?' Ariadne said faintly. 'You mean they disappeared into thin air? Like a conjuring trick?'

'Don't be a ninny, Ariadne.' Grace rolled her eyes. 'What do you mean by "vanished", Rosina?'

'Precisely that.' Rosina sank down onto the sofa. 'When I arrived home after the ball in London, my grandmother was gone and so was Dr Clarke. We haven't had a word from them since.'

Grace's hand flew to her mouth. 'Gracious, how exciting. Wait until I tell Papa. He will be furious.'

'I don't see why it would bother him,' Rosina said angrily. 'He abandoned Grandmama in a most callous manner. Dr Clarke has supported her and looked after her for years.'

'You think they have eloped?' Ariadne's eyes widened. 'But they are old.'

'I don't think anyone is too old to feel love for another person,' Rosina said slowly. 'Dr Clarke is devoted to Grandmama, and if they can find happiness together, I will be more than satisfied. It's just the not knowing that bothers me.'

'What are you doing about it?' Grace asked eagerly. 'Have you hired a detective to look for them?'

'Good heavens, no.' Rosina shook her head. 'Nothing like that. I'm hoping they will return when they're ready, and in any case, I have the children to worry about. I'm taking them up to London tomorrow. Lady Tring is going to look after them.'

'Poor little dears. That's all I can say.' Grace pulled a face. 'I don't know Lady Tring well, but I can say truthfully that she is not the sort of person I would think suited to bringing up children.'

'She is the only relative we can find,' Rosina said sadly. 'I will miss the girls terribly, but they should be with their family, and anyway, I haven't got the means to support them.'

'My papa settled a considerable sum on Miss Maddern. Surely that will help you, Rosina?' Grace eyed her curiously.

'That money belongs to Grandmama, not to me. I came here with nothing, and I will leave here with nothing.'

'She seems to have left you Moonshadow Manor.' Ariadne frowned. 'I would be happy to be the owner of such a house.'

'It does not belong to me, Ariadne. And I can't afford to pay Merry or Joshua, let alone find the money to buy provisions. I am going to London with Jack, and we will see that the girls are settled. After that, to be honest, I don't know what I am going to do.'

Chapter Nineteen

'I'm coming with you.' Grace climbed into the compartment and slumped down on the seat between Flora and Lottie.

'What do you mean you're coming with us?' Rosina demanded. 'We are simply taking the girls to London to stay with their great-aunt.'

'Does your father know you're going to London?' Jack eyed Grace warily. 'You know how he views your pranks, Grace. Is this another one?'

Grace rolled her eyes. 'Certainly not. I can't allow you and Rosina to have all the fun. I just hope that Ariadne doesn't have the same idea.'

'This is ridiculous,' Rosina said crossly. 'It isn't a game. You can't keep doing this, Grace.'

'Life is a game. You just have to learn how to play it without breaking too many rules. I am here, under your protection, Jack. With you as my chaperone, Rosina. And I am helping with these two adorable little girls.' Grace tickled Lottie, who responded with a gurgle of laughter.

Rosina glanced anxiously out of the window as the guard blew his whistle, and the train started to move. She half expected to see Ariadne racing along the platform, but there was no sign of her.

'What are you planning to do in London, Grace? We are going straight to Welbeck Street and when we've seen the girls settled, we are returning to Devonshire. Will you go to Cavendish Square?'

'Yes, of course. My sisters might have returned from the house party by now, and anyway, Papa left for town yesterday. I was annoyed that he did not ask me if I wanted to accompany him, but he can hardly say anything when I turn up today.'

'I imagine he will have quite a lot to say,' Jack said drily. 'But you're welcome to travel with us, Grace.'

'Would your sudden return to London have anything to do with Sir Francis Moulton?' Rosina asked, smiling.

'I might have arranged to meet him for tea at Gunter's,' Grace said casually. 'They serve delicious ice cream. You would love that, girls. You must ask Aunt Tring to take you there one day.'

Flora slid off the seat and held her arms out to Rosina. 'May I sit on your lap, please?'

'Of course.' Rosina put her arms around the small girl and lifted her onto her lap.

'I want to stay with you and Merry,' Flora said tearfully.

'I will miss you very much, dear. But your aunt wants to look after you and Lottie. She can give you so much more than I ever could. We will come and see you often, Flora.'

Lottie attempted to climb onto Grace's lap, but Grace moved away.

'I love you, Lottie, but I don't want my travelling gown to be creased.'

Lottie began to sniffle, but Jack reached out and swung her onto his lap. 'Look out of the window, Lottie. See all the cows in the fields.' He turned to Rosina. 'This isn't going to be easy, Rosie. I haven't had much to do with small children, but I can see that it's going to be hard, especially for you.'

Rosina nodded, swallowing back tears. 'It must be done, Jack. No matter how hard it is to part with them, it's for their own good. I think it is, anyway.' She rubbed her cheek against Flora's curly head of hair. Now that the time had come, she was beginning to have her doubts, but it was all arranged. There was nothing for it but to carry on and relinquish the girls to what was left of their family.

Grace leaned back in her seat. 'I don't see what all the fuss is about. They're like little animals. They'll be happy when they're well fed and well dressed. One thing Lady Tring doesn't lack and that is money.' She closed her eyes. 'Wake me up when we get to London.'

The journey progressed with Grace snoring gently on one side of the compartment, Flora sleeping soundly on Rosina's lap and Lottie curled up in Jack's arms. The children barely awakened when they had to change trains and Grace moved like a sleepwalker. However, once they were settled in another comfortable compartment all was peaceful until the train pulled into Paddington Station.

Jack led the way to the cab stand with Lottie on his shoulders, and Flora clutched Rosina's hand as if she would never let it go. Grace ambled after them, seeming reluctant to take a cab to Cavendish Square on her own.

'I'll come with you to Welbeck Street,' she said, yawning. 'Then you must come and have luncheon with me at Cavendish Square before you even think about the return journey.'

'That's fine by me.' Jack looked to Rosina for confirmation, and she nodded.

'Yes, thank you, Grace. I am rather hungry, and it is a lot of travelling to do in one day.'

Jack helped them all into a hackney carriage and climbed in after them, having given the cabbie instructions to drive to Welbeck Street.

When the butler opened the door, he seemed surprised to see the children, but he ushered them into the hallway and walked off in a stately fashion to announce their arrival.

Rosina had expected a few minutes at least with Lady Tring, and when the butler returned, she was surprised to be told that Lady Tring was not at home, but Mrs Debden, the housekeeper, would see them in the morning parlour. He led the way, leaving Rosina, Jack and Grace little alternative but to follow with the children. By this time, Flora was openly sobbing with Lottie joining in, even though she did not really understand what was happening.

Mrs Debden joined them almost immediately and her expression was not exactly welcoming. She eyed the children as if they were small animals who had escaped from the zoo. Rosina was tempted to leave there and then, taking Flora and Lottie with her, but the girls' needs were paramount, and Lady Tring could give them a far better life than she ever could.

'I was expecting to see Lady Tring herself,' Rosina said firmly.

'Her ladyship is a very busy woman.' Mrs Debden drew herself up to her full height, folding her arms and frowning. 'She is on many committees for charities that raise a great deal of money for good causes.'

'Yes, I am sure of that,' Jack said easily. 'But what about the children? Lady Tring promised they would be cared for and taken into the family.'

'She left instructions for them to be made at home in the nursery. A great deal of effort has been put into making a room suitable for such young people. A nanny has been employed, and she will be starting this afternoon. You have arrived earlier than expected.'

'Perhaps we should take the children now and bring them back later, when the nanny is here and maybe I can have a word with her ladyship,' Rosina said icily.

'There's no need. I will assign a servant to take care of them until Nanny arrives.' Mrs Debden stared down her nose at Flora. 'I trust that you are going to be a good child. I expect you to look after your sister and see that she behaves.'

Flora clung to Rosina's skirts, burying her face in the folds of the cloth.

'This is a lot for them to take in,' Rosina said hastily. She sent an anxious look in Jack's direction, and she could see from his worried expression that he was also concerned for the girls' wellbeing.

'Come with me, child, and don't be so silly.' Mrs Debden caught hold of Flora's hand.

'No. I won't go with you,' Flora cried desperately. 'Don't let her take us away, Rosina.'

'You need discipline, young lady,' Mrs Debden said through gritted teeth. 'You will change your attitude soon enough.'

'They are good children.' Rosina held on to Flora, who was growing hysterical. 'Let her go, ma'am. You're frightening her.'

Jack stepped in between them. 'You heard what Miss Wills said, ma'am. Release the child.'

Mrs Debden eyed him warily as she let go of Flora's hand. 'I will not be held responsible for bad behaviour, sir.'

'No, indeed you will not.' Rosina scooped Flora into her arms. 'This was a mistake. I can see that this house is not a fit place for young children.'

'That's right, Rosina,' Grace said, startled out of her apparent lethargy. 'You tell the old vixen.'

Mrs Debden turned on her, scowling. 'What did you say, miss?'

'Miss Wills is right, ma'am,' Jack said firmly. 'We will take the children with us.'

'I will call on Lady Tring later.' Rosina held Flora in a tender embrace. 'You can see how distressed she is, so we will take her away now, but unless Lady Tring can convince me that this will be a happy home for the girls, I will keep them with me. I've learned to love them in the short time I have been looking after them. I cannot bear to think of them being unloved and unhappy.'

'Well said.' Grace patted Rosina on the back. 'Come home with me, Rosina, and bring the little ones.' She glanced at Jack, who was cradling a near hysterical Lottie. 'You're a lawyer. I'm sure you can work something out legally.' She marched out of the room with Rosina following.

'Good day, ma'am.' Jack hurried after them.

* * *

It was only a short walk from the gloomy house in Welbeck Street to the open space of Cavendish Square with its circular garden and London plane trees wearing the tender green leaves of late spring. Horrocks let them into the house with no sign of surprise on his face.

'Have my sisters returned yet, Horrocks?' Grace asked cheerfully.

'No, Miss Grace. As I understand it, they will be away for another week at least.'

'Never mind, it means I can borrow whatever I like of Clarissa's best gowns.' Grace grinned mischievously. 'Please inform Cook that there will be five of us for luncheon, two of the party being rather small people.'

Horrocks's rigid expression softened slightly as he glanced at the tear-stained faces of the little girls. 'I'll pass the message on, Miss Grace.'

'We'll be in the drawing room, Horrocks,' Grace said calmly. 'We'll have coffee and some lemonade for the girls.' She sailed on ahead, as if used to commanding a fleet of servants.

Rosina and Jack exchanged amused glances as they followed Grace to the drawing room. She took off her gloves, bonnet and mantle and handed them to a maid who followed them at a discreet distance. She waited to take Rosina's outer garments and left them, balancing Jack's top hat and kid gloves with care.

Grace collapsed onto the sofa. 'Do make yourselves comfortable and tell me what the plan is now.'

'Plan?' Rosina sat down with Flora on her lap. 'There is no plan, as you put it, Grace.'

'But you've taken the little ones away from their family,' Grace said pointedly. 'You cannot be thinking of keeping them, Rosina. It was a grand gesture, but surely you will return them to Welbeck Street this afternoon.'

Rosina shook her head. 'I don't know about that. I didn't take to Lady Tring when I first met her, and the least she could have done was to be there to welcome the children.'

Grace turned to Jack. 'What do you think, Jack? Surely you can't condone kidnapping the girls?'

'I'm not kidnapping them,' Rosina said angrily. 'They were left in my care and I'm just doing my best for them.'

'We will speak to Lady Tring before we make any firm decisions,' Jack added. 'I suggest we leave it at that because we're upsetting Flora with all this talk.'

'Yes, exactly,' Rosina said, nodding. 'This is too important to take lightly. Their lives are in our hands, whether we like it or not.'

'Well, I am meeting Frank at Gunter's at four o'clock, but you are all welcome to stay here tonight if it's too late to return to Devonshire.'

'What will Sir Bertram say to that?' Jack frowned. 'It's an imposition at best.'

'You're Papa's lawyer, Jack,' Grace said breezily. 'He's always mixed up in some sort of deal where he needs legal advice. You above all people should realise that.'

Rosina shifted a sleeping Flora to a more comfortable position. 'I'm learning more about the misdeeds of my family every day. I wonder what my pa would say if he knew the truth.'

'Do you really imagine he was ignorant of your mother's family history, Rosie?' Jack set Lottie down on the sofa as she awakened and began to wriggle in his arms.

'I don't think he knew anything about Grandmama's affair with Sir Bertram,' Rosina said slowly. 'I imagine he must have known that Grandmama was unmarried, but it was never mentioned at home.'

'And yet he was happy to allow you to live with a woman who had been shunned by society for a mistake in her youth.' Jack shook his head. 'One day I would like to meet your father, Rosie. I have a few choice words I would like to say to him.'

Rosina opened her mouth to protest but at that moment a maid arrived with their refreshments, and the opportunity was lost.

'Thank you, Nell,' Grace said, smiling. 'That will be all for now.' She waited until the maid had left the room. 'I was going to mention having two rooms made ready in case you needed to stay, but that can wait until later when we know what you're going to do.'

'I think we ought to return to Welbeck Street after luncheon,' Rosina said slowly. 'I want to speak to Lady Tring, and I think Jack should be there as my legal adviser.'

'I don't want to go there,' Flora said softly. 'I don't like that house.'

Grace handed her a glass of lemonade. 'Well, then, Flora. How would you like to accompany me and my friend Frank to Gunter's for an ice cream?'

Flora clapped her hands. 'Yes, please.'

'Yes, please,' Lottie repeated, giggling excitedly.

'That's settled then.' Grace poured the coffee and handed a cup to Rosina and another to Jack. 'Gunter's it is.'

Rosina was determined not to leave the house in Welbeck Street until she had spoken to Lady Tring in person. Mrs Debden tried her best to make her agree to leave the children and return to Devonshire, but Rosina was having none of it. She stood her ground with Jack's backing, and she took a seat in the dreary drawing room, refusing to move until she had said her piece. Eventually, after Rosina had waited for nearly two hours, Lady Tring entered the room. She did not look pleased.

'This is inexcusable behaviour, Miss Wills. But

then what can one expect from the daughter of a cloth merchant and a woman of questionable lineage.'

Rosina jumped to her feet, shaking off Jack's restraining hand.

'How dare you insult my parents? They might not be wealthy and well connected as you are, but that does not give you an excuse to belittle them – or me, come to that.'

'What is it you want to say? Be quick as I have a card party to attend in half an hour.' Lady Tring eyed Rosina coldly, her lips disappearing into a thin pencil line.

'Do you really want to raise Flora and Lottie as if they were your own children, Lady Tring? Or are you taking them in because it is the correct thing to do, and it makes you look good in front of your society friends?'

Lady Tring recoiled as if Rosina had struck her in the face. 'How dare you insult me in my own drawing room? I want you to leave my house now.' She turned to Jack, scowling. 'And you, sir. You call yourself a man of the law? Well, I have just been slandered by that young woman. What are you going to do about it?'

Jack placed himself between Rosina and Lady Tring. 'I think we have heard enough, ma'am. It seems that your offer to take the children in was due more to duty than common kindness and family feeling.'

'How dare you, sir?' Lady Tring's cheeks flamed scarlet with anger.

'Miss Wills has developed a fondness for your great-nieces, and they return the affection,' Jack continued unabashed. 'Perhaps in the circumstances it would be best for all parties if you relinquished responsibility for the girls and gave them into her care. I can assure you they would have a kind and loving home.'

'Take them. I never wanted them in the first place.' Lady Tring shot an angry glance in Rosina's direction. 'The children are penniless. They have no fortune to inherit and from now on I wash my hands of them.' She turned on her heel and stalked out of the drawing room.

Rosina exhaled slowly. 'Did she just give the children to my care, Jack? Or did I imagine it?'

He wrapped his arms around her in a hug, releasing her quickly as if embarrassed by this show of affection.

'Yes, she did, Rosie. You've won, but are you sure this is what you really want? I know you love the children, but bringing them up is a huge task.'

'I'm prepared for that, Jack. I can't bear to think of them locked away in this hateful house.'

'Just think it through before we return to Cavendish Square. I agree that this isn't the ideal home for them, but Monty is their nearest relative. If you have any doubts as to your ability, financial or otherwise, I think you should speak to him first.

He is a gambler, but he could be persuaded to do his duty by his nieces.'

'No. Never, Jack. I saw what he was like after his drunken spree. I wouldn't leave a cat in his care, let alone two small girls. I will manage one way or another. I most definitely will.'

Jack smiled. 'Then I think it's time we joined Grace and Sir Francis in Gunter's and gave the children the good news.'

'Oh, that would be so good. I love ice cream, and I believe Gunter's serve delicious cakes as well. Let's get out of this place, Jack. Gunter's it is.'

The hansom cab dropped them off outside Gunter's teashop in Berkeley Square. Jack proffered his arm, and Rosina laid her hand on his sleeve as they entered the prestigious eatery. The scent of sugary confections, vanilla and the expensive perfumes of the ladies present filled the air, and the patrons presented a rainbow of coloured silks, lace and hats decorated with ostrich feathers and artificial flowers.

Rosina spotted Grace and the children seated at a far table, with Frank looking every inch a family man, and for the first time Rosina could envisage him and Grace as a couple. But a nudge from Jack made her turn her head at a party seated in the window. Their good-humoured chatter and laughter were contagious, and it was obvious that they were having a wonderful time.

'I don't know who they are, but they are enjoying themselves,' Rosina said, smiling.

'Look closer,' Jack said in a low voice. 'I think you know the lady in the striking purple gown and the ridiculous hat.'

Rosina followed his gaze and gasped in amazement. 'I don't believe it, Jack. It can't be her.'

'I'd recognise that laugh anywhere, and look at the gentleman seated at her left. There's no mistaking him, despite the smart outfit.'

'I've been worried out of my mind since Grandmama left without so much as a note to say where she had gone, and here she is having the time of her life.' Rosina marched over to the table.

'Grandmama!'

Jane looked up and smiled. 'This is a nice surprise, Rosina. I didn't know that you were in town.'

'You disappeared without a word,' Rosina said angrily. 'Now I find you in Gunter's, dressed to the nines and having a wonderful time.'

Jane glanced round at her circle of acquaintances. 'My granddaughter exaggerates.' She turned back to Rosina, smiling. 'I'm sure I left a note, my dear. You must have missed it.'

'I searched high and low but there was nothing. I think you owe me an explanation, and you, Dr Clarke. Your housekeeper was intending to report you to the police as a missing person,' Rosina's voice shook with emotion.

'I think we should leave them to finish their meal, Rosie.' Jack laid his hand on her shoulder. 'There will be plenty of time to discuss this later.'

'Quite right,' Dr Clarke said hastily. 'We can explain, Rosina.'

'Where are you staying, Grandmama?' Rosina demanded, frowning.

'At a hotel in Curzon Street. It's not too far from here,' Jane said in a low voice. 'Please don't make a scene.'

'Perhaps we could meet you later at your hotel?' Jack suggested hastily. 'We don't want to intrude.'

'Excellent idea, my boy.' Dr Clarke said, nodding. He took a visiting card from his pocket and handed it to Jack. 'The address is there. Give us an hour or so and then we can talk in private.'

Jack slipped his arm around Rosina's shoulders. 'I think that sounds sensible, don't you, Rosie?'

'Yes, I suppose so.' Rosina looked down as Flora tugged at her hand.

'Me and Lottie are at a table over there,' Flora said, pointing. 'We've had some ice cream.'

'We're coming to join you.' Rosina allowed Flora to lead her away and she did not look back. She was shocked to find her grandmother and Albert taking tea in Gunter's as if it were the most natural thing in the world, but she was also hurt and angry. It was hard to equate the garishly dressed woman with the grandmother she had come to know and love. It was even harder to accept that Grandmama did not seem to feel guilty for her thoughtless actions.

'Come on, Rosie,' Jack said softly. 'Don't let them see you're upset. We'll sort this out when we speak to them at the hotel.'

Rosina nodded mutely and allowed Flora to lead her to the table where Lottie was still eating her ice cream.

Frank rose to his feet and pulled out a chair for Rosina. 'Who are those people? I don't recognise them.'

'The lady in the hideous gown with the preposterous hat looks a bit like your grandmother, Rosina,' Grace said, craning her neck to get a better view. 'And the gentleman at her side looks suspiciously like Dr Clarke.'

Rosina sat down, taking a deep breath. 'You're right, Grace. That woman *is* my grandmother, and she is here with Albert. I don't know whether to be glad that she's safe and having a marvellous time, or furious with her for all the worry she has caused.'

'I think it's funny,' Grace said, giggling. 'Miss Maddern was at death's door when you first came to Ugstock. Now look at her.'

Frank cleared his throat. 'I think perhaps the least said about that the better, Grace.' He gave Rosina an encouraging smile. 'Would you like some ice cream or perhaps some cake?'

'A cup of tea would be nice,' Rosina said vaguely. 'And perhaps one of those fancy cakes.'

'What about you, Jack?' Frank signalled to the waitress, who hurried over to them.

'I'll have the same as Rosie, please.' Jack lifted Flora and set her down on the seat next to Lottie.

'What are you going to do about Miss Maddern?' Grace asked eagerly.

'We're going to meet them at their hotel in an hour,' Rosina said in a low voice. 'Would you mind taking the girls back to Cavendish Square?'

'Of course not.' Grace moved from her chair to sit beside Rosina. 'You must tell me everything at dinner tonight. You will be staying, of course.'

Rosina smiled reluctantly. 'I don't think we have any choice. I am not returning to Moonshadow Manor until I know exactly what my grandmother is planning, and more importantly, what she wants me to do with the house if she has decided to remain in London.'

'You need to ask Dr Clarke what his intentions are,' Grace said seriously.

'His intentions?' Rosina stared at her in surprise. 'Do you mean marriage?'

'Well, the poor lady has suffered enough from devoting herself to the wrong man, meaning my papa. Surely Dr Clarke ought to make an honest woman of her, so to speak.'

'I hadn't thought about it like that,' Rosina said thoughtfully. 'But you're right, Grace. He should do the honourable thing, and I am going to tell him so.'

Chapter Twenty

The hotel in Curzon Street had once been three separate dwellings but had been converted into one building. It was quiet, respectable and met with Rosina's approval as she sat in the comfortable lounge with Jack. They did not have long to wait until Jane and Albert joined them. Jane had abandoned the ridiculous hat and had changed into a more conservative watered-silk dinner gown in a shade of deep blue. Albert had also changed into a black evening suit with a frilled white shirt, and he fingered his cravat nervously.

Jack stood up but Rosina remained seated, eyeing her grandmother warily.

'I know what you must be thinking,' Jane said, clinging to Albert's arm.

'I am just amazed to find you both living like lords

in London while we have been worrying about you.' Rosina shrugged. 'But it seems as if you simply don't care.'

Albert led Jane to a chair, and she sat down.

'I'm not apologising for enjoying our first taste of life together,' Jane said calmly. 'But I am sorry to have upset you, Rosina. We would have explained everything on our return.'

'So, you did plan to come back to Moonshadow. How was I to know, Grandmama?' Rosina frowned. 'You left me with very little money to live on, and I had no idea where you had gone or for how long, or even if you intended to return at all.'

'I must take my share of the blame.' Albert took a seat next to Jane. 'I have been in love with your grandmother for many years, Rosina. But I had to wait until she discovered what sort of man your grandfather was before I told her how I felt.'

'I think we can both understand that much,' Jack said quickly. 'But you didn't need to run away. Surely you could have left a note for Rosie, or you could have given me some instructions regarding finance, Miss Maddern.'

'Yes, you're right, of course, Jack.' Jane looked away, biting her lip. 'But it all happened so fast, and I suppose I was carried away by that, and excited at the prospect of coming to London and being myself for the first time in years.'

'And I intend to do the honourable thing,' Albert

added firmly. 'I have proposed to Jane, and she has accepted my offer of marriage.'

'We plan to marry quietly before we return to Ugstock.' Jane smiled wistfully. 'I can't be a young bride, but at least I can be a respectable matron now.'

Rosina found herself weakening. The love she had for her grandmother overcame the anger and hurt she had experienced, and she was even more aware of the pain that Jane Maddern must have endured, being treated as a woman of ill repute and raising a fatherless child. 'No!' she said firmly. 'You must not do that, Grandmama.'

'No?' Jane stared at her aghast. 'You can't mean that, dear.'

'Rosie?' Jack gave her a questioning look.

'I mean it,' Rosina said calmly. 'For one thing, I doubt if anyone in the village will believe that you are legally wed, and for another, I hate to think of you having a hole-in-the-corner ceremony, Grandmama.'

Jane clutched Albert's hand and held it to her cheek. 'I don't care what people think. I'm used to being the scarlet woman of Ugstock.'

'Exactly,' Rosina said triumphantly. 'After all you have been through, I think you should have a proper wedding in the village church with everyone invited. We should make a big day of it.'

'I don't know about that,' Jane said nervously. 'I think I would prefer to marry Albert before we face the people at home.'

'No, Grandmama.' Rosina stood up and began to pace the floor. 'That won't do. You've lived in the shadows for too long. This must be done properly for all to witness.'

'I think Rosina might have a point, my love,' Albert said gently.

'I'm afraid people will laugh at us. They will say it is ridiculous to have a church wedding at our age.'

'No one will laugh at you, Miss Maddern.' Jack rose to his feet. 'I think Rosie is right. Perhaps this is what Moonshadow needs – a celebration of the love you two have for each other.'

'Yes, Grandmama,' Rosina said eagerly. 'Moonshadow has had more than its fair share of sadness and star-crossed lovers. A happy ending to your situation will cast out the shadows in the house that have lingered since Roxanne was forced to give up her baby son.'

'And you imagine a big wedding will accomplish that?' Jane shook her head. 'Roxanne has become something of a legend, mainly because she walked out onto the moor and disappeared. No one knows what happened to her.'

'There are a lot of people who think her disappearance suspicious,' Albert said slowly. 'But rumours spread quickly and become exaggerated over time.'

'All the more reason for putting the past behind you and celebrating your love for each other,' Rosina said triumphantly. 'Do you agree?'

Albert smiled and nodded. 'I believe I do.'

'And you, Grandmama?' Rosina continued eagerly.

Jane sighed. 'I think I am outnumbered. I leave it in your hands, Rosina, my dear.'

'You will enjoy it all, Grandmama.' Rosina eyed her thoughtfully. 'And, first of all, you need a wedding dress, and I know exactly the right person to take you shopping tomorrow.'

'I have a nice gown, Rosina,' Jane said firmly.

'I mean a gown fit for the occasion, Grandmama. Not that purple creation you wore to Gunter's. Grace will take you to the best shops in town. She will know exactly where to go and what is suitable.'

'It seems such a waste of money, Rosina.' Jane shook her head. 'I'm sure there are more important things to buy than a gown I will only wear once.'

'Think of it as an investment, Miss Maddern,' Jack said, smiling. 'There will be other situations that call for a splendid gown, maybe even another wedding closer to home.'

Rosina linked her hand through the crook of his arm. 'Maybe Grace will marry Frank. Anyway, I think it's time we returned to Cavendish Square, Jack. I have a lot to do.'

'Are you sure this is a good idea, Rosie?' Jack asked as they sat side by side in a hansom cab on the return to Cavendish Square. 'I mean, perhaps Albert and Jane *would* prefer to get married quietly.'

'I want my grandmother to take her rightful place in the village that has treated her so shabbily since she gave birth to my mother. I understand that she broke the rules because she was in love with Sir Bertram, but she is a good person, Jack. And I really do think that somehow Roxanne's spirit is woven into the very fabric of Moonshadow Manor. She was mistress there for such a short time, but she seems to have loved the place.'

'She also loved my great-grandfather,' Jack said drily. 'Roxanne was quite free with her favours.'

'I think she was in love with two men and probably made the wrong choice. Maybe she walked onto the moor just to get away from the situation in which she found herself. We will never know.'

'But you think that a big party will calm her restless spirit, if there is such a thing?'

'I think it worth a try. Everyone loves a wedding and it's time my grandmother was a bride in her own right, even if she has had to wait forty years for the privilege. You're a man and you can't know how a woman feels in these circumstances, but you'll see that Grace agrees with me when I explain everything.'

'We're about to find out,' Jack said as the cabbie reined in his horse outside the house in Cavendish Square. 'But I'm sure you're right. This is just the sort of thing that Grace would love.' He alighted and helped Rosina down to the pavement.

Horrocks opened the door so promptly that

Rosina suspected he had been waiting for their return. He ushered them into the drawing room and lingered in the doorway until Grace dismissed him. He left reluctantly, seeming to suspect that there was something of interest going on that was being kept from him.

Rosina could not wait to tell Grace everything, and she spared no details. Grace clapped her hands and uttered a cry of delight.

'A big wedding is just what Ugstock needs, Rosina. It's a wonderful idea. Ariadne will be furious because she is desperate to get married, but she will have to wait her turn.'

'You can hardly blame her, Grace,' Jack said with a mischievous grin. 'You seem to have stolen her beau.'

Grace tossed her head. 'Frank was never interested in Ariadne. He was just being polite and considerate, as is his wont. Anyway, I agree with Rosina. Jane and Albert should be married by the Reverend Matthew Horsfall in Ugstock church. But where will the reception be held, Rosina?'

'At Moonshadow, of course,' Rosina said firmly. 'I will have the large barn tidied up and decorated with flowers. We will have dancing outside if the weather is good, and in the barn if it rains. But I will need some help, Grace. I'm depending on you.'

'Of course. You know I have almost nothing to do. What comes first?'

'I want you to take Grandmama shopping tomorrow. She will need you to guide her firmly to get a truly wonderful wedding dress, or she might turn up in that dreadful purple creation.'

'In that case, Rosie, I suppose you are going to look after the children tomorrow,' Jack said casually.

'No, Jack. I think Nell is quite capable of keeping an eye on them for the day, if Grace agrees.' Rosina hesitated, gazing abstractedly out of the window. 'I think I should go and see my father before I return to Devonshire. I realise now just how important family is. I can't pretend to like my stepmother, but I want to see Pa. Maybe you would like to accompany me, Jack?'

'I think that is an excellent idea. I might want to have a word with your father, Rosie. And I would like to see your old home.'

'I don't know what you might have to say to Pa, but he's a man of the world. You will probably find him very interesting.' Rosina turned back to Grace, who was sipping her coffee. 'Now, about the wedding gown, Grace. Do you think perhaps a shade of silvery mauve might be appropriate, or perhaps a very pale blue?'

'Leave it to me. I'll make sure she chooses exactly the right gown. And a new bonnet, of course. Then there will be lace gloves and new shoes. I love spending money, particularly when it is someone else's.'

'I'm assuming that Grandmama can afford nice

things.' Rosina turned to Jack. 'You handle her finances, Jack.'

'I think I can advance her some of Sir Bertram's money for such important purchases,' Jack said, smiling. 'What about you, Rosie? You will need a new gown if you are to be maid of honour.'

'I hadn't thought about that. I'll think of something. The most important person to look after now is Grandmama, because, if I know her, she will try to limit the proceedings.'

'We must not allow that,' Grace said, shaking her head. 'I am on your side, Rosina. If all else fails, we will enlist Ariadne. She might be annoying, but she does know how to bring the best out in servants and tradespeople. We will work together to make this a wedding that the village will remember for all time.'

Next morning Rosina stepped down from the hansom cab and stood on the pavement outside her father's house in Islington. Jack paid the cabbie and moved to her side.

'Is this where you grew up, Rosie? It's a nice house.'

Rosina nodded. 'I can't complain. We weren't rich by the Charteris family standards, but I wanted for nothing.' She gazed at the double-fronted house with its distinctive arched windows on the ground floor and traditional sash windows on the floor above. The small front garden was protected by a low wall and iron railings.

'Well, are we going to stand here all morning and admire the architecture, or should I go and knock on the door?' Jack reached out to hold her hand. 'Come on, Rosie. Is it so hard to return home?'

She managed a weak smile. 'Not really. I have some happy memories of my life until Mama died. After that I have to admit that things were difficult.'

'You don't have to do this, you know. We can hire another cab and return to Cavendish Square, and no one will know the difference. It's not as if your father was expecting you to visit.'

'You're right, but I'm being silly. Of course I want to see Pa.' Rosina picked up her skirts and crossed the pavement to open the gate and let herself into the neatly kept garden.

Jack followed her and waited while she knocked on the door. Moments later it was opened by a maid whose stern expression melted into a warm smile.

'Miss Rosina. You've come home.'

'Good morning, Aggie. It's good to see you.' Rosina stepped inside and held her hand out to Jack. 'This gentleman is my grandmother's solicitor, Aggie. He accompanied me from Devonshire.'

Aggie bobbed a curtsey. 'May I take your hat and gloves, sir?'

Jack took off his gloves and top hat, which he handed to her. 'Thank you, Aggie.'

'Is my father at home?' Rosina asked anxiously.

'Yes, miss.' Aggie glanced up the stairs at the sound

of a baby howling. 'Master Oswald is teething. The mistress is with him.'

'Don't bother her then, Aggie,' Rosina said hastily. 'Where is my father? You don't need to announce us. I'd like to give him a surprise.'

'He's in his study, miss. I just took him some tea. Can I fetch some for you and the gentleman?'

'Yes, thank you, Aggie. That would be lovely.' Rosina turned to Jack with a smile. 'Follow me.' Rosina led the way. The house was simply laid out with two rooms on either side of the hallway, and the study overlooked a small back garden.

'Rosina?' Humphrey Wills rose from his seat behind a large kneehole desk and hurried round it with outstretched arms, which he wrapped round his daughter, hugging her until she could hardly breathe. 'You've come home.'

She wriggled free from his grasp, laughing. 'It's good to see you, Pa. I've missed you.'

'Not as much as I've missed my beautiful girl.' Humphrey wiped tears from his eyes on a large cotton handkerchief. He stared at Jack. 'And who is this, Rosie? Won't you introduce me?'

'Yes, of course. This is Grandmama's solicitor, Jack Dimond.'

Jack stepped forward, holding out his hand. 'How do you do, sir? I hope you don't mind us descending upon you like this?'

'Of course not, my boy.' Humphrey shook

his hand vigorously. 'Have you accompanied my daughter from Devonshire?'

'I have indeed. I am Miss Maddern's solicitor, but I count myself as her friend.'

'And a friend to Rosie, too.' Humphrey looked from one to the other, smiling. 'I'm assuming this is just a visit, Rosie, or are you home for good?'

Rosina put her head on one side as the faint painful cries of a teething baby filtered through the open window. 'I don't think there's room for me now, Pa, but that's not a complaint. I am quite settled in Moonshadow Manor with my grandmother. As a matter of fact, it is about her that we came today.'

'Is Jane all right? I hope her health isn't failing. That's why she sent for you, isn't it?'

'Actually, Pa, it's more an invitation to her wedding that brought us here. I wanted to see you anyway, so I thought this was a good opportunity.' Rosina sank down on a chair by the window.

'Jane is getting married? At her age? She must be in her sixties now.' Humphrey leaned against his desk. 'Who is she marrying?'

'Dr Clarke, Pa. I don't know if you've ever met him, but he's been her friend for many years and finally they decided to wed.'

Humphrey turned to Jack. 'Do you approve of this match, sir? I mean from a legal point of view. Does it affect my daughter's future? I assumed that Jane would leave the property to Rosina.'

'I think that Miss Maddern has Rosina's best interests at heart, sir.'

Humphrey motioned Jack to sit down. 'This is all a big surprise to me, but if Jane has finally met a man who will take care of her, I can only be thankful. My late wife would be delighted. I should ring for Aggie to bring refreshments. Where are my manners?'

Rosina laughed. 'It's all right, Pa. I took the liberty of ordering some tea when we arrived.'

'Of course, my dear. This is still and always will be your home, if you should choose to return to London.'

'I know, Pa. Although I don't fancy sleeping in the broom cupboard.' Rosina relented immediately. 'I'm just joking, Pa. Of course you need to look after your new family. I am old enough to take care of myself. But you haven't answered my question. Will you be able to come down to Devonshire for the wedding, and Dora, of course?'

'I would like to, but it all depends on my wife, especially with little Oswald having so much trouble teething. You do understand, don't you, Rosie?'

'Of course, Pa.'

Humphrey rose to his feet and went to open the door. 'I thought I heard the rattle of teacups, Aggie. Put the tray on my desk, please.' He glanced over his shoulder. 'You and Jack will stay for luncheon, won't you, my dear?'

'Thank you, Aggie.' Rosina smiled as Aggie passed

her a cup of tea. 'I'm sorry, Pa, we should get back to Cavendish Square. I'm taking care of two small girls, who were recently orphaned. I've left them with a maid, so I ought not be too late returning.'

Humphrey smiled indulgently. 'That is so typical of my daughter, Mr Dimond. When she was a little girl, she would bring in injured birds or other animals to care for. It seems she's graduated to children now.'

'Them hedgehogs was the worst,' Aggie said, lingering in the doorway. 'Full of fleas, they was.'

'Thank you, Aggie.' Humphrey waved her away with a mock frown. 'I'm sorry you can't stay longer, Rosie, but perhaps you could visit again before you return to Ugstock?'

'I will try, Pa. But Grace and I have a lot to do for Grandmama's wedding.'

Humphrey picked up his teacup. 'And who is Grace? I am getting confused by all these new people.'

Rosina laughed. 'She is my aunt, in fact, Pa. She is Sir Bertram Charteris's daughter, and I learned recently that he is my grandfather. It's a secret that Grandmama has been keeping for forty years or more and now it is in the open.'

'I suspected as much, although I couldn't prove anything. Your poor mama often wondered about the identity of her father.' Humphrey replaced his cup on the saucer without tasting the tea. 'But before you go, my dear. Would you go upstairs and greet your stepmother? I know it is difficult for you, but Dora would be very offended if you went without seeing her and Oswald.'

'Yes, Pa,' Rosina said reluctantly.

'Jack and I can have a chat while you are gone, my dear.'

Rosina had no particular desire to speak to Dora, but she went upstairs anyway. It was no surprise that Dora was not best pleased to see her. She was pacing the floor with baby Oswald in her arms, and it was difficult to talk above his continuous wailing. After a few polite words, Rosina made her escape and returned to the study.

Humphrey looked up as she entered the room. 'Jack tells me that you have been working on a market stall, Rosie. You should have let me know that you were in need of money. I'm not a wealthy man but I could have sent you a bank draft.'

'I'm no longer your responsibility, Pa,' Rosina said firmly. 'I enjoyed the challenge.'

'I thought that Jane would take care of you financially, but now she is getting married that puts a different complexion on the matter. Her husband will control her finances, and he might not wish to support you.'

'I hadn't thought of it like that, Pa. I just need to think of a way to earn my own living.'

'I'm sure you will marry soon enough, and your husband will support you, but I was talking it over with Jack, and I might have an idea of how you can become financially independent.'

Rosina glanced at Jack, who nodded in agreement. 'I'm intrigued. Tell me more about this scheme, Pa.'

'You won't remember my late brother, Dudley, because you only met him once when he came home on leave from Bombay where he was assistant to the ambassador.'

Rosina shook her head. 'No, I don't remember him.'

'To be brief, Dudley was a collector of art and foreign antiquities. He had them shipped home at regular intervals and stored in a warehouse at London Dock.'

Rosina frowned. 'That's fascinating, Pa. But how does it affect me?'

'Dudley never married, and he left everything to me. There was no money involved as he had spent it all on his passion for collecting, but I have no use for all those foreign gewgaws.'

'Your father suggested that you might have them sent to Ugstock where you could set up a business selling the articles to collectors,' Jack said eagerly. 'That sounds eminently sensible to me, Rosie.'

'Yes, my love,' Humphrey added, smiling. 'What do you think?'

Chapter Twenty-One

Rosina and Jack returned to Cavendish Square after a brief visit to the warehouse in the docks. All the artefacts were crated up, but a random examination of the contents of the nearest box revealed items that were both intricate, beautiful and no doubt worth a considerable sum of money. Rosina did not hesitate to take the proof of ownership to the dock office, and she made arrangements for the entire contents to be sent to Moonshadow Manor. It cost every penny she had, but Jack promised to back her until she started earning, and he was as enthusiastic about the scheme as she was.

It was mid-afternoon by the time they entered the Charteris house to find Jane had gone to lie down, exhausted by her shopping trip with Grace. Francis had taken pity on Albert and had taken him to

Boodle's for the comparative peace and quiet of a gentlemen's club. Nell had taken the children to the Zoological Gardens, and Grace was on her own in the drawing room, seated at the escritoire, writing lists. She jumped to her feet when Rosina and Jack entered the room.

'I'm afraid I have worn your grandmother out, Rosina. We went to every shop and department store, and in the end, we found a wonderful gown in Marshall & Snelgrove.'

'You did well, Grace.' Rosina sank down on the sofa. 'Did you get shoes to go with the gown?'

'We did,' Grace said triumphantly. 'And stockings and gloves, as well as a dear little hat that perches on the top of her head, with silk roses and a short veil. She will look amazing on the big day.'

'You did well,' Rosina said, smiling.

'And I found a lovely gown for myself, and I chose one for you, too, Rosina. I have it on approval, but I will send it back if it doesn't fit or if you dislike it.'

'I really don't think I can afford a new gown,' Rosina said, eyeing Jack warily. She thought he had not heard, but he looked up from the copy of *The Times* he had picked up from a side table.

'I told you not to worry about expense, Rosie. I am handling Miss Maddern's budget for the wedding, as I told you. I think your gown as maid of honour must come out of that.'

Rosina was not in a position to argue and, if she

were being honest, she was eager to see the gown that Grace had chosen for her.

'All right,' Rosina said cautiously. 'I'll try it on, Grace, but if it's not appropriate it will have to be returned to the shop.'

'It's in my room. Come with me now and you can see for yourself.' Grace caught Rosina by the hand, giving her little chance to protest. She glanced over her shoulder as she opened the door. 'You must be the judge, Jack. I'll insist that she comes downstairs for your opinion.'

The gown that lay spread out on Grace's bed was white muslin with sprigs of tiny pink roses and green leaves. The frilled neckline and short puff sleeves added a touch of youthful elegance to the beautiful creation.

'Try it on,' Grace insisted as she unbuttoned Rosina's grey morning gown. 'I'm tired of seeing you dress like a governess, Rosina. You shouldn't wear dowdy clothes – you're much too pretty.'

Rosina started to protest but she was no match for a determined Grace, and within minutes her plain corded-cotton gown lay on the floor and Grace was tying on the hoops that formed the crinoline, followed by a froth of lace-trimmed petticoats.

'I didn't realise how much work there was in getting a lady dressed,' Grace said as she lifted the gown over Rosina's head and began fastening the bodice, which fitted as though it had been made for her. Adjusting the neckline and shaking out the creases in the voluminous skirts, Grace smiled delightedly. 'I knew I was right, Rosina. You look beautiful and the gown is perfect for a country wedding.' She plucked a dainty bonnet from the pillows and fastened it over Rosina's luxuriant dark hair. 'Perfect. You look so amazing you could be the bride. Now take a peek in the mirror and see if you agree with me.'

Rosina studied her reflection in the cheval mirror and for a moment she thought she was gazing at a stranger. Grace was right, the gown was perfect, but she dared not think about the cost.

'It is a lovely gown, Grace,' Rosina said grudgingly. 'You have excellent taste, but I think it's too grand for me.'

'Nonsense. Go downstairs and show Jack.' Grace shoved her unceremoniously out of the room, leaving Rosina little alternative but to return to the drawing room.

Jack's expression when he saw her allayed any doubts she might have felt. He rose to his feet and took her hands in his as he looked her up and down.

'You look stunning, Rosie. The gown is beautiful and so are you.'

'You don't think it too much for a village wedding? I feel overdressed.'

'Nonsense. It is perfect and so is that silly little hat, but it looks wonderful. I know that your grandmother would agree. Grace could not have chosen better.' He held her hands a moment longer than necessary. 'I had an interesting conversation with your father when you were upstairs being nice to your stepmother.'

Rosina pulled a face. 'I do try to be a better person, but Dora is not easy to get along with, especially when she has a teething baby in her arms. What was it you spoke about to Pa?'

Before he could answer the door burst open and Flora rushed into the room, followed by Lottie, with Nell following close behind.

'I'm so sorry, miss,' Nell said breathlessly. 'They ran on ahead and I couldn't catch them.'

'We saw animals,' Lottie lisped. 'Big animals.'

'Elephants,' Flora said firmly. 'We saw elephants, Lottie.'

'That is very exciting,' Rosina agreed, smiling. 'You can tell me all about it later, but you'd better go with Nell now and take off your outdoor clothes.'

Flora moved closer to Rosina, gazing up at her with a rapturous smile. 'You look beautiful, Rosie.'

Nell shook her head. 'It's Miss Wills to you, Miss Flora. Where are your manners?'

'It's all right, Nell,' Rosina said hastily. 'She didn't mean to be rude, and I appreciate the compliment.'

Nell held her hands out to the children. 'Let's go to the kitchen and ask Cook if she has any cakes or biscuits.'

That seemed to do the trick, and the girls hurried to her side, reaching up to clasp Nell's hands.

Rosina watched them go with a smile. She had grown fond of the little girls, even in such a short space of time, and she could not bear to think of them living in an unhappy home, unloved and miserable. She turned to Jack.

'What were you going to say?'

'It can wait. I'll tell you later, but now we should make arrangements to go home. I have clients waiting and you have a wedding to arrange.'

'Yes, of course, Jack. And I have to be at Moonshadow when the carters arrive with all my foreign treasures.'

'I think we should leave tomorrow, but perhaps you should talk to your grandmother first, Rosie.'

'I will, Jack. I'll go upstairs and change back into my day clothes and then I'll have a word with Grandmama.'

The journey home next day was planned for the morning. Jane and Albert opted to remain in London for another couple of days, but they promised faithfully to return to Moonshadow when they were ready. Rosina was bothered by this, but in no position to argue. She had enough to do with a last-minute dash to the department store to purchase more clothes for the children, which she accomplished with Grace's help. Another problem had arisen when Flora and Lottie discovered that Nell was to remain in Cavendish Square. The children sobbed and begged her to stay with them and in the end, Grace suggested that Nell might be taken on as their nanny. Rosina was doubtful at first, mainly because she could not afford to pay Nell's wages, but Jack stepped in and assured her that funds would be forthcoming, if only on a temporary basis, and she would need extra help if she was to start a business working from home. Grace was consulted and she spoke to the housekeeper, arranging Nell's release from her position in Cavendish Square. Nell accepted the change in her status enthusiastically, and she lost no time in packing up her meagre belongings.

At first Grace had decided to remain in London, as her romance with Sir Francis was becoming increasingly intense. However, she changed her mind at the last minute.

'I'm coming with you,' she announced as Rosina prepared to leave with Jack, Nell and the children.

'I thought you were getting on so well with Frank that you wanted to remain in London,' Rosina said, frowning. 'Why the change of heart, Grace?'

'Horrocks has received a message informing him that Aunt Eugenie and my sisters are returning tomorrow.' Grace pulled a face. 'Clarissa set her cap at Frank, and she'll accuse me of stealing her beau. Then Cecy will join in and probably Aunt Eugenie, and I'll be outnumbered.'

Rosina laughed. 'I would think you were a match for your sisters and an aged aunt.'

'I am, but it's tiring, and a waste of time. If Frank really wants me, he will follow me down to Devonshire. Anyway, we have a wedding to arrange, and I must admit I'm curious about your unexpected inheritance. I can't wait to see all those amazing things that your late uncle collected abroad.'

'It is rather exciting.' Rosina slipped her arm around Grace's shoulders. 'Come on, Aunt Grace, you and I will set the world to rights and maybe we'll make a fortune.' She turned to Jack, smiling. 'What do you think?'

'If I were a betting man, I'd say the odds would be in your favour.' Jack opened the front door. 'There are two cabs outside. Nell can take the children in the first one with the luggage, and we will take the second.' He picked up Lottie and carried her to the cab, holding her until Nell was seated before lifting her onto Nell's lap.

Rosina supervised the loading of their luggage, which seemed to have increased hugely since they first arrived in Cavendish Square, and then she allowed Jack to help her into the next cab. She sank down on the seat next to Grace.

'I do hope that Grandmama and Albert join us in a couple of days, as they promised.'

'You can't rely on these young lovers,' Grace said, giggling. 'The next thing we know my papa, your grandpapa, will turn up with some beautiful ballet dancer on his arm, and announce that he is getting married for a second time.'

'You never know what is around the next corner.' Rosina smiled at Jack as he climbed into the cab and sat opposite her.

'What are you talking about?' Jack settled himself against the squabs and tapped the roof with his silver-topped cane.

Rosina laughed. 'I'll tell you later. No, that was what you said when you had been speaking to my papa. You never did elaborate, Jack.'

'I will, when the time is right.' Jack glanced out of the window. 'I think that is Frank who has just arrived at your house, Grace. Do you want to stop the cab and speak to him?'

'No. The servants will tell him he's too late. I want to see if he will race after us and try to catch me before I board the train.'

'Aunt Grace, you are terrible,' Rosina said with mock severity. 'What sort of example are you setting for your poor innocent niece?'

Grace narrowed her eyes. 'If you call me Aunt Grace once more, I will not be responsible for my actions.'

Jack held up his hands. 'Now, now, ladies. Let us have peace during the journey home, or I will be forced to put both of you in the guard's van with the rest of the luggage.'

'I'm teasing her, Jack,' Rosina said hastily.

'And I'm just joking,' Grace added. 'No one would believe that I was old enough to be anyone's aunt, anyway.' She glanced out of the window. 'I can't see Frank following us. I hope Horrocks told him that we are on our way to the railway station.'

Rosina doubted whether Frank had the heart and soul of a knight errant, but she kept her thoughts to herself. Arguments with Grace were inclined to end up going round in circles. They might be related by blood, but Rosina thought that sometimes Grace was simply too much.

As it happened, Frank did not turn up at the station, and Grace sulked all the way to Exeter, where they changed trains. She was still grumpy when they reached Ivybridge, and she insisted that Jack should find her a cab to take her home to Glazewood Hall, even though the servants would not be expecting her. Rosina tried to persuade her to accompany her and Nell to Moonshadow Manor, but Grace was adamant that she wanted to go home. However, the only transport available turned out to be Seth Tully's farm cart. He had stayed on when the market closed and had been enjoying a few pints of cider in the pub. Jack was concerned about his ability to handle the reins, but Rosina assured him that she could take over should Seth fall asleep en route. The children were tired, but they seemed to find a wagon filled with straw the most exciting thing that had ever happened to them. Nell climbed onto it with help from Seth, who held on to her hand rather too long, and kept winking at her.

'I'm not sure about this,' Jack said worriedly. 'Maybe I ought to drive.'

'No, boss. I'm fine,' Seth said, grinning. 'The ladies are safe with me.'

'I'm sure we are.' Rosina waited while Grace climbed onto the wagon. 'Please don't worry, Jack. We'll be fine. All I want to do now is to get home and settle the children down. They must be exhausted.'

Jack laughed, eyeing the girls, who were scrabbling about in the straw. 'They seem to have found a new lease of life, but I take your point. What about Grace?'

Rosina glanced over her shoulder at Grace, who was frowning and shifting uncomfortably on the wooden floor of the cart. 'She can stay with us tonight and I'll get Joshua to drive her to Glazewood tomorrow, or maybe Sir Francis will have caught up with us by then.'

'I'll ride over as soon as I've seen my clients.' Jack frowned. 'Are you sure you'll be all right with Seth?'

'I am quite sure.' Rosina accepted a helping hand as she joined Grace in the wagon and Seth fixed the tailgate before leaping onto the driver's seat and flicking the reins above his patient horse's head. It ambled off at a steady walking pace, and Rosina settled down for a long and rather uncomfortable drive home.

Merry was surprised to see them and delighted to welcome them home, but she looked askance at Nell, who was being ogled by Joshua, which made Rosina nervous. She had liked Nell instantly and she was very good with the children, but she was also very pretty, which was something Rosina had not taken into consideration. Seth was hanging around, now sober after the long drive from Ivybridge, and he was taking longer than necessary to unload their luggage from the cart, all the while eyeing Joshua as if daring him to say something to Nell. However, the girls had fallen asleep for the last hour or so of the journey and Nell was more concerned with getting them into the house than in flirting with her two new admirers.

Rosina was quick to introduce Nell to Merry. 'I think we should give the children some bread and milk and put them to bed,' Rosina said firmly.

Merry lifted Flora in her arms. 'Come with me, maidy. We'll do as Miss Rosina says, shall we?'

Flora nodded tiredly and laid her head on Merry's shoulder as she walked across the yard and entered the house.

'And you two can stop gawking,' Grace said crossly. 'Anyone would think you hadn't seen a pretty girl before.' She caught Joshua across the ear with a swipe of her hand. 'Get on with your work.'

Joshua backed away, rubbing the afflicted part of his head. 'Yes, Miss Grace.'

'He's not working for you, Grace,' Rosina said angrily. 'There's no need to hit him.'

'He's still a servant.' Grace tossed her head. 'You have to be firm with them, Rosina, or they will walk all over you.' She marched into the house and slammed the door.

Rosina sighed. 'Thank you for the lift, Seth. How much do I owe you?'

'Put a good word in for me with Miss Nell,' Seth said dreamily. 'And we'll call it quits. I was coming this way, so it's nothing to me.'

'That's very kind of you.' Rosina shook his hand. 'I will be needing some help in a day or two, if you're interested in some paid work.'

'That I be, miss. What do you want done?'

'I have a couple of wagons coming from London and the contents will need to be unloaded and put in the barn, which will need a good clear out first. I wonder if you and Merry's uncles Tom and Sid could come tomorrow and make a start. I will pay the going rate.'

'And will the young lady be here for a while?' Seth's face flushed and his eyes lit with anticipation.

'Yes, to that. Nell is going to look after the two little girls until I find a suitable family to adopt them.'

'I'll be here as soon as I've finished my chores on the farm. I'll see if Merry's uncles are free to help as well.' Seth climbed onto the driver's seat and drove off with a wave of his hand.

Rosina turned to Joshua, who was standing by the pile of luggage.

'Would you take the cases indoors, please? You may leave them in the hall at the foot of the stairs. We can sort them out from there.' Rosina picked up the smallest valise. 'Thank you, Joshua.' She entered the house and was met by a savoury smell of roasting meat. It was good to be home.

The kettle was bubbling on the hob, and Rosina made a pot of tea while she waited for Merry.

'I've put Nell in with the little ones, miss,' Merry said cheerfully. 'She seems nice enough, although a bit too pretty, if you ask me. She's going to cause trouble in the village.'

'She's good with the children. That is all that matters, Merry.' Rosina filled three cups with tea and passed one to Merry. 'I'm sure she knows how to keep young men at bay. She must have had plenty of practice in London.'

'They'll be round here like a flock of starlings, all clamouring for her attention because she's as exotic as one of them foreign birds with pink feathers, I saw in a picture book.'

Rosina laughed. 'I don't think starlings are very interested in flamingos, but I understand what you're saying. We just have to wait and see.' Rosina pulled up a chair and sat down. She was about to give Merry the good news that she had found her grandmother and Dr Clarke, but it was obvious that Merry had something she wanted to share. 'You're obviously bursting with news, Merry. What has happened while I was away?'

'Well, as a matter of fact there is something that's caused a stir in the village.' Merry settled down at the table. 'Someone has moved into Conjuror's Cottage on the far side of the village. It's been empty for years after the school mistress, Miss Foster, died, and people say it's haunted, but I don't believe that. Maybe she won't stay there for long.'

Rosina stirred her tea and took a sip. 'Surely it's a good thing to have a new tenant?'

'I suppose so,' Merry said doubtfully. 'But this person is a very old lady. She keeps herself to herself and no one knows who she is or why she has come to Ugstock.'

Rosina smiled. 'Perhaps she likes the peace and quiet of the village.'

'Uncle Fred says she doesn't leave the cottage. Her maid brings a list of things they need to the shop, and they have their groceries delivered, even though the cottage is only a stone's throw away. She seems to have money, according to Uncle Fred. Now why would a woman of means want to live in a near derelict cottage in Ugstock? And why would she keep to herself, I'd like to know.'

Rosina was losing interest, but she made an effort

to concentrate as Merry was obviously intrigued by the newcomer. 'Maybe the old lady cannot walk far. Have you thought of that?'

'I dare say you're right.' Merry rose to her feet. 'I'd better start making supper. I had a feeling you might return soon so I baked a ham. It was fortunate I did, in the circumstances.'

'Yes, indeed. I'm starving and I expect Grace is hungry, too. I suppose she's sorting out a room for herself.' Rosina could not hold back the exciting news a moment longer. 'We have a lot to do, Merry. For one thing I have inherited a collection of foreign artefacts that I intend to sell, and for another we have a wedding to plan.'

Merry dropped the knife she had been using to pare carrots. 'You're getting married, miss? Did Mr Dimond propose in London?'

Rosina stared at her in astonishment. 'Whatever gave you that idea, Merry? Mr Dimond is just a friend.'

'If you say so, miss.' Merry bent down to retrieve the knife. 'I just thought . . .'

'Never mind that,' Rosina said hastily. 'We found my grandmother and Dr Clarke in London. They planned to get married in secret, but I persuaded them to have a lovely wedding here in Ugstock. I want to invite the whole village and make a huge celebration of their union.'

'Well now, that's a plan indeed.' Merry concentrated on peeling a large carrot.

'You don't think it's a good idea?'

'Miss Jane has had to put up with years of gossip, and people who should know better looking down on her because of her having a child out of wedlock. Ugstock is very traditional, and people might think it inappropriate in the circumstances.'

Rosina shook her head. 'I can't believe that the people who have known my grandmother all her life would be so judgemental.'

'Like I say, miss. This is Ugstock.'

Grace breezed into the kitchen at that moment and came to a halt. 'What have I missed? Why so serious, Rosina? What is this about Ugstock?'

'Merry doesn't think a large wedding for my grandmother and Dr Clarke would be appropriate, Grace.'

'Why should we let that bother us, Rosie?' Grace reached for her cup of tea. 'Everyone loves a party, and the locals won't say no to free food and drink. We made a plan and I say we should stick to it. Tonight, after supper, we'll start on the guest list and go on from there.'

'You're right,' Rosina said slowly. 'I made a promise to Grandmama, and I can't break it. We'll need your help, Merry, as I don't know everyone in the village.'

'Yes, miss. Of course, I'll do all I can.' Merry began chopping the carrots with a determined frown.

'I'm going to check on the children,' Rosina said,

rising to her feet. 'I'll ask Nell to come down for supper when it's ready. We'll all eat in the kitchen this evening, Merry. No need to lay up the table in the dining room. We're all tired and I for one am going to have an early night. Tomorrow the hard work begins in earnest.'

Chapter Twenty-Two

Seth Tully and Merry's uncles Tom and Sid Bragg turned up early next day and began clearing out the old barn with such enthusiasm that it was done in a day. After that Rosina set them about whitewashing the walls and scrubbing the tiled floor. It was ready in time for the arrival of the two wagons laden with crates and boxes, and they were unloaded and stacked neatly against the back wall.

Rosina paid Seth and the Braggs and sent them off to the kitchen for a midday meal while she, Grace, Merry and Nell began unpacking and sorting the items. Flora and Lottie were running round excitedly, not helping at all but thoroughly enjoying themselves. Rosina set everything out on the odd assortment of tables and benches that she had found in the old dairy and the coach house. There were dozens of ornate brass jugs, bowls and trays, some of them decorated with colourful enamel. There were musical instruments that none of them had ever seen before and could not name, and there were several tea chests filled with ornaments, religious icons and strangely shaped oil lamps. They unpacked exotic paintings and bolts of silk, damask and chintz. Days passed and they had not yet begun sorting the porcelain dinner and tea services, nor the unusual teapots. There was even a samovar packed in its own box with a dozen or so glass cups in silver holders. An excited cry from Flora made Rosina turn with a start and she smiled when she saw the case packed with French dolls, which had caught Flora's attention.

Grace stood back, eyeing the collection wide-eyed. 'This is amazing, Rosie. Your uncle must have been collecting these things for years.'

Merry stopped unwrapping teacups to wipe sweat from her brow. 'Must have spent all his money on this stuff. I pity his wife.'

'He never married, as far as I know,' Rosina said hastily. 'This seems to have been his life's work, and I intend to do it justice.'

'What are you going to do with all this?' Grace picked up a strangely shaped teapot and put it down again, pulling a face. 'Who would want these odd things?'

Rosina smiled. 'I will try to sell them, but I have

no idea what they are worth. I think I need to take advice from an expert.'

Grace fingered a bolt of shot silk. 'I would like a dress made from this.'

'You may have it. Call it wages for helping me,' Rosina said airily. 'You will need a new gown for the wedding of the year, or maybe your own nuptials. I hear that Sir Francis is staying with Jack.'

Grace pulled a face. 'Yes, he is, but that minx Ariadne has found out and Hugo has invited Frank to dine at Daumerle House. I know who put him up to that. Ariadne is determined to get engaged before I do.'

'If Frank is so fickle and can change his mind overnight, then he's not worth having, Grace.' Rosina gave her a hug. 'Anyway, we still have the big wedding to arrange. I will lock all these beauties in the barn for the present, or at least until I can get some expert advice.'

'Do you know anyone who might help?' Grace tucked the bolt of material under her arm. 'I will accept this. I love the colour.'

'There is someone, Grace. I can't recall his name but there was an antique dealer at the Fairbanks' bankruptcy sale. I expect Jack remembers him. I want to do this properly, if only to honour my late uncle's memory.'

'Quite right,' Grace said firmly. 'I personally have had enough of this dusty old stuff for today. I am going indoors to wash my hands and face and change into a clean gown.'

'I should give the little ones some food, miss.' Nell grabbed Lottie by the hand and beckoned to Flora, who was cuddling one of the dolls. 'Put that dolly down, please, Miss Flora. She does not belong to you.'

'It's all right.' Rosina glanced at the doll, which had suffered a slight accident in transit so that its head wobbled, causing one eye to open while the other remained closed. 'Flora can keep that one.'

'And me.'

Rosina looked down to see Lottie clutching a carved wooden bear that seemed to be a nutcracker, although it appeared to be broken and had lost one ear, which gave it a slightly endearing lopsided appearance.

'Yes, Lottie. You may have the bear. Now go with Nell, there's good girls. Merry and I will finish up here and then we'll come in for luncheon.'

'Yes, miss.' Nell took the children and followed Grace from the barn, leaving Rosina and Merry to finish their task.

'There's a powerful lot of stuff here, Miss Rosina,' Merry said, brushing dust from her apron. 'Are we going to set up shop or take it to the market?'

Rosina frowned thoughtfully. 'I hadn't considered the market. My idea was to do business from the barn.'

'This wedding you keep talking about, when is it going to be? I mean, if it's going to be held here at

Moonshadow we have a lot of preparations to make, and with all this going on I can't see us managing.'

Rosina met Merry's worried gaze with an attempt at a confident smile, but in her heart she knew it was not going to be easy.

'I want my grandmother to have a wonderful day, Merry. She and the doctor ought to have followed us from London, but it's been a week now and no sign of them. I've made out the guest list, which includes just about everyone in Ugstock, but I can't do anything until they return.'

'The banns must be read, miss. Three Sundays before the actual wedding, if I recall rightly.'

'You're right. I'd quite forgotten that detail.' Rosina shook her head. 'Maybe it wasn't such a good idea of mine. Perhaps I ought to have allowed them to do what they really wanted, which was to have a quiet wedding in London.'

Merry laughed. 'They're old enough to know their own minds. I doubt if you could force either one of them to do anything against their will.'

'I expect you're right. Anyway, I can't do a thing until they return, so I'll have to concentrate on my collection of oddities. Let's go indoors and have something to eat, Merry.'

'There's just one other thing, miss?' Merry said tentatively.

Rosina hesitated in the doorway. 'What is that?'

'Are we keeping the children? I don't want to get

too fond of them if they're going to be whisked away to another family.'

'Their uncle is too irresponsible to have them, and although their great-aunt said she would give them a home, it was done with obvious reluctance, which is why I brought them here to Moonshadow. I've grown fond of them, and I would gladly keep them here, but I don't know if the law will allow it, as we're not related. I need to speak to Jack.'

Merry glanced over Rosina's shoulder. 'Well, now's your chance, miss. Jack Dimond has just ridden into the stable yard together with that titled gentleman from London.'

Rosina turned to see Jack dismount and she hurried out into the warm sunshine.

'I was just talking about you, Jack,' she said smiling.

'If you were put out because I haven't been in contact for a few days, I apologise. But I've been very busy.'

Frank dismounted and handed the reins to Joshua. 'I'm afraid some of that is my fault, Rosina. I must add my apologies, too.'

'But we were involved in business negotiations,' Jack added hastily. 'I think you had better give Grace the good news, Frank,' he added as Grace emerged from the house and came hurrying towards them.

'What is going on?' Grace demanded crossly. 'Why are you looking so smug, Frank? If you have something to say, please get it over and done with.'

'Perhaps we could go for a walk on the moor,' Frank said shyly. 'Just a short walk, Grace.'

'I don't know what cannot be said in front of my friends, but if you insist, Frank. Mind you, I do not like walking, so it had better be a very short stroll.'

He proffered his arm. 'I promise.'

'You know I hate surprises as much as I loathe long walks.' Grace took his arm, and they set off slowly towards the moor.

'What was that all about?' Rosina demanded. 'We have so many problems, Jack. I hope Frank isn't going to add to them.'

Jack glanced into the barn. 'I see you've unpacked your treasure. Might I have a look?'

'Of course, but first I want to know what is going on. You're hiding something, Jack. I can tell by your expression.'

'The business deal I mentioned is to do with Glazewood Hall. You know that Sir Bertram wanted to sell it in order to purchase Grandtor House?'

Rosina stepped back into the barn and a shiver ran down her spine, which was not entirely due to the coolness inside the old building.

'No, Jack, I didn't know that.'

'Frank made an offer for the estate and Sir Bertram accepted it. The new owner of Glazewood Hall is Sir Francis Moulton.'

Rosina stared at him in amazement. 'I didn't realise that Frank was so wealthy.'

'He isn't the sort of chap to go around flaunting his assets, Rosie. Besides which, he has a special reason for wanting to purchase Grace's family home.'

'He's going to propose?' Rosina faced him eagerly. 'Is that why he was being so mysterious?'

'He's spent all morning trying to pluck up the courage to ask Grace to marry him. He seems to think he's not good enough for her.'

'That is nonsense, of course. I think Grace will be overjoyed. For one thing, she is in love with him, although she would not admit to having such a tender feeling, but she knows that her sister Clarissa had hopes in that direction. Then there's Ariadne, who is terrified of being left on the shelf and is growing ever more desperate. She's even persuaded Hugo to invite Frank to dine at Daumerle.'

Jack picked up a porcelain dinner plate and examined it closely. 'This is nice. It would make a good wedding present.'

'For whom, Jack? Don't forget there's my grandmother and her devoted Albert, as well as Frank and Grace.'

Jack put the plate down, avoiding meeting her gaze. 'That is the problem, Rosie. I know you had your heart set on giving your grandmother the best and biggest wedding that Ugstock has ever seen, but I'm afraid that it is out of the question now.'

Rosina's hand flew to cover her mouth. 'Oh, no. They can't have called the wedding off. After all they've been through over the years . . .' She came to a halt, eyeing Jack suspiciously.

'What is it? You said there was something else.'

He moved closer and took her hands in his. 'I'm sorry, Rosie. I received a letter from your grandmother this morning. She asked me to tell you that she and Albert decided they couldn't wait any longer. They were married by special licence in London, a couple of days ago. I presume they're now on their honeymoon. She hoped you would understand.'

'But they thought a wedding witnessed by the entire community was a good idea,' Rosina said faintly. 'I wanted everyone to see how happy they are together.'

Jack raised her hands to his lips. 'And they will. The gossips will be silenced for ever when Jane and Albert Clarke return home. The past will be put aside, if not forgotten, and they will be able to enjoy the rest of their lives together, as it was meant to be.'

'I suppose you're right. It's fortunate that I haven't sent out any invitations. I do understand why they wanted to make it official. Perhaps I pressed them too hard for a decision. Sometimes I don't think things through.' Rosina withdrew her hands gently. 'I only wanted Grandmama to be happy. Maybe I tried too hard.' She sank down on an upturned tea chest.

'You only did what you thought best,' Jack said quickly. 'But you were dealing with two battle-hardened people well past their salad days, who knew exactly what they wanted.'

'I understand, and I'm happy for them. Anyway, I have plenty to do now that my inheritance has arrived. What do you think of my uncle's gift to me? To be honest, I'm a little overwhelmed by the size of the collection.'

'What do you intend to do with it all?' Jack asked, gazing round at the laden tables and benches. 'Are you going to take it all to market, or try to sell it from here, as you originally intended?'

'I have no idea of the value of any of this, Jack. I need professional advice.' Rosina frowned. 'What was the name of that man we met at the Fairbanks' sale? I believe you said he was a dealer.'

'That would be Donald Patterson. He is a dealer in antiques.'

'Do you know where I could find him?' Rosina asked eagerly. 'I need to know what I should ask for when I put them up for sale.'

'I believe he has a showroom in Exeter. As a matter of fact, I have a client being seen at the County Assizes in Exeter Guildhall next week. I'll be in the town, so I can look up Mr Patterson, if you so wish.'

'Please do,' Rosina said earnestly. 'That would be very helpful, Jack.'

He smiled. 'Anything to wipe that worried frown from your brow. Now you don't have to fret about anything, thanks to your grandmother and the good doctor deciding to take matters into their own hands.'

Rosina nodded. 'That is a bit of a disappointment,

but I still need to find a permanent home for my little girls. They are so happy here with Nell, but I'm not their legal guardian, and I'm going to be very busy from now on, which doesn't seem fair to them. I feel they ought to be with a proper family. Neither Lady Tring nor Monty is ideal in that role.'

'There is one other possibility, Rosie,' Jack said slowly. 'If you were married with a husband who also cared about the children, that would make you a proper family.'

Rosina met his intense gaze, and she felt the blood rush to her cheeks. She was suddenly breathless. 'What are you saying, Jack?'

'You must know how I feel about you, Rosie. It's obvious to everyone else, but there's never been the right moment for me to tell you.'

'I don't understand. Are you saying you would marry me so that we could adopt the girls?'

'I most certainly wouldn't put it that way, but it would be an answer to the problem.'

Rosina jumped to her feet. 'That must count as one of the worst proposals of marriage that any woman ever received.'

'It wasn't meant that way, Rosie. It just came out in a rush. I've been trying to think of a way to tell you how I feel since the first day we met. I'm not good with words when it comes to emotions.'

'Utter nonsense,' Rosina said angrily. 'You spend your life using words to persuade magistrates and judges to be lenient with offenders. You are treating me like a court case.'

'No, indeed I'm not. I'm sorry if I put things badly, but I do want to marry you.'

'You may be in need of a wife, but you had better look elsewhere. I believe Ariadne is looking for a husband. Maybe she would be a better candidate, although I doubt if you are wealthy enough to attract her.'

'That is unfair, Rosina. I'm trying to tell you how I feel, and you've thrown it back in my face.'

'Yes, I have. You might try a little harder next time you decide to put a proposition to a woman, Jack Dimond. I am not interested. I am going indoors, and I don't want you to follow me.'

Rosina was angry and hurt by his lack of sensitivity to her feelings. She marched across the stable yard, entered the house and slammed the door behind her. However, she could not resist the temptation to peer out of the scullery window. Jack stood for a few moments, staring after her, and then he mounted Judge and rode off in a cloud of dust. Rosina struggled with a maelstrom of emotions. She had won the argument, but she experienced a huge sense of loss. Her feelings for Jack had been developing slowly. She had not fallen in love with him at first sight, but as they had come to know each other better she had been more and more at ease in his company. She valued his opinion, and she missed him when he was not with her. If that was being in love it was far from the descriptions of the emotion she had read in romantic novels. In fact, she had spent so much time worrying about everyone else that she had given her own thoughts and feelings short shrift.

The sound of childish voices, and Nell's voice reprimanding the girls for making such a noise, brought Rosina back to reality. When she heard Merry talking to Nell and their voices grew closer, she knew she could not face them. One look at her and they would know that all was not well. Rosina was in no mood to share confidences with anyone, and she took the back stairs, heading for the privacy of her own room. She threw herself down on the bed, covering her ears with her hands in an attempt to shut out the voices clamouring inside her head. She was angry with Jack and furious with herself. Moreover, she realised that despite their differences, she had lost the one good friend she had relied on since she first came to Moonshadow Manor.

Gradually common sense reasserted itself and Rosina sat up, brushing her dishevelled hair from her face. She told herself that there was no point hiding away, and she was about to go downstairs when the door burst open and Grace rushed into the room, waving her left hand so that the large diamond ring flashed in the sunlight that streamed through the window.

'Frank proposed. Look at my ring, Rosie. Isn't it splendid?'

Rosina managed to dodge Grace's flailing hand. 'It is the largest diamond I've ever seen, Grace. Congratulations.'

'You'll never guess what Frank has done for me.' Grace did a twirl before subsiding onto the bed. 'He's bought Glazewood Hall. I had no idea he loved me so much, or that he was so wealthy.'

'That's wonderful, Grace,' Rosina said, smiling. 'I'm happy for you.'

Grace gave her a hug. 'I can't stay here chatting. Frank is waiting for me downstairs. We're returning to London this afternoon so that I can begin planning the wedding, and I'll need to visit my dressmaker or maybe even visit a modiste in town. Frank is going to take me to Venice for our honeymoon, isn't that exciting?'

'It all sounds wonderful, Grace. I'm truly happy for you.'

Grace's smile faded. 'But I won't be able to help you with your collection or the wedding plans for Jane and Albert.'

'I still have to get advice about the items I need to sell, and Jack told me that Grandmama and Albert have already done the deed. They married by special licence in London.'

'I'm so sorry, Rosie. I know you planned to make it a memorable occasion. You must be disappointed.'

Grace patted her on the shoulder. 'But never mind. You can help me to organise my nuptials. I have yet to decide whether I want to get married from home or from Cavendish Square.' She raised her hand to gaze at her diamond ring. 'I haven't shared the good news with Merry and Nell. I must do that and then I will get my things together for the journey to London.'

'I'm going downstairs, too.' Rosina stood up and shook the crease out of her skirts. 'Come on, Grace. Let's pass on the good news.'

Grace and Frank left soon after and a sense of quietness descended on Moonshadow Manor. Rosina left Merry and Nell to entertain the children while she went into the barn and began cataloguing the contents. She put all thoughts of Jack and his outlandish proposal out of her head as she worked until her hand and wrist ached from making notes. Merry brought her a cup of tea.

'We have a visitor, miss,' Merry said, frowning. 'It's the strange new lady who bought Conjuror's Cottage.'

'What does she want? I'm very busy.' Rosina took the cup and saucer from her. 'But this is most welcome. I didn't realise how hard it would be to list everything.'

'She didn't say, miss. Just that she would like to see you. She's very old and she walks with a stick.

Maybe she's a witch. They say that it was a witch who first lived in that cottage.'

'I don't believe in witches and wizards any more than I believe in Roxanne's ghost wandering the moor,' Rosina said firmly. 'Perhaps the woman is just being neighbourly. I'll drink my tea and then I'll come in and see her.'

'Very well, miss. I just hope she don't turn me into a frog or something if I say the wrong thing.' Merry marched off in the direction of the house, leaving Rosina with a picture of her suddenly transformed into a small green frog. However, curiosity overcame her desire to finish her task, and she drank her tea quickly before hurrying into the house.

'She's in the drawing room,' Merry said in a conspiratorial whisper. 'I gave her a cup of tea and a slice of saffron cake.'

'I'll go and find out what she has to say.' Rosina shot a sideways glance at Merry. 'And no more talk of witches, please.' She did not wait for an answer, and she walked quickly through the house to the drawing room.

Seated in Jane's favourite chair by the empty grate was a woman of indeterminate age. Despite the pallor of her papery skin there were traces of past beauty in her lined face and her dark eyes were bright with intelligence. Her grey hair, streaked with silver, was pulled back into a severe chignon, and she was dressed all in black from the lace cap on her head to her booted feet. Rosina could see immediately why Merry had associated the elderly woman with the dark arts, although the smile that lit her face dispelled any doubts that Rosina might have had. She moved slowly towards her.

'How do you do, ma'am?'

The woman extended a bony hand encased in a lace mitten. 'How do you do? I believe you are Miss Wills.'

'Yes, I am. Might I know your name?'

'Please sit down, Miss Wills, looking up to you is making my neck ache. I am Lady Greenstead, and I am presently renting Conjuror's Cottage. Do you own this property, Miss Wills?'

'No, my lady. Moonshadow Manor belongs to my grandmother, Mrs Albert Clarke.'

'I was hoping to see her, Miss Wills, but your servant told me that her employer is in London.'

'I don't know when she will come home, ma'am. I believe she is on her honeymoon in Italy.'

'How fortunate for her. Perhaps I will call again when she returns. I'm sure someone in the village will let me know when she is at home.'

'May I ask what this is about, so that I can tell my grandmother?'

'I prefer to keep my reasons to myself for the time being, Miss Wills.' Lady Greenstead reached for her silver-headed cane and rose somewhat stiffly to her feet.

'Can you not give me a hint as to what you want with my grandmother?' Rosina asked urgently. There was something strange about this woman that had Rosina baffled and she was reluctant to let her go without knowing a little more.

Lady Greenstead moved slowly towards the doorway. 'You will find out soon enough, Miss Wills.'

Chapter Twenty-Three

Cataloguing all the items in the barn kept Rosina busy for the next two days. She had been mystified by the unexplained visit from Lady Greenstead, as had the rest of the community, according to Merry and Nell. Merry was convinced that the woman was a witch and Nell agreed with her. Seth Tully had become a frequent visitor on the vaguest of pretences, although it was obvious he fancied Merry, and he, too, insisted that there was something very mystical and probably evil about an old woman who lived alone. He insisted that she had a black cat tucked away somewhere in Conjuror's Cottage, or perhaps she had a raven as her familiar, but there was something strange going on. Apparently, the entire population of Ugstock agreed with him. Rosina might have agreed with them, but common sense told her that their fear was based on superstition and Lady Greenstead was simply an elderly woman, living on her own. She made up her mind to call upon her when she had finished sorting out her newly acquired possessions.

Rosina worked hard, hoping to put Jack's clumsy proposal out of her mind, but she had a nagging feeling that she might have been unfair to him. In his awkward way he had tried to express his emotions, but she had refused to listen. However, her full attention now must be given to making enough money to pay the servants, although to Rosina they were more like family, and they all had to be fed. Then there were general household expenses, which usually came out of Grandmama's purse, but in Jane's absence these had become Rosina's responsibility.

When one morning, Nell pointed out that Flora and Lottie needed new shoes, which would entail a visit to the shoemaker in Ivybridge, Rosina knew that she would have to go to Jack and ask for an advance on her grandmother's money. She also needed to get in touch with Donald Patterson so that she could start selling the articles in the barn. Perhaps she owed Jack an apology for the way she had treated his clumsy proposal of marriage, or maybe he would be the one to say he was sorry for upsetting her by speaking out of turn. She made up her mind to settle things one way or another, and decided to take Nell, Merry and the children to Ivybridge. She would get the funds needed while Nell and Merry took the girls to the shoemaker's to be fitted for new boots.

It was a tight fit to get everyone in the chaise, but they managed to squash together, and Joshua drove them to town. Merry, Nell and the girls went off to the shoemaker's shop, leaving Rosina to visit Jack's house.

Mrs Tarr opened the door and her smile when she saw Rosina was genuine.

'Do come in, miss. We haven't seen you in an age. I was beginning to think the worst.'

'Is Mr Dimond at home, Mrs Tarr? I need to see him urgently.'

Mrs Tarr's smile faded. 'Oh, dearie me. I do hope nothing is wrong.'

'No, it's a money problem that could soon be solved. Is he at home?'

'As a matter of fact, he's in the parlour with a business gentleman. Shall I announce you, miss?'

'If he's got a client with him, you'd better enquire if it's convenient to see me. I won't take up much of his time.'

'Very well, miss. Why don't you come into the dining room? I'll bring you some coffee if the master is going to keep you waiting.'

'Thank you, Mrs Tarr.'

Rosina followed her to the dining room and took a seat by the window, which overlooked the small garden at the back of the house. She remembered the last time she was here, when she had eaten luncheon with Jack. Things had seemed much simpler then, and she was suddenly nervous. She did not know how he was going to receive her or even how she was going to respond to him. She looked round as the door opened, expecting to see Mrs Tarr, but it was Jack who strode into the room. He came to a halt, the welcoming smile on his face fading.

'Rosie?'

She stood up, eyeing him warily. 'Jack! I'm sorry to bother you but, not to mince words, I need some of Grandmama's money. I know she didn't make provision for me before she left with Albert, but I wonder if you could make an exception and release a small amount.'

'I can't use her funds, but I don't think she imagined she would be away for so long. How much do you need, Rosie? I can help you.'

'The children need new shoes. Nell and Merry are taking them to the shoemaker as we speak, and to be honest I need provisions from the village shop.' Rosina looked away as the blood rushed to her cheeks. 'Jack, I . . .'

He was at her side before she could finish the sentence and he grasped both her hands. 'I was coming to see you today, Rosie. I shouldn't have left it so long, but I've been trying to get in touch with Patterson.'

Rosina stared down at their intertwined fingers. 'I was very short with you when we last met, Jack. I'm sorry.'

He squeezed her hand gently. 'No, it's I who must apologise, Rosie. I made a fool of myself, blurting out a proposal like an idiot. You were right to protest. I am truly ashamed of myself. Can you forgive me?'

She looked up and met his anxious gaze with a tremulous smile. 'Of course I can, Jack. I value your friendship more than anything.'

'Then I will have to be satisfied with that, for the time being.' Jack smiled and released her hand. 'Don't worry about the money. The girls may have new shoes, and I'll give you as much as you need to keep everything going, at least until Jane and Albert return.'

'Thank you, Jack. That is a huge relief, but I don't want you to think I came here only for the money. I was genuinely ashamed of myself for treating you so harshly.'

'The fault, as I said, was mine. Now come with me, Rosie. There's someone I want you to meet.' Jack opened the door and led the way to the front parlour where he ushered Rosina into the room. 'Donald, just by chance, the lady I was talking about has graced us with her presence.' He turned to Rosina, smiling. 'Rosina, I want you to meet Donald Patterson. I dare say you will remember him from the bankrupt sale at Fairbanks House.'

Donald stepped forward, extending his hand. 'Miss Wills, it's a pleasure to meet you. Our first meeting was very brief, but here we are again, and Jack tells me that you have a wonderful collection of foreign artefacts that you want to sell.'

Rosina nodded. 'Yes, Mr Patterson. My uncle left his life's collection to me, but I have no idea how much the items are worth. Would it be possible for you to value them for me?'

'It would be my pleasure. I have a client to visit this afternoon, but I could come to Moonshadow Manor tomorrow morning, if that is convenient?'

'That would be excellent,' Rosina said, smiling. 'I've catalogued everything to the best of my ability.'

'That's good. It will make my job much easier. From what Jack tells me it is an exceptional collection. I might even be tempted to purchase part of it myself.' Donald turned to Jack. 'I'm afraid I must leave now as I have to travel to Plymouth for my next meeting, but I will be back tomorrow.'

'If you come here first, I'll accompany you to Moonshadow Manor. It's off the beaten track so I can act as guide.'

'Thank you, Miss Wills. I'll say good day to you, and I look forward to seeing you again tomorrow.' Donald walked to the door. 'Don't worry about seeing me out, Jack. I know the way. Goodbye for now.' He left the room, closing the door behind him.

'I wasn't expecting to find him here today.' Rosina

sat down on the small sofa with a sigh of relief. 'He seems nice, Jack. It would be wonderful if he did want to purchase part of the collection.'

'I'm no judge of such things, Rosie. But I would say that everything your uncle left you is of the highest quality. That must count for a lot, but we'll see what Donald says tomorrow.' He held up his hand, smiling. 'I know you need to go to the shoemaker, and you require money. Wait here while I get some from the safe in my office, and I'll go with you.'

'Thank you, Jack. I'm so glad we've settled our differences,' Rosina said earnestly.

'Don't imagine that my feelings have changed, Rosie.' Jack hesitated in the doorway, regarding her with a rueful smile. 'I must make sure that next time I propose to you I do it in the right way and at the right time. I have no intention of giving up easily, that's one thing you have yet to learn about me.'

Rosina had meant to tell him about the strange lady who had called at Moonshadow Manor, but for some reason it had slipped her mind. She would mention it casually as they walked to the shoemaker's shop.

With her hand tucked in the crook of Jack's arm, Rosina walked at his side as they headed into town.

'And you have no idea why this stranger wanted to see your grandmother?' Jack said, frowning.

'No, Jack. Lady Greenstead wouldn't say anything

else, and I didn't like to press her for an explanation. It was hard to guess her age, but I'd say she is in her eighties and very well preserved.'

'She must be an acquaintance from many years ago, although if you are correct about her age she would be much older than Jane.'

'I know. It's a real mystery, just like her sudden arrival in Ugstock and renting Conjuror's Cottage. No one in the village seems to know anything about her.'

'I'm sure someone will solve the mystery, or we might have to wait for the honeymooners to return,' Jack said thoughtfully. 'I expect it's all round the village that Miss Maddern and Dr Clarke are married.'

'I'm sure it is.' Rosina leaned on his arm. It was a relief to be able to share her concerns with Jack. She realised now just how much she had missed him, even though they had only been apart for a short time. It was nice to chat about inconsequential things and to laugh at a shared joke.

They arrived at the shop to find Flora in tears, with Nell and Merry trying to calm her down.

'What's the matter?' Rosina asked anxiously.

Flora pointed to a pair of red leather child's shoes with sparkling paste buckles that were hanging in the window.

'She saw them and now she's obsessed by them,' Merry said grimly.

'They are very fine shoes.' Rosina leaned down to wipe tears from Flora's cheeks with her hanky. 'But they are not practical.'

Flora wailed even louder, and Rosina straightened up. She turned to the shoemaker. 'Are the shoes in the window for a reason, Mr Chubb?'

He blinked and took off his steel-rimmed spectacles, wiping the lenses on his apron. 'I made them for a customer from Teignmouth, miss. But they never came to collect, nor did they pay for them. What child round here wears fancy shoes like that?'

'It appears that young Flora has fallen in love with them,' Jack said, ruffling Flora's hair. 'Perhaps you ought to try them on. They might not fit you.'

Flora wiped her eyes on her sleeve. 'May I, Rosina?'

'They ain't suitable,' Nell said crossly. 'Them's party shoes for a rich nipper.'

'If you would kindly take them down, Flora may try the shoes on, Mr Chubb.' Rosina met Jack's amused look with a frown. 'You shouldn't encourage her.'

'If the shoes are too small that will be the end of the conversation.' Jack stood aside as Mr Chubb reached up to unhook the tiny shoes.

'Sit down on the stool, young lady.' Mr Chubb bent down to put the shoes on Flora's stockinged feet as she had already taken off her serviceable boots.

'They fit me.' Flora jumped off the stool and

danced round the shop. The paste buckles flashed as they caught the sunlight streaming through the window. 'I can dance.'

'Well done, Jack,' Rosina said sarcastically. 'You need to be the one to tell her she can't have them.'

He laughed as he watched Flora's antics. 'Look how happy she is, Rosie. After all these little mites have been through, don't you think she deserves some fun?'

'They aren't suitable,' Nell repeated, frowning. 'If you give in to her every time she will become a brat, sir.'

'I'll do a very special price for you, sir,' Mr Chubb said hastily. 'You may have the shoes for the cost of the leather and the fancy buckles.'

'We came to get sensible boots for the girls, Jack,' Rosina said firmly. 'The red shoes will be worn out in a week or two.'

'And Flora will have had the time of her life wearing them.' Jack nodded to Mr Chubb. 'Put them on the bill, if you please. And whatever else the children need.'

'Very good, sir.' Mr Chubb turned to Rosina. 'Will that be all, miss?'

'Me wants shoes,' Lottie said, pointing to her sister's feet. 'Like Flora.'

Merry rolled her eyes. 'See what you've started, Mr Dimond. We'd only just had their feet measured for new boots.'

Jack scooped Lottie up in his arms. 'When you are Flora's age you may have red shoes with sparkly buckles, Lottie. Do you understand?'

Lottie plugged her thumb into her mouth, nodding.

'That's a good girl. Now as you've been so helpful perhaps you would like to come with me to the bakery, and I'll treat you to a cake.'

'Me, too,' Flora cried excitedly.

Jack took her by the hand. 'Yes, of course, Flora.'

'You're spoiling them,' Rosina said, laughing.

'You will ruin them, sir.' Nell shook her head, but her lips curved in a smile.

Merry put her head on one side. 'Are we all included in that, Mr Dimond? I have a fancy for a slice of cake.'

'What have you started, Jack?' Rosina demanded as she opened the shop door to allow him to pass, with Lottie clinging round his neck and Flora grasping his hand.

They walked in procession to the baker's and Jack bought cakes for everyone, which they ate on their way back to his house.

Joshua was walking Pixie, but on seeing them he drew the chaise to a halt. Merry and Nell climbed in first and Jack lifted the children into the vehicle. He held his hand out to Rosina. 'I would take you in my carriage, but I have paperwork that must be completed today.'

'That's quite all right, Jack. I'll see you tomorrow

with Mr Patterson.' Rosina hesitated, lowering her voice. 'I don't know how you would go about it, but perhaps you could find out more about the mysterious Lady Greenstead?'

'I was planning on doing that, Rosie.' Jack helped her into the chaise. 'Drive on, Joshua.'

Rosina could not resist the temptation to look back as they headed in the direction of home, and she had the satisfaction of seeing Jack standing outside his house, watching them drive away.

'He's a real gent, is Mr Dimond,' Nell said in a loud voice. 'And he's so good with the children. I wonder that no one has snapped him up before now.'

'I never used to like him when he came here as Miss Jane's solicitor,' Merry added. 'But he's changed since I first met him.' She shot a sly glance in Rosina's direction. 'I wonder what caused that to happen.'

Rosina said nothing. She settled down to enjoy the journey back to Moonshadow Manor. The sun was warm on her face, and she was feeling more optimistic than she had for some time. Tomorrow Donald Patterson would examine the contents of the barn and give her his opinion as to their value, and she would see Jack again. Suddenly that seemed the most important thing of all.

Donald Patterson spent an hour walking round the barn, examining the contents in detail and making notes in a small black book. Rosina and Jack could do nothing other than stand in the doorway and watch.

'Did you make any enquiries about Lady Greenstead?' Rosina asked in a low voice.

'I had a word with the mayor, who happens to be a client of mine. He told me that the Greenstead family have a large estate to the north of the moor. They made their money in tin mining.'

Rosina shook her head. 'But why would a wealthy woman of a certain age, travel all the way to Ugstock and rent a rundown cottage on the edge of the village? It doesn't make sense.'

'There's only one way to find out, Rosie. One of us must ask her.'

'Preferably not me,' Rosina said, smiling. 'I found her quite intimidating. Anyway, the most important thing now is to hear what Mr Patterson has to say.' She waited breathlessly as Patterson approached them. 'Mr Patterson, what is your verdict?'

'A most impressive collection, Miss Wills.' Patterson closed his book and placed his pencil in his jacket pocket. 'Your late uncle was a man of taste and discernment.'

'But the value, Donald,' Jack said firmly. 'That is the main question. How much do you think the items are worth?'

'A considerable sum, Jack. I can't give you an exact quote without taking each article into consideration, but I would be prepared to offer a generous amount for the items that I would like to purchase for my gallery in Mayfair.'

'That sounds exciting,' Rosina said eagerly. 'How much were you thinking of offering, Mr Patterson?'

'Donald, please,' he said, smiling. 'I can see that we are going to do business in the future, Rosina, if I may call you that.'

'Please do, but you haven't answered my question.'

'I need a little longer to work it out, but I will give you a price by midday. As to the rest of the collection, I think you will do very well to price them individually. When I've worked out my offer I will go through the remaining stock with you, if that is convenient for you, Rosina?'

'Yes, indeed. It's more than I could have hoped for.' Rosina turned to Jack, smiling. 'Isn't that wonderful?'

'It is very fair, as I knew it would be. I suggest we leave Donald to get on with his task in peace. Maybe this is the moment for us to visit the mysterious woman in Conjuror's Cottage.'

'I'll see you later then,' Patterson said hurriedly. 'I can't wait to examine these artefacts closer. Don't worry about me, I'm more than happy to be left on my own.'

'I'll ask Merry to bring you out a cup of tea.' Rosina clutched Jack's arm. 'Let's hope that the mysterious Lady Greenstead isn't practising the dark arts, as her predecessors apparently did in that cottage.'

'I suggest we walk to the village, Rosie. It's a lovely day and we have plenty of time.'

'I suppose it would be easier to hop back to Moonshadow if she should decide to turn us into a pair of green frogs,' Rosina said, laughing. 'After all you wouldn't be able to hold the reins in your little stubby frog fingers.'

'But if you were to kiss me, I might turn into a prince,' Jack said with a wry smile.

'We will have to wait and see, Jack. In the meantime, I need to fetch my bonnet and gloves. It wouldn't do to turn up looking dishevelled. I have a feeling that Lady Greenstead would not be impressed.'

They walked slowly back to the house. Rosina went to her room to put on her bonnet and lace gloves, leaving Jack to ask Merry to provide Donald with tea and maybe a couple of her saffron buns.

The sun was high in the sky, and it was hot for the time of year as they made their way to the edge of the village where Conjuror's Cottage stood alone against a background of open moorland. Its dark windows gazed sightlessly out onto an overgrown garden, and ivy battled with brambles as if attempting to invade the property.

Rosina held back a little, clutching Jack's hand. 'Why would a wealthy woman want to live here? Heaven knows what it's like inside.'

'There's only one way to find out.' Jack gave her hand a gentle squeeze. 'She can't eat us, Rosie.'

'You obviously haven't read the story of Hansel and Gretel,' Rosina said nervously. 'The wicked witch lured children into her house, planning to gobble them up.'

'If we should have children, I will forbid you to read anything by the Grimm brothers. Their tales are much too violent for nicely brought up youngsters.'

'There you go again, Jack. Do you find it amusing to pretend that we are going to be married?'

He took both her hands in his, looking into her eyes with an intense gaze. 'I love you, Rosie. I would be honoured if you would agree to be my wife.' He leaned over to kiss her briefly on the lips. 'Please say yes before we risk being eaten or imprisoned by the wicked witch.'

'Are you serious, Jack? I never know if you are teasing me.'

'I am very serious. I couldn't be more so. Marry me, Rosie, and I will love you and care for you for the rest of our lives.'

Rosina felt her resolve melt away. She had deliberately put aside any tender feelings she had been harbouring for Jack. Her grandmother's ill-fated passion for Sir Bertram had made Rosina wary of allowing herself to fall in love, but somehow the emotion had crept up on her and she could no longer pretend indifference.

'Will you marry me, Rosie?' Jack said again, his voice breaking with emotion.

She looked into his eyes, and his feelings for her were unashamedly laid bare. She knew there could only be one response. 'Yes, Jack, with all my heart, I will marry you.'

He held her in an embrace that sent her senses reeling, and she returned his kiss with a hunger and enthusiasm she could never have imagined. Jack released her with gentle kisses on her forehead, cheeks and then her lips.

Rosina held him at arm's length, smiling dazedly. 'I think you'd better knock on the door, Jack. I don't think the wicked witch can hurt us now.'

'Nothing can ever come between us, Rosie. Let the witch do her worst.' Jack thumped on the door knocker and the sound echoed through the small cottage, but there was no response.

Rosina held on to his hand. She was still reeling from the suddenness of the change in their relationship, but almost impossibly happy. She could face even the wickedest witch with Jack at her side.

'It's no use knocking, sir. She ain't there now.'

Rosina and Jack turned to see Bob Pavey, the coalman, standing at the gate.

'Do you mean she's left the village?' Jack frowned. 'Do you know why she left?'

Bob Pavey's lined face creased into a grin. 'The likes of her don't tell the likes of I nothing, sir. But she's gone and good riddance. I've just collected the sack of coal I delivered afore she upped sticks and left. I can't afford to lose money on unpaid bills.' He tipped his cap and walked away.

'We've done our bit, Rosie,' Jack said firmly. 'The lady has gone, and we will probably never see her again. Besides which, we have more important matters to discuss.'

'I don't understand why she didn't wait to speak to Grandmama. There's something strange going on, and I won't rest until I discover the truth.'

'I suggest we put everything behind us and concentrate on our future, Rosie.' Jack proffered his arm. 'You were going to plan a big wedding for your grandmother, but I think you need to make it for us now. I want the whole of Ugstock, if not the entire county, to celebrate our nuptials, and the sooner the better.'

'That would be wonderful, but, Jack, I have business to discuss with Donald, and I can't really plan anything until Grandmama returns.'

Jack tucked her hand in the crook of his arm. 'I suggest we call in at the vicarage on the way home. We'll give the good news to the vicar and arrange for the first reading of the banns on Sunday. Then it's official and tomorrow, if you have nothing better to do, I will take you to Plymouth to buy you an engagement ring. What do you think, Rosie?'

Chapter Twenty-Four

The Reverend Matthew Horsfall was only too pleased to agree to the reading of the banns, having first rendered a long speech on the sanctity of marriage, which left Rosina feeling slightly dazed. Everything had happened so quickly that she would not have been surprised to wake up and find it was all a dream. However, when she and Jack returned to Moonshadow Manor they were met by Merry, whose expression was anything but happy.

'Thank goodness you've come back,' Merry said tearfully. 'I sent Joshua to get you, but he couldn't find you.'

'We've been to see the vicar,' Rosina said faintly. 'What is that you're holding, Merry?'

'It came just like this. It was folded but not sealed. I didn't mean to open it, but somehow it fell open.'

Merry handed the sheet of vellum to Rosina. The heading was painfully clear. It read, in black gothic lettering: 'Notice of Eviction', and the address of the premises was noted below.

'But this must be a mistake.' Rosina's hand shook as she handed the paper to Jack.

He read it, shaking his head. 'Who delivered this, Merry?'

'A messenger on horseback, sir. He didn't say anything. He just gave it to me and rode off again.'

'Let's go indoors, Rosie,' Jack said slowly. 'I need to study this, but it is addressed to your grandmother, and it seems to have been instigated by the Greenstead estate. I have no idea how that is possible.'

'I knew Lady Greenstead was up to no good, Jack. And now she's run away, having sent something like this.' Rosina was about to follow him into the house when Donald Patterson emerged from the barn.

'You're back, Rosina. I have been through everything, and I have an offer to make.'

Rosina hesitated. 'Could it wait a while, please, Donald?'

'No, I'm sorry. I need to be on the road soon. This has taken up more of my time than I bargained for, but it's good news.' Patterson crossed the yard and handed her a piece of paper. 'That's the sum I'm offering for the entire contents of the first two tables, which is about a third of your stock.'

Rosina blinked as the figures seemed to jumble together before settling in a sensible order.

'That's a generous offer, Donald.'

'Do you accept?'

'I would be a fool to turn it down, but what about the rest of the collection?'

'I've left notes on the benches as to what I think you might expect for each item. Do you plan to sell them from here? Or were you thinking of renting a premises in Ivybridge?'

'I haven't had time to consider it in detail, and now something serious has turned up that might change everything, but I accept your offer, Donald.'

'I'm glad you're happy to go ahead, Rosina. I'll pay the money by banker's draft, so you know the payment is secure. I have to go now but I will be happy to help or advise you in any way in the future. Jack knows how to get in touch with me.' Patterson shook her hand. 'I must say it was a pleasure to be involved in such a glorious collection of artefacts. I wish I had known your uncle. He must have been a very astute businessman.'

'Thank you, Donald.' Rosina watched him as he walked away and climbed into his chaise, taking the reins from Joshua. He drove off with a cheery wave of his hand.

'Should I put Mr Dimond's horse in harness, miss?' Joshua asked as she was about to turn away.

'Not yet, Joshua. We have some business to

discuss. I'll let you know when he is ready to leave.' Rosina hurried into the house, avoiding the kitchen where she could hear Merry and Nell talking in low voices with the squeals and giggles from the children as they vied for attention.

Rosina found Jack in the study, seated at the desk with the eviction notice in front of him.

'Is that legal, Jack? Can they really evict Grandmama and me for no reason?'

'That is what I am going to find out. I intend to visit the Greenstead solicitors who instigated these court proceedings.'

'What do we do if it is legal?' Rosina asked tremulously. 'Grandmama was born in this house and so was my mama. It's been in the family for generations.'

'I will get to the truth of the matter, Rosie. You mustn't worry. Whatever happens, I will look after you and the children. Jane is married to Albert, so he will protect her.'

'But what will happen to Moonshadow?' Rosina stifled a sob. 'I've grown to love this old house more than I can say, and it was supposed to come to me eventually. I can't bear to think of someone else living here.'

'I feel the same, but I can't allow emotions to cloud my judgement. I'm sorry, but you will have to wait a while longer until I can take you to buy an engagement ring.'

'I don't mind waiting,' Rosina said, sniffing. 'But we can't arrange our wedding if we're going to be thrown out on the streets.'

Jack rose to his feet and wrapped his arms around her. 'We have a month's grace, according to this vile document, but I am going to fight it with everything I have in me. They won't rob you of your inheritance, my love.'

'I want to go with you tomorrow, Jack. I can speak up for myself.' Rosina rested her head against his shoulder, taking comfort from the strength of his arms around her and the intoxicating scent that was his alone.

Jack stroked her hair gently. 'The meeting will be one solicitor to another. I will challenge the decision, of course, and if we're forced to take them to court you will have your chance to speak then. As it is, you would do better to remain here and keep everything going.'

'I will, if you think it best, but I'd rather be with you.'

'We will never be apart once we're married, Rosie. One thing I need to do is to get in touch with the newlyweds. They did not seem to think we might need to know where they are, but I mean to find them somehow, as Jane is the legal owner of Moonshadow.'

'What can I do? I feel so helpless, and I hate that.'

Jack held her at arm's length, his dark eyes twinkling. 'You can search for that huge guest list that you made for Jane and Albert. If the worst happens, we will at least have one splendid last party at Moonshadow Manor.'

'Don't say that, Jack,' Rosina said urgently. 'We can't lose Moonshadow. It would break Grandmama's heart.'

'I hope our celebrations will be the first of many, Rosie. I want to see our children playing in the garden and riding out on the moor on their first ponies, and that includes Flora and Lottie. We can't abandon them now.'

Rosina slid her arms around his neck. 'I do love you, Jack. Whatever happens, nothing will change that. I don't care if we end up living in the barn with the girls and our children running wild on the moor.'

'I'm a successful lawyer, Rosie. It won't come to that, even if the other side win. I can support my family. We might never be wealthy like Hugo or Sir Bertram, but we will have a happy and loving family. Neither of them can say that.'

A timid knock on the door made them pull apart.

'Come in.' Jack held on to Rosina's hand.

Merry opened the door. 'What's happened, miss? Are we going to lose our home?'

'Not if I have anything to do with it,' Jack said, firmly. 'We have a problem, but it will be solved one way or another. However, we have good news as well, Merry.'

She glanced anxiously from one to the other. 'Good news, sir?'

Jack slipped his arm around Rosina's shoulders. 'Rosina has done me the honour of agreeing to be my wife. You are the first to know, apart from the vicar.'

Merry's eyes filled with tears, and she clapped her hands. 'Oh, sir! That's wonderful. Miss Rosina, that's the best news I've had for ages.'

'Thank you, Merry. I was so happy until I saw this hateful document. It's quite ruined my day.'

'We won't allow it to spoil things, my love,' Jack said gently. 'I will sort it out. You should concentrate of the wedding plans.'

'I know I won't sleep a wink tonight.' Rosina sank down on a chair in front of the desk. 'I wish you would change your mind about me travelling with you tomorrow.'

'You are needed here, Rosie. I will come back to Moonshadow when I've dealt with Lady Greenstead's solicitors, and I'll tell you everything.' Jack turned to Merry. 'I'd best leave now. Please ask Joshua to harness Judge.'

'Yes, of course sir.' Merry hurried from the room.

'It will all work out, Rosie,' Jack said firmly. 'You'll see.'

That evening, after dinner, the children were in bed, leaving Nell and Merry free to play cards and chatter excitedly about the coming wedding. Rosina escaped to the barn and went through the notes that Patterson had left for her. Outside the light was fading fast and she lit a lantern so that she could continue her work. Through the open doors she could see bats circling crazily in the half-light and, although she tried her best to concentrate on labelling the items she wanted to sell, her thoughts kept straying to the notice of eviction. Most puzzling of all was the reason why the Greenstead estate claimed to own Moonshadow Manor and its grounds. Eventually she was overcome by fatigue, and she extinguished the lantern before leaving the barn and locking the doors.

As she crossed the yard, she was aware of a light in the coach house, and she came to a halt as an idea struck her forcibly. Jack might have refused to take her with him to visit the Greenstead estate's lawyers, but surely the person who had instigated the court action must be Lady Greenstead herself. That might well explain her reason for coming to Ugstock in the first place, although why she had left in such a hurry was another mystery and one that Rosina was determined to solve. Never someone who would settle for standing idly by when the world seemed to be tilting on its axis, Rosina walked over to the coach house and knocked on the door.

It was opened by a startled Joshua. 'What's the matter, miss? Is anything wrong?'

'Joshua, I want you to do something for me.'

'Yes, miss, anything.'

'Do you know how to get to the Greenstead estate? I believe it's north of Tavistock.'

'Yes, miss. I know it well. I was born in Tavistock.'

'I want you to drive me there first thing tomorrow morning, Joshua. We should leave before the others are up and about.'

'I'll be ready, miss.'

'Six o'clock, Joshua. Don't oversleep.'

'No, miss. You can count on me.'

Rosina nodded. 'Good night, Joshua.'

She headed back to the house and went straight to her room as she had no intention of sharing the reason for her early start next morning. Lady Greenstead might have instigated the court action, but Rosina was determined to discover her reasons for so doing. It seemed impossible that a family living so far away could own Moonshadow Manor, especially when its history was so well documented. Lady Greenstead must have a good reason for her actions, and she would have to explain herself. Rosina wrote a brief explanatory note for Merry, which she would leave on the kitchen table next morning. She went to bed feeling exhausted but set on her purpose.

The Greenstead estate was protected by a high brick wall extending as far as the eye could see, and ornate wrought-iron gates guarded the entrance. The gatekeeper emerged from his cottage and, after a brief discussion, during which Rosina managed to convince him that she was well known to Lady Greenstead, he rather grudgingly opened the gates. A long avenue of horse chestnut trees led up to the mansion, which sprawled in a rather haphazard way in the midst of a deer park. It seemed that different generations of the Greenstead family had built extensions in the architectural style that was fashionable at the time, and the result was slightly eccentric but interesting. However, Rosina was not interested in the building; she was intent on seeing Lady Greenstead in person.

After a brief argument with the butler, Rosina was instructed to wait in the entrance hall while he checked if her ladyship was available. He returned minutes later with a disapproving look on his face.

'Follow me, if you please.' He strutted off with Rosina close on his well-polished heels.

The morning parlour, as the butler called it, was larger than the drawing room at Moonshadow, although probably on a par with the one at Glazewood Hall, and a little smaller than a similar room at Daumerle House. Rosina, however, was not impressed. She waited while the butler announced her in a pompous manner that might have been amusing at any other time.

'So, you've come all this way to see me, Miss Wills.' Lady Greenstead eyed her with cold indifference. 'I think I can guess why.'

'You admit that it was on your instructions

that we received that despicable notice of eviction. Moonshadow belongs to my grandmother, and it was handed down from her father.'

'And that person won it in a card game. I am told that Phillip Maddern cheated Jabez Dimond out of the property in question.'

'How could you possibly know that? It happened more than sixty years ago. Besides which, from what I've heard of Jabez Dimond, he would have challenged the result if he suspected that Phillip had cheated. Anyway, with due respect, ma'am, what has it got to do with you?'

For a moment Rosina thought she had gone too far. Normally she would not have been so blunt, but she had come a long way, and she was faced with the threat of losing her home.

Lady Greenstead's taut expression relaxed a little and she laughed. 'You are forthright to the point of rudeness, Miss Wills.'

'My family have a lot to lose, ma'am. You, it seems, are extremely wealthy and you live in luxury. Why would you want to take Moonshadow away from us?'

'That property belonged to the Dimond family and Phillip Maddern was a cheat. I want to see a wrong set right. That is my reason, and it is why I came to Ugstock and stayed in that disgusting hovel. I'm not prepared to discuss the matter further, Miss Wills. It is now in the hands of my lawyers.'

'But you can't just claim ownership without some proof,' Rosina said in desperation.

'The truth will come out in court, Miss Wills. Moonshadow will return to its rightful owner.'

'Are you saying that you are a member of the Dimond family?' Rosina demanded angrily.

'I don't have to explain myself to you, or anyone else. I think it's time you left, Miss Wills.'

'You are very much in the wrong,' Rosina said boldly. She could see that she was getting nowhere and there seemed to be nothing more to lose. 'You cannot possibly have a claim to the Moonshadow estate. Perhaps it amuses you to see people suffer.'

'I suffered.' Lady Greenstead's eyes glittered with malice. 'You have no idea what it is like to go through the things I had to endure as a young woman. I may not have many more years left, but I am intent on seeing justice done at last.' She reached up and tugged at a bell pull. 'You may go, Miss Wills. I admire your nerve in coming here, but your journey was in vain. Go back to Ugstock and enjoy your last few weeks in Moonshadow Manor. I can assure you they are coming to an end. You should return to your father's house in London. You see, I know all about you. I spent my time well while I stayed in Ugstock.'

'You are a bitter old woman,' Rosina said angrily. 'Just because life has not treated you as you might wish, you want to ruin the lives of others. I can tell you in my case that I am engaged to be married to a wonderful man. I will have a happy family with the one I love. My grandmother has married a man who is devoted to her. She has thrown off the shackles that bound her to Moonshadow for all those years when she was bringing up my mother and disgraced by the community. She is happy now and nothing you can say or do will take that away.'

The door opened and the butler stood on the threshold.

Lady Greenstead sat forward in her seat. 'Show Miss Wills out, Cadbury. She is leaving and she is not to be allowed back into the grounds. Inform the gatekeeper, please.'

'This way, please, miss.' Cadbury held the door open.

Rosina backed away, keeping her eyes fixed on Lady Greenstead's lined and faded face that had been ravaged by time, but her dark eyes burned with intensity.

'I will send you an invitation to my wedding, my lady. Perhaps you need to come and watch the village celebrate. You will see what it means to love and be loved.' Rosina turned on her heel and marched out of the room. 'I can find my own way out, thank you, Mr Cadbury.'

'I'll go on ahead and summon your coachman, miss.'

'Have you been with Lady Greenstead for long, Mr Cadbury?' Rosina could not allow him simply to walk away.

Cadbury eyed her curiously. 'I've been with her ladyship for many years, miss.'

'It's none of my business, of course, but has she any family? She seems quite lonely.'

'None that I know of, miss.' Cadbury walked on, quickening his pace and putting an end to any attempt at conversation, leaving Rosina with little more understanding of the situation than she'd had before she came.

It was a relief to climb into the chaise and set off on the journey home. Joshua remained silent, speaking only when spoken to, and Rosina found herself drifting off to sleep, rocked by the swaying motion of the vehicle.

Merry was eager for news when Rosina arrived back at Moonshadow, but Rosina could only tell her what Lady Greenstead had said, which did not go down well at all.

'I would have told the old besom a thing or two.' Merry shook her head. 'She can't take Moonshadow away from you, can she, miss?'

'I certainly hope not,' Rosina said sadly. 'But she is obviously very wealthy, and money, it seems, can buy almost anything. I hope that Jack has had more luck with the lawyers in Plymouth.'

'If anyone can sort things out, it will be Mr Dimond.' Merry gave Rosina a searching look. 'You're exhausted, miss. Go and sit in the drawing room. I lit a fire earlier and I'll bring you some supper, if you wish. Me and Nell ate with the children. She's putting them to bed as we speak.'

'Thank you, Merry. I'm not very hungry but some soup would be nice, if that's what I can smell simmering on the hob.'

'My vegetable broth always goes down well,' Merry said proudly. 'And there's fresh baked bread to go with it. I'll bring it to you when you've had time to take off your bonnet and mantle. Maybe a glass of sherry wine will bring the colour back to your cheeks. You do look a bit wan, miss.'

Rosina laughed. 'What would I do without you, Merry?'

Rosina left the kitchen and went straight to her bedroom where she took off her outer garments. Merry had, as always, had the forethought to light a fire in here, too. It might be late spring, and the temperature soared in the day, but it was still chilly at night. Rosina tidied her hair and went downstairs to the drawing room where Merry had placed a glass of sherry on the small table beside Rosina's chair. She sat down and sipped the drink, staring into the bright flames that licked round the coal and logs. The scent of apple wood filled the room, and Rosina felt a sudden desire to cry. The thought of leaving Moonshadow Manor was almost too much to bear, and it seemed that Lady Greenstead had money and probably powerful friends in the judiciary if her confidence was anything to go by.

Minutes later, Merry arrived with a tray of supper. The vegetable broth looked and smelled enticing and the bread was still warm from the oven. Rosina found that her appetite had returned, and she ate hungrily. She had just finished and placed the tray on a table, together with her empty glass, when the door opened and Jack walked into the room. She jumped to her feet.

'Jack. I wasn't expecting to see you tonight. I thought you would go home after your journey to Plymouth.'

He swept her into his arms and kissed her, which she returned with equal fervour. She was the first to pull away gently.

'You must be tired, Jack. Have you eaten?'

He shook his head. 'Merry has already questioned me and given me a lecture on looking after myself. She's going to bring me something.' Jack sank down on the sofa and patted the seat beside him. 'Come and sit down. Merry told me you've been to see Lady Greenstead. What was that all about?'

'She should have left it to me to tell you that.' Rosina sank down on the sofa beside him. 'I wanted to see her in her own home, and I wanted to find out why she was being so vindictive.'

'What did she say, Rosie?'

'Not very much actually.' Rosina sighed. 'She is not a nice person, Jack. She seems very bitter about something or someone. She's obsessed with setting things to rights, at least in her own mind. She wouldn't say anything more, so I am no wiser now than I was before.'

'Her solicitors are adamant that she wants Moonshadow and she is prepared to go to court to get it.'

'Can she evict us just like that?'

'I couldn't get much out of her solicitors, so I've lodged an appeal against the eviction notice.'

'Her home is very grand,' Rosina said wistfully. 'She is obviously very wealthy. I really don't understand why she wants this property, which is small in comparison.'

Jack placed his arm around Rosina's shoulders and drew her closer to him.

'Sometimes a lonely person will latch on to something from the past that brings back memories. It's a pity that your grandmother isn't here. She might know something.'

'Is there anything more we can do before the appeal goes through the court?'

Jack smiled and put his hand in his jacket pocket. He took out a small shagreen-covered box and flicked it open.

'I know I was going to take you to Plymouth to choose a ring, but I was looking in the jeweller's window and I saw this. It was so exactly what I envisaged that I had to buy it, but if you dislike it we will take it back to the shop and you may choose whatever you want.' He held the box so that she could see the magnificent central diamond with a heart-shaped ruby on either side, set in ornate rose-gold.

Rosina caught her breath at the sight of such a beautiful jewel.

'It's wonderful, Jack. I love it. I hope it fits.'

'The jeweller assured me that he could alter it if necessary.' Jack took the dainty ring from the box and slipped it onto Rosina's finger. 'It could have been made for you, my darling.'

Rosina held her hand up so that the jewels sparkled in the firelight. 'I will never take it off, Jack. I love it and I love you.'

Their passionate embrace was interrupted by Merry, who entered bearing another tray of food. She came to a halt.

'Oh, I'm sorry. I'll come back later.'

Rosina drew away, smiling. 'No, come in, Merry. Look at my ring, isn't it the most exquisite thing you've ever seen.' She waved her left hand.

Merry abandoned the tray and bent over to examine the ring.

'Mr Jack, you've outdone yourself. The Queen wouldn't have anything better. Come and show Nell, miss. I don't think I've got words to describe your ring.'

Rosina glanced at Jack, and he nodded.

'Go on, Rosie. I've just realised how hungry I am

and that soup smells wonderful. You can't eat a jewel but I'm going to do justice to that soup.'

Rosina followed Merry to the kitchen where Nell was tidying up, but she stopped immediately and came over to examine the engagement ring.

'Don't wear that if you go to market, miss,' Nell said gloomily. 'There are them as would cut your finger off to get a prize like that. It must be worth a fortune.'

Rosina covered the ring with her right hand. 'Don't say such things, Nell. This isn't London.'

'She's right, though, miss,' Merry added seriously. 'You should wear gloves so that no one dangerous can catch sight of it.'

Rosina laughed. 'Maybe I should have a bodyguard. Perhaps Seth Tully would accompany me everywhere.' She left them giggling at the idea as she returned to the drawing room.

'You should stay here tonight, Jack,' Rosina said seriously. 'It's getting late and it's a long ride to Ivybridge. I don't want Roxanne's phantom luring you onto the moor, or any such things like evil pixies that the local people believe roam the marsh at night.'

Jack finished the last drop of soup. 'That was delicious. But I must go, Rosie. I have a meeting first thing in the morning, and I want to get the paperwork done for the appeal. We've got less than three weeks until the wedding. There's a lot to be done.'

Rosina nodded. 'You're right, of course. Tomorrow I will work out the guest list. I have the list I made when it was going to be Grandmama's wedding to Albert, so I'll start with that.'

Jack rose to his feet and gave her a hug. 'I'll leave you now, reluctantly, I might add. But in three weeks we will be together for ever, Rosie. I can't wait to call you my wife.'

Rosina slid her arms around his neck. 'You and I will be happy wherever we live, but that doesn't mean I'm not going to fight for what is ours.'

Chapter Twenty-Five

For the next two weeks Rosina barely saw Jack. She was fully occupied with wedding plans and sorting out items for the first sale in Moonshadow barn. Donald Patterson had circulated the date and time amongst his business colleagues. At first Rosina had been reluctant to have the sale so close to her wedding, but it was a way of keeping nerves at bay, and, besides, the eviction notice still hung over their heads. To lose Moonshadow would be a terrible blow to all of them, but it would also mean finding another home for the artefacts inherited from her uncle. This made having the sale as soon as possible a necessity, and eventually the date settled upon was a week prior to the wedding. Rosina had seriously considered renting shop premises, but with the appeal taking place soon after the wedding, and its outcome far from certain, Jack had persuaded Rosina to think again.

The day of the sale dawned bright, with a clear sky and the promise of a fine day ahead. Nell and Merry were as excited as the children, but Rosina was nervous. Patterson had agreed to conduct the sale, which was to be an auction rather than merely selling at fixed prices. Everything had been divided into lots, and a catalogue had been printed. Rosina was in the barn first thing that morning, checking and rechecking the arrangements. The sale had been advertised in the local paper and by word of mouth. There was nothing left to do other than hope everything went well. Rosina returned to the house where Merry and Nell were having breakfast with the children.

'Sit down and have something to eat, miss,' Merry said firmly. 'It's going to be a big day today.'

'Get it over before the more important celebrations,' Nell added, smiling. 'Flora and Lottie are going to be flower girls, isn't that right, girls?'

Rosina took her seat at the table. 'I hadn't thought of that. I've had so much else to do. But it's a lovely idea.'

'Me and Nell have been making their dresses,' Merry said proudly.

'I'm sure they will both look lovely.' Rosina accepted a bowl of porridge from Merry. 'Thank you. I'm not very hungry, but I'll try to eat. I keep thinking how awful it will be if no one turns up for the sale.'

Nell giggled. 'Worry more about the groom not turning up for the wedding.'

'Nell!' Merry said in a shocked voice. 'That's no way to talk.'

'I was joking.' Nell blushed rosily. 'I meant to make you laugh, Miss Rosina.'

'It's all right, Nell.' Rosina swallowed a mouthful of porridge. 'Perhaps the only thing I'm certain of is Jack being there at the altar. Being in business is very nerve racking. I'll be glad when the auction is over.' She pushed the plate away. 'I don't think I can eat any more, Merry.'

'My mum would make me sit at the table until my plate was clean,' Merry said severely. She was suddenly alert, and she ran to the window. 'There's a carriage pulled up in the stable yard, miss. Isn't it a bit early for the sale to start?'

Rosina jumped to her feet and went to look over Merry's shoulder.

'Oh, my goodness! It's Dr Clarke, and he's helping Grandmama from the carriage.'

Rosina hurried from the kitchen and crossed the yard at a run. 'You've come home. I thought you were in Italy.' She hugged her grandmother. 'You look wonderful. Being married suits you, Grandmama.'

Albert patted her on the shoulder. 'We decided to stay in London after all, Rosina.'

'Yes, we did all the things I've always wanted to. We went to the Zoological Gardens and the Tower of London, and Madame Tussauds.'

'We ate at some of the best restaurants. They were delightful, but very expensive,' Albert added, pulling a face.

'And we went to the theatre almost every night.' Jane smiled happily. 'Now we've come home, Rosina. What has been happening here?'

'You'd better come indoors, Grandmama,' Rosina said gently. 'There's a lot to tell and I'm afraid not all of it is good.' She ushered them into the house and settled them in the drawing room. They both declined breakfast, having eaten at a wayside inn.

'We came by road,' Albert explained cheerfully. 'We wanted to prolong the honeymoon and enjoy the countryside.' He gave Rosina a searching look. 'But I can tell there is something bothering you, my dear.'

'Yes, what is it, Rosina?' Jane sank down on her favourite chair. 'What has happened?'

'I hardly know where to begin.' Rosina paced the floor agitatedly. 'So much has occurred in such a short time.'

'You can begin by telling us about that lovely ring you're wearing,' Jane said gently. 'Are congratulations in order?'

Rosina came to a halt, gazing down at her ring with a tender smile. 'You will be surprised to hear that I'm marrying Jack in just over a week's time.'

Jane rose to her feet and enveloped Rosina in a hug. 'My dear, I was expecting it, perhaps not quite so soon, but it was obvious to anyone that you two were the ideal match.'

'Really?' Rosina shook her head. 'It took us long enough to realise it, Grandmama. Anyway, you will be here for our wedding, which is wonderful. I've invited my pa and Dora, but I don't know if they will make the journey.'

'Well, it's wonderful news, but that is not all, is it? What is it you are worrying about?' Jane resumed her seat, reaching out to clutch Albert's hand.

'Do you know anything about the Greenstead family, Grandmama? They have an estate to the north of Tavistock.'

'I've heard of them, of course. I believe Bertram knew Sir Willoughby, but that's all.'

'Which makes it even more mysterious,' Rosina said slowly. 'Lady Greenstead claims ownership of Moonshadow Manor, and we have received a notice of eviction. Jack is appealing against it, but at the moment it stands.'

Jane and Albert exchanged worried glances. 'But that is so strange. It can't be true.' Jane frowned. 'I can't see how Lady Greenstead could have any claim to this house, or why she would want it.'

'Unless she is related in some way to the Dimond family,' Albert said slowly. 'But Jack ought to know, if that is the case.'

'I don't want to seem rude, Grandmama.' Rosina cleared her throat nervously. 'But do you and Albert intend to live here?'

'I have a perfectly good house, and if Jane doesn't wish to stay there, we can always purchase something more suited to our needs. We have discussed this at length.' Albert raised Jane's hand to his lips. 'Don't worry about us, Rosina.'

Rosina was about to respond when Merry burst into the room. 'Mr Patterson has arrived, miss. And there are carriages pulling up in the yard and outside. It looks as if the whole world is coming to the sale.'

'The sale, Rosina?' Jane stared at her aghast. 'What are you selling?'

'I can't stop to explain now, Grandmama. Come to the barn in a while and you'll find out.' Rosina turned back to Merry. 'I've asked Joshua to direct the prospective purchasers to the barn.' Rosina followed Merry from the drawing room.

'Mr Patterson is in the morning parlour, miss. I thought that was the best place to put him, considering the fact that Miss Jane has returned so unexpectedly.'

'Quite right, Merry. I'll go and speak to him now.'

Jack arrived just in time for the start of the sale and the barn was packed, with people queuing outside and waiting their chance to slip in and bid for the item of their choice. Patterson was masterly in handling the bidding and it was obvious to Rosina that he had performed this task many times before. All she could do was stand back and admire his expertise. She leaned against Jack, who gave her a reassuring smile.

'I've done all I can for the appeal,' he said in a low voice.

'Do you know when it will be held, Jack?'

'Ironically, it's going to court the day after our wedding. Let's hope it is a present worth waiting for.'

Rosina was suddenly alert. 'That's the last lot coming up now, Jack.' She held her breath as Patterson took the bids, cleverly urging the buyers to pay more until the gavel went down. He thanked everyone for their attendance and closed his book before stepping down from the temporary rostrum.

'That went well, Rosina,' Patterson said, smiling. 'In fact, it will have made more than I expected. Everything has been sold. Your late uncle had a rare talent for selecting the most desirable and valuable items to collect.'

'How much have we made, Donald?' Jack asked casually.

'My clerk will let you know when he's totted up the figures, but it's quite substantial.'

'Come into the house, Donald,' Rosina said eagerly. 'We should celebrate, although I'm afraid it will have to be sherry or a nice cup of tea.'

Patterson laughed. 'A cup of tea will suit me

very well. We'll leave Anderson to make sure the buyers get the right articles. He's been with me for years.' Patterson saluted his clerk, who grinned and nodded.

'I'll send my maid out with some refreshment for you, Mr Anderson,' Rosina said as she was about to leave the barn. 'Thank you for all your hard work.'

When Anderson produced the final amount of money made that day it was impressive, even allowing for the ten-per-cent commission that Patterson charged for his part in the proceedings. Rosina knew that he could have asked for more, but everyone was happy with the result.

Jane and Albert left in the middle of the afternoon with Jane promising to return next day to discuss any wedding arrangements that were outstanding. With the visitors gone and the stable yard empty apart from Jack's chaise, a sense of tranquillity descended on the property. Merry and Nell had taken the over-excited children to the village to visit Fred Pavey's shop with a promise to buy them some boiled sweets if they were good.

'It's strangely quiet,' Rosina said as she and Jack surveyed the now empty barn. 'Who would have thought the sale would go so well?'

'At least you have enough to keep the house going for a while, assuming that our appeal is upheld.' Jack placed his arm around her shoulders. 'One thing we haven't discussed is where we will live after we're married, Rosie? Supposing the appeal fails, and we lose Moonshadow.'

She shot him a sideways glance. 'I've just assumed we would live here, Jack. Your house is very nice but it's not big enough for all of us. We can't lose Moonshadow. It means as much to you as it does to me. After all, it did belong to your family in the first place.'

'We'll fight it all the way. Maybe I ought to visit Lady Greenstead at her home. I want to know why she insists that Moonshadow belongs to her.'

'If you do, I hope you have more success than I did, Jack.' Rosina smiled ruefully. 'If anything, I think I made matters worse.'

Jack shook his head. 'I doubt that, Rosie darling. But from now on I think you should concentrate on the wedding. Forget Lady Greenstead and leave the legal matters to me. It doesn't matter if it's the last party we have at Moonshadow or the first of many, we will have a celebration that everyone will remember for years to come.'

Rosina did her best to put her worries out of her mind as the day of the wedding drew nearer. Jane helped her with the final arrangements, including the food for the wedding breakfast, which she organised with the help of Merry and Nell. Tables and chairs were borrowed from numerous sources so that the guests could eat inside, should the weather turn on them.

Grace came down from London, insisting that she would be the maid of honour, and giving Rosina little choice in the matter. This annoyed Ariadne who also laid claim to that position, but she had to settle for being chief bridesmaid and Hugo was to be Jack's best man. When it came to bridal wear, Rosina had intended to wear her plain silk gown, but she was almost deafened by the chorus of indignation from Jane and the others. She found herself at their mercy and a dressmaker was summoned, patterns were pored over, and swatches of material went from hand to hand until everyone was satisfied. With only two days to go, the dress was completed with the aid of a sewing machine and many willing hands. The gown that Grace had chosen for Rosina in London was to be worn for the party in the evening, where the local band would play for them. Bob Pavey played the fiddle with his brother Fred on the bass drum, Seth Tully on the cymbals, and Sid Bragg had recently mastered the flute – more or less, anyway.

Rosina had sent an invitation to her father and Dora with little hope of them making the journey to Devonshire, but to her surprise they arrived the day before the wedding, together with a young nursemaid and Oswald.

'I'm so glad you came, Pa,' Rosina said, smiling. 'I would have had to ask Albert to give me away if you had been unable to attend.'

Humphrey kissed her on the cheek. 'It's my duty

and my pleasure to give you away to a man who obviously loves you, Rosie. I'm sorry to hear you might lose this old house, but you will find somewhere else to live and make it a happy home.' He glanced over his shoulder as Oswald began to bawl, and Dora handed him over to the young nanny.

'Take Master Oswald and put him to bed,' Dora said impatiently. 'He obviously needs to sleep.'

Merry cleared her throat. 'Er, excuse me, missis. Maybe some fresh air would soothe the baby. Nell is taking the girls for a walk. I'm sure she would be happy to take Master Oswald as well.'

'Anything to stop him crying,' Dora cried passionately. 'I need to rest, Humphrey. I'm going to our room. Please don't disturb me until it's time to dress for dinner.'

'Very well, dear.' Humphrey sank down on the sofa. 'She's very highly strung, Rosie. Poor Oswald is a difficult child. He gets colic and he seems to be teething continuously. I'm sure you were no such trouble.'

'He'll grow out of it, Pa,' Rosina said hopefully. 'Leave him to Nell for a few days. She is marvellous with babies and small children.'

'That will be a relief. Anyway, my dear girl, it leaves us free to have a chat. Tell me what happened to your late uncle's collection.'

Rosina sat down beside him and recounted the details of the sale and the amount of money it had raised.

'That's wonderful, Rosie,' Humphrey said, smiling. 'You have inherited my head for business, and my brother obviously had excellent taste. I know you will do well in life, my dear. You were never one to give up easily.'

Rosina was about to reply when the door opened, and Jane walked in, followed by Albert.

'I've bought you some satin slippers to wear with your wedding gown, Rosie,' Jane said eagerly. 'You need to try them on to make sure they fit.' She turned to Albert with a meaningful look. 'Didn't you have a suggestion to make, my dear?'

'Yes, of course.' Albert turned to Humphrey. 'I suggest we leave the ladies to their task, Humphrey. You might like to come to the village inn with me, and you can meet some of the locals.'

Humphrey was on his feet without a second bidding. 'Excellent idea, Albert. I'm afraid Dora has a headache and she's resting, but I'm sure she won't mind if I go with you.'

'Leave Dora to us, Humphrey,' Jane said firmly. 'We will keep an eye on her.' She waited until they had left the room. 'Poor Humphrey has been hen-pecked into submission. It will do him good to get away from that woman for an hour or two.'

Rosina laughed. 'I believe you planned that, Grandmama.'

'I've known your father for more years than I care to recall. He was happy with your poor dear mama, but I'm afraid Dora has him very much under her thumb.'

'At least he's come here to give me away,' Rosina said cheerfully. 'Now where are these satin slippers, Grandmama? I can't wait to try them on.'

The white satin slippers fitted perfectly, and they complemented the ivory silk gown. On the morning of the wedding, Rosina stood still while Grace did up the tiny buttons at the back of her bodice, and Ariadne waited, holding the headdress of orange blossom and the long veil. Rosina would have been happy with a small hat and a short veil, but she had been outvoted by her grandmother and her friends, who all claimed to be experts on wedding attire.

Earlier that morning it had felt as though there were hours before the ceremony at midday, but suddenly the time had slipped away and Merry put her head round the door to announce the arrival of the bridal carriage. Nell had already taken the flower girls to the church and the congregation would almost certainly be settled in the pews by now. Rosina was suddenly nervous. She was happy and excited, but she had an ominous feeling that something unexpected would happen.

'It's just wedding nerves,' Jane said firmly. 'I expect Jack is feeling exactly the same. Come on, Rosie. It's time to leave for the church. Your father will be there waiting to walk you down the aisle.'

She ushered Rosina from the bedroom and followed her downstairs.

Rosina took a deep breath as she walked across the yard to the landau, borrowed for the occasion from Daumerle House. It was decorated with flowers, greenery and white satin bows. Joshua jumped down from the driver's seat to assist her into the vehicle, followed by Jane. It had been decided that Grace and Ariadne would meet them at the church, with Flora and Lottie ready to walk on ahead with their baskets of flower petals.

It was a short carriage ride to the church and Humphrey was waiting for them, looking almost as nervous as Rosina, but he managed a smile and proffered his arm. Rosina laid her hand on his arm and, clutching her bouquet of hothouse flowers from Glazewood Hall, she followed the flower girls up the aisle to the strains of the 'Bridal Chorus' from *Lohengrin*. The church organist, who was known to be keen rather than talented, must have been practising for weeks as he played with only a few missed notes, but all eyes were on Rosina as she walked slowly towards the altar where Jack was waiting with Hugo at his side. The church was packed with familiar faces, but Rosina almost came to a halt when close to the front she saw Sir Bertram standing in a pew with Clarissa, Cecily and Miss Templeton. Sir Bertram smiled and nodded to her as she walked past him, but she could not bring herself to smile back. She held her head high and walked on to stand beside Jack, and the ceremony began.

Humphrey did his part, giving his daughter's hand in marriage, but when they reached the point where the vicar asked if anyone had good reason to object there was a sudden commotion. The church door opened noisily, and there was a sudden hush as all heads turned to see the latecomer. Dressed in black from head to foot, Lady Greenstead walked into the nave, her booted feet echoing off the high vaulted ceiling and her cane tapping on the tiled floor.

The vicar hesitated, gazing at her nervously, but she shuffled into a back pew and sat down. The ceremony continued uninterrupted until Rosina and Jack were pronounced man and wife. They went to the vestry to sign the register, but as they prepared to leave and the organist struck up the first bars of Mendelssohn's 'Wedding March', Lady Greenstead stood up and blocked the aisle. The organist hit a wrong note and stopped playing.

'What is going on, ma'am?' Jack demanded angrily. 'Please allow us to pass.'

Lady Greenstead leaned heavily on her walking stick.

'I will say what I have to say in front of the whole congregation.'

Matthew Horsfall edged past the bride and groom. 'Really, my lady. Could this not wait until you are outside? Remember this is a holy place.'

'I know that, young man,' Lady Greenstead said coldly. 'But what I have to say needs to be heard by all and sundry. I suffered from gossipmongering in my youth, and I want my heirs to live free from scandal and falsehoods.'

'Please, ma'am. Let's do as Mr Horsfall says and take this out of the church,' Rosina said anxiously.

'No. I am determined to have my say. Heaven knows, enough has been said about me and now it is my turn to speak.'

Jack held up his hand as a ripple of comments threatened to engulf them. 'Please, everyone, allow Lady Greenstead to speak.'

'Thank you, Jack.' Lady Greenstead took a deep breath, glancing round at the expectant faces with a hint of a smile. 'I have withdrawn the claim to Moonshadow Manor. It was never mine even though I married into the Maddern family.' She paused dramatically at the sound of gasps from the congregation. 'Yes, I am she. Those of you old enough to remember me will know what I am about to say, but for the younger people, I will put the record straight. I gave birth out of wedlock to the son of Jabez Dimond, the true owner of Moonshadow Manor. Jabez was already married, and I was a young defenceless girl of fifteen, so I gave up my son on condition that he was raised by his father. I was alone and desperate when I married Phillip Maddern, but I discovered that he had cheated the Dimond family out of their family home, and Moonshadow Manor never truly belonged to the Maddern family. I realised too late that I had made a mistake, and I ran away, onto the moor that I loved.'

Jack stepped forward. 'You are Roxanne?'

A wry smile twisted Lady Greenstead's lips. 'I am Roxanne, but as you can see, I am still very much alive. I was found wandering the moor and saved by the man who became my husband, Sir Tristram Greenstead.'

'But why didn't you tell us who you are? Why did you threaten to evict us?' Rosina demanded tremulously.

'I wanted to right a wrong. I wanted to give Moonshadow Manor back to the Dimond family, but I can see now that my help was not needed. Fate has stepped in and done my work for me. Honour is satisfied and my part in the drama is done.' Lady Greenstead turned and walked slowly from the church.

The confused organist started to play the wedding march, but Rosina and Jack raced after Lady Greenstead with the congregation scrambling to follow them. Grace and Ariadne snatched Flora and Lottie up in their arms to keep them from being trampled and everyone poured out into the sunshine.

'Where are you going, Lady Greenstead?' Rosina demanded, tossing her bouquet to Ariadne, who caught it one handed. 'You can't just walk away.'

'Why not?' Roxanne faced her with a wry smile. 'I've done this before. It's what I do.'

'Not this time,' Jack said evenly. 'If all this is true, and you are my great-grandmother, I can't allow you to leave like this.'

'You don't owe me anything, Jack Dimond. I was going to evict the Madderns so that I could give Moonshadow to you, but I see that is no longer necessary. You and Rosina are uniting the two families. I'll go back to my abode, and you will get on with your lives.'

'Nonsense,' Rosina said hotly. 'You should come with us now, Lady Greenstead. You are part of Jack's family and mine, too. There is no reason for you to be separated again.'

Jane hurried up to them. 'You are Roxanne? You are a legend, my lady. I can't believe it's you.'

'Who are you, ma'am?' Roxanne stared at her, shaking her head.

'I am Phillip Maddern's daughter, Jane Clarke. You haunted our home for years. You were supposed to be a ghost roaming the moor. Now we see that you are flesh and blood, like the rest of us.'

'I'm sorry to disappoint everyone,' Roxanne said with a smile that transformed her lined face into a semblance of the looks that had bewitched men in her youth.

'You must join us for the wedding breakfast,' Rosina said firmly. 'We can't allow you to walk away now that we know the truth.' She glanced around at the curious onlookers. 'You have so many questions to answer, and so many people who are eager to get to know your story.'

'You are not going to disappear onto the moor again, Great-grandmama,' Jack said firmly. 'You are part of our family now and always. You will be guest of honour at our wedding breakfast.'

Humphrey stepped forward. 'It would be an honour if you will ride in the carriage with me and my wife, ma'am.' He shot a stern look at Dora, who opened her mouth as if to disagree.

'We'd be honoured, your ladyship,' Dora said with a weak smile.

Sir Bertram edged towards them through the crowd of eager onlookers. 'You are Lady Greenstead?'

Roxanne turned to give him a withering look. 'I am she, and I know who you are, Sir Bertram.'

'What is it, Papa?' Grace asked anxiously. 'Please don't make a scene.'

'I've no intention of doing anything so vulgar, my love. But I believe that this woman, Lady Greenstead, has pipped me at the post, so to speak, in the purchase of Grandtor House.'

Lady Greenstead laughed. 'My late husband left me very well off, Sir Bertram. I decided I would like to live nearer to Moonshadow, the house that my dear Jabez loved. I have purchased Grandtor House, and I intend to live there, especially now that I have made amends with my family. I hope to survive a few more years and welcome my great-great-grandchildren into the world. Jabez would have approved.'

Sir Bertram's face was suffused with purple as he turned away in disgust.

'It's good to see someone get the better of you at last, Bertram,' Jane said, laughing as she clutched Albert's arm. 'I, for one, am delighted that you have set the record straight after all these years, Roxanne. You have stared down at me from your portrait for so long that I feel I know you, and I hope we may become further acquainted when you move to Grandtor House.'

'I suggest we all make for Moonshadow Manor,' Jack said loudly. 'Everyone is welcome.' He bent down and lifted Lottie in his arms as she began to cry, and he held out his hand to Flora. 'You may ride in our carriage, girls. We are a family now.' He placed Lottie in the carriage and set Flora on the seat next to her. He turned to Rosina, taking her in his arms and kissing her on the lips.

'I will love you for ever, Rosie.'

She returned the kiss, encouraged by a round of applause from the crowd. 'Our family will live at Moonshadow Manor for generations to come, Jack. This is just the beginning.'